BY THE WAYSIDE

A NOVEL BY

JEFF PUTNAM

BASKERVILLE
PUBLISHERS, LTD
DALLAS · NEW YORK · DUBLIN

BASKERVILLE Publishers, Ltd.
7540 LBJ/Suite 125, Dallas, TX 75251-1008

Library of Congress Catalog Card Number: 91-077771
ISBN: 0-9627509-5-6

Manufactured in the United States of America
First Printing

BARCELONA

1

"Yaaainhhh..."

That could have been the cry of a newborn, all right, and I was looking for it on the living room floor beneath the couch she was on.

No, the noise had come from Elena, the Cuban woman who was about to have our baby.

"This is it, honey. It's more than contractions. Something's coming out. Jesus, the pain. We'd better get down there."

She meant the Maternidad, the Barcelona charity hospital where the baby's welcome was scheduled for a month and a half hence.

It was sunup and we'd returned to the flat two hours ago from a trip to southern France. Elena had slept on the ride home, had had no false labor on the trip. She'd wanted to make the trip, had been asleep when I'd done the fast driving...

I was already rehearsing the things I'd tell her mother when she showed up. If our baby didn't make it her parents would add murder to the list of my crimes. At the top of it was "soft on Castro." They were disgusted with Elena for getting pregnant by me. They disapproved of everything but my height genes.

It was a good thing we had the rent-car outside because it was hard to get a cab up on the outskirts of the Sarriá district. I drove the deserted streets so fast that the cops must have thought I wasn't worth the bother, or there weren't any cops awake at that hour.

In a quavering voice Elena translated what the interns were saying. The baby had stuck its arm through her cervix, the arm was without circulation, it would take too much time to set up a spinal. She'd have to have general anesthesia.

"A general..." A smile was decorating her gritted teeth. "What I wanted all along."

This wasn't sarcasm. She'd been disappointed to find out that the doctors here didn't believe in general anesthesia for normal childbirth, preferred not to use it for their C-sections.

She wasn't afraid of blood. She wasn't afraid of dying. True, she'd probably have worried about her doctors' competence if she could have heard what they were saying as they worked on her. She was brilliant, much smarter than any of these harried, hardworking medical people could have known, and she didn't trust anyone to decide what was best for her. That wasn't the main reason she wanted to go under, though.

Sleep was Lena's favorite state of being. She hated being on her feet for more than a couple of hours each day, and if you were with her when she had to be, it was sure to be your fault. I'd known her to cry when she couldn't get out of walking a certain distance, always a distance I'd have called short. Sometimes she'd sit right down by the side of the road and sob.

Being gassed and knocked out this way was almost as good as going into a coma. The time unconscious was short, yes, but compared to the kind of snooze she was getting with me this was a high order of stupor, insensibility deluxe.

Elena was wheeled away gratefully supine. One of the doctors told me where to wait. There wasn't any paperwork yet, a big improvement on Monty Python. There were other people waiting here, nurses coming and going, a Lenin's tomb affair with a green curtain behind which the newborn were arrayed with names at their feet. I was the only husband waiting alone. Every time a family was notified that their baby could be viewed I went along.

I viewed many babies, none of whom bore a name close to mine or Elena's. The nurses kept saying things to me I couldn't understand, but it was clear that I was meant to go back and keep waiting.

I waited all day. I was sure that our baby was somewhere in a pail. It had learned all it would ever know of life outside the womb while it flexed one tiny hand. Elena, too, had not survived. She'd been knocking at Death's door all her life and finally she'd been taken in. The nurses had seen how distraught I was getting. By afternoon the doctors had had a look, too. There were conferences behind cupped hands. No one had the guts to give me the bad news. They'd wait until I gave up and went home so they could send me a postcard.

By five PM I was feeling feverish, which I thought unusual for someone who hadn't eaten. Dehydration could cause hot dry skin, but I'd been getting up every ten minutes or so to go into my night watchman routine, which I finished with a swallow of water before facing five more minutes of waiting.

It occurred to me that I might be losing my mind, and what a good thing that would be, because then I could barge through the double doors and get a straight answer or start going through their pails. A few seconds after I got that idea I acted on it.

The people in green were surprised to see me, surprised that I'd found anything here worth the visit, the tourist treatment. They were accustomed to having people like Elena wheeled in and out of their lives, but this hot-browed, hand-waving person spoke little Spanish and was a head taller than anyone at the hospital. In spite of his growth of beard and the sweat darkening his clothes he was clearly a tourist of some kind, and should be directed to the Tourist Charity Hospital where he could use one of his credit cards...

I finally got through to one of them when I clutched my

right forearm and waggled my hand, then pointed between the legs of one of the nurses. At last I had been identified, I was OK. "Of course, Mr. Cabezón. But your woman is gone from here this morning early, operation quick, she rest now, nurse take you."

Nurse did, just like that—one of the same nurses who'd heard me saying Lena's last name all day. (I'd said "Bancroft," too, in case Lena had changed her mind before she went under. We'd agreed in advance that her name would cause less trouble.)

Lena was already sitting up in bed, reading an illustrated magazine, looking less bored than usual. If she had been a gum-chewer she'd have been chewing it with her mouth open.

"Lo, hon'. I was sure you'd gone out for a few."

"You're all right? The baby...?"

"They didn't tell you? A girl. She'll have to spend two or three weeks in the premature care unit, but they expect her to be all right."

"The arm? She won't lose it?"

"No. Supposedly she's going to have full use of it soon. Have a seat. Hungry? The Boixes brought these. Sorry they're almost gone."

In my relief I'd forgotten how hungry I was and I scarcely looked to see what she was offering. Irrelevant pastry of some kind. Or perhaps it was the very thing that Catalans brought after a caesarian. The Boches—the Catalans pronounce Boix just as the French pronounce "boche"—had been driving me crazy ever since we came with their ritual Catalanism.

Lena told me I could go see the baby, but only through a glass window, and only by yelling "Cabezón," and I might not really be able to see anything if Lenita were asleep. If I wanted to go...she had no objection. If I wanted to come back and say what the baby looked like...fine.

The page made a snapping sound and slithered into alignment.

Before I rushed off I thought to tell Lena how glad I was that she'd come through surgery in one piece, even if there was a little cut in it, and was in such good spirits. She glanced up, frowning slightly, as if she thought I had a motive.

"It's hard to believe we're taking charity," I said, looking around. "Private room, private bath." There was a leather couch that might have doubled as an examining table and there were two comfortable chairs.

"Thanks for coming." She went back to her magazine.

Acting bored was never a pose with Lena. She'd had her baby and life was back to normal. She was in bed with something to nibble on and something to read. She'd have been less bored back at our flat with the things I cooked for her and served her in bed, and her books on romance philology. Her books covered one wall in her little bedroom whenever the spirit moved me to clear the floor of them. Lena had just finished a year of doctoral work at the University of Barcelona and she needed a lot of books to make up for all the classes that had conflicted with her hours of sleep.

2

I might have been back sooner than she expected.

"I'd have hung around longer if they'd have let me touch her, but do you know what it is they've got her in? It's like a big, glassed-in gazebo. It's a merry-go-round with the parents circling the place, bobbing up and down. The nurses fetch the bundles of fur and mouth words. The parents mouth words back at the nurses. The babies are crying lustily. In the slice of nursery where they've got Nena none of the babies can be touched. In sign language they let me know she's fine. A blue-eyed nurse pointed at her blue eyes. Of course they all have blue eyes now, don't they? Perhaps she meant, 'homo sapiens.' Her color is dark red and she's got black hair and her swaddling is nun-white. I couldn't see her very well and I'm not sure they wanted me to see her better. I came away feeling grateful for the nurses. They seem happy with their work, they all have the blush of young motherhood about them, and considering what the noise must be like in there, you have to wonder what it is about life they might not like. Anyway, it's a good excuse to watch women working, and I'm sorry I didn't know about it before this." I was high on Degas and fly-on-the-wall views in general.

"All right, Gordon. Why don't you get something to eat. This must have been a strain for you, wondering if we were dead or alive on an empty stomach."

"Can I stay in this room with you if I come back at a reasonable time?"

"I don't know. Why don't you go home, you'll have enough of us soon. You'll want to drink a bit, won't you? Drink and sing the way you do."

"The thought has crossed my mind. Relief will get me into a barroom even quicker than disappointment. I'm too tired to get in trouble, though."

"I'm not taking any chances." She held out her hand and I put the keys to the rent-car in it. This was a carryover from our brief time together in the United States, when she'd entrusted me with her sports car. She liked the idea that she could prevent disasters by managing me, though nothing had come of it. Anyway, from lunchtime on people in Spain had alcohol on their breath, and it's well known that Spanish drunk drivers are skillful and considerate. In other words, I'd have had to leave the roadway to attract attention.

"Take the keys, then, but I guess you know you're practically forcing me to celebrate in the bars."

"Take a cab home. You've got money. How much money have you got, anyway? You haven't got the money for

France on you...?"

"No. Do you want me to count up in front of you so you can decide what size celebration I can afford?"

"My mother might be here at any time, you know..."

"You told her! You broke your word. I'd better head for France tomorrow, then. Your mother wasn't going to show until the baby came home."

"Please, Gordon, you've got to stay until she gets here. Otherwise she'll think you've abandoned me the way the Boches have been telling my parents you're sure to do sooner or later. She'll force me to come back to the States with her...In my weakened condition...Not a word in front of her about going to France to *look* for work. My parents would never understand how you could leave me at a time like this..."

Elena's father, Enrique, was a romance philologist...an attorney...a substitute teacher...But the best way to describe Enrique was as an embittered Cuban immigrant. He'd lost a fortune when Castro threw him out, which was shortly after the revolution. He'd made back his fortune in the United States by working as a Spanish teacher while his wife slaved in satanic sewingrooms. This unusual recipe for success was effective because Enrique and family never ate in a restaurant or went to a motion picture or a play or a concert or even the zoo. For decades Enrique and Isabel's sole recreation was watching the Spanish language channel in their pyjamas.

Since Castro had let him take all his books when he threw him out, Enrique was assured of enough to read for the rest of his life. He already knew some thirty languages and was fluent in five of them (though he never left the city limits of Palo Alto). His wife made all their clothes and cooked when she wasn't slaving in the sewingroom, so she didn't have time to read. She couldn't even spare much time for Spanish TV.

Elena's folks lived in Palo Alto, California, then, and I'd met them and given them some charming arias before Lena and I left for Spain. I'd liked Isabel a lot. I thought she might have secretly admired me for spending every penny I ever earned in bars and restaurants. Lena's folks didn't approve of us going

7

off to Europe together, but Lena at 34 was almost as old and wise as I was.

They were aghast when they found out Lena had got herself knocked up, which news didn't reach them until Lena was five months gone and we'd already been in Europe for better than half a year. Lena had informed them that we planned to get married even though we'd never been anything but "good friends who enjoyed sex with each other once in a while," and that "Gordon and I have decided that our baby was conceived at a hotel in Nice where he was having a reunion with some old friends and we'd both had too much to drink."

She played down our attraction to each other when she had to answer to her parents. She knew she was infuriating them by taking matrimony and procreation so lightly, but if she'd let her father find out how important our sex was she'd have broken his heart.

Yes, there'd been a reunion in Nice and I'd seen a lot of faces I'd missed seeing, and our glasses had seethed with Belgian ale that I'd missed drinking, but my happiest memory of that night was wallowing in Lena's body till the sun came to the window full of flowers and made us feel like part of a brochure.

We may well have conceived our child that night because there was nothing habitual about our sex. Sometimes we wouldn't touch each other for days. It was her doing, I can see that now. Elena liked sex to be total, some would say dirty. Flowerboxes were irrelevant. The floor was as good as the bed. She needed to bore herself for a few days to get ready for one of our frenzies, chirping about linguistic discoveries until they were as dull as the rates and rules that were nailed to our hotel doors.

She was a gifted linguist. No school had ever let her pay tuition in spite of the income from her ranch. Her money, her studies, her parents were all drawbacks where I was concerned. We weren't right for each other, didn't even like each other, but the yen we had for each other kept us together. Just about the time I'd start wondering why we wanted to keep on boring each other with our different interests and vices we'd have another all-night frenzy and I'd stagger away like a branded calf. Elena was affected just as strongly. She'd lie crumpled in bed all day listening to the birdies sing, or now that we were in Europe, street repairs.

Elena was bar non the kinkiest woman I'd ever known, but she had nothing in common with the sort who'd turned themselves into tidbits and whispered out of the shadows in the back of men's magazines.

She was a smouldering Latin beauty with straight brown hair and huge dark eyes. Her figure was good to look at, though her sleep habits had made her flesh so spongy that I jumped back in alarm the first time I held her. She had full lips that thinned quickly at the corners and one of her slow smiles was sexier than anything you'd find in a pile of magazines.

I could never describe her well enough to do justice to the effect she had on me. She had my number, then, but in an unobtrusive way, like a cat. Also catlike was the way she always took the path of least resistance and made her life as comfortable as possible. Catlike too was the way she seemed to know all the dark secrets of life without losing her innocence. If I never thought of a cat while I was with her it must have been because a black cat from the quarry next door had adopted me. I called her Behemoth and she was a lot more demanding than Elena.

You can't call someone kinky because of her smile. What would you say of a person who would imperiously extend her arm for *frôlage* in the middle of a discussion of Catalunya's utopian textile towns? I'd gone with her on a recent field trip, done some reading...Just like that her milky flesh was between us, quivering slightly...sure, the effort, but there was expectation here, bated breath. *L'invitation au frôlage...*

She wanted it whenever the thought crossed her mind. Wind currents I couldn't even feel put her in the mood. She never bothered to catch my eye first, just put out her arm. The point was to caress her so lightly that she couldn't be sure whether I was caressing her or not. Something on the order of a zephyr was what I tried to manage, making her down stand electrically, avoiding her dermis. When I was in form I could even manage to avoid the odd petechia. It was exhausting work since she never tired of my doing it, and it gave her such pleasure that I had to be near collapse to feel good about stopping. What man could want to end a woman's ecstasy if he had the means to prolong it?

We were both eager to be parents. Since I was broke and childless after two divorces I felt like the luckiest man alive. Lena was well-to-do after her divorce eight years ago. I was not only going to be a father, but the child wouldn't have to starve on my account.

Heretofore the women in my life had just got the abortionist on the line whenever a relationship with me proved fruitful. The thought of me as a father would have made most people laugh: the women, certainly; the regulars at Hennessey's bar. Oh, no one had ever doubted my ability to get girls in trouble, least of all the girls—that was part of my appeal.

I'd given up drinking continuously some time ago while there was still something left of my mind. I found that I'd learned how to do a lot of things besides fly while I'd been on automatic pilot. I had so many skills that I couldn't remember them all. Once I started work as a trainee before I realized I'd done the job before.

I'd also picked up a history which was what made the girls laugh when they thought of having me for a husband or imagined me a father. Prospective employers laughed right along with the girls. People who'd had lives like mine had to pay for them. You'd think I'd been having the time of my life lying in the gutter, that there was nothing in the world Mr. Personnel Director would rather have done, with shit in his pants, if possible. It was the kind of jealousy you'd expect from a faithful husband who drools over his friend's exploits. A policeman's jealousy.

Neither the booze nor the hard work—longshore, loading jobs—had fazed me. None of the rules that kept my friends in lock-step were holding me back. I had a dream, and an unknown old tenor in California, and a famous old tenor in France had made sure that this dream would never leave me: not to sing leads on a big stage, but to be able to sing like the old singers, the singers of the Golden Age. To help preserve an old technique, then, as they had before me.

I'd worked like a madman on my voice for the last seven years and lived by my wits. When it wasn't possible to do something I knew how to do for a living, it was often possible to find work teaching others how to do it. I improved my French as a waiter in French restaurants. When I left for France I escaped my background altogether and was thought of thereafter in terms of what I could do instead of what I had done.

In France for five years I'd worked my way from bits to third and second leads. After some minor career damage during my time with Elena I planned to go back to France and try for the top. My mentor, the famous French tenor, had been willing to co-sponsor a book I'd been writing about voice. Because of his reception during a brief visit while we'd been traveling, Lena had had great hopes for my book. It helped that she had recognized my friend from the LPs in record stores. Then in Spain, while a baby had been forming inside Elena, the old soldier had faded away. When I'd last showed up with Lena and my theoretical homage to the way the old man had sung and could still sing there had only been one old woman who remembered me, glaring through her tears and squeezing my hands.

I may not have had high hopes for my book at the moment, but I wasn't even close to giving up on my voice. When I'd hit rock bottom years ago there'd been a famous old tenor from the Vienna State Opera braving the junkies and whores in a Manhattan hotel to beg me to take free lessons. Then my problem had been pride.

Under various aliases I'd written to some French opera companies and had been scheduled for auditions. I intended to keep knocking on doors until my money ran out, and I expected someone to take me while I still had a good sum left. With that I'd rent a cottage in the French countryside. Lena and Lenita would come to live with me in it. The dream that was sustaining me was simple as that. There were no bundles of French currency under the floorboards. There might have been fruit trees on the property, or farm equipment, or nothing but high grass and briar patches—this wasn't the kind of dream that could be shattered.

Probably it wasn't a dream at all, but just a hunch that in France something would go right for me. The French respected the way I spoke their language. I could be reckless in French and still be comfortable with anything the French might think of me. When there was room for recklessness in what I wanted to do, I couldn't lose.

3

I'd just left the hospital when a thunderstorm was bouncing water off the street and I ducked into one of those little bars that has FRANKFURT on the awning. What better way to celebrate? Bratwurst and German-style beer...

For someone who'd lived in Spain for so long, my Spanish was rotten, I'd made absolutely no attempt to learn it yet because I rarely came face to face with Spanish people I wanted to talk to. I did the buying for us, yes, and I understood all the numbers and price-words as well as any Spaniard, but I still had to point at a lot of the things I wanted or sculpt them in the air.

Here in the bratwurst bar before I had my first beer down I'd told everybody that I'd become a father today in brazen bad Spanish and the bartender set up the next one on the house and the guy sitting next to me the one after.

To judge from the number of children on the Barcelona streets it was surprising that Spaniards would make such a fuss over another one. But when the new arrival in question belonged to a tourist, to someone who couldn't even speak their language...?

Trying to assign a motive was hopeless. Being this close to the Maternidad the jolly bartender must have had men just become fathers popping in every day, and what's more important, men whose reason for being in this neighborhood had just ended. He'd have been an idiot to give away drinks on the basis of paternity, and he couldn't have been an idiot—this bar was well-stocked, -maintained, -patronized. Something in their conditioning, some experience of childhood had predisposed these people to open their arms to a stranger who looked like something that had just crawled out of a vacant lot.

To make a long evening short, I got shit-face drunk, and spent so little I had enough for a cab when I emerged. The rain had stopped, so even if a cab didn't come right away, it was a beautiful night to be standing on the street full of the drinks good people had sported me, thinking of Nena tucked away in her nursery and France in slumber not so very far away where I'd be able to express myself again.

All the lights were out on our street in Sarriá, but it wasn't that late. My head had cleared on the ride home and instead of wishing for a soft place to lay it I was ready to celebrate some more. Being dry again wasn't the reason, there was plenty of good sherry upstairs. I needed to unbosom the gratitude and joy that was still welling up inside.

I'd heard of private clubs where one could drink all night. The cab driver knew where there was a good one. I had him wait outside our place while upstairs I shaved and put on the safari jacket Lena had bought me "for shopping." I'd vowed never to wear it unless I were stalking game, but it had pockets with snug buttons where some of my France money would be safe...Safer than it was in the hiding place.

The cab driver had been completely mistaken about the

13

all-night bar. I'd used the words *fiesta, felíz* and others gleaned from packaging and Christmas cards to describe what I was looking for. What I found was a kind of drug-dream atmosphere. Actually, the layout was interesting and would have been fortunate if anyone had wanted to talk—lots of levels and comfortable places to plop down. Yet no one was talking. Everyone was listening to hyper-repetitive modern music and seemed to be dealing with an inner torment that had all the earmarks of withdrawal. Yes, but not from alcohol or there would have been more drinking going on. This must have been where rich junkies came to nod.

I stayed at the bar and threw down a few quick zombies. I kept scanning the large irregular room to see if anyone was coming out of it. Drunk as I was I knew enough not to mention newborn children in a crowd like this.

The bartenders might have been giving me dirty looks. No doubt my wellbeing was out of place, but I'd been watching a clock all day and had lost interest in what it had to say.

Everything was getting hazy, but that didn't keep me from reading a lot into it.

Ever since I'd been in Barcelona with Elena we'd only gone out four or five times, excluding the trips we'd made with the Boches during our first two months to places of historical interest. This was my big night out on the town, my blowout...and breakfast couldn't come soon enough.

This time my cabdriver spoke English, but I'd have been better off if he hadn't. In chatting with him I mentioned that I planned to leave for France soon to look for work singing opera. He must have known that I didn't know Barcelona because he dropped me at the Opera Bar well down the Ramblas. There I was having *café con leche* in what I learned was one of the principal meeting places of Barcelona vicelords and thieves.

4

When I came to, a woman was leaning over my table kissing me, her hands on both sides of my head. Instinctively I felt for the upper left pocket of the safari jacket. Unbuttoned, empty. Then I felt the upper right, the lower left, the lower right and the secret pockets. Buttoned and empty, all. I started on the pants pockets.

Meanwhile the girl had stopped trying to resuscitate me. Even before she said, "I'm sorry, I know what they did to you," I knew she was an American.

"I nodded off.." She nodded herself and then squinted at me, amazed that I was taking everything so well.

If getting on my good side was her game, she ought to have known two things that I wasn't going to tell her. In the first place, people who've never had any money take large losses better than millionaires take small ones. Secondly, if she knew what had happened she had seen what had happened, knew that a large sum was involved and wasn't troubling herself to help me recover it. If my sensible analysis of the situation was even close, I didn't want her on my side...

For long. She'd been kissing me and she was beautiful and I wanted to know if she were interested in me for anything but more of what had been taken from my pocket. Also, if she were from Iowa, as she seemed to be, and worked in the Barcelona underground, my all-night blowout would have led to something interesting. If she wanted me to be on her side I might not have wasted my thousand after all.

We went to another place and had a bite together and it turned out that she was a tourist from Illinois, and had been trying to console me. She'd been as innocent as I to have gone to the Opera Bar in the morning. She too had thought the people looked sinister. She too had been up all night drinking. Yet she'd seen so many sinister-looking Spaniards by now who had turned out to be nice...

"I'm afraid it's my fault you got robbed. I knew you were pretty far gone when I sat with you, but so was I. It happened while I was in the restroom. I didn't get a good look at the people who ran out because they were in silhouette."

"Don't trouble yourself. This kind of thing happens now and then when I've had too much to drink. It's the price I have to pay. Still, it seems excessive. I haven't had a good soak in a long time. The way I feel about it, I ought to be able to drink trouble-free from morning to night for the next three months."

"You seem so blasé. Weren't you going to France to find a job?"

"Yes, but something will turn up here now that it has to. They didn't get everything. I live here."

"You've certainly got a good attitude. I'm going to stay here a while and look for work teaching English. I don't want to go home till the fall. I'm staying in the hotel on the Plaça de Pi. It's a pretty place, but noisy. You could walk me there, it's not far. I was going to sleep till afternoon. If you want to come by then we could do something together. It might be good for you to have some fun."

"Thanks, but I guess I've had enough fun to last me a while. Time to face the music. There are certain people who might be annoyed if they knew I'd just been dancing to it. Take the woman who had my baby yesterday at the charity hospital, or her mother who's due to arrive at any moment from the United States."

My companion, whose name I forget, had backed away from the table and transferred her weight to her feet so that she could leap into the air before she was overcome by the sulphurous fumes that poured from my mouth or transfixed by the green fire in my eyes.

"Then you're not a good person at all!"

"Well, now...I won't pretend that you're the only person ever to have this opinion of me, but compared to the people you'll find at the Opera Bar...There's no question in my mind that you left with the right person, even if I'm not the one with the most money. Not a prince, perhaps..."

She was leaving. Her Reeboks were immaculate.

I had some paper money in my pants pocket and could

pay our bill, which was goodsized thanks to her ideas about the right thing for us to eat and drink.

5

I was broke when I straggled up to the Plaça Catalunya to join the hippies and pigeons...Hadn't left enough for the trip out to the hospital, reasoning thus: "This beer will do me good now. The walk will do me good later."

I was such a newcomer to Barcelona's downtown dynamics I didn't know that the Plaça Catalunya was a terrible place to sit and wait for life to regain meaning—was like being on the infield of a speedway.

"Excuse me. Is there a chance you speak English?"

One look and I knew it had happened again. When would I snap out of it and get a step up on these confrontations that were happening over and over all my life? I ought to have been waiting for this man with open arms.

Whenever I was wiped out, as low as I could go, without any money or prospects or friends, utterly without hope, when the meaning of life was being enunciated for all time by a bird pulling a worm out of the ground and leaving a little turd behind, when Nature was opening a mouth of some kind everywhere I looked and the sound of eating was loud in my ears and the only use I could possibly have in the cosmic scheme of things was as food for creatures that wiggle and crawl—at the precise moment that I'd attained enough dignity never again to bother with all the human nonsense, and the courage to strip the flesh off my own bones—then, then came the tap on the shoulder, the tug on the sleeve, and it was time to be a Good Samaritan again. I should have had a standard response by now—"Shirt off my back, is it?"—but no, dullard that I was in learning the lessons of life, I took one look at this poor soul and was his.

"Jesus Christ, man, how did you do this to yourself?" Decent dehydrated English type. "You're right in the middle of a big city and you look as if you've been crawling in the desert."

"Exactly right. I'm Owen Hughes. Could you buy me a *café con leche?*"

"I'll try. Short myself. Hang in there, I've thought how I can help you...We'll help each other." I'd heard French words issue from the crowd to our right and I was a master at scrounging from French people.

I went slow with him until he'd got the coffee down. He perked up then and wasn't trembling when he confessed that it was his second *café con leche* of the day. I told him we could afford a pastry with what was left over and he had that, too, with a glass of water. I'd been wondering how he could be suffering from dehydration with all the public fountains. It was clear that he was starving after he ate the pastry. A fish back in water.

Outside I told him straightway how far it was to my place in Sarriá. "If you can hang on, there's plenty of food, you can stuff yourself and stay the night. Maybe longer. Wait here."

I went inside a bookstore and asked to use the phone...for a call to the Maternidad..."Certainly!"

"When is she coming?"

"She won't be here for a week at least, maybe two...Where are you?"

"All right, Owen," I said emerging. "You're in for two weeks, maybe three if I know that woman of mine."

We went to get his bike where he had it chained and he told me enough about himself so that I knew he wasn't mad, though he'd been a tormented man before he left England.

"I had a bike shop. Sold, repaired them, was breaking

even." The fact of the bike and his cycling attire should have been a relief. I could have been dealing with an athlete who had pushed himself too far. Yet I knew there was more. "It was trouble with my wife and daughter that made up my mind. One day I just locked the shop, jumped on my bike and here I am."

"You make it sound easy, but look at you."

"I left from Kent, spent half my money on the night ferry. I could eat off the side of the road till Zaragoza. It's a desert from there to Barcelona, though—two days of hell. Nothing to eat. Almost no water."

"But there are people, man, a few people here and there. Did you really have too much pride to ask for anything?"

"You see, I haven't got a word of Spanish. I'd taken trips to France before. Seemed to get along there with almost no French. I don't know why I settled on Barcelona, really. The Mediterranean, the port. I knew the necessities weren't dear. Bread, wine..."

He went on to tell me that his wife had been involved with another man, and his teenaged daughter had known of the involvement and protected her mother. He'd left the bike shop in the keeping of his partner, who was his best friend. Owen had been an army man, a bandsman, he'd played the cornet in places that were once called Aden and Bechuanaland. Prior to opening his bike shop he'd spent many years as a commercial traveler, and had done well. He felt the lack of a good education—"I don't even have A levels"—but he'd read widely in recent years and wasn't afraid to teach himself Spanish.

"I'm forty-nine. They say a person my age is apt to be slow to learn a foreign language. I've known fellows who don't expect much of themselves at fifty years of age, but I've nothing in common with that lot. I'm closer in spirit to my daughter than I am to my wife, however much I've made the latter sound adventurous. Curiosity is what makes me tick, or so I'd like to think. Would you care to tell me something about yourself? If you don't mind my saying so, you don't seem to be any more fit than I am to make a climb like this today."

"You're right. Yesterday I didn't eat. Had some sausages

19

in the late evening, a bite of pastry this morning, but my blood is running cold...I'll hold the story of my life till we get home."

Moments later I was obliged to burst into a Chinese restaurant during their lunch service yelling, *"Pan! Pan!"* One of the waiters gave me a stick of bread and I ate it sitting on the street before we continued on our way.

Owen had watched this performance with nervous admiration, nervousness ascendant, and I expected him to be downright queasy about the incident in retrospect.

"Do you dine there regularly?" he asked during a pause to swallow.

I shook my head and kept chewing.

"Someone you know?"

Still unimpressed by my solemnity.

"No," I told him when the bread was gone. "When I need something, I ask for it, and the person who doesn't need it as bad as I do gives it to me. In my world this is what's called 'life,' though for some poor souls, I admit, what I call 'life' is nothing but a euphemism for survival. Anyway, we're not the same type. You're a desert rat. Independent. You accept your lot and make the best of it. I like the desert, too, for about a half hour. Then I'd like to be back inside drinking gin and tonic with what's-her-name."

He laughed. "I'm not what I seem at the moment. No, we're a lot more alike than you think. There's nothing like a bit of travel when you can be comfortable at night. You understand, I was in a bit of a rage when I rode all the way down here. For some reason I felt that if I survived I'd find a new purpose in life and accept the past."

"Well, you're in great physical shape, and that didn't happen in one trip, but I still think you might be in a bad way from all you've been through, and I hope you'll do a lot of eating and sleeping and not much else for the next few days."

Before we start with the eating again—why was Owen agog as he labored up steeper and steeper hills with his bicycle? The Sarriá district is a mossy old cemetery in the north of Barcelona where the rent is high since the streets all peter out into huge estates, vegetable gardens, railroad tracks or piles of sand, and where it's comparatively hard to get run over or robbed.

Our little apartment house stood high above Sarriá on a dead-end that petered out into an abandoned quarry. Since it was cut into a mountain, our street was dead as well from the middle to the end on one side, where there was a stone escarpment. In the distance our apartment house looked like a survivor, but drawing near it could be seen that all of our neighbors lived in older and better buildings, mansions, and our apartment house was an outpost.

The eating started as soon as we came through the door and went on for some time with nothing but a drop of sherry and parts of sentences having to do with which food where, the salt, and so on, to break the monotony. Finally we were sprawled out in the living room with our sherry glasses and bottles where we could reach them.

Knowing all that was in him I could give some thought to what he looked like. Till now I'd only been sneaking looks at him. Unless you were a doctor it would have been impolite to rest your eyes on him for long.

His body was composed of steel bands from years of riding his bicycle where ordinary people put the car in low gear or didn't go at all. He had huge gray-blue eyes with so much of the white showing that you wondered how he kept them in his head when he was tying his shoelaces. He had enormous ears, and the lobes of them might have contained the only fat molecules he had left. All his stores had been wiped out to feed his churning legs.

Because he had massive cheekbones and a prominent jaw, but no cheeks, his face made me think of a praying mantis. So did his alertness around food, at least for a few days. Sprawled in the living room I eased him into accepting my unlimited hospitality by letting him think that he was part of a plan. (He was, but I was making it up as I went along.) Owen's being there was really a help, because I needed a plan almost as much as he needed a place to stay.

"So this woman is a Cuban...-American? Is that it? Palo Alto...California? An immigrant doing doctoral work. That's quite impressive, isn't it? I don't know much about you Americans."

"She has a ranch in the hills near the place you named. Her parents rent a place in town. You've heard of Palo Alto, I'm sure?"

"Oh, yes. She's here as a student, then, and you're..."

"You'd like to know my exact relationship to her."

"Not in the least! I'm sure it's none of my business. I do wonder what you've found to do with yourself in Barcelona. You see, we might be faced with the same situation."

"Bullshit, you wonder if I'm not over here just sponging off this woman."

"Well, I hardly...Not after she's just had your baby."

"I must say it's a breath of fresh air to be around someone who can be made to squirm over such minor evidence of a bad character."

"I assure you..."

"Can it. I paid my way over. Had high hopes for a collaboration with a French tenor, once my teacher. He died a few months back. I work for my keep, but I guess I love Elena. I'm crazy about her, anyway."

"It's curious that you've been here so long and don't speak any Spanish. What have you done with your time?"

"Sing, write about singing, study opera scores and foreign languages besides Spanish. I'm an operatic baritone. Something you could put up with, would you say?"

"Playing in a band didn't affect my taste in music."

"I don't want an audience. I practice a lot, though. By now the whole neighborhood is used to me. In fact, if I don't get something going before long, somebody's sure to come poking around to see if I'm all right."

"I'd be delighted to hear what it is you do."

He meant it. I shot him the prologue to *Pagliacci* with a few real fortes. He was bracing himself in his chair.

"Amazing! I've heard opera before, though I'm not what

you'd call an opera lover. I had no idea how loud it was...Tell me...Is it possible to hear the orchestra when you're all singing at once?"

"It's the stone walls in here. Your horn would have been just as loud."

"How the devil could this woman of yours stand it—pregnant, no less? I'm sorry, I shouldn't have put it that way. I was moved by that soft passage before the end."

"Lena never hears me unless I'm performing somewhere. I sing while she's at school. When we've got guests who want to hear me I go into that abandoned quarry next door. I practice there, too, when I'm sure all the dogs are indoors."

"The dogs...Yes! Quite! Seriously, I wonder how you learned to do such a thing. You mentioned a teacher."

"Yes. The sound comes from an old recipe. Perhaps by mistake one day my old teacher put on a record of a Golden Age singer at 16 and 2/3 RPMs. This was an LP made from the old 78s, so the record had been slowed by half. He noticed something peculiar about the man's vibrato, and then he began to notice the same thing with a lot of old singers. The swing of their *vibrati* was from the fundamental to a whole or a half-tone higher, and back. With most modern singers the swing was below the fundamental, as if their *vibrati* were trying to pull them flat."

"The old singers all sounded sharp?"

"No. The fundamental is most of what we hear. But given a great instrument to begin with, if the voice is unforced the vibrato will be very regular, a little quicker than the kind we're used to hearing today, and it will create a shimmer. I don't know what it is...A vibrato within the vibrato that buoys the voice, gives it a kind of magnetic lift. Our spirits soar in sympathy by the same magic. Alas, the forced voice is all we hear today, its doubtful pitch spinning a dark shroud. You wait for the person carrying its dead weight to quit. The vibrato slows, becomes irregular, complains. It's the classic sound of a mechanism when we ask too much—think of a car that won't start."

"Surely something has come out of this knowledge..."

I knew what was troubling him.

"Why am I here in Spain with this Cuban woman? Why haven't I done something with my secret?"

"Not in so many words." The way Owen said "yes."

"My failure is more troubling than you think. I took seriously what my old teacher had discovered. It seemed obvious to me that if I could reproduce characteristics of the vibrato that were common to so many Golden Age singers, de facto I'd be in functional alignment with a Stracciari or a Ruffo. A correct technique would be handed to me."

"And was it? Were you satisfied?"

"It took 15 years of work with friends and with a tape recorder, singing phrases every kind of way. There are thousands of variables in singing. You might think it's a matter of tongue and teeth and lips and the famous diaphragm, but there are sensations that help us to check our position, focal points where we feel a vibration. There are images that cause incredibly subtle muscle movements that profoundly affect a tone. If you think of singing to the person in the back row, for example, the muscular adjustments will be different than they would be if you were trying to sing for someone right in front of you."

"I see. But you did succeed."

"No doubt of it. I won't go into all the strange things I discovered, but the tone I was making had many of the characteristics we were hearing on the old records. Using fancy equipment at a university, we mapped it. We'd turned back the clock and created a Golden Age singer. Maybe not one of the greatest Golden Age singers, but I sounded a hell of a lot better than those tinny old records."

"I'm reminded of the Faust story. But you weren't your teacher's only pupil, I imagine."

"The only one for whom singing wasn't a hobby. He was too old, too strange for my competition. He'd made his career in eastern Europe, didn't know anyone in America to open doors."

"How sad. Then it was up to you."

"Alas. I let him down. We quarreled. Then I went to France and had the greatest tenor of France behind me, and his teacher, in his nineties—a force of nature, that old man—he'd sung with Caruso. There was still gold in that throat."

"Surely you didn't quarrel with them."

"They both died. First the old man, while I was back in the States, then my teacher—only 64—after I came back to do a book with him. With his name behind that book we'd have had hundreds of young singers, at least in France, avoiding the pitfalls I'd climbed out of."

"What about the old teacher back in the States? What happened there?"

Enough of his probing. "Acid happened! Alcohol happened! Black eyes would have happened if we kept being in love with the same woman. I'd have been the injured party, he really was an old man. Typical genius. Sexually potent to the end."

"Still, if you find work on the stage somewhere you can share your secret with the world." I nodded and he raised his glass. "Gordon Bancroft may yet be a famous name."

"Jeremy Locke. I can't leave traces at my age."

"I doubt you're forty."

"My age is such a well-kept secret even I don't know it. But going on forty is old in my game, Owen. Too old for contests, too old to break in."

"Are you sure? If you'd sing for someone important..."

"Sing and stay out of cafes, you're right."

"So women and booze are still a problem for you."

"Only when I project myself to a town in France, a provincial town, a dingy room, a need to live outdoors, to sit in cafes all day. You know how it is in France. If they let you buy them a drink, you're in..."

Before his body couldn't take any more Owen wanted a short lesson to see if he could "make one decent sound."

I refused, of course. He'd have passed out in a minute, and I didn't want him to be left with the impression that I was a fanatic just waiting for someone like him to come along.

He was amenable to more sherry, still wanting to clear the air of things that bothered him about his new situation, or perhaps merely to see how I would handle more sherry myself...

No, it was Elena that had him worried. I'd tried to touch on her lightly, but the moment you tried to keep Lena in the back of your mind she went on the prowl.

"You've been leading a monastic existence, by the sound of it. Surely she'll understand a need to celebrate at such a time...Perhaps you needn't be unduly ashamed, that is."

"I feel like a fool, but I don't think I'm crawling with shame...yet. I might be when she gets through with me."

I'd already explained about the stolen money, and the fact that I would have to straggle down to the hospital sooner or later today to face Elena.

"You see, Lena would never let on that there's a payoff down the line for my singing and writings in voice pedagogy. She likes to think that I'm here as her servant for room and board. Let's face it, she couldn't have come here without me. I plan everything. She can't...it wears her out to make a cup of coffee. She'd starve if it weren't for me. All she wants to do is lounge on that bed of hers and ply her brain with the latest theories in transformational grammar. I take care of the crumbs, the coffee cups. I keep order. I do all the shopping. She even sends me ahead in her pursuit of a Ph.D. I keep her supplied with books, I make phone calls to the English speakers in her classes to find out what she missed. I draw the line at doing laundry, but I'd be doing that, too, if it weren't the one thing she enjoys doing. Oh, I collect the dirty clothes and put them in, but she presses the buttons and believe it or not, when the cycle ends, she pulls out the clean clothes by herself before she needs me again."

"Dear, dear..." He was rubbing his chin. "I don't know about this. I don't think I should try to stay on when she comes home. You won't tell her about me, of course?"

"Depends on when her mother comes. It might be wise to prepare the ground with Lena before the mama gets here."

"The mother, that's right. What sort is she? I'm almost afraid to ask."

"Don't be fooled by her size, she's as soft as Elena. Not a muscle to her name. She makes a loud noise, but it's my experience that she doesn't mean anything by it unless you take her seriously. Think of her as a vicious dog. Snap right back at her, and whatever you do, don't let her get you on the run."

"Dear, dear. This has me quite as frightened as any of the recent things I've done."

"Relax. When you see these two plumped-up pillows..."

"I can quite imagine them carrying a bit of weight."

"But only a bit. It's a puffed-up quality I'm getting at. You want to keep them full of themselves, full of food, as well. Keep dishing up the compliments and sweet nothings. You should be great at it, Owen, the little I've known you. 'Is there anything you'd like at the store? You haven't had any nougat since Thursday, my sweet.'"

"Surely you're not suggesting I take over for you."

"I wasn't suggesting it, but I was hoping you might, in time. I need to find work in France to escape the Boches before their case against me gets any stronger."

"And who are the Boches, I wonder?"

"Another time. They really are a little scary. I'm off to the Maternidad. Eat and drink all you like and don't worry about these Cubans of mine. You're welcome to stay here as long as you like. I really do have some say in the matter as Lena's lifeline. Being mothered again would be a big step down for her."

6

"You *imbecil.*" When she was put out with me Lena would lapse into Spanish, and this explained the vile aspect of my Spanish vocabulary. "*Idiota!* Don't think the Boches won't help me get rid of you..."

"Where will you find someone abject enough to do everything for you that needs doing except turn pages and move your bowels? Think how you'd like it there in your bed without the pitter-patter of my size 13s."

"Stop trying to drum up importance for your chores. Anyone could replace you. It's not as if I live in luxury. It might do me good to start taking care of a few things again."

"Maybe so, but you'd been letting everything slide for a long time before I found you on your lily pad." This was a reference to her waterbed in Palo Alto. "Anyway, there's work for me in France, a costume with my name on it or maybe just a slot in a clock somewhere that's waiting for my timecard."

"Enough. How can you expect any good to come of a crusade like this when you can't be out of the house for 24 hours without losing every penny you've got to your name? If you hadn't been living like a monk the whole time since I've known you you'd have been mugged a long time ago."

"Why will France be better? Because I can talk to people, I can assert my views and screw up their logic. Here the logic is beyond me. I'm swept along."

"What logic? Logic?"

"Everything that happened to me yesterday, last night and this morning was completely logical...Everything from the moment Nena started wiggling her fingers."

"What was logical about that? Because I'd lost my waters? I still wasn't due for a month and a half!"

"No, she was behaving illogically, and you don't expect that of a fetus, even though you can rely on it in a child. This may be the first evidence of precocity. But I'm talking about the logic of what happened to me. Everything that happened can be traced to the fact that I don't speak Spanish. If I could have made myself understood to the nurses and doctors they would have been able to tell me about your operation and where they'd taken you and when I could see you. I could have gone with Nena to the gazebo. What was going on here at the hospital would have been a process that included me, one that I could have influenced in some small way, and not one that was building like a tidal wave."

"To sweep you into a bar with all your money sticking out of your pocket."

"No, hear me out. Because of the screw-up here at the hospital I hadn't eaten all day, my nerves were shot. Because of the downpour which began just as I was leaving the hospital grounds, I was forced into the first bar I found. I couldn't eat quite enough bratwurst to restore me. I'd gone without food for so long that the first beer went right to my head..."

"Then why didn't you stop?"

"They were buying me, lining them up! I'd told them I became a father today, and they were celebrating with me. It was the best-hearted bunch of people I'd ever found in a bar. In a place like Cuba the people would have risen up to follow them—put them on billboards a block long! What was I going to do, just turn my back on them? Notice I'm leaving the keys out of this. If you hadn't taken my keys I'd have driven home. From all the shopping I've done there are people in the cafes who know my face by now. Within walking distance of our flat there are cafes that serve people who are jumping for joy. I guess I haven't left the keys out after all, but dammit, that's the way it is when everything is perfectly logical. All the new details that come to light fit right in. As soon as I came in to see you today you told me, 'Sorry, honey, you could have stayed here after all.' Just as I thought, all the Catholic shit here in Spain is just for naming things and showing respect for the past. The fathers of the children born here can fornicate with the mothers of them while the nuns mop the floor outside. I could have gone out and brought back a couple of bottles of champagne. I could go up to Sarriá right now for some things and we could live here till you're strong enough to go home."

"This is such a load of shit, really. So what if you ate sausages with these good people and got drunk? That's just what I expected of you. Right, perfectly logical. All that waiting. Nothing to eat. The long period of worry and the sudden relief—I know a little about you, Gordon. I know how emotional you are, how much it means for you to have a good laugh or a good cry. But why for fuck sake did you go back home and go out again with all your money on you?"

"I swear, leaving the bratwurst bar I was ready to curl up at home and have pleasant dreams, but by the time we got there I was wired again, a tickertape parade wouldn't have been exciting enough. Sure, I was thirsty. I wanted fancy drinks with ice cubes and not that warm sherry of ours. But I really think what was driving me at the time was the desire to tell someone, to make a friend, to find just one friendly English-speaking person..."

"Don't hand me that shit about how lonely you are, how if we don't go out more often and find someone to speak English with, your treatise will suffer."

"The hell with my treatise, we're talking about a child here. Yes, I do think it's a factor that I don't have a single friend I can turn to in a big city like this and say, 'Why don't you come over. I just became a father.' Look at your Boches. They got here before I did."

"The hell with your logic is what I say. Taking over $1,000 with you to a disco in the middle of the night to look for a friendly, English-speaking person who would want to celebrate the fact that you've become a father is about the dumbest thing I ever heard of..."

"I wasn't looking for a disco, don't you see? It was my lack of Spanish that was getting me in trouble again. I was trying to find a place that was open, that's all, a place full of respectable people who work weird hours. Instead I ended up with the jet set."

"But that's not where you were robbed."

"And for good reason. I had the good sense to be wearing

the safari jacket you'd had the good sense to buy me, and I was determined to stay awake, which I've always been able to do in the past by keeping the drinks coming and talking to people. But the crucial bit of logic comes next."

"I doubt it, or they'd have found your naked body outside that disco somewhere..."

"The driver who took me for breakfast spoke English."

"There you have it. You finally connect with someone who speaks your language and he dumps you in a hellhole down off the Ramblas. And why? Listen to this logic. Because you told him what you were looking for. A woman who would still spread her legs for a stinking drunk."

"No, I just asked him for a good place to meet English speakers. But the reason he dumped me in a den of thieves had nothing to do with the words between us. He hated my guts and was throwing me to the wolves because of where he picked me up, at a disco for rich druggies."

"Well, did you find any friendly English speakers down on the Ramblas?"

"Yes, but I don't remember meeting her. She only penetrated my consciousness after the loss."

"What a shame. Since you were unconscious you didn't have the chance to step in and thwart all the diabolical logic. You'll say you didn't know what you were doing, but I know. You were trying to think of a way to get between her legs. I doubt you mentioned your daughter the whole time you were there. If you had, according to the well-known laws of Spanish logic, even the crime czars would have bought you a drink and called off their dogs."

"You might have put your finger on it. In any event, I did find an English speaker, and there's something positive about the end of my story."

"You're going to move in with this girl?"

"I didn't mean, positive for me. For us. For you and Nena and your mama. When I leave for France I've found someone to carry the heavy groceries."

"Oh, Jesus. You've dragged someone home again. As

often as that used to happen back in California I thought I'd be safe here in Spain."

"You'll be completely safe, I'd stake my life on it. It's an Englishman."

"An Englishman with no place to stay? A wanted murderer, no doubt. Don't you know they repatriate Englishmen who are stranded here? If he isn't a criminal all he has to do is go to his consulate."

"He doesn't want to go back. He left an unfaithful wife there and rode his bike all the way to Barcelona."

In the long pause that followed Lena didn't appear to be considering what I'd told her. Her large, brown, heavy-lidded eyes were upon me but I wasn't in them. I'd seen her eyes this way when she looked out the window. "I see," she said at last. "When I come home from the hospital, when baby comes home, when my mother comes there will be a madman in the apartment to look after us."

"It may sound like a crazy thing to have done, but there was something wonderful about it, too, and he isn't a bit mad. His name is Owen Hughes, must be a transplanted Welshman, and he used to play the cornet in army bands in places like Aden. He's got a very pleasant way of speaking, he's bright and sensitive, and in spite of his postings I don't think he's much of an imperialist or racist. When he uses the word 'wog' you can sense he regards brown people with affection."

"What is it with you? What happened? Is it the baby? The Gordon Bancroft I knew in California and thought I was taking to Europe with me was a well-traveled man, someone who'd already spent years in France, someone who'd lived by his wits. I admired you for managing to have such an interesting life even if you couldn't always manage it at your own expense, and I didn't mind shelling out for you. I thought you'd be good company, and you were, the first two months here, when we traveled. I guess I've blundered into the truth of the matter, haven't I? You have to keep moving to keep your wits about you. As soon as you settle down you start to get dull. Your imagination goes stale. You lose the crustiness that makes you so much fun around new people. You start making romances about the idiots with whom we're in everyday contact. That milkman of ours, for example. That imbecile, Joaquín. Any Spanish speaker would know what he is in five seconds. You think all his little jokes and *dichos* are clever, and you'd still think so if you could translate them yourself. You've gone soft in the head, in other words. Yes, go to France, go starve, go through hell up there, I know you will and I'm beginning to think that's the only way you can give the best that's in you. We're just too far apart to live together. You have to have your back against the wall to do anything with your life. I have to have mine down on something soft."

"You won't consider coming to live in my little cottage in an exurb of wherever it is I'm going to be singing opera?"

"Gordon, I won't even consider spending another day with you in our apartment unless you get that Englishman out of there."

"You know what a beautiful, sensitive and intelligent woman once told me? 'In an emergency, when bombs are falling, the English are the most helpful people on earth.' Now isn't an Englishman someone you'd like to have around while your mother and I are trying to get along?"

"There aren't any English people. They're a multeity. The nation's another melting pot. He could be anyone."

"You're judging by our country. The American pot has been on high heat for too long. People's identifying edges have turned to goo. In the English pot you've got fibrous integrity. Only someone lacking a sense of humor altogether could fail to admire their haters. Anyway, never mind Owen. I want you to know how confident I am about this trip to France. You can count on me to succeed. This is the chance I've been waiting for to show my stuff."

"Go to France and see what you can do with your life. So far all the evidence points to the fact that you're a loser, and if you are, I don't want to have anything to do with you, even if you happen to be the natural father of my child."

"It might be too soon to bring this up, but what about our

all-night orgies? Won't you regret running me off the next time you get horny?"

"The way I feel I doubt if I'll ever get horny again. I want a man who can be a good father to my girl, and if you're not him, goodbye."

"All the more reason to give Owen a chance."

"I don't want to hear another word about him. Get him out. Today."

"This is a family man, Elena. A hard worker. I didn't tell you all the good things about him. He had a bike shop back in England."

She clenched her teeth. I thought she might be in pain and asked about her stitches. "No, it's you," she said angrily, pulling the covers up to her neck and squeezing her eyes shut. "You know how I feel about grueling sports."

"Hear me out. He had a little business. He's raised a daughter. The daughter was protecting the wife, you know how it goes. Really, it might be hard for people like us to see any problem when a woman that age wants to fuck around. If I had a wife in her late forties and liked to work on bikes as much as he does..."

"Never mind. What does he look like? Don't worry, I wouldn't be interested in a million years, even if this would be a chance to give Nena a real father. If I'm going to meet him I want to have some idea what to expect. If this is some kind of English queer you're involved with..."

"Come on, nothing of the kind. He has enormous ears...Remember LBJ's? But Owen's stick out more. He's ridden his bike so much over the past years that even his cheeks have disappeared, and that probably makes his teeth look bigger than they are. He smiles a lot for someone starving..."

"Get rid of him. I've heard enough."

But of course I didn't have to get rid of Owen, all I had to do to soften her up was tell her more good things about him each day when I came to visit.

7

Owen was asleep when I got back from the hospital, but not in the same house. Not a trace remained of our banqueting and bibbing. Even the little sherry glasses had been washed and set out to drain, the bottles bunged and returned to the shelves where they'd been taken down. The place he'd chosen to sleep showed great sensitivity, I thought—a keen reading of his present circumstances and those he would confront soon.

There was a small bedroom off my own that I'd been using for storing the junk we'd found in the fascist's apartment, and there was still a narrow bed in there, but Owen hadn't wanted us to embarrass each other with the various sounds of sleep or relief. He'd gone to sleep in the tiny room I used as a study, spreading out his oilskin under the drawing table I used for writing. The thin carpet wouldn't have made the tiles any softer, but he looked comfortable snoring away in there except for his feet, which protruded from beneath the table and could be seen from the entry, huge and sore. Since there had been no one to ask, the poor man hadn't even taken one of our blankets.

8

In the next days, while Nena was turning from dark red to pink, and Lena was becoming morose, Owen ate and drank and slept plenty, took voice lessons, and tried to find out more about me and his new neighbors.

"Every time I look out the window that huge Alsatian is looking at me. I don't suppose you used to feed him?"

"Yes, that's *Box* (pronounced Botch), means 'mad' in Catalan. He's never known any kindness but mine. It's a good job he stayed sane. Throw down food whenever. Give it a good heave, though, or it'll end up on the path to the fascist's. If you throw Botch food he'll recognize your scent when you walk in front of that compound and he won't try to bite your head off."

"I see. Someone lives there, then? It's an enormous place, I realize, but I haven't seen anyone about but the woman who feeds our friend, and she's surely just the caretaker or the caretaker's wife."

"They go out of town a lot, but we'll have to deal with them, all right. Especially if someone else is feeding their dog."

"I take it they've already given you trouble on that score."

"No, they gave the trouble to the fascist, the fascist gave it to Lena, and she gave it to me."

"'The fascist' would seem to be a man of some importance."

"He owns this apartment house and lives in that palace down on the side of the hill. The drive between us and Botch's compound is to his place, though you'll never see him, just his daughters. I think he has a secret passage."

"His daughters, then. Two beautiful girls..."

"Walking as if in the company of a creature whose fleece is white as snow?"

"Very much like."

"Beautiful, mysterious, probably heartbroken..."

He nodded and flashed the whites of his eyes.

"Those are his daughters. I know nothing about them. They must be on orders not to look at other people as a way of safeguarding them from strangers."

"What about the fascist himself?"

"The most imposing presence of any man you will ever meet. Inside he is nothing but pulleys and cogwheels, but outwardly...The way he dresses...God, the nobility of his bearing! There's death in his eyes, ice on his lips."

"All this right there at the bottom of that little drive. Yet he doesn't venture out much, I understood you to say."

"That's right. He'll only be interested in you if he finds out you're staying here, and his only interest will be to raise our rent and put you on the contract."

"Unless I feed the dog."

"A formality. Of course it's wrong of us to feed another man's dog, but how can he stop us when my only motive is to keep the dog from trying to tear my head off each time I go by with a bag of groceries? Think—does he want to risk annoying us to please a neighbor whose manse is even more imposing than his own?"

"Quite right. How silly of me. I shall feed him, then, old mad dog. I love animals. You've never had one here?"

"Yes, there's a black cat over in the quarry who answers to the name of Behemoth. She was mine. Elena decided to get rid of her for good luck."

"Quite a place you've got here with your fascists and black cats."

"Hang on, I haven't even told you how the man talks. We had to meet him at contract-signing time. That's Spain for you, the attorney cost us a hundred bucks. Anyway, here the old fellow keeps looking at me and muttering. Finally he can't contain himself, he's walking in circles around me and asking Lena questions. She translated later. He'd been impressed with me for weighing over a hundred kilos and had wanted to know something about my habits, what I ate. 'Politically North America is a cesspool,' he told Lena, 'but they know how to eat, they like to compete, they kill the yellows and crush the blacks.'"

Owen shook his head, but in general I think he was pleased with his new home and might have wanted to stay on even after the women and the baby arrived, even after he'd found a job, for the sake of making a proper start in Spain.

He was already making trips all over town to apply for work as an English teacher—the direct method, of course—and had his eye on a bosomy Scot at the London School.

The Boches worried him, though. He'd been able to imagine a horrible outcome from his dealings with the fascist, the dog opposite and my Cuban friends, but he was able to put them out of his mind. Where the Boches were concerned he kept wanting to know more.

I'd been right to think Owen was sensitive. He had a nose for shit as keen as any dog's.

"All right, Owen, there is a reason I don't get along with these people. There's a shameful secret. I want you to know it, but before you judge me too harshly, you should also know that the Boche woman is the very same who has just told Lena, after hearing about the money I lost, that it wasn't stolen from me at all. I've hidden it away in an account so it won't be spent on the baby. She thinks I'm planning to blow it in France. That's the kind of mind...But there was bad blood or she wouldn't think this way. It started...God, do I really have to tell you this?"

"Please don't if you've got it in manuscript."

He knew that I kept a diary. I gave it to him.

9

(date) Montserrat/funicular. Lena had the trip day wrong. Boches couldn't have picked a worse morning. The night before had demonstration of cricopharyngeus muscle for L.'s American friend from school (Yaya?) who's been 'dying' to meet me. First thought 'bats her eyes a lot for someone moribund.' Later she puked her dinner all over the bathroom and turned blue-gray. Her blind date, Jordi (Lena's professor friend who knows seven languages) is good company. Gave the impression he understood what I was saying, though I'm quite sure he missed most of it.

I fail to disguise being somewhat tremulous as we ride out of Barcelona. For some reason I'm always in the death seat contorting myself to talk to the ladies. Another milestone has been reached in our deteriorating relations. In the beginning the Boches worried that I might drink too much, now they are sure that I do. My doing the cleaning, shopping and cooking has come under increasing suspicion. They think I will never be good for much else and Lena will be better off having a maid. Where in the beginning they seemed delighted or perhaps even flattered by my attempts to say "marvelous," "fantastic," "extraordinary," "my life has been changed forever," etc., now they ignore me and glance at each other.

We stop in an ugly little town twenty minutes west of Barcelona that couldn't be the Mecca of the Catalans. (It is impossible to visit Catalunya without seeing pictures of Montserrat.) The town is still asleep. Magically a young girl emerges from a nondescript stone house. In English Lena tells me that this is Mary of the Angels, that she is 14 years old and the daughter of some great friends of her great friends, that she is coming with us to see the sacred relics and to ride with us into the clouds.

The Angel in the back seat changes everything. The slogans of the Catalan nationalists scrawled on the old stones, the mutilations of the countryside, heavy equipment abandoned where the wounds are fresh—everywhere the hand of man has been recently I feel violated, I feel a wrenching horror. Her presence intensifies these images of violation. I imagine the happiness I would find if I could protect her somehow from the unrelenting crudeness and random cruelty that will always be waiting outside the window.

We climb the mountain fastness, the laboring engine of our little car like a clanking chain, my stomach full of slag, my emotions careening wildly between panic, fits of laughter and nose-cone passivity. Remorse over my wasted life is weighing on me and becoming so unbearable that by the time we arrive I want to end it all by throwing myself under a tour bus full of Germans.

Shiny two-story buses are parked all over the place. Half of Europe has made the pilgrimage this morning. Perhaps a statue I don't know about has been moved to tears. On my feet I no longer feel that I'm about to die, or that I ought to kill myself. All that will be needed to make the world bearable for a few more hours will be something to drink. As we near the hub I am ecstatic at the sight of a bar tunneling into the holy rock, jammed. God bless the characteristic thirstiness of Spaniards, and thank God the trait has carried over to the Catalans, no matter how earnestly they believe themselves to be different from the rest of Spain, and thank God I've got some Spanish currency on me.

I'm excusing myself to take a piss leaving the Angel and her unworthy hosts to go on without me or remain in the hubbub as they prefer. I'm drinking glasses of beer at a swallow, 5 in under a minute. I've drawn a small crowd and in several languages I've expressed admiration for the bones of the saints, excepting their dryness.

Emerging the Angel takes my hand. Alcohol hasn't changed my perception of her. I am aware now that she is taller than the rest, that her body is completely that of a woman, shapely in a way that turns every head. Openmouthed, both men and women watch her pass. She saunters and lets her hip brush my upper thigh. When we pause she leans against my arm, letting me feel for a few holy moments the weight of her angelic breast. Only Lena and the Boches ignore her.

I go into my swallowing act again and this time Lena and the Boches move on. The Angel tarries at the entrance with love in her eyes. These are dark blue eyes without a hint of invitation in them, only innocence, but an innocence that is yearning for experience. She is feeling love as a possibility, but does not know how to express it, what form it should take.

She is squeezing my hand hard now the whole time, and harder still at intervals when she wants to stop our ascent, stand close, take deep breaths and plunge into each others' eyes. In all this time she has never spoken a word to me, has spoken very little generally except to answer questions of the Boches in Catalan, or of Lena in Castilian. Her voice is husky, it scatters words on the ground.

I can feel the blood in my penis but perhaps I'm too worn out to have an erection that will embarrass me or make it impossible to continue the pilgrimage. At the moment, awaiting definite signals, my prick has climbed into the bulge of my trousers which is widening horizontally as we continue up from the street to the holy stairway.

I'm not alert to an opportunity to hold the Angel in my arms, I'm not planning to give the slip to Lena and the rest. There's warmth in the air now, and perfume. In spite of the tumult in all the various seats of my emotions and between my legs I never budge from the reality of our situation. Even when her divine breath is in my nostrils, or when she lodges a breast against me for a moment, or a bit of her hair brushes my neck— I credit the way we're taken along, the surprises underfoot. I know that she wants to be against me, wants to be a woman for me, but I persist in my fatherly keeping, leading and holding firm.

By the time we're back in the car it seems that our love is already centuries old. The mists that arise from the hills speak more of us than of the Visigoths. She is in my lap in the front seat, her head nestled under my chin. She can't be comfortable, I'm not, but our awkwardness is gentled by an ocean of feeling. The way we stab each other when we're tossed is pleasure itself.

There is general uneasiness in the funicular, as well there should be if there is anything telltale in our expressions. She's on my lap again. Her eyes brim with contentment. This is love, love at last in the arms of a madman, his desire contained but firm and to be counted upon, hands gentle, eyes full of tears.

There is whispering in the cabin, so many people changing position that the conveyance has begun to sway. The Cuban-Catalans are shouting about the rock-climbers scaling the cliffs below, a supreme example of reckless exhibitionism. My love and I only have eyes for the quilted countryside spread out behind us, a shouldering crowd of colors. From where we sit swaying in the mountain shadows we notice the excited people around us the way one looks at a plate of food on someone else's table in a restaurant. We know exactly what is possible, we are content with what is ours.

We scamper about on top of the mountain along with the

others, father and daughter again, forgiven everything by those who've come up with us, who are eager to have been mistaken. Now we *are* father and daughter I'm the old man helping her up. She's laughing and prancing, not needing my help, not wanting to let go. Our tryst in the inner place, the holy place, is ended. We have emerged needing the air and the sun and the others. From here on we'll be going back.

Looking grave she rides with the women in back when we take her home. She's probably hungry—I am. We ate sandwiches for an *almuerzo* back in Montserrat, but I'm ready to pack away some heavy food—feeling faint from the effort of behaving myself.

There's a moment of sad fondness when she takes my hand for the last time. Elena says they will just be a minute inside, suggests that I stretch out as best I can in the car. I'm glad not to meet the Angel's parents in my sodden condition and produce more correct behavior. I memorize the street, the neighborhood, the way everything looks here. This is her world, this is what I will take with me. A few years hence much more will be possible. Of course it's extremely unlikely that we will find each other again, but what was the chance I would find myself living in Spain with someone like Lena?

When Lena and her friends emerge an hour later I'm in a fury. How could she leave me so long in the little metal hotbox with nothing to drink?

"Oh, it wasn't so long..."

"It was an eternity! What fucking manners! I feel like baggage you brought along. How will that girl ever respect me when she sees that I'm nothing but a suitcase full of English?"

The fatal blow is struck on the way out of town when I bring my fist down on the dashboard.

As it gets sorted out later I realize that I've been mistaken about some things that have happened this day. True, the girl was charmed by me, but she began to feel ashamed of her feelings and was afraid to reveal them in front of her parents. As for my being shitfaced, no one was fooled by all my trips to the john, but they thought I'd held myself pretty well considering all the climbing I'd had to do and the fact that I'd been up all night trying to be a good host and hadn't slept well in weeks. Not for one moment, says Lena, were the Boches upset about my comportment with Mary of the Angels. They thought I'd behaved like a good father, considering we'd had nothing to say to each other. In fact, everything had gone all right—or passably well—until I attacked the Boche automobile, and this attack would never be comprehensible, would never be pardoned.

"You see, honey, in spite of all the places they've taken us and all the meals and so forth, my friends really don't have that much money, and that little car is precious to them."

"I never dented the dashboard. I know how to do these things even when I'm shitfaced."

"I know, but it's the idea. You can't take your frustrations out on other people's possessions."

"They care more for that cruddy little car of theirs than they do for that girl's virginity?"

"Honey, they know you'll never see her again. There wasn't a beach or a forest or someplace where you could go crawling off together. It was a cultural trip and it was the morning."

"All right. I've got it. It's all clear. But let me tell you something. If I could ever find my way back to that village and find her little house I'd wait outside for the next ten years. I'd wait till her head was full of shit from school and she had nothing in mind for the future but things like the Club Med and washing machines. I'd wait till she'd been totally fucked by this society of people with sacred relics and then I'd take her back to the top of that mountain and find a place to crawl off to, if I had to dig it out with my bare hands."

"But she wouldn't be innocent then, you see."

That stopped me. "You're right. She wouldn't have anything to do with someone who digs with his hands."

"Now do you see why I tell you not to drink so much? You get everything so overblown. She'll find a nice young Catalan boy and go to the top of the mountain eating *churros*

43

and she won't miss a thing there is to do there or see. Cultur-
ally, at least, you spoiled the trip for her, but I wouldn't be
surprised if she's been there before."

Owen was grinning nervously when he handed back the
spiral notebook full of ravings that I called my diary. The hell
with the good opinion of an Englishman, I was thinking.

"I don't know quite what to make of that," Owen was
telling me. "Very funny, I think."

"Then why aren't you laughing?"

"I found it strange, too."

I leafed ahead and gave back the notebook. "This was the
last time I saw them. This is how it stands."

(date) Open warfare with the Boches from now on. They
show up today to see if Lena's still alive and I can't bring
myself to greet them at the door. They follow me down the hall,
I point at the room where Lena is asleep under her reading
matter. I slam the door to my closet, read a story by Raymond
Carver. When the buzzing has stopped for a while I emerge.

"You've got to get a regular job, honey," she tells me.

"What could be more regular than my runs to the market?
What about our regular meals? This is Spain, you'd think
they'd know about servants. Don't tell me they think I'm living
too high on the hog. They know the little I'm getting out of
this...And they can see that you're living like a fairy princess,
so what's the problem?"

"They're afraid this will go on forever because I'm not
strong enough to throw you out."

"Well, they've got that right. You're barely strong
enough to pick your nose. But you've never wanted to throw
me out. What they're really saying is that you're not strong
enough to do their bidding, and of course they're right, you're
not a Panzer division, you're not even a lone terrorist. It must
drive them crazy to think of all the good night's sleep I've had
with you..."

Owen thought that these notes about my life with Lena had been interesting, but he was still at a loss to understand why I would want to be her husband and try to raise a child with her.

"Perhaps it's not my place to say so, having abandoned my own family, but I don't think you owe her the rest of your life. I can quite understand why you might like to give fatherhood a try. I did myself and I'm glad I did, no matter how badly things worked out. If you're going to make a go of it, though, your expectations ought not to be so high."

"Do you think they'd be too high if I set my sights on being a family man like you?"

"Lord, no."

"Well, that's what I want to be, and to me it's not such a modest goal. You're a big success in my eyes."

I may have had other motives in wanting to be a family man. I did have a vague idea that being the father of a small child would make it easier to ask for work. "All right, maybe I've had lousy jobs all my life, and I haven't stuck with them," I wanted to be able to say, "but now I've got a little mouth to feed."

10

Owen's good character emerged with a vengeance after a few days of heavy eating and deep sleep. He scrambled out from under my writing table whenever I came near the room. If I felt like doing a little writing he urgently needed to go for a stroll in the private hunting preserves rimming the hills above our neighborhood.

Never in the time I knew him was his company anything but desirable. Even before Lena came he lingered with his dinner when I lingered, finishing only seconds earlier or later than I did, and he considered the washing up a privilege. He worked with such speed and efficiency that he appeared fearful. His formative years could well have been spent cringing beneath a heavy spoon.

When Lena came home she was so eager to be abed that she scarcely noticed Owen. Later she told me he was more of a wreck than she'd expected, but she'd known at a glance that he had a servile character and would be someone she could enjoy living with. High praise.

I'd pegged him right. Owen's long years as a soldier had been an exhaustive preparation for family life. He could mend anything, he could probably have made his wife's clothes if she'd wanted him to, he was a wizard at removing stains. He had an aversion to smudges, and in no time we were seeing so well out of certain windows that we realized we had flower boxes, and later the same day they were full of flowers from the hunting grounds.

Owen introduced a small cat into our *ménage* as a means of controlling insect pests and other small creatures that came in the night. He showed us how the cat should be cared for, bringing sand in from the abandoned quarry. He named the cat Hermione after his wife, and it came when he called it.

Owen repaired what was nonfunctional in the apartment, which is to say just about everything, including the tiles in the living room that I could never get to stop chattering no matter how carefully I removed the old mortar and applied the new. I watched him work on these tiles with interest. I couldn't see how his method of work was so different from mine, yet the result spoke for itself. I was soon able to slither about the house as quietly as the cat.

He knew about electrical outlets and plumbing. He could repair and install locks which made Lena's supine existence more bearable, and I enjoyed being able to lock the door when I went to the bathroom.

Owen Hughes wasn't just a family man. He was *the* family man. I wouldn't have to be all he was to satisfy my detractors that they'd been mistaken about me. All I would have to do was imitate him fairly well and extract a few principles from his behavior.

Never take anything for granted. The foundation of family life. Never take for granted the smallest kindness of a loved one. If she hands you a cup of tea, it should always be for the first time ever, and gratitude should ooze from your eyes.

Never take for granted the fact that your family life isn't in danger simply because all your little machines are working, you can see out of your windows and back at yourself from your mirrors, and see vague reflections of yourself from everything you own that can be made to shine, and no sign of yourself wherever you sit or walk or lean or place your head. Nothing is ever clean enough to be taken for granted, not for a minute, and breakdowns are imminent all over the place if only you are family man enough to look for them.

A family man only rests and reads his paper and makes a little mess when his wife insists that he do so, insists that she will be able to live with the gathering dust and the dreadful possibility of a blackout or an explosion for the next ten minutes, or the time it takes to cross and uncross your legs at least twice.

Of course with an ostensible wife like Lena you never got your cup of tea or your smoke break or anything else. Insecurity was all on the side of the family man because you never got any thanks and you never knew when you were going to get your dismissal. All you got from Lena was the occasional clearing of the throat or muffled eructation which meant that she was still alive in there.

Now that there were locks on the doors it was almost impossible to have a private conversation with her. I longed to know what she thought of Owen but that was one thing I could never ask her at mealtimes.

"Oh, he's all right," she said when I finally cornered her.

"Don't you think he'd make a perfect husband?"

"If you like the type," she said, starting to sound bored. "He's too tidy for me. I don't like someone who never stops fiddling with things. Of course, it's not his fault. This place is falling apart, and he's used to living with steel. Needing a good fuck is probably all that's eating him. Too bad he's too good for just about anybody, at least in your book. I really do admire him for trying so hard to get a job in a country where he doesn't speak the language. If you had a tenth of his determination I wouldn't have to listen to so much shit about you from everyone who knows you're the father."

Which brings us to the second great principle of family manhood. *Always look for a job.* If you already have a job, look for a better one, or for increased duties. Working two jobs and still finding time for family and housework will qualify you for the family man's hall of fame, which differs from the others in that there is absolutely nothing memorable about any of its members.

Alas, before I could fill my head with dreams about being eternally forgotten I had to hunker down and find a way to disappear for a mere three or four hours each day.

"The least you can do is take IOUs for his voice lesson."

"Sure, and wait for his debut season to collect."

Our sessions were in the quarry, but Lena had evidently heard an improvement in the odd sound that floated over the dog chorus.

Bicycling from one school of English to another Owen ultimately found one that believed in the direct method of teaching, i.e., where not one word of Spanish would ever be spoken to his pupils or to anyone else. Owen would be pardoned the occasional lapse, surely, for he had learned to say things like *"vale"* and *"es igual"* which were very Spanish and a perfect response to a host of situations, including imminent death.

"If Owen can get a job here with thirteen words of Spanish, you can, too," Lena told me, stating the obvious. "It isn't that I don't think what you're writing is important, but be honest, the people who could help you sell it have all died out. You're whistling in the wind. If you got a job of some kind it would make it a lot easier for my parents to accept you as father of my child. I'm tired of lying when people want to know what you do with your days."

"Come on, the Boches are the only ones who've been prying, and they're the ones who've got your parents interested. We've got to stop everyone from having ideas of what I should be doing. I warn you, if I'm pressured into a job I detest I'm going to be a terrible husband and father."

"Isn't it clear to you by now that economic support is all you've got to offer us?"

"Think, Elena. Remember. You were a sex-fiend when I met you. If you'd been a prostitute I'd have said you were giving away the store. Maybe sex was all we had, but do you realize how rare it is for people to have such strong desire six months into a pregnancy...over a year in all? We didn't need other partners to stay interested. We didn't need to be away from each other to bring on the need for another orgy. An attraction like ours was so rare that the only possible explanation is destiny. Destiny wanted us to want each other so badly that we'd create that child in spite of all the things we don't have in common, in spite of oral contraceptives, in spite of..."

"Destiny wanted me to forget to take my pill?"

"What?"

"I lost two days. It was all the drinking."

"Why didn't you tell me before this?"

"I didn't want you to think I was trapping you into a marriage. Now I don't care what you think."

"Because you don't want me."

"For a husband? An aspiring opera singer in his late thirties? Someone who used to roll in the gutter who's turned into an ascetic who only drinks when he feels like passing out in a den of thieves? Someone who has to change countries when he needs to find a job?"

"That's where Owen comes in. I've been learning how to be a family man from him. But if you don't trust me to get it right, we could keep him with us if you'd give him thirty minutes of one of those nights we used to have."

"You want a *ménage à trois?*"

49

Jeff Putnam

"Why not? I don't see the three of us in bed together, but Owen's a great guy and that wife of his really got him down. I think it would be great of you to see if you could put some spring back into his step. Who knows how much he'd get done around here if he had some incentive."

"So that's your little scheme! You want me to shell out for him so you'll have nothing but time to fool around with those opera roles."

"For a while. I want to have something to sell when I get to France."

"I can see what's coming when my mother gets here," she said bitterly. "She's going to want me to go back to the States."

"I could understand her wanting a move like that to spite us, but I hope you won't go along. Where would that leave Owen?"

"Back on his bicycle!"

"Don't be a fool. Nena would be much better off here in Europe with one vigorous parent than she would be back in the States with a lot of anti-Castro armchair wadding and a role model who's nothing but a bulge in the bed."

"The one vigorous parent being Owen, I take it."

"Who else? He may not be a natural parent, but he wouldn't feel as unnatural as you or I in the part. If there were something in it for him, something as worthwhile as your ass..."

"I've told you, he's too old. I don't find him attractive. He's deferential enough to be someone I could live with, but that wouldn't last if he had an ounce of clout. He's genuinely obligated to us for giving him a chance to get his life sorted out, but he's someone who loves his independence. Just wait till he has a sanctum of his own, you'll see."

"I won't ask again. When he's got a few more classes and some money saved I know he'll make a play for that Scottish girl and try to get her to start at the bottom with him."

"You think I should offer him a chance to start at the top."

"The timing is right. You'll never again be in such a good position to do him a favor. I'm sure he's thought how much

50

better a husband and father he'd make you. All of the shitwork and cooking that takes me 5 or 6 hours a day he could probably accomplish in two. He'd work full time on top of that and still have time to play with the baby. That's the main thing. He'd give the baby something to live for."

"I don't know. I don't trust him."

"You're afraid he'd get your money and get rid of you?"

"Something like that, yes. Model your behavior after Owen all you want—you're not a bit like him. I wanted you here with me because you have an unusual mix of qualities: you're noble, humble and degenerate."

"Degenerate? Granted, I used to be."

"Well, if not, you're amoral, which is important to me. And you've settled down a lot in the past year. I wouldn't have thought you had it in you."

11

I didn't blame Elena for not visiting Nena, since the child's growth and convalescence couldn't be seen, and Lena was still convalescing herself. When it was time for Nena to come home, Lena came with me willingly to receive her.

The nurses had handed back a lot of kids by this time. There wasn't a hint of suspicion on their faces that we weren't everything that good parents should be. They seemed pleased that I had my hands out.

Taking a newborn for the first time is a heady experience. Nena weighed next to nothing, and suddenly I did, too. I felt myself rising and passed her off to Lena before my feet left the ground. I should have realized that Nena weighed a ton to

Elena, who hadn't had anything heavier than a book in her hands for years. Like a hot potato Lena gave me the baby back. Though I had some idea of what to expect now, when I looked at her delicate features I got dizzy all over again. The hospital grounds were parklike so we let the cab wait, promenaded and passed Nena back and forth for a while. By the time the feral cats were out in force Nena was a heavy enough bundle to bring home.

For a couple of years when I was a child my mother had taken in foster children—babies—and I'd learned to care for them. Since I wasn't a major league prospect yet my father didn't object to my being a nursemaid, and of course my mother needed all the help she could get.

Whatever my deficiencies as a provider, I knew what I was doing with Nena and loved doing it when the bitches would let me. I'd stopped working on my book now that Nena was with us, and this caused an improvement in my spirits, as if I'd shaken off a long illness.

Owen wasn't much interested in Nena, but there may not have been anything odd in that since Nena stayed with Elena and Mama and all those books and it was hard to see anything, though it was clear where all the sounds and smells were coming from.

Since Elena wanted her mother to think she was having a quasi-normal relationship with me, and that we sometimes slept in the same bed together, or at least could lie on the covers with our clothes on without embarrassing each other, I'd infiltrate the place from time to time and lie there in the midst of all the mothering until no one could breathe.

Isabel was a changed woman away from Enrique. I'd remembered her as being a quiet and cheerful sort, a bustler who never stood still long enough to give pain a chance. I'd never heard a complaint cross her lips.

Now that was all we heard, in a loud voice. Before she'd met Owen or said hello to me she'd seen Hermione and started spouting. She didn't speak a word of English and I couldn't tell what was wrong, or what she was feeling.

Lena hastily translated. Cats were well known to scratch infants' eyes out and suffocate them in their sleep. Lena didn't care if this was nothing but an old wives' tale, the cat had to go before her mother would consent to stay with us.

"All right, but I don't like the way cats who hate us are accumulating in that quarry."

Mama still bustled, but she didn't do anything, she just moved things around and made my job tougher, or Owen's job, because he was trying to relieve me of my duties and take full credit for the housekeeping.

Owen was amazed that his washing-up routine attracted so little attention. The only way he could show the ladies how fast he was moving was by making noise every time he touched a dish.

Mama complained about the noise he was making.

Lena translated.

Our first evening all together Owen demonstrated his skill in repairing Spanish floor tiles. Isabel's only comment had to do with the fact that our apartment was a *porquería*. All day she'd been telling us this whenever she looked around and the word was starting to characterize our apartment the way the word "fuck" might characterize a mining camp.

Undaunted Owen continued to justify my choice of him as role model. Except at mealtimes he was seldom to be seen without a cleaning utensil in his hand. He'd have worn a uniform if we could have found him one. He was like me in this one respect at least—he had no shame. So what if he had to dance to the tune of these nincompoops for a while, there were better times ahead!

His bicycle was stolen. Fine, he started taking the Metro, he had a little money now.

He moved to another school of English because of the influence of a new friend, a Catalan fellow who had a huge empty apartment near the center of town that had belonged to his very good old family for centuries and for which the upkeep was a pittance. Owen didn't have to tell me he hoped he'd be given a small room—after all, his friend lived alone—maybe a dozen rooms. Such an address would raise him in the eyes of his private pupils and he might even persuade his Scottish girlfriend to live with him.

The day after I'd heard all this from him he was fired from his job at the new school, presumably for not submitting to the advances of his mentor, though he didn't want to be specific.

All of the changes in his situation had taken a matter of days. The school he had been influenced to leave had replaced him, so he'd be looking for work again tomorrow, he told us. We got all this bad news at once over a seafood casserole of mine. Owen was a big fan of my cooking and I'd wondered while I was at work in the kitchen if he'd tell us tonight that he was relocating to the center of town, and how much he'd appreciated all we'd done for him. If so, what a nice touch it would be that we could be seeing him off with such a good meal.

Instead, for the first time he didn't match us bite for bite, didn't have a word to say about the food, didn't have a word to say at all until he'd polished off two glasses of white wine.

"A pouf. I was done by a bloody pouf."

"It's understandable, old man. He was offering more money, you were impressed by his apartment. I know how eager you are to have more privacy, there's no shame in it."

"You shouldn't feel unwelcome just because my mother is here," said Elena. "As long as you stay in Gordon's writing room you don't put us out much at all."

"What do you mean, put us out?" She wasn't expecting this many decibels. "He's been busting his ass around here for nothing!"

Isabel might have been able to pick up a word now and then but she didn't know what was going on. To keep her husband happy she hadn't danced or listened to any English since 1960 and she'd forgotten what she had learned in Cuba. Still, decades of fiddling with the dial had taught her something. Lena was telling her that Owen had lost his job and confirming something the old lady already knew.

I'd expected a consoling glance in Owen's direction from

Isabel, a sad look at her plate if she couldn't bear to face him.
I wasn't ready for the outburst that came.

"What's she saying?"

"She says that Owen should never have had the right to
eat with us, even if he could pay," said Lena, ignoring Owen.
"She said that seafood is skyhigh in the markets here, and
shouldn't be given to servants."

"That does it..." Before Owen could excuse himself and
take another trip on the wind I slammed my fist down on the
table. "He's a damned sight more welcome here than you are,
you waddling, overfed bitch!" This to Mama, of course. "I'm
sick to death of your bellyaching and the airs you've been
giving yourself since you decided that your daughter is a rich
landowner. This man is worth ten of you, and he's just lost his
job!"

"I'm grateful for your interest, Gordon, but I can find
another place to stay."

"Like hell you will. Let the fat bitch go stay in a hotel if
she doesn't like it here."

"Aren't you forgetting who pays the rent on this place?"
Lena.

"*Es una porquería...*"

"And that's another thing that's gonna stop right now.
Owen and I work plenty hard to keep this place clean and I'm
tired of this fat bitch calling it a shithouse."

"I won't have you referring to my mother that way."

"Really, don't you people think you could sort things out
more satisfactorily if I were off now?"

"Stay right where you are, Owen. The two of you might
not have any respect for me, and that's just fine. I've had it easy
for a few months and I've been able to get some work done, and
I owe it all to you, Lena. No amount of drudgery would be
thanks enough for the freedom I've had with you shut up in
your room—and I never expected to be thanked for the things
I've done for you. But before you get the idea you've got me
where you want me, I want you to think hard about the way
you've taken this man for granted. I brought him here as a

guest, and he had every right to be treated as one. Instead you've been using his insecurity to make a slave out of him."

"Really, I don't think my treatment has been quite that awful."

"Tell your mother how he lost his wife and daughter, how he came to be here."

"She knows about that..."

"Ask her how she'd like to provide for herself in a foreign country without a word of the language and be a role model for someone like me."

"I hear the baby," said Lena, leaving the table. Her mother trotted after her. Owen was on his feet, too, collecting the dishes.

So much for dessert, but no one cared what they were missing.

"Leave 'em, Owen. Let Mama take care of the dishes tonight."

"Best if it's a last gesture on my part. If things were left a mess I'd be afraid to come up here to see you."

"You've got nothing to be afraid of. Isabel's been bullied all her life, and now that she's seen what I'm capable of she'll take me seriously as a husband for Lena. In fact, she'll be such a staunch ally that she'll prevent the police from coming, and she may even go to bat for me when the Boches start trying to enmesh her in their lies. Believe me, after tonight you're safe here."

Owen trusted me. We talked till 3 AM in my writing room, keeping our voices down. The baby was waking in the night, and going right back to sleep, but there was a lot more noise than usual in Lena's room next door, whispers turning into drumrolls, thunderbolts turning into whispers.

The Boches would have to intercede before Isabel could be turned against me, and that wasn't going to happen as long as the baby was too small to go anywhere, since Mama wouldn't let the baby out of her sight, and the Boches were too scared of me to come to our house any more.

12

From the night of the seafood casserole till the day I left for France Mama said *porquería* no more and smiled at Owen whenever he came into her line of sight. She only made a nuisance of herself by repeatedly suggesting that Elena and I marry.

"We've been through all this a hundred times," Lena kept telling me she was telling her. "The Spanish wouldn't marry us because we couldn't produce papers to show that our last marriages had ended properly in divorce."

Elena had been married to someone eight years ago and divorced him after a brief agony. Both of my divorces had been in impressive Mexican Spanish but I had no idea what had happened to these documents. I was sure they existed. The people who had boxes of my papers in their garages were the best people I'd ever known, and all of them were still friends, even the ones who'd been storing my things for a lot of years, but I'd never had the gall to ask one of them to find something for me.

The Spanish functionary in charge of preventing our marriage had advised us to go to Gibraltar where the British imperialists would marry anything with a bloom on its cheeks...transvestites...even mandrills. He'd given us precise information on how to reach Gibraltar from Madríd.

I'd never had any objection to marrying Lena. Her pregnancy had inured me to the prospect. I didn't object to the rock and the apes and the British army, we both had a feeling for the absurd.

Elena was the one who wouldn't budge. She objected to the change of planes in Madríd. All the walking, that's what I thought. We decided to lie to her parents, and of course my mother had always had a hard time keeping track of my gyrations and we didn't have to tell her the truth, either.

Elena frequently had trouble keeping her lies straight and it might have been a slip of the tongue when she told her folks long distance that we were nothing but good friends. She may have been trying to suggest that her child would have a better chance with parents who were friends than with parents who were exclusively lovers. Or she could have been giving her father a hard time. She'd been a frustrated delinquent all her life. There's no telling how much pain she'd have caused her parents if it had only been easier for her to do things.

Marriage was all we talked about now and I thought fondly of our *porquería* days.

The change in Owen's status was underlined when Isabel asked him, through Lena, his thoughts about marriage.

"Really? Yes, I do have an opinion. Tell her I think it's very important. Without marriage we'd have something like chaos, wouldn't we?" Lena kept a running translation going and from the look on the old lady's face it was clear that Owen had been promoted from servant who ought to be eating scraps in the kitchen to guest of honor in a matter of days.

"As far back as I can remember everyone in my family has been married. All my uncles were married to my aunts, my grandfathers were married to my grandmothers, my greatgrandfathers were married to my greatgrandmothers..."

"She wonders if you have brothers and sisters."

"Right. Sundry, tell her. All of my brothers are married to my sisters-in-law and my sisters are married to my brothers-in-law."

"What about the daughter you have at home? Your only child?"

"Ah, yes. Not a pleasant situation. She's eighteen years old and still unmarried. She might be capable of having children, but she's never said she wanted them, or a husband, either. I can tell you one thing—if she ever gets near a man, it had better be someone she wants to marry. If she's not serious about a bloke, I don't approve of her holding his hand."

"If she's eighteen years old and she hasn't even held a fellow's hand," I interjected, "my guess is she's a lesbian."

This remark was duly translated since Lena was getting into the spirit of things, but a cloud came over Mama's countenance and we ate in silence for half a minute.

"It's not true, you know," said Owen, awkwardly breaking the silence with his knife and fork poised. "Oh, not about my daughter. She's a lesbian, right enough." He paused for the transmission. "But I'm a bastard, myself, and a shameless one at that, because I don't care who knows it."

Isabel chose to treat this as a joke. Because of the drip of seconds all the small noises we made for the next minute sounded expressly atonal and arrhythmic.

"Marriage...yes." Owen again, like hair-growth after death. "You see where it got me. I spent twenty years of my life learning more and more about a fascinating person. She became my universe. That was the trouble, of course. I needed her too much, and she began to be too sure of me. Don't worry, when she started playing around, I did, too. I wasn't going to let her make a fool of me. But it was totally empty for me with other women—sex, the lot. Marriage was never unnatural, never a hell for me until she didn't want to live with me any more. I still think well of the institution, mind you—how can I turn my back on 20 years of happiness..."

"Nineteen," I put in, "unless you rode your bike all the way to Barcelona because of a one-night stand."

I began to wonder if Lena was translating every excruciating word because Mama was offering Owen a plate of *judías* with a big smile on her face and a string of Spanish words that might have belonged on a greeting card or above a fireplace.

"What did she say?" Owen asked Lena.

"She says that she'll heat them up for you if you like. She knows that you like them because she's seen you fill your plate with them before."

"That's very kind. I was distracted. I'll have them just as they are." He served himself competently with nothing but a small fork and suddenly he was revealed to me like an open clam. This was the kind of dinnertable discussion he'd known as a paterfamilias back in England.

"The odd American will put Tabasco sauce on his green beans," I told him. "Like to try them that way?"

"I'd rather not, they're so very good the way you've prepared them. Superb, actually."

"A remarkable bean in every respect. Lena, why aren't you translating any of this? Owen, I insist it doesn't make sense for you to thank marriage for bringing you so much happiness—let's say twenty years' worth, in round figures. You were just the lucky beneficiary of the fact that it took Hermione that long to meet Mr. Right."

Lena started laughing before she'd finished her translation, so Mama went along, but there was fear in her eyes, and then it was all over her face when she got the rest of the words.

The gist of Mama's long speech at that point was that Lena and I should be ashamed of ourselves for making fun of a man like Owen—a "faithful, loving husband," etc., whose marriage had been ruined by a sinning wife.

"I'd like to respond to all of this, if I may," said Owen, who deserved the floor and probably a sound system. "I'm afraid that my wife and I aren't well enough known to you to be the subject of discussion. You see, we'd both been knocking it off behind each other's backs for years, especially during the time that I was a commercial traveler. Sin, per se, was completely irrelevant to our marriage, because neither of us had anything remotely like a moral code, and we've brought up our daughter without one."

Mama was shaking her head when these ideas caught up with her.

"...I flatter myself that what we had in place of a code of some kind was an ability to think for ourselves and understand each other. We didn't want our life together to depend on roles and customary ways of being. We both wanted to grow in our own way, and the essence of what held us together was the desire not to frustrate each other, but to encourage, consult and console."

"Doesn't sound like any marriage I've ever heard of," I broke in. "Not between a man and a wife. A marriage of true minds, maybe. Something convenient between a couple of founding fathers."

"Shut up and let him finish," Lena was saying, and her mother, too, no doubt.

"That's all I want to say. I don't mind Gordon's thrusts. We've had long talks about the kind of people we are. He's only trying to keep me entertained."

"No, I'm not. I'm trying to keep you from romanticizing what you had with that bitch. Let's not get excited, ladies. This is a difficult situation. Alliances may not be a good way to ensure personal growth. Who knows, maybe a man and wife can grow in different ways, though. Maybe the wife felt that she didn't want to belong to anyone anymore and the husband had come to feel that the most important thing was to belong."

"Do you suppose we could talk about something else, Gordon? This really is too painful, even when you leave my name out of it."

"Sure. Same tyranny, different subjects. Lena, ask your mother what's so special about her marriage that makes her want to recommend it to other people. I've only spent a couple of days in her husband's company, and all I thought about was escape."

Lena was capable of almost anything where the truth was concerned, but I think she gave my question to her mother straight. Mama's face seemed to fill with air and her mouth came forward full of ridges just like the mouth of a balloon. Next thing her tongue was flapping around in her mouth as she let all the air out, then she filled up and repeated the process a dozen times. I'd cleared the dinner dishes and put on the dessert before she was done.

"Faith, that would be a rousing defense, I'm after thinkin'."

Lena gave me a long dirty look. "Don't start with that Irish shit," she said, turning to Owen for succor. "Think of our guest."

"Have you Irish blood?" asked Owen. "That would be a surprise."

"By the bowels of the virgin, I haven't a drop. It's just a habit of mind I picked up from the crowd at Hennessey's, and there was too much fiction altogether when I was but a child."

I didn't affect a strong accent, but Mama sensed a further derangement and was leaning across the table the better to listen to me, her face a slack bag, slits for eyes, mouth a black, flat M.

"That's not what he told me," said Lena, still refusing to bring her mother into the discussion. "He told me that Irishness, especially affected Irishness, is a way of showing solidarity with Cuba."

"How, I wonder. Really, this interests me."

Proving his versatility once again Owen was also showing interest in dessert, a pastry I'd improved with fruit.

"Sure, there are a power of ways the two countries are like," I explained. "Ireland and Cuba on the one side, the United States and Britain on t'other. A bit of sweet in your gob'd keep the flies out," I said for Mama's benefit, since Lena was translating again. "Think on't. Haven't we got an unfartunate colonial period in both places, and wealthy imperialists using them for a playground, and their women corrupted and their men brought to disgrace. The way of Guantánamo and Ulster, aren't the imperialists keeping a foothold, whatever the Protestants would have to say about it who have no business in Ireland in the first place?"

"It's clear what sort of people they are at Hennessey's," said Owen. "Surely there's no case against the Protestants remaining in Ireland since they're as Irish as anyone, whatever you think of the British presence."

"You say what's right. It's the British presence I mean to decry, no reason to bring religion into it. It's by way of being a bastard that yeer not Welsh, yerself, with a name like Owen

Hughes?"

"No, it's by way of never having set foot in Wales. I knew my father, more's the pity."

"Then it's a drop of Gaelic blood ye have as well."

"Stop it, Gordon. He can go on like this for days."

"As a recent mother, why don't you tell us your views on marriage, Elena?" Owen said. "I'd like to know what your mother was saying, too, if it could be summarized."

"My mother wasn't talking about her own marriage. She was bawling us out for lying about being married, and for not taking ourselves seriously as parents. She knows I'm worried about what my dad might think."

"Sure it's a complaint she has about us when the word *malhecho* is mixed up in it."

"Shut up, Gordon. It's about time someone wanted to know my thoughts on the subject."

"May the divvil scald my scrotum if I haven't welcomed yeer thoughts these many months. It's the sharp tongue of ye I can't abide."

"I don't believe in marriage," Lena began, "except to protect children." She watched me pour a big glass of sherry and leave the bottle open beside it. "Where Gordon and I are concerned it makes no sense at all, since he can't contribute a peseta to help raise our child. This might be to Lenita's benefit, though. If the burden of her support falls on my parents, she'll have everything she needs."

A tear was trickling down her mother's cheek and onto her dessert dish. Since the bit of dessert on it was gone, I started to clear.

"You couldn't see any advantage for yourself?"

She thought again. "Not really. Gordon won't be a role model, so whether he stays with us or not isn't a problem for me. Extended visits might be the best arrangement." There was new hope in her eyes. "At the very least I hope we can be cordial. Gordon may not know it, but I tend to have more energy when I'm visiting or being visited. When Nena learns to walk I'll have another good reason not to spend so much time in bed..."

Her energy had been falling off for some time, and she went to join the sleeping baby at that point.

When Mama, too, had taken her leave I abandoned my bogtrotter routine.

13

The amount of learning that was going on in our little flat was staggering—learning of all kinds. Nena's learning was mechanical at this stage, and not very interesting unless you had something she wanted. Elena had the milk she wanted and didn't complain about having to give it to her as long as she could go on with her studies. This she did with a book in one hand, a breast in the other, and Mama to keep the baby from falling off the bed. Learning was business as usual for Elena, it was all she ever did, along with forgetting, but what she learned and what she forgot was known only to Lena now that she'd dropped out of her program of studies at the university.

Owen was the big learner. He had a habit of acquiring words and phrases, having picked up the English he knew by eavesdropping and having fantasy conversations among the dunes. He was studying English grammar now along with Spanish grammar, which was a convenient arrangement since all the language books I was feeding him had the English grammar right alongside the Spanish.

I was learning a lot of Spanish, finally, and trying to brush up my French, and I was learning a lot from Owen about

British English—the fact that "frightfully interesting" meant "dreadfully boring" to English ears, and Owen wasn't old enough remember when it had not.

Mama Isabel was the only non-learner. She learned nothing new about her daughter, or English or American people. Not one of our words or ideas got through to her. Back in Palo Alto she took orders from Enrique; here in Barcelona she took them from little Nena. Her husband's erudite muttering, the baby's gurgles were distinct imperatives. She knew what needed doing.

She didn't want anyone else to know. To prevent them finding out, the entire time that Nena was sensible to the world around her—sprawled next to Lena in the little room—Isabel blocked the way to bedside. The room was so small that when I wanted to do something for the baby I had to crawl to it from the foot of the bed, which is why the surviving photograph of this period, taken by Mama Isabel, makes perfect sense.

There are the proud parents, like a pair of Spanish quotation marks around the straining child. The part of my face showing reveals that I am smiling, enough of the baby's can be seen to reveal that she is screaming. The photo is very dark where Lena's face shows, but she is evidently smiling back at me.

The tiniest details bring back great slabs of time. A bit of iron from the fascist's bed. A chip in the wall. By the span of my shoulders it can be seen that the bed would be too small for me to sleep on alone, and the presence of the others brings to mind a refugee camp, crowding of Cambodian or even Siamese intensity. My black t-shirt fits right in, and once again it's too dark where Lena is to see that her bedclothes and jewels would fetch enough to send a boatload of us across the South China Sea. Dark as it is against the wall, I remember her expression, it was well known to me. Her amused look. I saw as much of it as I did her look of annoyance, which made up her entire expressive repertoire. When we had relations, or near-relations, with my hand skimming over her body, her eyes were closed and face opaque.

It is what I don't remember about this photo, however, that strikes me with most force now. Something I couldn't have known at the time. Something Isabel had seen again and again during her stay and would never forget.

I have straight, fine hair, but it's long and untidy in this picture. The way my head is canted to view the baby, with my hair off my neck, a secondary growth of hair is revealed of which I'd been ignorant: dark curls well down toward my back, wet and matted.

There were plenty of messes in my life at this time and I was aware of most of them, and perhaps even proud that I was aware. The biggest mess of all was on the back of my neck and I wasn't aware of it? Isabel and Lena and Owen and everyone else who had to do with me—even Joaquín, the milkman—knew precisely what was happening on my neck and must have assumed I did. I suppose I should have been grateful to all the people who'd known about the mess on my neck and treated me passably.

All except Lena. Again much later I would become aware of another sign that I was turning into a troll, and she would make me aware by laughing at me.

Too fine to be seen in any photo of this period, too fine to be seen in any of the hazy mirrors where I turned up from time to time—too fine to be felt, apparently, or caught in women's jewelry—blond hairs were growing from my ears, from the tops of them, the pinnae, the lobes, and vying with the darker hairs inside. Gossamer thin blond hairs that were four inches long by the time Lena laughed at me and told me she was sorry she'd laughed—now she'd never get to see the day I was caught in my own web.

She meant it. She'd thought I had a master plan. She'd thought so all along, she said. Quoting from Sartre or somebody she assured me that the person I was then was the person I had wanted to be, that I'd created myself.

I laughed, too, but later found myself wondering about what she'd said—and the way she said it. Her eyes were telling me, "Come on, cut the crap, you know what I'm talking about."

I thought I did, finally. The way her mother was always taking orders gave me a clue. Lena thought everyone was the product of indulgence, as she was. People became what they were in order to please themselves, there was no question of carelessness, or failed responsibility. Now that her parents were no longer available to carry out her wishes, she did so herself. Whenever she felt like saying, "No, I won't, I don't want..." she went to sleep.

She thought that I'd become the way I was because I didn't care about my appearance, didn't care what anyone thought. She admired me for not caring, it was our point of contact. It would have scared her to know how many people besides myself I'd tried to please.

BORDEAUX

14

Here I was back in France and it was just like the old days, dragging around in the dark and the rain looking for the cheapest room and ending up with a room that cost more than some I'd already seen because I was too tired to keep looking.

Forget the old days—I had to. Nothing would be the same now that I was trying to get a job for Nena's sake. Oh, it would be impossible to live any more cheaply than I had in the past, not unless I felt like sitting around all day on the street behind a horror story on cardboard.

In Nice I'd put myself over with a tenth of the voice I had now precisely because I was willing to wait for another chance somewhere, nothing was ever do or die. Good fortune was just a matter of time. Possible employers were so grateful for my lack of urgency that, had they known about each other, they would have bid for the chance to be my benefactor.

What I didn't have now was time. By definition I'd always have time to survive, but Lena wanted quick results or she'd leave with the baby and I'd have to be offering her a castle and liveried servants to lure her back to Europe. Following her was out of the question, too. I knew Lena and her folks well enough to realize that I'd never be able to horn in if they got a domestic scene going back in the States.

No mistakes. The next day I found a cheap room that was so pleasant it was hard to imagine poor people coming to die in it. I reported to the opera house and let them know I was in town for my audition three days hence, asked for and was given the use of a practice room.

I took long walks when the rain stopped, ate lots of fresh fruit, cleansed my body with mineral water, went over my audition arias a million times in my head along with the speeches I intended to give when asked about my background.

When I took the stage in front of thousands of empty seats and the three uncomfortable souls who'd invited me to sing I was ready. Perhaps because I hadn't auditioned in such a long time I didn't feel like someone with a throat full of cotton, about to submit to a surgeon. I felt as I had when I'd enjoyed performing and had an audience with me.

At the end of the first aria my attitude was, "Wait till you hear the next one," but a member of my little audience was rushing down the aisle, shouting at me over the orchestra pit.

"Bravo, Monsieur Locke! Splendid! What a shame all the important roles have been cast. We must find a way to keep you with us. We will make room for you! Can you be reached at the address you've given us? Monsieur Poirot is out of town, but if you can wait here ten days he will put you under contract right away. Truly impressive, *monsieur...*"

15

Before I drifted away drunk with praise the accompanist came running after me, removing her glasses and saying she wanted to know me better. My cue to invite her for a cup of coffee. Good form demanded she refuse a couple of times and try to entice me into some semi-official chitchat in an office here on the premises. I was certain the *régisseur, artistes des choeurs* had put her on to me to try to find out everything she could and jolly me into staying in town until the head man could hear me.

"Let's be honest with each other, Madame..." I was on the verge of telling her that I was aware of her mission for the company... She shouldn't feel compromised by having a coffee with me. We could have it in the *Grand Café* across from the opera house where anyone could see we were all business, even at a little table in the corner...

Then I saw her for the first time. Until now I'd shut everything out of my mind but what I was going to sing, how I was going to look and sound up there on the stage. Before I'd taken the stage she'd been someone with glasses who smiled a lot, and while I was singing I'd taken for granted all the right notes she gave me, I'd only have been aware of a person behind those notes if she'd held me back or rushed me. The *régisseur* had given me such a swelled head that I hadn't really noticed her on the way out, either, even when I'd thanked her for playing so nicely.

God was in his heaven, all was right with the world: a dangerous state of affairs for me. Every detail that caught my eye would seem to be part of the reason I was so happy. This could have been the woman of my life standing in front of me with a straining bosom and warmth in her eyes. What a disaster to lump her in with all the little details that were just right!

She'd grown tired of waiting for me to find the right words. "I'll have coffee with you at the *Grand Café*. Everyone knows me there."

Good. We were moving again. I switched my music case

to my other hand and began to feel her skirt against my leg. "You must have thought I was trying to find the right French word just now, but no, Madame. I was trying to find a polite way of saying that I knew you had a job to do for the company."

"*Monsieur*, I'm not some person they keep to entertain visiting opera stars."

"Then I've insulted you."

"I'm afraid you have. I am more than a staff accompanist. I've been a musical director here in Bordeaux. If you were a French singer trying for a part with us you would have heard of me, you'd be flattered by my interest in your voice."

"I am, but not because of your eminence in the opera world. Just now, in spite of my entirely unjustified and reprehensible notion that you were a spy, I was going to suggest that we could still be comrades and hear each other's stories, and that I couldn't have thought of a better way to spend an evening, when all of a sudden..."

No doubt because of her keen sense of rhythm she'd stopped our progress in the shadows so that I wouldn't finish what I was trying to say in front of the concierge.

"...All of a sudden you were a beautiful woman standing in front of me, and the music was gone, and so was the point of being fellow musicians..."

She hid her mouth with both hands, but I couldn't be sure a husband had come between us, French women were inconsistent about rings. He was nowhere to be found in her eyes. I was looking so deep she gave an involuntary start and rushed us outside on the strength of it.

After crossing the wide boulevard and taking seats off by ourselves in the cafe, something was already settled between us. I'll stop short of saying we'd acknowledged an attraction for each other, but we must have known we'd have to be more than friends.

We were of one mind about not wanting coffee. Sipping Grand Marnier we shared the kind of information that friends would have about each other—proceeded quickly to the naked truth about each other, in fact—but not as friends would do, for the sake of being comfortable. We were making each other squirm.

Amazingly, I let her go first. The pattern when I met someone I liked was for *me* to reel off a dozen unpleasant facts about myself, forcing a tacit declaration of love on her part if she were undaunted.

Yes, she had a husband. She still loved him. They were separated. She gave the last fact looking away, her lips hard. She didn't want to be involved with anyone right now. She hadn't been sleeping around since the husband left. She loved her work at the opera, she'd lived for her work. No man had ever meant more to her than her work as an artist, her pianism. No, her husband was no musician, no artist, though he loved the arts. He did research of some kind. She muttered something about cannibalism, a laboratory. She didn't want to bore me.

Over our next round I countered with a grisly account of Lena's safaris into the Romance languages. I told her how I had kept my dishtowel quiet to hear Elena explain the precise way a Latin word was mangled by the migrating tribes of Europe. I told her how I'd been reduced to singing in a quarry, to giving voice lessons there. As if she hadn't heard enough to decide that I was an existential laughingstock, I explained why my pupil didn't pay me, that he was a curious Englishman who'd bicycled down to Barcelona to give his wife something to think about.

Not to be outdone she told me how she'd made a fool of herself over Placido Domingo. And he hadn't been the only one...She was partial to tenors, but I'd reached her with some of my high notes.

"It's a spiritual communion." She nibbled on her drink, set the glass down tenderly, tapped on the rim. "A man who is jealous is going to drive me crazy." She'd narrowed her eyes as she said this. Now she closed them. "Crazy. I will never give him a reason to be jealous. But if he is jealous of me for no reason, I will betray him instantly." She was merry again when she opened her eyes, as if she hadn't meant to be taken seriously.

"I was telling you what is in my heart when I hear a beautiful voice," she added, touching the back of my hand. "I was moved by your singing today." She whisked her hand away and asked me to order for us while she went to the ladies'.

I thought hard about her while she was gone. I still wanted to believe she was the perfect woman for me, but the strange darting intimacy I felt with her from time to time, the look of pain on her face when she looked away, her need to reassure me of her virtue...I could well have been getting in over my head.

Before she'd come back I'd decided I ought to thank God if her personal life was a shambles. How long would some tidy well-adjusted type put up with a life like mine—voice or no voice? It was clear that her emotions were all over the place, but what was I to expect after I'd just sung my heart out at an audition and then blurted the fact that her beauty was causing me to forget everything I'd just done? She'd been around singers all her life, she knew what auditions were like. For a singer not to talk about his voice nonstop for hours after an audition was rare in itself, but to score a hit the way I had *sur le champ* and have my head turned so quickly by her...This must have been the single most flattering occurrence in her life.

She *was* beautiful even if she had been gilded by the God-in-heaven effect. I hadn't been fooled in any way. I'd seen between the ripples when she left moments ago. I may not have known it until now but this was my type: longhaired, longlimbed, bosomy, bigassed. Willowy and ample. Wonderful to stroke or squeeze.

Intelligent? She had to be. All opera coaches were geniuses, complete students of the species. No emotion was strange to them. They could be carried away by romantic music while they were looking at the cracks between your teeth. Superficially they may have had something else in common with dentists, being just as quick to interpret muffled sounds, but coaches were interested in so much more than what was inside or what came out of a person's mouth. They were healers, holistic of course. They could draw up a horoscope, invent placebos. They could convert you to the religion of your choice, or the diet. They could marry you to the right person, divorce you from the wrong one, make you a better parent or pet-owner. They could bring you to orgasm without taking their fingers off the keys.

I'd had a lot of coaches but until I met Sylvie I'd never known one who wasn't holloweyed and hollowcheeked, a nail-biter, a chronic masturbator, strung tight in some way, that is, and trying to find relief in the wrong things, more tobacco, more caffeine, more work. Those who were genial drunks or good-time Charleys thought of themselves as performers *manqués* and gravitated to piano bars.

All in all, coaches were the most self-destructive people you'd ever want to meet and it seemed a miracle that so many careers had fattened on their bony fingers. However, like all people who could be inspired by anyone who came through the door they lived to a ripe old age, if you could call it living.

I had Sylvie pegged, though. She'd removed her glasses and looked me in the eye to let me know that she was more than a coach, more than another genius who wanted to coax beauty from me. She had her own beauty to give the world and she wanted me to see the abundance of it.

16

She was wary when she returned, as if she knew what I must have been thinking about her. She was more sober. The real purpose of her trip?

I took her hand and felt her resist.

"You know the truth about the woman who bore me a

child. You told me the truth about your husband because you let me see how it upsets you. You told me your feelings for great singers you've worked with..."

She wanted her hand back.

"...I was moved by what you told me. I don't think your feelings are silly in any way. You hear so much singing day after day, it's amazing that you can still respond to beauty in it..."

She was squeezing back now.

"...And not just to the acclaimed singers, but to a nobody like me when he has a good day."

She took back her hand and threw herself into a "mock-reproof" mode.

"You must never call yourself a nobody! You have worked very hard to be where you are. I don't know your roles, but it is impossible that you have not done leading roles somewhere. You must not be ashamed of your experience, no matter how humble! I will help you to find your way in Bordeaux. I know the people who will be sincerely interested in helping you make a career. You think you are too old, no? Thirty-nine? Thirty-five? My age exactly. I have heard about you Americans, trying to be children to the last minute. You will make a big career starting today. In France you are an artist, not a piece of paper full of numbers..."

I told her I was grateful for her interest and acknowledged needing to be taken in hand. "I meant what I said about your beauty, though. I know I couldn't resist you, no matter what was at stake."

"A wife? A child?"

"She isn't my wife. When she was my lover it was a case of mistaken identity or something very like it. I didn't even like her that much before I came here..."

"Ah, but now you know what it means to miss someone."

"That must be it. I feel sorry for her. Well, I always did, but I'm so much more aware now of what she has to offer and how it's going to waste. I would like very much to be someone she could count on, and to be a good father to that child."

By the Wayside

She sat back from the table as if she'd just become aware of poison in her drink. "And what do you want me for, then? A friend? A confidante? A mistress? Yes, a mistress, that must be it. I'm not the sort of woman...You've seen too many French movies, eh, Monsieur Locke?"

"Locke isn't my name, really."

"Then it's all a trick..."

"Bringing you here? I was hypnotized. Your charm, your beauty..."

"Nonsense. Day and night men are telling me how beautiful I am. Let it be so. I no longer need to be convinced. Deep in your soul, though, weren't you attracted by my piano-playing?"

"Of course I was. It must have been the way we fit together that made it feel wrong for me to leave..."

"That's it! The fitting. I felt it, too. I was a mighty, storm-tossed tree shaking off my notes like little birds. You took them like the wind and flung them across the sky, glittering white in the turning currents. You were there for me at the climax as well, a small dead bird in my trembling hands."

"It's probably the wrong time to say so, but I just had the depressing thought that sex doesn't mean much to you, with another body, that is." I flicked my head at an occupied table nearby. "I realize it will be difficult to talk about copulation in a place like this."

"What does it mean to you?"

"I'm not sure. I don't go into it looking for meaning the way you strain to see a blackboard. Anyway, sex is self-explanatory, isn't it? Love, I mean. While you're involved that way all the meaning of life comes unravelled before your eyes."

She burst out laughing. "What a cynic you are," she said with near-complicity. "But of course, you are much more. You have a healthy appetite for life. I like this in you. It is not enough for you to conquer M. *le régisseur*. You must conquer a beautiful, talented woman to round out the day. Then in the morning you will board your train..."

75

"Not so. I hadn't given a thought to what would happen between us. I blurted out what I felt, is all, and ever since I've just been stringing along...Wait. Please hear what I've got to say. Do you feel like a beer? My throat is too hot. *Une chope, s'il vous plaît!* Have one yourself, or anything else you'd like. As I was saying, I don't have a clue what's going on, or where it might lead. I'd be very sad if I offended you in some way. Now that I know how well you play, of course I'd like to have you help me with my repertoire, but the trouble is, and has been, how can I work with someone who attracts me the way you do?"

"You want to work with me, then? You will stay here and wait for Monsieur Poirot to return?"

I nodded redundantly.

"Then we shall be friends. Take your hand away!"

"You don't feel anything for me, then?"

"Of course I do, you fool, but I know the people who just sat down over there. Until they leave you will entertain me with your stories, drink lots of beer. I will pretend to be bored. Never mind anything you think about the way I'm behaving. Tell me about yourself." She slapped me across the face and a *chope* landed in front of me. Everything was happening so smoothly I wondered if her friends had arrived on cue.

She'd seen my résumé and knew I'd worked in France, but I couldn't talk about France for fear of letting slip a word that would lead to a broken heart or a wounded ego.

"Make me laugh," she was saying to encourage me.

Surely she'd forgive the antics of a 22-year-old without needing to know he was a part-time postman who was experimenting with LSD.

"It won't be hard to make you laugh if I tell you about my first job in the opera. A chorister, of course, the youngest one. The wedding scene from *Nozze di Figaro.* That was my biggest disaster. Grounds for divorce. You know the moment the rustics come in with garlands, festoons, whatever the word is in French—each couple is holding one up between them."

"I've seen it staged that way. Go on."

"Well, I had a big strong lady on the other end of mine, and I took the turn too wide..." She was starting to catch on, chewing her sweet lips. "I didn't come in center stage rear like the rest but ran into the cyclorama. Our garland fell apart. No one else could come in on time. Instead of entering a couple from the left, a couple from the right, they were sliding by each other, their garlands were getting tangled. So many forgot to sing that the first ones in were singing solo."

We sang the chorus together like comrades of old. She had a sweet voice.

"How wonderful! I'd have given anything to see it! Oh, I love Mozart...But after playing that little chorus a million times. You understand...You were fired?"

"Actually, no. I had the sense to resign. No one pays too much attention when choristers are falling all over each other, but when the painted scenery starts making trouble..."

"You didn't bring it down!"

"This was one of the biggest stages in the opera world, Sylvie. A cyke of iron, the entire chorus couldn't have brought it down. However, running into it at a trot, young and strong as I was then, I did cause it to undulate. The forest around was undulating, the distant lakes were heaving, the mountains were jelly."

"Splendid! But how sad to be banned from performing again after one such mishap."

"There were plenty of others! *Nozze* was one of the last shows. The miracle was I lasted so long."

"Please tell me the others..."

"Well, there was the time I was overdresssed wrong in *Boris*."

"Surely no one could get in trouble for being overdressed in that opera."

"I'm using the wrong word again. For the sake of quick scene changes we had on our pilgrim costumes over our boyar costumes, and our boyar costumes over our revolutionary rabble costumes—that was how a select group was supposed to be dressed, anyhow. I was one of the select group, unfortunately, chosen for my ability to survive intense heat and because I really could pass for a boyar in those days, one of the czar's trusted nobles. Trouble was, when I came to the czar's council with my staff of office—quite a dramatic entrance, we were on risers to either side of him—I was dressed as one of the revolutionary rabble."

"Brilliant! Ah, but if you didn't lose your job for that, one of the dressers surely must have. Poor things, how did they let something like that get past them?"

"No reason to feel sorry for them. Two of them removed my peasant attire after the boyar scene. That's the way they think, you know. 'Scene change. Whatever's on comes off.' That's the way they thought in San Francisco. Horrible as they must have felt to see a peasant up there advising the czar, off came my peasant clothes the moment the scene ended. They might have been rough about it—I don't know, I was feeling no pain. In the final scene when the peasants rushed off to make their revolution, a lone boyar lay downstage right, asleep against a stone wall."

"You must be a legend."

"I've probably ruined more opera in one season than any living chorister, but audiences don't really sit up and take notice unless the international stars are falling into the pit."

"You never fell on top of an orchestra..."

"No, but I stepped on somebody's robe and he did. No fault of mine. We were the capuchin friars in *Don Carlo*. They're always afraid of too much ankle showing when they're bringing on the clergy. Robes meant to be stepped on when there are stairs to climb."

"How exciting! Was he injured? Which section of the orchestra did he fall on?"

"Into one of our tubas. When you consider how much a brass player has invested in his embouchure, it was lucky for that tubist he wasn't playing at the time. As for my fellow basso, he went to the hospital and died two weeks later of a bleeding ulcer. Completely unrelated to the accident. He'd been drinking too much whiskey for years. I probably gave him an extra week of life because he couldn't have been drinking whiskey all day while he was in the hospital recovering from broken ribs."

"I love to hear your stories but they scare me, too. I probably should let the other *chef* know about Jeremy Locke before he makes up his mind about you. I'm teasing!"

"Madame, forget this alias, I beg you. I use a different name everywhere I audition. If I ever go back to Nice or San Francisco I'll dye my hair, shave my beard and wear lifts. Anyway, I'm not in France to sabotage provincial opera. Since all your friends are sure to find out about my baby, it's best if I've diddled my last wigmistress..."

She smiled to herself then, her eyes all glinty, and if I hadn't known her better I'd have sworn I was seeing lust.

"Tell me about Nice. I want to hear everything. Yes, about the women...But not here. I'm going to leave and walk up the *Cours de l'Intendance*. I'll be staying on this side, looking in the shop windows. Have another beer. That'll look just right. When you catch up to me, stay nearby, but not too close. Follow me at a distance. It's very difficult for me to leave the *centre ville* without being seen..."

"There's no way to take a taxicab discreetly? Two cabs?"

"Not while the sun shines!" The sun hadn't come out yet in the short time I'd been in Bordeaux, but it wasn't the time for pleasantries about the weather. Not while she was panting after secrecy, wild to escape her routine...

17

I was lost in no time, and I'd been keeping her in view—she didn't dress to be less striking. All the turns would have made sense if she were shopping. If she had been walking faster I'd have given up, certain she was trying to lose me, but she was stopping a lot, talking to people. Maybe she really was well-known in Bordeaux, and not just to singers and other musicians.

Then I lost her. She'd vanished into a building. There weren't many shops here, wherever here was. I kept on, looking into the stores. There was a music store midway down the block, but she wasn't inside. There was a slender alley on the other side of the store, and she was beckoning from the rear of it, half behind the building.

She'd left the door open. There was a rug, a concert grand, a hard sofa, a million opera scores on the wall. She was taking one down as I came in. Without looking inside she opened the book and placed it on a music stand. I recognized the Dutchman's piteous plea to his guardian angel from his aria near the top of the show, *Die frist ist um*...No clips to hold the pages open. She must have worked with a lot of baritones to break the binding.

"See how this is for you. You do the Dutchman?" I nodded. "I'm very excited to hear you." She began the notes leading up to my entrance, *molto tremolo*.

I, too, was atremble. Arguably the most difficult aria in the baritone literature, mastering this long monologue had been the goal of my work with the great French tenor in Nice who had died suddenly six months ago. It had been his feeling that a top German house would hire me on the spot if I could bring it off. "No baritone of the present day can sing the Dutchman full voice."

Neither could I, to start with, even though I considered myself a baritone of the past. I'd slaved for a year to bring my voice up to the challenges in that role. In the end I'd been up to it, if not yet comfortable, when news that a friend was dying persuaded me to return to the States and I began the long forced march up event and down dilemma which led to my returning to Europe as Lena's factotum.

I wasn't trembling from fear, but from excitement. For the first time in the last years there seemed to be some continuity in my life. I was no longer a man like other men feeling appropriate emotions: alienation, confusion, dread, disgust, remorse. I was the Dutchman, doomed to roam the oceans for eternity in seven-year installments, venturing onto land between them only to have hope extinguished yet again, cynicism justified, unable to find a woman who would be faithful until death, that my troubled soul might rest in peace.

The following English translation is standard and may be heard in the odd wilderness workshop or junior high school version.

> *Thee I beseech, kind angel sent from heaven...*
> *Thou who for me didst win unlooked-for grace,*
> *Was there a fruitless hope to mock me given,*
> *When thou didst show me how to find release?*
> *The hope is fruitless! All is quite in vain!*
> *On earth a love unchanging none can gain!*

In the whole 19th century couscous there isn't a better psychological portrait of Adolf Hitler, with the single difference that Hitler's soul could never rest until every hand was raised to him. It was the odd person who *didn't* believe in him that was keeping him awake at night. Anyway, whether an entire people can be faithful or not, it's probably easier to believe that they are, with thousands of policemen wielding a truncheon for you, than it would be to believe that a woman is faithful, even if you've got her locked in the basement.

Sylvie was hunkering in the manner of a born soloist as she attacked the keys. I seemed to be "doing it for her" so well with my voice that my words and notes were being taken for granted. Being treated like the recorded version by a coach was high praise. She kept right on going to the end of the aria without once looking at me—eyes closed the whole time. Quite a feat.

> *A single hope with me remaineth,*
> > *but one alone yet standeth fast;*
> *Though earth its frame long time retaineth,*
> > *in ruin it must fall at last.*
> *Great day of Judgment, nearing slow,*
> > *when wilt thou dawn to end my night?*
> *When comes it, that o'erwhelming blow,*
> > *to strike our world with crushing might?*
> *When all the dead arise again,*
> > *destruction I shall then attain.* (Three times.)
> *Ye planets, from your courses fall!*
> *Welcome, eternal end of all!*

In my defense I'd never felt any solidarity with the Dutchman when he was going on in this vein. Yet I gave his doom and gloom every ounce of planet-deviating emotion I could muster. I'd always got the feeling I was making a big impression singing this stuff, even though there was a good chance I wasn't getting any sympathy for the character. True, he was dead—a serious impediment to sympathy from word one. We were being asked to take pity on this poor soul for its inability to expunge itself. Having wandered the earth for a good portion of eternity already, we could understand it wanting an end to the whole mess.

Clearly space travel was the mode of choice for souls in torment. You didn't have to be a Norwegian fisherman to know that a shipful skulking about on our oceans was a bad business.

My feelings may have been unlike those of a normal man my age because she'd aroused me by means of this offbeat operatic exercise. Though I was putting everything I had into the Dutchman, his terror and torment never fazed me.

Even before she'd played for me in her studio I was aware that she had an erotic interest in betrayal. Betrayal was the horrible outcome that dogged the Dutchman, the unvarying result of all his yearning, his poetry, his treasure, his tenderness. But I was quite sure that there was nothing about the story of the Dutchman that captivated her. She didn't give a fig for his poetry or his treasure or his blackmasted ship with its blood-red sails. She was interested in the blood-red mast I was erecting at the moment, that was vying with my music stand. That's where she looked when she opened her eyes.

She motioned me to the seat beside her. I straddled the seat and tried to turn her, to take her into my arms. She let herself be turned, but when I tried to kiss her lips she quickly gave me her cheek and tried to push me away.

"You don't understand..." I waited for more. "I don't want to make love to you. I want to make love to Wagner."

Contempt for her came up so quick that I was remembering the air outside on the redolent streets of Bordeaux like the smell of life to someone about to emerge from a cave.

"Crap. There's a lot of beautiful music here, but the ideas behind it are downright silly."

"How can you say such a thing after they've lain so beautifully in your mouth?"

"All right, so senseless actions can be beautiful." I was trying not to feel sorry for her. "Marching armies can be beautiful if you're far enough away. But that's stretching it..."

"I'm crushed to hear you say this. I thought our souls were in harmony."

I put my hand on her back and she was crushed enough not to flinch.

"While you were playing you were right there for me. If we'd have done that well on the stage a while ago that *régisseur* would have taken me home with him and given me the master bedroom. Working with you has been a tremendous experience. I'm sorry if I get the signals wrong. But you're not just an artist—always an artist, are you? When you motioned to me just now I was sure that you wanted me to kiss you, at least. It's obvious that you were sexually aroused..."

"Wagner does this to me. During the music I was wanting

you inside me. Now I am feeling very shy, very much another man's wife. It would be a violation. Let me tell you something. All my life I have been under a pressure to give myself to men. They were trying to have sex with me before I was a woman."

"How sad. I understand. You have every reason to be timid, then, and I'm sorry I raised the issue."

"You still don't understand. It's not your fault. If you were French you would know right away that I have given in to the pressure. Not always, but many times. Our culture teaches us that it is a good thing to be desirable, and that it is not necessarily a bad thing to have many lovers. Now I am married. I won't pretend to you that I have always been faithful to this man. In a way, I have, though. I think it's possible to give the body and remain committed as a wife."

"Music to my ears, as it would be to any man alone with you right now."

"Do you think I could give you my body *a tempo*? For art, if that doesn't sound too banal? My body will be yours, but let me give my feelings to Wagner."

"You want me to screw you while I'm singing *Die frist ist um*? While you're playing it? Jesus Christ!"

"Exactly. I'll show you how we can manage it." She was off the bench now, pulling off her sweater, unbuttoning her blouse. I didn't believe my eyes—all the more reason to keep them peeled. I had to get my hands on her, even if she were looking the other way, even if she were cracked, not of age, poxy. The fact that she wasn't cracked or feebleminded, a few years younger than I and—being a wife, faithless or no—not likely to be venereally tainted just made having her that much more urgent. My red mast was aching to set sail.

How to take her while she was playing, though? From behind wouldn't be any good. I couldn't feature putting it to her in the ass, not if what was about to happen were to partake of high art. My absolute bar-none favorite way to mast a girl was to have her in my lap facing me, especially if she weighed less than a hundred and eighty pounds. Sylvie was longlimbed, as I've said, but in spite of a heavy bosom, which was all business at the moment, and a blooming rear end, which she was just now bringing into view, I doubt she weighed a hundred and twenty-five. She would have been perfect to dandle in my lap, but how the devil was she going to play the piano behind a back as big as mine?

She was watching me watch now. It took your breath away to see her. There wasn't enough left to sing two notes of an aria, but she'd said she was going to show me how to manage it. When she'd had her fiasco I was going to take over, throw her on the rug and let the sales clerk from the music store provide the accompaniment by pounding on the walls.

"If Wagner is the man you're after I guess I should just unzip my fly."

She smiled uncertainly as if the weirdness of what she wanted was coming home to her. She came to the bench with jerky movements, desire taking her forward, fear taking her back. Good with her hands as she was she managed to get the pants out of the way without spilling any blood...No mean feat, I was pushing hard. She considered what she saw for a moment like someone about to have a car crash, then she fell on it with a groan and promptly gagged herself. Victim or beneficiary of this I could have kept from laughing, but it was hard for an innocent bystander.

Now that I was wet she directed me to straddle her bench again and sat down to play with me inside. I was in the classical position to turn pages for her, but I was beginning to realize this would never be necessary. She had other plans for my hands.

Ever since an adolescent experience in a shabby theater on 42nd Street I'd been suspicious of the various "positions" for lovemaking which are possible for our species. Books pertaining to same were for laughs. From the time I was interested in sex I knew instinctively that everything had to happen like a roll of the dice, like chips falling where they may. Where you ended up didn't matter. There was always a mess after.

Better not to analyze at all. When there is passion and no woman we think about her many parts, we pass them in review, right down to the last peeping fold, the last straggling hair. When the woman is there the whole is much greater than the sum of its parts, and greater still according to her desire. But we're talking about Wagner here, not flesh and blood. One can listen to an orchestra to identify the various instruments, or one can let the music have its effect.

All this being said, on to a brief analysis, because where Sylvie was concerned all the how-to books and how-to pornhouses would at least point you in the right direction. But who would find her in her studio off the back of an alley in Bordeaux, find her and sing the Dutchman well enough to turn her on...in seven years? Fourteen? In her procreative lifetime? In spite of the broken binding on the score she gave me, in spite of the way she thought she could "manage" bringing us together, I felt pretty sure I was the only person who'd ever managed to be managed.

It was more than the difficulty of the aria that made me feel so unique. It was the difficulty of getting it up during such a morbid piece. It's well known that thoughts of death will fell a hard-on in seconds. The image that always worked in school when I was called to the blackboard was of an old woman in a death camp pissing into a pail.

But those were the early days. I was still completely uninterested in dead bodies. I could be turned off by a woman with a slight cough. However, because of all the years that I'd been screwing in a semi-anesthetized state, after too much to drink, that is, I did rather like the idea that *I* was a dead body, a nonentity, an object that my woman of the moment was masturbating with. As an object it was less embarrassing to watch her transports, to study all the minute changes wrought by her desire. In line with what I've said above, in the transports of love the details merge, the spectacle of life regains its primal oneness and us beings our primal awe. However, a drunk can't feel love, can only reenact some scene. The most a drunk can hope for is a good eyeful.

That's what I felt was going on here—sophisticated pornography. Nothing the least bit unpleasant about it. It recalled bizarre interludes with a woman I used to call "the papayatrice"—a practising psychiatrist who was as susceptible to categories as a Des Esseintes. She'd made a fool of herself in the toolshed as well as the pantry.

I'd never sung opera whilst screwing or being screwed. This was the first first. I'd been in a woman this way before, but only in passing, when she was trying to keep me inside her while getting into or out of the doggie position.

Being sideways to Sylvie as well as perpendicular was just as good as drunkenness for inducing the right amount of deadness to play with her and watch her respond. Her nipples felt like walnuts. When I got my finger down between her legs her clitoris was pecan-sized, and as hard. My left hand was cleaning a pumpkin, recalling another childhood mystery.

I wasn't singing full voice, of course—not with my mouth an inch from her pink right ear. I must have had the volume just right because it was clear that she was coming the whole time we rehearsed.

In retrospect what was most amazing about her performance was how she could take her weight off me every time she attacked the keys—and her attacks were endless oceanic assault waves. I remembered the duckwalks we'd had to do in football practice. In that exercise ten minutes was an eternity. This amazing woman would have played through the entire score of the Dutchman that night if I hadn't complained of a cramp in my leg.

There had been no cramp, but I'd been so hard for so long that I was sore, and unless she threw me a glance or let me know in some other small way that she was aware of my existence as something besides a cock and a voice, relief was nowhere in sight.

She was wild-eyed when I left her, trembling all over, her soft hair full of sweat. I needed another beer.

I had a few beers in her quarter and took a cab back to my humble hotel room. I was up to here with Wagner and the Dutchman and music in general. It was one of the few times in all my years abroad that I was homesick. I'd have given anything for a hot dog, a cold beer, a baseball game. Sunshine, of course.

Instead I waited for sleep with my toes clasping the rails at the foot of my bed, listening to the rain.

18

The night I met Sylvie I'd spent nearly all of the money I'd have needed to eat and sleep for the next ten days awaiting the return of the man who was going to hire me. So what, I thought, when he returns I'll tell him the truth about my situation. He could put me under contract right away and give me an advance. They'd done that in Nice.

I started to worry when I'd visited the opera house three days running to see Sylvie and had been told by the concierge that she hadn't come in that day, or wasn't available. I knew he was getting rid of me, but I refused to believe that she would shut me out of her life after a coaching session such as the one we'd had the other day.

I didn't try to find my way back to her studio. I thought she might have been embarrassed by how wild things had got during the first day of our knowing each other—afraid that she wouldn't be able to conceal an affair like ours from her husband.

I thought she was overdoing it, even though her marriage was at stake. With a strong lock on the door and no holes in the wall to inform our friend the clerk, the sounds in her studio were innocence itself, even with me singing half-voice. Morbid German was the very soul of innocence outside of Germany.

A week after my audition I visited the stage entrance again and the concierge informed me that Sylvie's husband was the leading baritone with the company, one of the most respected singers in France. He went on to say that he could tell from my demeanor that I was smitten by Sylvie, and that the best thing would be to forget it. If I went ahead as if nothing were amiss, and acknowledged Sylvie as a colleague, there would still be a chance for me, though I should forget about any role her husband was doing and ask for a contract as a bass. He very kindly told me what roles would be a waste of my time, and one of them was, of course, the Dutchman.

I was already broke and there were three days to go. I cashed in my train ticket to Nantes. The head man in Bordeaux would want to hear me when he returned and I would have to be strong—devil-may-care, preferably. After ten days Poirot still wasn't back and I was sore because I was broke again, though my hotel was paid.

In long walks around the town I'd become friendly with a group of clochards who were grubbing a living in a little square off the *voie piétonne* not far from *centre ville*. There were shrubs and small trees, little benches arranged so that men could sit and pass the time. Quite unusual for such men to gather so near the center, I thought. There were two cafes with large *terrasses* on this square, no less.

When the clochards found out I could sing they had me doing a street pitch, and with the coins I picked up on a good afternoon we'd have enough for wine and something to eat.

It was after tossing off the aria I'd auditioned with at the *Grand Théâtre* that I was surprised by the man who'd auditioned me in the company of the man who must have been Poirot, the long-awaited impresario.

I'd been getting a healthy round of applause, people on the terraces across were applauding. They were still applauding after I'd sat down again next to the men, who were roasting a chicken over a large tin can. My eyes were drawn to two men who were not applauding. Who were consulting. When I met their gaze I knew I was done for in Bordeaux.

Sure enough, I got the flowery letter telling me my services weren't required two days later.

BARCELONA

19

Back in Barcelona Botch welcomed me enthusiastically.
No one else did.
No one else was there.
"America! America!" shouted the *portero* after I'd yanked
him out of his hole under a wing of the house.
"All right, Invidio, where are my books, my belong-
ings?"
"Inglés! Inglés!"
"I can see some of that stuff is mine. Right there! Piled
right behind you!" I was speaking a mixture of French, English
and Spanish that nobody but Invidio could have understood.
He tried to block the door of his hovel.
"Out of my way, you. I want everything that's mine!"
He handed me some soft porn.
"That shit isn't mine."
I put my fist in his face and he backed into his hole trying
to get the door between us.
I followed him in. God, was the place rank. What to
expect. He lived his entire life in this one small room. Nothing
could be worse than being an illiterate who took orders from
our fascist. I'd never felt anything but disgust at the sight of this
slinking knave, but standing in his miserable dwelling, in the

presence of the things he was trying to steal from me, I felt pity for the first time.

I examined the stacks of my things. Suddenly none of it mattered. These weren't the books I treasured. Light reading, mostly. Baggage.

I put the books back where he had had them and watched gratitude come into his eyes. I wanted to touch him on the shoulder before I left but he was still too afraid.

"El inglés tiene todo," he said from the darkness as I emerged.

I looked down at the fascist's *palacio* for a moment. No, Elena must have known I would never ask the fascist for anything, even news of my daughter.

Of course Owen was keeping everything that Elena thought I deserved—probably not much. A letter from her would be enough. I knew exactly where she was and what had happened. I wasn't counting on being invited to Palo Alto. I didn't particularly want to go. But I did need to know what was expected of me, what my penance was. How big did my castle have to be before she'd come back to me with the baby? What new chores would I be taking on?

I found Owen right away because before leaving he'd given me the name of a cafe—in case. He was sitting next to his Scottish girlfriend, Brenda, having tea when I came upon him.

Owen might have been glad to see me but Brenda was just surprised and staring hard. Perhaps she'd had a different idea of what I looked like. And why not, so had Owen, who didn't waste any time asking me about all the weight I'd lost.

He was indeed keeping a letter from Lena for me and some of my books. I was appalled by the change in his English since he'd become a teacher. He'd stopped framing his sentences and seemed capable of saying any old thing. I asked him how things were in the English racket.

"We're both giving lots of classes, but it's the same old thing," Owen told me. "The schools give everybody a small piece of the pie because people are loyal on the brink of poverty. And the private pupils keep shopping around for a new teacher."

"As soon as they find out there are teachers like Brenda."

"No, it's my method. It's too much at once, they don't feel like they're getting anywhere. The direct method is fine in front of a class. I never lose my composure. But when you're alone with some fellow asking where is the bloody WC, and he keeps looking at you blankly..."

"I understand. Well, English teaching's not for me. I saw some buskers on the way down here, up by the Galerías..."

"On the Puerta del Angel," said Brenda. "It's closed to traffic now." She meant, at midday.

"A lot of them come in here to change their coins for notes," said Owen. "Stick around till two or three, you'll meet some. English speakers."

"Good friends, they are," said Brenda, "which is amazing when you think how they compete out there."

"I know the scene from my days in France. What I can't figure is why everyone's doing a street pitch. There's a lot more money working the terraces with a bottler. Take the Zurich Bar up on Plaça Catalunya. I was thinking of trying it tonight, and I was going to ask you to bottle for me, Owen. The money'd be better if Brenda would do it. But not the first time out. Balls will be all right. Owen's got that direct method..."

"You just want me to pass the hat for you, then?"

"I'll do a couple of songs and you whizz past the tables and get people to throw coins. You'll probably come up with some olive pits, but no mind."

Owen was smiling. "You bastard. Sure, I'll help you out. Let's get you a room in the pension. Cheapest I've found and right above this place. I hope you know what to expect, though, Gordon. This is rock bottom."

Owen started off, then turned back to Brenda pulling his thin lower lip.

"That's all right," she said. "I've got to see someone about a class."

There was a middleaged Galician couple at the desk. She

clung to the man's arm at the sight of me. They called Owen *"el profesor"* to impress me.

"You've gone up in the world, man," I told him at the top of the second flight of stairs. "From mad cyclist to professor and all you had to do was change your domicile."

Owen had the keys and opened the door to my room for me. He was a head shorter and kept going. I didn't make it past the first beam. He turned when he heard the sound and watched me fall.

"I should have warned you! Don't try to get up yet, Gordon. These places are all like that. I took it for granted you knew. Remember the rule: when you have to stoop to go through a door, keep the position. You'll get used to walking with your head down after a while. Think how much more it'll mean to be able to go outside."

I had no response to any of this but amazement.

His room was bigger than mine and I could stand up in half of it. We paid the same, but he was *"el profesor..."* I picked up Elena's letter and those of my books Owen couldn't use to teach English.

Dear Honeybear:

I'm sure it's better for all of us, but especially the baby, if mom and I go back to California with her. The medical care is so much better there. And mom and dad are eager to take care of Lenita while she's a baby. Who knows, they might even adopt her if it turns out I can't be a very good mother and then you'll be free to write and sing and have the life you've always wanted in a foreign land, safe from your enemies, free as a bird. If you ever come into some really big money be sure to write and we can discuss a way for you to get the baby back, cuz my parents won't live forever, and my mother is close to death even as I write from the filthy conditions we're living in, which is just one more reason we have to leave. I'm sure she'll be better when we get back and Lenita will be receiving the same wonderful care from her.

When I spoke to daddy on the phone I think the thing that made him maddest was not you getting drunk and having your money robbed but the fact that you left a helpless baby in the company of an Englishman who might be insane. He says you should go to AA if you can get drunk enough to be robbed and that you should go back to college and stay till you've got at least a master's (he knows your age). Of course he never did think you were good enough for me because of your lack of political insight.

Lenita moves her fingers, kicks her legs, blows bubbles and cries a lot. I wish you could see her but I'll send pictures.

Love, Lena

Since I was not in possession of an intercontinental ballistic missile there was no way to reply to this letter. I knew I would eventually, to give her my address so that she could send me pictures of the baby. But for the moment this free bird had things to think about besides Nena and her bubbles.

I *was* rock bottom, broke and stranded in a country where I didn't speak the language. Still, I had more going for me than a lot of the people in this pension. I had both my legs, I had no incurable lung disease. I hadn't come here to die. There were plenty of beggars scattered all over Barcelona and only the crazy ones looked like they were starving—the ones who spent all their money on children's toys.

Was this another line of shit I was handing myself? No, I could feel it in my bones. I was ready for anything. To hell with trying to be the right person to go with my voice. To hell with being dedicated to another age like a one-man medieval monastery. It was time to live life and stop watching at the window.

I'd been making forced moves for so long that I'd forgotten how to push back at life. What a place to start pushing! I was twice the size of anybody in the neighborhood. I felt a surge of energy that I hadn't felt since the days when I ran around with the Foreign Legion.

Better not to get carried away. I was counting on these poor, miserable people to help me stay alive, and they might be reluctant to help a John Wayne type. Not to worry, I'd find a formula, I had a few days to tinker with the equation before it was me and the wall.

20

It was drizzling when I came for Owen.

"Sure we're going to do it. It won't be raining on *them.* They'll be sitting there watching the rest of us run." I gave him a watch cap of mine to bottle with. "Hey, where's your cycling cap?"

"Jesus, Gordon, I couldn't see the point of it. I'd feel like an idiot."

"That *is* the point, man. You're much too distinguished-looking to need money, or to be stuck in the rain. They'll think you want a match, or directions, maybe, and they'll be sore to find out otherwise. Poke your head in with nothing but that colored cap and your big ears to recommend you! They'll be scared and give you money to go away. That's the ticket. In and out before the restaurant puts the cops on us."

"It's legal here, though, Gordon—busking is, I'm sure of it."

"All those guys are doing a street pitch. Doesn't it strike you as a bit peculiar that nobody's ever working the terraces? Get the hat, would you? Trust me."

Owen was into me for too many favors, the poor bastard. God was he a sight in civvies with that hat on. Almost as good as having a clown go around for me.

The Zurich Bar was going full blast on both terraces. I was scared shitless, but I didn't want Owen to know it. He was scared, too, and there was no way for him not to show it. The cap squeezing his head could have been the reason his ears looked so big and his eyes so wide, but there was no mistaking the fact that he wasn't afraid of anything in front of him. What was scaring him to death was happening inside.

He stood behind me while I sang, "Old Man River." I was trying to keep my head inside the awning, but cold rivulets were coming down the back of my neck.

Some poor soul applauded. I felt Owen trying to push past me and had to hold him back. "The show's not over just 'cause you're shitting in your pants! After the next one..."

Some waiters were taking notice. The look of the bewildered Spaniard I recognized from the times I had the words wrong. ("The frogs in this part of Catalunya certainly are productive.") I began to see it was Owen who had their interest, lurking behind me with his red-and-white headgear. Nothing wrong with the singing...so far.

I gave them "Wagon Wheels" and turned Owen loose right at the end. This time three or four folks applauded. They were beginning to realize that this was a performance of some kind. The applause stopped abruptly when Owen bounded into the picture stretching my watch cap to the size of a manhole.

For a moment I thought everyone was going to scatter. He was thrusting my cap right into their faces, you'd have thought he was trying to get them to eat out of it or give back some of their sorbet. Had the poor bugger never seen this done in France? Maybe not, maybe he'd clung to the back roads where the only cafes had a petrol pump out front.

I was laughing my head off well inside the awning and the

waiters were worried now. This was clearly some kind of invasion but they couldn't yet figure by whom and why. Owen was the star of the show. He had all the eyes and was getting a few pesetas as well. It was the way he moved that had me in stitches. Instead of sliding through the aisle the way the waiters did he was jumping up and down, bounding between the tables, forgetting someone, bounding back. He couldn't have covered the crowd any better if he'd been sprayed at them.

He came flying by me still holding my cap out in front. Bit of a point at the bottom now.

"Let's go!"

"Where? Who's shooting? Shit, man, we've got to work the other side. These waiters probably don't even know the ones over there."

"Are you mad? We'll be arrested! Didn't you see the looks they were giving me?"

"Sure did. They're crazy about you. I'll bet you could get a regular job here entertaining at night. Wait'll summer and the Germans come. By God, that cap of mine will be dragging the ground."

We were rounding the cafe, well out in the rainy night. We could go for the other side, go down the steps to the Metro or bolt into the busy traffic, the quickest way out. That was sweat on his forehead now, not rain, and I was worried about him.

"All right, Owen, let's take a break. We'll go across for coffee and talk this over."

"Can I take off my bloody cap?"

"If you expect me to be seen with you, you'd bloody better."

We had two *cafés con leche* while we were counting up. After the coffee we would still have 400 pesetas.

"What do you think of that, Owen? Five hundred pesetas for ten minutes work. Two hundred and fifty for you and you only had to work four minutes, if that."

"Four minutes? You've got to be joking! It seemed like forever."

"You don't like this line of work."

"You're damned right I don't. I thought I was going to die. I've never been so humiliated in my life. The looks they gave me! You'd have thought I was pointing a gun at them! And the things they were saying. I didn't get the Spanish, but it must have been, 'Fuck off, you fruitcake.'"

He shuddered and his eyes moved like an express train past a local stop.

"It's a shame, is all, because you'd do a lot better with me than you'll ever do with your classes. You're a bottler born. Christ, even I wanted to give you some money. In time you'd learn to use the hat better. You don't want to make the world go dark on 'em! Put the hat closer to the man's hand, close to his coins if he's got any on the table. People don't carry their money in their mouths, even in a place as dangerous as Barcelona."

But Owen couldn't stick it. He'd grown fond of being *"el profesor," "el loco"* just wasn't in him. Some English people are *born* with a terror of being ridiculous.

21

I went out the next day on my own. The rain had stopped, light was pouring down on me, and I had the confidence of someone submitting to unnecessary surgery.

A sad weary *"señor"* was all the policeman needed to say. I was relieved. Now I'd find a spot and do a street pitch and take my chances with the rest.

"Just another street performer..."

Devil take the legitimate musicians, but particularly the

opera singers, who were out to prove who could bark the loudest and show off their tricks. When I thought of past solo appearances I sometimes wondered if singing professionally had been something I liked or still wanted to do. I thought of the dollops of dread melting in my chest, the unpleasantness between fellow performers—or the forced pleasantness, which might have been worse. I remembered the emptiness after a show, the feeling that I'd never know the truth about my performance from the people who told me about it.

A lot of things I'd learned about singing didn't matter now. I didn't even have to get the notes right. All I had to do to lay claim to a spot was make some kind of noise. And that was why I knew I was going to enjoy performing now as I never had before. I'd be doing as I pleased with my voice, and trying to please with it. No conductor would be prodding me with his baton, there would be no orchestra to magnify my presence or absence, not even an old lady at the piano to wonder if I'd come in on time. The point was merely to make some beautiful sounds, surprise myself with them and maybe a few other people who happened by.

Competition was still there for those who wanted it, but since we didn't perform for each other it consisted in silly comparisons of the day's take.

I glanced at my case from time to time, I loved to watch the money turning into a pile, I couldn't have been any happier laying golden eggs, but I never had to bother about the money when I sang because the money was often better when I sang well. I was on my way.

A lot of people who passed in front of me must have thought I was doing what I had to, but that was never strictly true, even when I was hard up. I'd never enjoyed a job so much in my life.

As usual when the road took a propitious turn I felt the need of a god to be grateful to, or really a way to thank the chaos of my life for causing me to do something I would never have done willingly, and giving me the chance to find out how much I liked it.

As usual, too, I only knew how to give thanks by emptying my head and using the tiny muscles in my throat to gift-wrap a song.

22

I've been on the street for some days, feeling my way. Doorways contain my voice, I want to be under awnings. I'm not trying to hide, but it's better if the crowds don't know where all the sound is coming from. If they could see me they'd give me a wide berth. Near the source opera sounds a lot like pain to the uninitiated.

When Marina comes to stand next to me I know my luck has changed. Her three-year-old is twirling in a white dress. By now I'm used to the peripheral patch of color that indicates a listener. The other buskers call it an "edge" when a semicircle forms in front of you. I can only keep an edge briefly here in the heavy traffic, and it's a thin one at that, never two deep. Very rare are those who slide along the buildingfronts as this little girl and her mother have done.

The twirling child is dramatizing my situation. Her fearless continuity inspires me. An end of fear is close, but my offerings are still too tentative to get the crowd with me. I recall adolescent gropings, the fear then. Isolated contacts are a victory, but they need to be sustained and repeated many times before they slur into a caress.

Marina touches my arm when I've delivered the climactic phrase of the *Pagliacci* aria. There's more, but that's for the purists who are studying me from across the street, and the hell with them.

She tells me her name and her daughter's—Ana, Anita.

Marina's got a great Spanish face, all nose and beret.

By the Wayside

She tells me she's a *vasca*, so I tell her she's got a great Basque face. Yes, she'll have coffee.

Her English is poor, she says, but she's already decided it's better than my Spanish. Her daughter is singing to me not to be silly...*no dice tonterías*...

After I've packed up and we're moving off I tell her about Elena and the baby.

Anita keeps buzzing around, dancing ahead, stopping our progress as she jams her head between her mother's thighs.

Marina yanks the child's collar to keep her off the street, puts a guiding hand into her blond curls from time to time, never loses her train of thought no matter what the child does.

Her husband is having an affair with a woman who sells *bocadillos* on the Ramblas. Not from a stall, these are home-made sandwiches she sells to the vendors. Nuria...She is known by everyone on the street. So is Virgilio, her husband. So is she.

The fraternity of buskers I'm so happy to have joined, which already includes screevers, clowns and magicians, has just been enlarged to include all the rest of the people on the street who are trying to get attention: the anarchists with their pamphlets, the tricksters spieling like a power drill, the whores who open their jackets and gently cradle a breast while they're looking right through you. I want to know them all, I tell her. If they have a private language like the street people of France, I want to speak it.

Marina has heard of my act before she heard my voice, she tells me over lemon tea. She doesn't know anything about opera, but she knows at a glance I need help if I want to make money busking. I should carry a book of opera songs...Was there such a thing?

"An anthology. I've got a couple."

"This is exactly. You look in the book when you finish, you are resting. The others know you are not giving up your spot. Catalan people respect very much what comes from a book. They are not loving opera is possible, but they are afraid to ignore something so loud from a big book."

I'm aware that the Basques think of the Catalans as the other master race of Spain, but her cultural trappings are suddenly a disguise, her *boina* or beret is no more Basque than mine. But no, she's as Basque as they come, full of stories about Basque food and song, Basque brothers and Basque lovers. Her language is an example of history on her side. But history's not always on her side, say I, or we wouldn't have these bombings.

She tells me I'll never understand the E.T.A., but I tell her I want to. "If you're one of them I'll even help you blow up modern buildings, preferably banks."

"I'm not a separatist," she tells me, full of good humor. "I'm an anarchist. My husband is from one of the oldest anarchist families of Spain."

"I'm an anarchist, too. I know our traditions are different. Back in the States we haven't got an anarchist party, as you may know, so it was hard for me to fit into the political life of my country. Probably aren't enough anarchists for a dinner party. People confuse them with terrorists, the fault of the anarchists we did have once, assassins and mad bombers, you remember the type. Now that I'm in a country with an anarchist party, however, I want to join the opera squadron of the vegetarian pacifist wing."

"But OK you are placing bombs for the separatists."

"If you'd been a separatist...Let's face it, I want you to be my friend, maybe my lover, if there's any chance you want to get even with your husband." She smiles. She's already told me that Ana doesn't understand a word of English but the child's pulling at her mother's sleeve and I'm beginning to wonder. "Even if I can't have you I want to pick your brains."

She's still smiling and I'm not sure she understands half of what I'm telling her, but she's determined to hear me out.

"Holding an anthology while I sing? That was brilliant, Marina. I need that kind of help. I need to make a lot of money on the street. I don't want to follow my child back to the States. I want her mother to bring her back to me."

"You want to keep going a family by operasinging

on the street?"

"Bingo."

"Maybe so a Cuban. They are tough, loving life."

"Not this one. Take my word. I'm really up against it, but after the freedom I've had singing out there I don't think I ever want to tiptoe into favor at an operahouse."

She's so excited she's taken both my hands. "The *boina* is just right. This coat is very good, I like." She's pulling the lapels of the best coat I ever owned, a double-breasted blazer made for me by an opera-mad tailor in Nice.

She lets go of me, disappointed. I should hold the little gadget that sounds like an harmonica (my pitchpipe) in my right hand, stop fishing it out of my pocket. To legitimize my opera performances on the street a pitchpipe is better than an orchestra. She's adamant: any fool could switch on a tape-player, but I knew the difference between F# and G.

"You ought to manage me," I tell her when she's been on me for a while. "You ought to manage all of us." She's keeping a laugh back. Maybe she already does.

Before she has to go she finally comments on the possibility of visiting my pension above the Tapas Bar.

"I was going to try to be faithful to Elena, but I see that's impossible. I guess I'd better be discreet, though, in case I succeed in getting her back."

"Yes, discreet. So many are whores."

I glance at her daughter. Marina smiles and tells her to order a chocolate. The child revives like a paper flower.

"Because of my poor Spanish no one wants my ideas, so it's very clear to me when someone wants my money."

"Soon I will start working as a secretary again. I can come to you in early morning. I promise you we will have everything that I am already wanting very much..."

Virgilio has published a book of poetry, but his main contribution to their marriage is a huge flat full of elderly anarchists. A dozen old women to fuss over Anita! I'm invited to come and stay for dinner whenever I like, to stay the night. Nuria comes all the time...

23

I take my hat off to the Barcelona police, the Guardia Urbana, who see to it we buskers respect each other. The competition, the musical wooing is most intense on the Puerta del Angel, a gateway between the old Barcelona and the new, between the commercial sector and the historical. Here the industrious Catalan people are on their way to dine in the *barrio gótico* or on their way back to work. Motor transport is forbidden at the busy times. The elaborate façades of office buildings, the irregularities of storefronts, the quirky way the street divides to enter the barrio...all account for twenty or so little territories where music can be contained and musicians won't obstruct the flow of foot traffic. These spots are traditional. The police know them and defend our right to take them on a first-come basis. If one of us stops playing to blow his nose, the police will move on some newcomer trying to start up across the street.

I've had all the trouble I'm going to have, I think. I was moved on the first day and couldn't understand why for a moment. People were throwing coins at me from upper stories. I recognized the word *biblioteca* while the cop was taking my arm. I'd given some students a few laughs. Good thing I got out of there before the students wanted to get rid of me.

That cop was an old fellow. The best cops are older. They show you to a free spot and wish you luck. When they want to tell you something the rule with the cops is to let you finish your song. In my case they wait across the street. No one ever waits to talk to me in the line of fire except children and once in a while a teasing woman, usually a whore.

Scrambling for a good spot I question how we buskers can be such good friends. The hatred rises in me when I find someone I've never seen in a spot I've made my own for three or four days in a row. In three weeks some faces are starting to be friendly. Amazing how many people pass the same spot each day, usually twice.

I gather I'm one of the few street people who respects the

police. A fellow American might know how I feel. I don't have to look over my shoulder any more. When in my life had I not been looking over my shoulder in a public place? The jobs where I wore a suit, the New York jobs, but I'd been young then, I never looked over my shoulder in those days even when I couldn't remember the damage of the night before. I had no need of remorse. The people I'd hurt were always up ahead shaking their heads or their fists.

24

I owe everything to the Spanish. They seem gullible to be so good to me. They force me to take myself seriously.

The money I'm piling up will be enough to bring Lena back. Sometimes the thought of what I'm going to ask her to do is more preposterous to me than it will be to her.

I'm getting my money from the Spanish, the tourists just smile or take pictures. There are exceptions and once in a while I'll give up my spot to be a tourist with them. Operalovers, mostly. So far they seem to come from Northern countries, though I'm good with French people, especially those who think France and Spain are at war over the relative cost and quality of their farm products. They think it takes guts to sing in French in broad daylight as I'm doing...

I sent two such French maniacs to Hewitson for a lecture on the Spanish character. When he gave it to me it went like this: "Simplicity can look like coarseness. Openness can look like innocence. The humble can look servile. In the simplicity of the Spaniard I see nobility. I have walked the streets of France, Gordon. I love the country, but what happens on the street looks like cinema. Life obeys rules, like an art form. Here it just happens, and you can look deeper and deeper because there's no predetermined significance. Take that whore over there. Yes, anyone could see that's what she is. Go across and talk to her. Meet her gaze and tell me what you find. Better yet, go to bed with her and see what happens. Put away your phrasebook and let Spain into your blood..."

Hewitson's dead serious. He's taken incredible chances.

He has a good job conducting interviews of English speakers for the *Vanguardia*. He's a liaison, a mystery man. The newspaper people are probably afraid of him and this is why he can spend most of his time out on the streets rallying the performers.

A few days ago I was flattered to be taken under his wing.

Half of Barcelona is under there with me! Hewitson is a one-man chamber of commerce. He tells Spaniards about the glories of Spain. He never shuts up about how lucky they are to walk home amid the splendors that spring from the ends of his waving hands. You can walk clear across town with him and never once catch a glimpse of your shoes. After one of his spiels born losers forget the back rent, dance back inside their tenements and click their heels in front of their hungry kids.

Hewitson is an Irish-Australian who looks like Errol Flynn on carrot juice. Un-Spanish as Flynn was, Hewitson can't help following in his footsteps. It's probably just a cultural thing, but Hewitson has a pot-smoking hand and a drinking hand and he's got them both going at once whenever he's loose from the job. He favors bars that are open to the street. His hands are still waving. He knows everybody. He quiets down when he's doping and drinking incessantly, but not as much as you'd expect.

Hewitson reminds me of one of the characters out of Henry Miller's Paris books. He's obsessed, in a hurry. He's always talking to me as if we have a host of things in common, but the difference between me and Henry Miller is that I wish I *did* have these things in common with him. Right away when I met him I thought, he's obsessed, he's good for laughs, but he's sure to get boring, no one could keep this up, he'll start repeating himself. No, when Hewitson says, "Look at that!," you're seeing it for the first time. He gets funnier as he goes along. Deeper, if you stay with him.

I've known him a couple of weeks when he decides I'm ready to come home and meet the wife and kids. I could have made the scene at his place sooner, but I've been putting him off. I don't want to miss work, the money's too good, I've been finding these terrific spots...

Now I'm ready for him to roll over me, I've decided I can walk out on the streets with my music case at any time of day or night and make enough to stay alive...Stay ahead. One day's hard work is enough to put me a week ahead of an empty stomach.

"You're going to love Lidia, I've been telling her about you." I'm in a cafe near the cathedral counting up. I sip lemon tea and make stacks of the coins that have been thrown at me all day, stacks my friend Antonio is going to turn into notes. "Looks like you've been getting good drops. Why don't you tuck that away and be my guest for a couple of days? Eduardo won't be staying (a conga man we're going to meet somewhere. I've never seen him when he's not beating his drum.)..."

I want to stay as long as he'll have me. I don't know what I'm getting into, can't imagine what Hewitson will be like indoors around the same faces and furnishings. He's told me that his place takes up the entire top floor of a building on the Diagonal. It would have to be a labyrinth. It seems like many years since I've been in a place big enough to explore.

We've got time to kill so he's taking me on a tour of parts of the barrio I've been told to avoid. There's no danger here in spite of the men in the shadows with glittering eyes. Hewitson is too sure of where he's going, he's obviously someone who belongs. He seems to welcome confrontations in these narrow streets, looks like he wants to give everyone a hug, and everyone shrinks back.

We're looking for a little bar that sells Asturian cider and *cabrales* cheese. I'll never be able to find this place again without him. He's raving about the tastes so much that I'm swallowing continuously to bail out my mouth.

"Look at this place!" I note there are steps down. "Empty! Always! Adolfo!" he booms. Now he's chirping away so fast in Spanish that he loses me.

Adolfo is a gangling brute of 50 or so who looks as if he's lost as many fights as he's won. Even though Hewitson is his only customer, maybe the reason he's still in business, there is no more than a trace of a smile to make my friend welcome. It's questionable if we're really in public any more.

Depending on the kind of person Adolfo turns out to be, this place may be my first choice for entertaining whores. Dark, cheap, private—the opposite of flashy. A note of music would show disrespect for the cider, whose bursting bubbles are the main sign of life here.

The cider-pouring is a big production, like something from the movies. The point is to pour from over your head into a bowl at your hip so that half the product is wasted. The cider must be aerated, Hewitson insists.

I have a hunch Adolfo is a trifle insane. An empty bar, so much waste. He keeps pouring us glass after glass this way, splashing cider prodigally about his workspace and onto himself while Hewitson's This is Spain! expression glows in the dark. I can't help but feel I've hit on one of the reasons this isn't Germany.

The cider's fine, but the cheese is so good that I want Hewitson to run my life for a while and tell me everything to eat.

"This reminds me of the best cheese I ever tasted..." I meant this comment to gush right along with his.

"And what would that be?" He's put out, but he'll stop pouting if I'm recalling a Spanish cheese.

"A gorgonzola I bought in Nice..."

He's harrumphing, is all. It's hard to forget a visit to Gorgonzola...

"I waited more than two weeks for a slice of that cheese. You know how it comes, huge cylinder like so, they cut through with the wire, take out the wedges, chunk, chunk, chunk; they make the second horizontal cut, chunk, chunk,

chunk. All this takes time, the ones who buy these cuts aren't crazy about this cheese, but when they reach the bottom you've got to hurry. That's where a blue cheese like this can stagger you. Mushy with butterfat, pinkish meat. Someone tipped me off that the butterfat goes to the bottom."

"Good, you know something about cheese. Still, it bothers me that you call a cheese like this second best..."

"I didn't mean to. For years I never tasted a gorgonzola as good as that one I waited for. It's all in my head. Anyway, while this cheese is in my mouth...Well, it would be like a woman thinking of the neighbor kid while she's having one of her own. I'd love it no less if it were the only cheese in the world. In some ways it is..."

"Bravo. That's how I feel. Not only here...I've been here in Spain for twelve years, a big part of my adult life, and I still feel that way . No matter where I am, there's no place I would rather be. So many good times...It irritates me to reminisce...An old friend shows up and I'm lucky if I can remember his name. He's telling us about the time of his life he had with us and all we can remember is a day like any other. A cornucopia is meant to induce a state of mind, you don't touch a thing..."

The cider is more alcoholic than French cider and I'm really feeling it but Hewitson is taking me somewhere to drink Galician *aguardiente*, something to brighten our spirits after an hour in that dank hole wallowing in cider and strong cheese.

Hewitson never gets drunk. He reminds me of types called "merry" when they've had too much, but that's not going far enough. He free-associates. The coherence is in what's around him, the coexisting images that set him off. He greets an old gypsy woman, she's not persistent when he pushes on. She calls after us, telling me that I'm going to live to be 84, according to Hewitson. I'm beginning to think I want to.

"When we go out with Lidia...It's amazing, the gypsies recognize her, they gather around...A few paces back. They adore her. At the festival in Almería...She brings them good luck, I suppose..."

We pass a sex shop. "I met Lidia in Almería, working in a sex bar. Not selling herself. Her father owned a big section of the Diagonal, I was told. I'd heard this kind of thing before in sex bars. Then I woke up with a view over the Diagonal and found it was all true. This place has the best *jamón serrano* in the world. You wouldn't expect to find good food in a neighborhood like this, eh? Have you tried this ham? They cure it in the snow, you know."

"So much history next to boxed plastic dildos."

His face tells me he rejoices in the juxtaposition.

"How is it you've lived so long in Spain," I'm asking him moments later, "and traveled as much as they say you have?"

"Who says I have?"

"The Germans. Franz for one—Frankenstein."

"They heard it from Klaus. I traveled with him. I'll tell you more sometime. Poor Klaus. Yes, I kept moving for three, four years. My first years away from home. I wasn't in Spain long the first time. In Africa after I left, Greece, Crete, I knew I was coming back. Finally I had to. The memories were too strong. Lidia and I take a trip from time to time. I'd like to see the United States. The west, I think. Poor Klaus. I saw him recently and again he said, 'I want to go down.' He'd made some progress that way since I first heard those words. We spent weeks in Nepal practically on top of one another smoking opium...Traveled half the world together...He never found a Lidia..."

25

We're into the wee hours and Hewitson shows no sign of slowing down. He's on his back spouting in the middle of one of his living rooms, stopping only for a toke or a sip of his drink. Eduardo and I are on the sofa, sodden. Lidia is lounging back against my legs. Eduardo's hands are dead on the vellum, supporting his head. The room is spinning. Hewitson's words are all I can hang on to. There's a comforting domesticity about them, as of things on a clothesline I've just recognized as mine.

I was the one got him started on his travels. Puffs of experience become a miasma.

"Timor...my God. I was traveling with a Frenchman and this Dutch guy. Quite a friend, as it turned out, the Dutchman. We went on together all the way to Thailand. The ship was manned by Malays. Falling apart. They hated us...We were last in line for the shower. They recycled the water. You came out smelling worse than when you went in. The shitter was incredible. None of us could eat.

"We dock, debark. They make us wait in a hut while an official examines our passports. This is Portuguese Timor, the eastern part of the island. The Portuguese are hanging on, it's a Christian country, but leftists are everywhere. There's about to be a revolution that will send the Portuguese packing. You may remember what happened in '75. The leftist independence faction did have control for a while, but then the Indonesians moved in and wouldn't let go.

"Outside a hole in the hut there are hundreds of people vying for the chance to breathe down our necks. It's a furnace out there, hotter where we are. The idiot looking at our passports has a slave fanning him.

"For half an hour the brute paws our travel documents and gives us dirty looks. Granted, the photographs are of people who aren't unshaven and filthy. Our clothes are soaked through and have been for days. But the problem isn't matching the people with the photos or he'd have spent more time looking back and forth. If he's not taking his time to give himself importance, if he has some reason to suspect us, perhaps it's because we're each from a different country, traveling together. Anyway, we're weak, starving, not that much better off than the wretches outside waiting to kill us for our shoelaces...

"Finally he passes us and we climb into a jitney for our ride into town. You've seen these things in the Orient that are covered with amulets, regular little traveling altars. All during the ride to town our driver has a cheap tape machine playing the same song, blaring it. A sixty-minute tape of his only record— we heard it all. The song is meant to increase our apprehension. DOWNTOWN, da da da da DA da da da DA, DOWNTOWN. Some black woman from the States. After five minutes of being shaken apart on the road and listening to this woman I wanted to tear her larynx out with my bare hands, we could have torn her to pieces in minutes, we were beginning to be more like our old selves. We never thought we'd get out of the place alive, but we'd stopped being afraid.

"Dili is the capital. This is what the savages call 'downtown.' Dili. It's where you get the expression, a 'dilly,' which means an imbecile in Australia...

"As we enter town a well-fed fellow comes running out of a substantial house. A man of importance—dressed, at least. He's tearing us away from the jitney. The driver's happy to be paid, he's blessing us through missing teeth. From what we can judge from the driver's expression we seem to be doing the right thing by going with this energetic little fellow who's forcing us up the stairs to his house, up more stairs. He's pushed us into a room with a bed.

"There's an old woman on it, obviously ill, the smell is unbearable. It must be his dying mother. Our host is annoyed to see that she's still in the bed. He pitches her onto the floor and starts kicking her toward the door.

"The old woman is too weak to make her feet, she helps by crawling, her moans are involuntary, they're not related to the blows which must be as familiar to her as the bullets on the roof during the Northern Monsoon.

"We're trying to leave, to find a place to be sick, but the good citizen won't think of us going. Room for all! No one turned away! This is no inn of Bethlehem. He makes us wait, he won't let go of our clothes.

"A girl appears—a daughter, evidently. There's another behind her in the shadows, old enough to have grown three feet of hair. The girl he's showing us is his pride and joy. He rips off her clothes and points to her breasts.

"We're past the point of responding to anything. He must be able to tell by our expressions that we're appalled, struggling not to be sick.

"He clouts his daughter on the head and she offers her breasts. Her lips part and she shows us what's left of her teeth in what is meant to be a smile, but it was a look of pure terror.

"We were reeling when we reached the street, but it was a Christian country, thank God, and it was possible to get something to drink. Blind drunk is the only way you take some of those places. Alcohol has a different function entirely in that part of the world. It doesn't cause retching, it prevents it..."

When Lidia goes to bed Hewitson is on his feet again, he's rifling his sources, books, records. A million cassettes. He brings down a hundred that contain Spike Milligan. He's discovered that I'm dim about The Goon Show, though I've heard excerpts.

"Yeah, I heard he was certified, that Spike shot a guy in his backyard for picking fruit or something. Didn't kill him. Turned up in court wearing a Nazi helmet. Probably a lie."

"That's exactly right, even if the facts aren't. Who cares, the real Spike is all here. We've got all night. Tomorrow, the next day, who cares, if you're a fan. I've got all his shows. He's not the only one...But we'll limit ourselves, it's better. We won't do him justice by skipping around. Listen to this one..."

I can recognize Peter Sellers's voice. Hewitson starts at the top with Spike, Peter and Harry as British colonial army staff at war with the wogs, planning a retreat to keep the proper distance from their attackers. I'm drunk and stoned but I swear I can remember what it was like to be alive at the time these

113

shows were done. We were all breathing the same airwaves...

"How about it, Eduardo?"

I'm interrupting Hewitson and the Goons as well, but our host is being a sport.

Eduardo musters a shrug. He might be an acute observer. He might be an undemonstrative drunk. I've seen him playing in a salsa band ruled by a trumpet-wielding strongman. The cops moved them on when I got a spot they wanted and they set up across from me. We became friendly when I gave up my spot to them—"After all, five mouths to feed."

We've discussed the salsa band tonight. Hewitson and Eduardo concur, the trumpeter's nuts. I don't know him but I've seen him hit someone over the head with his trumpet...his bread and butter...His victim was another busker. But Eduardo keeps beating his drum for him and Hewitson keeps asking the trumpeter as well as Eduardo to come on picnics with his 9-year-old girl. They're all crazy except for Lidia and the 9-year-old, whose bright ideas seem to have been manured by common sense. Lidia's magnetic, though. That's what brings the gypsies, a physical attraction. I don't know what it is but I've felt it. The one-year-old is crazy as hell.

We're still listening to Goon Shows when the sun comes up. My brain is numb, though I've stopped smoking and drinking and so has Eduardo. I observe aloud that I feel as if a long flight has ended. Bill is rebuking me for wanting the night to end just as Lidia enters in her nightgown with an open robe, looking rested, making me long for a homelife of some kind, a double bed with a woman in it, so what if the bathroom is down the hall past the snores of people I will never know.

Lidia is planning breakfast. *Butifarra* sausages with whiskey chasers, a separate menu for the children.

I haven't eaten a sausage since army days, but Bill talks me into it. The whiskey is easier after a few bites. Delicious, whatever my stomach wants to make of it. Couldn't be any more confused than my liver.

Eduardo's head keeps sinking lower while breakfast is cooking and reaches the plate before his sausages.

The plan: I will help Bill carry him down to the car, he will be dropped off. We will then barbecue rabbits somewhere in the hills above the Costa Brava. I will hunt for wild mushrooms with daughter Leela. After dinner I will give a concert of French art song—Debussy, Fauré, Duparc.

Everything happens as planned except that Eduardo is with us, having revived in the car, so that my art songs are accompanied by conga drum and Bill snarling on the harmonica. Unseen Catalan campers applaud.

We lose Eduardo on the way back when he disappears from a service station on the outskirts of Barcelona, presumably because of getting into the wrong car and making himself welcome somehow. We deliver his drum to the Tapas Bar.

Here we are back in the living room at the Hewitson's and it seems to have got dark suddenly. Friends have arrived who don't look like street musicians, but they see nothing amiss in the fact that I am drinking whiskey out of a bottle and spewing into a blue plastic laundry tub that has been placed under the left arm of my chair.

I have difficulty following but Bill is talking about people I know. Later I realize, my friends on the street. Apparently some of these people are a lot funnier than I'd ever found them.

The talk goes on all night and I have my lucid moments, clear about every word and trying some of my own.

Franz had a fight with Klaus when he visited...

"Hell with Klaus..." I've been told he's someone I'm not likely to meet. "Franz is an enigma to me. I want to know more about him."

"He's no longer welcome here..."

"I cleaned the creatures off him." It's Lidia's voice behind me somewhere. "I carefully bathed him."

"He took a suit of my clothes." Bill.

"He comes back in a week all ragged," his wife again.

"Now he wants money. I tell him I can't. His guitar's been stolen. What happened to the cord? I ask. He hasn't had this guitar long enough to chain it to his leg. Oh, I can't stand to see a man that strong feeling sorry for himself. Maybe that's what was bothering Klaus."

"No, you misremember," said Lidia. "Klaus is a seeking man like Billy, but some pain has come."

"He wants to go down. He wants to fight with Franz. He doesn't care how he comes out."

With a jolt I realize that this explanation is for me. They've been addressing me right along, Lidia from beneath the right arm of my chair (obviously). The friends have left or are in another part of the house.

"Perhaps Klaus is on a Sufi trip like the path of Malamat," I offer, sensing that my words are bringing relief. "You know, inviting blame. Purposely pissing people off."

"That might be something like what's going on, but I don't think you've got it quite right. If this were some mystical device he'd have been using it to heighten his awareness, he wouldn't talk about going down. Anyway, he managed to get our friend Franz in such a state that there was no calming him. By the time the police came to drag Franz out they'd done a million pesetas worth of damage. The neighbors called the police, of course. Lidia and I wanted to hit Franz with something that wouldn't kill him, but it's hard to find something to wield in this apartment that isn't extremely valuable. They'd already smashed all the bottles."

"Did they charge him?"

"No, no. This is Spain! Just kept him overnight. It was a disagreement, there was nothing premeditated. What the police wanted to know was how he got into our apartment. Refused to believe I'd invited him. Thought I was trying to protect him from a burglary charge..."

26

Midway in my third night at the Hewitson's I get lost and am sucked down by a studio couch in an alcove.

With morning light at the windows of rooms I can't remember I grope through what seems to be an empty house until I find a way out. I'm still drunk, but pleasantly, under the circumstances.

The two-headed Galician Cerberus is glad to see me back. The woman-half is wringing its hands for joy. It may have given me up for dead. Except...my effects are still in the room. They'd be giving me a different reception if they thought I'd gone slinking off to find another pension. They're back in bed with smiles on their faces.

The rest of Barcelona isn't awake yet. Maybe I'll be able to sleep through the sound of the Damm truck loaded with empty beer bottles that jiggles past my window every morning and is harder to get used to than the crash of the metal blinds, the *persianas*, that shopkeepers fling up with great force prior to opening their doors.

Someone's pounding at my door. I've been settled two minutes. Has to be the Galicians, who've remembered that I owe back rent and want to make sure I know...I go to the door in my drawers. I already have zero respect for this couple. I'm paying my room with *rubias*, the tiny yellow one-peseta coins that I dump from my music case every few days into a paper bag and from the bag onto my landlady's kitchen table—the little coins we call ratshit. My hostess counts them into piles while I watch, ignoring me, her eyes glittering...

Marina!

"How did you get past them?"

"Never mind. I have not much time. I am to be at work." She's peeling off her clothes so quickly that I already feel overdressed in my dirty undershirt and my dirty drawers and my dirty socks.

She's naked now and I've never seen anything but her face and hands before. I drift to one side of the bed and then the other to look for a place to sit, but the only place is between her legs facing away and that won't do. I raise up her right leg and ease under and onto one elbow.

There's a wonderful smell coming from her. Both the large and small folds are engorged. Must have been playing with herself on the way over. Clearly she wants me to eat her. I give her a few half-hearted strokes of the blade, all the passion of someone making a sandwich.

"You couldn't have come at a worse time. I've been up for three days."

She answers by reaching between her legs and turning herself inside out. There was a time when I'd have died for the sight of her this way.

"I've just been with a child prostitute on Portuguese Timor."

"Now you have a real woman."

Between her legs she's perfect. There are healthy emanations. I've been trying to tell her I can't fuck her after all I've put myself through, not only at Hewitson's...Can't we go on being friends?...She can grope me under the table the way she did the other day in front of her husband. Trouble is, I like her husband and if Marina and I are going to have an affair I don't want him to know.

Life's door and death's door are starting to be the same, now. Passing in, passing out. In eating a woman I feel that it's my love of life, my appreciation of her involved...Not a throbbing sexual desire that wants to force pleasure to such a high pitch that it all gets lost. In fucking, her beauty, her wonderful languorous womanliness is gone and while I'm pulling myself out of the abyss there are moments when I wonder if all I've done is take the bait, if her body isn't some kind of trap, she's so much vaster than I am and there's no falling away for her when pleasure is at the peak—she goes on and on, and I'm not in her eyes, they're full of the sky, she's just pulling me along, urging me, digging in my flanks, pulling my hair. I'm something to ride. She's for the transports, I'm the transportation.

Marina is writhing beneath my tongue without yet knowing why I won't be putting anything more inside her. What's
this, though? Not much feeling. Probably a pee hard-on, but
so what, if I could finish her with it.

Yes, but won't the Galicians start pounding on the door
the minute I bounce the bed? Am I going to continue to
misunderstand the ordinary workings of life? What difference
does it make, I have to have her, even if I'm forced to tell the
Galicians to go away and leave me alone the whole time I'm
plunging it in.

"No, don't! Please don't! I'm not protected!"

Why is she here, then? She forgot! I'm sure of it!

I put it in anyway. She's tensing, it's like rigor mortis. I
recall the idiotic things I heard as a kid about women who
"clamp up on you."

"I won't come. I've got that much self-control. Just let
me slide it around a little so that I can remind myself what it's
for. I've wanted you too long. I won't even make you suck me
off or jack me off when the time comes..."

"I want to! Take it out now and let me suck. I swallow
it. I rub my body. I eat off my breast..."

She's gone so taut she's starting to tremble, and under
mine she's trying to bring her legs together.

It's no good, there's no mistaking the fear she feels, no
pretending that the vibrations that are chasing up and down her
taut strings have something to do with orgasm. Only a rapist
could find a continuation...

I withdraw, still firm, but I'm beginning to lose it.

She takes hold of me and I know she wants me in her
mouth somehow. Because of the tiny bed this isn't going to
happen without a certain amount of scrambling. Clearly I
should be where she's been and vice versa, but I want her to
figure this out for herself.

I'm so exhausted I need to be on my back anyhow. I know
I'll enjoy playing with her tits and watching her make good her
promises. Pornography should always be live. The memory
coddles it then and calls it up in mint condition. What she's

talking about will probably be there during my last moments when I'm eighty-four and the high spots are flashing before my eyes.

She wants to suck me off in midair from the head of the bed but she can't raise up high enough to compass it...for long. I ease her off the bed and supplant her. I'd have picked her up bodily if I'd been fit.

I'm quasi-bored by the time she starts to work on me, but by the sounds she's making I can tell she enjoys sucking. She's down there with the rocket when I lift off. She stays right with me during the ascent, the loss of booster, orbit, fetal acrobatics, free-fall, splashdown...

"I'm late to work," she says at last, exploring her chin with a handkerchief. "I'm sorry I didn't come sooner and we have more time, this is all, but later we find out what is possible. I keep you in my mouth when I say hello to those idiots, goodbye. Of course they are knowing but they are too afraid to say to your face. You are not to worry about this type."

I'm asleep the moment she closes the door.

27

When I go back to my routine on the streets I feel as if I'm returning to a job I don't know very well, a feeling I remember from days when I was always new in my jobs and the weekend breaks seemed like a goodsized vacation. All the faces are familiar and the names, even if they are right, don't seem as if they should be. By the end of the third or fourth two-hour set, though, I'm reassured, reestablished, reaccepted. I'm learning two songs from my anthologies that I've never heard sung, picking out the notes on my pitchpipe, mumbling the words into the restorative steam of my tea.

Marina comes to me twice on the street during the coming week, both times at night when I'm ready to quit. She doesn't seem to have sex in mind, but that could be my doing. My recent debauch is still a weight in my chest, a clinging strain that's composing my behavior like the presence of death. It's the rather sad and dry composure of elderly cancer victims, or others who've decided that they don't have anything to live for but aren't upset by people who do.

After a big night with a crowd of friends Virgilio and Marina take me home with them. The place is huge but there's no bed for me and they make me comfortable on the living room floor.

In the morning the grannies give me quite a start on their way into the kitchen. A word of explanation will lower the noise level in there, but not if I put my head in while I'm still wildhaired and red-eyed.

There are so many old folks that there isn't room at the table for everyone, they eat in shifts. The noise is tremendous, especially since the ones who are waiting to eat have nothing to do but talk and apparently enjoy having the eaters at a disadvantage.

Marina and Virgilio at the head of the table remind me why I never play around with married women if I can help it, never...unless I don't find out till I'm already hard or the woman has convinced me that her husband is a vicious bastard of some kind.

I've been around the block too many times not to recognize the kind of behavior that makes a marriage work. She's interested in what he has to say, listens when he says it. She gives him encouragement. He does the same for her, as much as he's able.

They'll stay together even if they don't know why they want to, no matter how much they screw others, even if they have very good reasons for wanting to.

28

Inside a week Virgilio is inviting me away from the Puerta del Angel in the afternoon. I feel like drinking beer and calling it a day. He's taking me to a cafe on a teeming little square near the Ciudadela Park. I was here once before with an English dame.

"I know all about you and my wife," he tells me over a cup of coffee. "I've known from the first day."

"I thought you might." Virgilio emphatically does not want to teach me Spanish, and I can't blame him. His English is good and he's got some French that's a help when he gets stuck.

"You know about Nuria. According to my wife you have been spying on us."

"Never. We bumped into you one night in a children's playground near the Sagrada Familia. She might have wanted the sandbox for us. She wasn't trying to catch you in the act."

"Why didn't you tell us you were there?"

"You had your hand up her dress. It wasn't a good time."

"Anyway, Nuria and I would like to spend more time together, but you know my situation at home. If I left, Marina might look for another man to help her with the child. My old relatives live for the child. That child helps them to ride a little further in their old wooden tumbrels..."

"Don't leave. We've got to make the best of things..."

"Marina is in love with you." He orders a beer.

"That's the last thing...It isn't true. Women think they're in love with me until they find out the kind of mess I make. Singing on the streets gives me an appearance of steadiness."

"Relax, Gordon. I know you care about Marina. Maybe your feelings aren't as strong as hers..."

"She's yours, and she should be yours. I know she loves you because I've seen it with my own eyes."

"We're great friends, but the spark of love is gone."

"What's the matter with you? I'm not good for Marina."

"She thinks you would be. What I am proposing...Look,

there isn't much room, but I would like Nuria to come live with us, with me, and I'd like to invite you to come live with my wife."

When Virgilio's beer arrives I order two Voll-Damms. Soon my hosts will be trying their rusty German.

"Relax, Gordon. This is not a time for tension."

"It isn't? Do we take turns on the bed?"

"My great-uncle is very ill. His bed will be free any day now."

"When you carry him out there will be room on his deathbed for your wife and me."

"Actually, Nuria and I had hoped to go in there. It's farther from the child."

"Ah, yes. The child. Forgotten her myself, though I was beginning to see how a bunch of old anarchists wouldn't make too much of a fuss about communal living on such a small scale."

"The more people we cram into that apartment, the happier they will be."

"But they don't want to explain why mommy doesn't sleep with daddy any more."

"I am thinking this will not be such a problem for Anita if she sees that we are together every day and there is no change in the way we treat each other. Anita is very fond of you, don't forget."

"Crap, she hardly knows me. I'd feel better about this if you weren't trying so hard to convince yourself."

"But I am not. You are a foreigner, you fascinate the child. Anyway, more people in the house means more attention..."

"It's clear that Marina put you up to this."

"She did not! A Basque woman cannot imagine this arrangement. She's no real anarchist."

I toss off a full glass of beer. "I can't say no if Marina will go along. It's not going to work if one granny has second thoughts. The arrangement should be understood as a noble experiment, whatever the average Spaniard would think of it.

There are going to be some problems. For one thing, if Marina is going to be my woman, you'll have to give up the right to quarrel with her. That won't be easy, but I can't have you making her upset. All her quarrels are with me from now on."

"Nuria will keep me busy. We already fight a lot, imagine what it will be like to live with her. As for Marina, we never fight anymore at all. If we were a couple of old people, you'd say we are getting along perfectly. What a shame my wife and I never had a chance to live in beautiful surroundings in the country, far from the traffic noise and the mouths of my relatives. Our life together has been harmonious, our natures flowing together in a single stream..."

"Time to pull the chain, though."

"Exactly. As long as the child is not taken away. You must promise, Gordon. No matter what happens you won't make a home for Marina somewhere else."

"How could I do that when I have a small child of my own that needs a home?"

"Is this so? I thought you were a father from something you said once."

"Marina didn't tell you? I told her to keep quiet about it, but I didn't expect her to keep it from you. Yes, I had a little daughter by a Cuban woman here at the Maternidad last summer. She left me to raise her in the States with help from her parents."

"You would go back to your country to be with her?"

"I might if I could save the fare. I make a lot of money singing but it's hell to keep."

He leans across the table and puts his hands together, hands that look frail as the wrists emerge from his thick wool coat. "You are prevented from leaving...by your subconscious. You don't really want to go."

"No. I'm prevented leaving by the fact that living in a state of exaltation is incredibly boring."

"I don't follow you."

"All the singing I do outdoors creates a state of heightened awareness. Change the air, change the air...That's all I do all day, by the numbers."

"Amazing...Heightened...Yes!"

"Nothing amazing about it. It would happen to anyone who could sing that long."

"Does it happen in opera houses?"

"No. Not with a conductor. Only when there's no one to please and I'm content with whatever rolls out of my mouth."

"Content? A moment ago you said, 'bored.'"

"I didn't say it right. I'm flying. All that life can give is mine and I don't need anything. Everything is fine the way it is, I wouldn't change anything, I'm neutral. But if nothing is ugly, beauty gets old. When the waiter asks what I want I don't know what to say."

"That sounds like hell."

"Hell, heaven, call it anything you like."

"So you spend all your money to end the boredom. It's true, the poor are never bored."

"I drink to stay interested, that's it. After a couple of beers I feel like I've been nailed to my stool. I have weight again. Other people have things that I want, especially the women. I want to touch them all, touch everything. Things that aren't going anywhere have an inner life. Things in motion bring in other things. Poetry, music is everywhere. The world is a joyous flow and I'm in and out of it like a fish..."

"You can have all that from drinking shit like this?"

"For a few hours. Some of the magic is even off the women after three days of throwing them down. Then I have my good times through my friends, and with friends as crazy as Hewitson you can understand why I laugh a lot."

"Yes, yes, I have known this is your medicine. No harm can come to someone who is always laughing."

I let this pass.

"I have to ask you...for Marina's sake...You have a child of your own to raise. And Cubans are very wonderful to fuck..."

"Before the child, she was."

"Then it's the child. You want to be a father. Sometimes

it makes no difference who the mother is."

"That might be it. The child. Being a father."

"I think it would hurt Marina to become deeply involved with you...Only to lose you the moment there's money enough to leave. You wouldn't come back?"

"I'm not a fortuneteller. I might wake up tomorrow morning in Tierra del Fuego."

"I do understand..."

In spite of the frail appearance of his hands, perhaps because of excessive clothing, Virgilio's neck and face are almost pudgy. There's a suggestion of a stoop whether he's sitting or on the go. He'd be called a teddy bear back in the States if it weren't for the tape holding his glasses together and his suspect clothes. Anyway, Virgilio is a man who lives with problems, his own and other people's, all the time. He doesn't intend to solve any. He toys with them, amuses himself with problems. He gives himself importance by the dextrous way he handles them, but nothing ever changes because of him. Problems for Virgilio are exactly like memories for old people. "...I understand. Could the child be brought here, then? Anita would have a playmate. We could make room."

"Not without bringing her mother. That would take a tremendous windfall."

"Wait, it's not as simple as that. Suppose you married the mother of your child, this Cuban...and divorced her! Then you could insist on the child's right to be with you a part of each year. Once your daughter is living here with us, and Anita is her best friend, and she's got a dozen women looking after her, I doubt she'd want to go back to her Cuban refugees."

"Best you don't think of them as refugees. They've been Americans for nearly a quarter of a century. Compared to the way she's living now, for Elena to move in with you would be like going to Dachau."

"We really do have a problem," he says, blowing smoke into his beer. "Marina is in love with you..."

He isn't looking at me. He doesn't need for me to be hanging around. He has all the elements of an equation and all that remains now is to play with it till he's got it right.

"Something has to be done for Nuria's sake. It's hell where she is now...Having a mistress is an acceptable idea, my family can understand that, but it would be an affront to the senior members to give Nuria a room to herself, and there's no sneaking around in a flat like ours. But you've got to come. It will be better for the child. My wife will have something to live for. Without love it has been a great strain for her to work at the office all day and take care of the child at night. Perhaps you know my wife—for love she will do anything. I feel she will be hurt by you if the day comes you will leave, but she will understand what it is to yearn for a child. There is a possibility we haven't touched. Would you still be so eager to leave Spain if the Cuban woman falls in love with someone in the United States?"

He wants input. I've grown accustomed to thinking of this as Virgilio's problem. He's the one with the hots, after all. "I might..."

"She must be very beautiful. So soon after a baby..."

"She didn't change much having the baby. She's extremely elastic. Think of an amoeba."

"I don't understand. Something is wrong with her?"

"Not exactly. She's bedridden, yes."

"Ah! Paralyzed! They say there's nothing so good in bed as a paralyzed woman, a living doll. Now it's clear. You don't love her, but you feel obligated to care for her. You're a noble man, Gordon. I've always thought so. How'd it happen?"

"It's a paralysis of the will."

"What? I see. A neurotic. I suppose that should be a relief. She just doesn't want to get out of bed, then?"

"She doesn't see the point. Neither does anyone else."

"I see. There's plenty to think about...You'll come to our home? I can take this up with Marina tonight."

"I feel like the dives. Maybe in a week or two..."

"Why don't you have one more and go home to bed?"

"Because I have a certain kind of place in mind and when I've had too much to drink, it's where I belong."

"All right, but be careful. I've seen where you like to go. Very dangerous. Sometimes when we are drinking we don't see ourselves as others do."

"I don't want to see myself at all. And as far as the others are concerned, I know I won't be seeing them as they are, I know I'll be seeing things that aren't there and ignoring unfavorable things that are, but seeing doesn't matter that much to me when I'm gone. Touching does. Holding someone. I don't care what lies beyond. If I've got a woman to hold I don't care if there's nothing to look at but the wall..." The agony on his face is unbearable. "I don't mean any insult to your wife..."

"Of course not!"

29

Virgilio's invitation hangs over me for many weeks, an insistent beckoning finger pulling a string that tightens my gut. When I run into Marina, or rather when she runs into me, since I'm easy to find when I'm working, she's acting like an old friend. All the energy she puts into smiles and confidences is meant to keep me from feeling her pain. It doesn't work because every forced move is pointing to her sad core.

Sitting with her during one of my tea ceremonies I hear that I've been remarked more than once in the company of a beautiful girl named Maribel...who is a notorious whore. She reminds me of my vows regarding Elena.

By the Wayside

"The whores Elena could understand...maybe forgive. Not if she knew what good women some of them are, but she'll never know more than I'm willing to tell her. But you, Marina, you're too much like someone who should be married to me. The perfect woman if busking is going to be my career..."

We both know Maribel would be just as good for me.

A scene of poignant kindness: Maribel in her bathrobe feeding me and making chocolate. I am too tired to talk, too tired to fuck when she opens her robe. The last time I see her face there's pleasure on it because I want her to fall asleep in my arms. She slides a pillow over the crook of my shoulder. We fall asleep with my face in her hair...

Marina wants to know if Maribel has been the only whore. I nod and she looks hurt. "The only one who's a friend. They're on me like flies when I work the Plaça de Pi."

"You will go back to her."

"Maybe not. I'm afraid of getting involved with anyone while I'm here alone. I want Elena back, and the baby."

"Does she write letters? She is coming?"

"Not yet. But she will when I'm a success."

"Going with whores you take a big chance."

"Becoming attached is too easy?"

"To Maribel, yes."

"Does she want me to be her pimp? I suppose I should be flattered..."

"No. She has problems in the life. You would pay the support, she would belong to you 24 hours. She is in love with you. I see her once with you walking, I know this..."

"I'm going to level with you. I don't want sex with these girls. This isn't France where self-destruction is a game. There people get together briefly to share methods or try to convert each other. Vice works because the people seem to know what they're doing, they take pride in their ability to rope you in. Here...even with Maribel sometimes it's like sticking it to your kid sister."

"There is brotherhood on the streets is sure. But she is seeing the money in your *maletín*. You are a foreigner not speaking the language well and has nothing but in his throat something, in his mind."

"I grant you I'm a champ out there sucking up the small change. Say I'm the best opera singer who ever set up shop in the gutter, that's probably not saying too much, my status is still way beneath the business types who pay Maribel, any one of whom could support her better than I could." Marina's not getting my drift. "The men in suits are getting two thousand pesetas worth of cupped breasts and I'm getting fifty pesetas of consolation..."

She laughs, but her gaze is fixed and there's no mistaking I'm the stooge again, amusing her. "You know what means you are jealous..." So she thinks my pride has been wounded not to be worthy of enticement when my errands take me past decorated doorways...?

I cut her off. As far as I'm concerned these breasts are being cupped out of a sincere desire to please. My friend Hewitson swears these women haven't been dehumanized, and I believe him. Their invitations excite them—are probably the only excitement left. They shiver as the hook goes in. All the rest of it is no more exciting than cleaning a fish, but one does what one must to put dinner on the table, or the drug in the bloodstream.

"Let's face it, for people who are waiting for a miracle there are worse ways to be occupied. Secretaries like you are falling asleep trying to get the words right, fully conscious that the words would be absurd if it weren't for your wage. And before long, it's bound to happen, you will know everyone you're going to know, everyone will have noticed you and you'll still be a slave. The only way out is to look for more important words and numbers. There's no danger Maribel will fall asleep when she's occupied with another body, there's too much danger. Every new face represents hope. And there's hope when the old clients turn up, because something might have changed for them."

"What hope? One of these men will try to own her? Keep her in the birdcage?"

By the Wayside

"No, that someone will see her specialness. Whatever it is that makes her much more than a whore, that enables her to laugh at the destruction of her body and the assumptions of those who think they have a right to it."

Marina's in a fury now, which is the usual thing if we spend too much time chatting and there's nothing going on under the table. According to her I'm as much a romantic imbecile as Maribel..She's struck with the resemblance between us, as I am listening to her. It's this belief that there is something special...

Maribel's no different than a lot of Spanish girls, according to Marina. Offering your body to all comers is a way of expressing contempt and gaining the moral high ground.

"With someone like you," a Maribel is saying to her clients, "nothing but a body could be of interest." Since the *democracia* to fall in love is an asexual phenomenon, and it's important to have the existential sophistication (what used to be called hipness, I think) to understand it as such. This is why Maribel and the other prostitutes attracted to me look moonfaced and melancholy. Their robes are always open, figuratively speaking, but they are secretly rejoicing that I want them to keep their secrets, deem them suitable companions for tea-taking, am willing to spend the odd fifty pesetas which I need much more than they.

"You've convinced me that Maribel and the rest aren't after my money, and are genuinely melancholy on my account, but explain why you want me to share your bed."

"This is Virgilio's bed, Virgilio's reason. I prefer you are staying in the barrio where I am visiting privately."

One of her fingers is visiting the palm of my hand.

"Once in two months? So there's no privacy at the home for old anarchists?"

"Because my daughter. Not only this. My husband will not permit offenses to his relatives."

"Then he's inviting me...He needs the money?"

"This is mainly the reason. I agree with him, everything is for your benefit..." She goes on to tell me how much I need

131

looking after; how much better it would be for me to be having her from behind in a closet than taking chances in the public places of whores no matter how special; how being a part-time father to Anita will make it easier to bear the separation from Lenita; how my Spanish will improve...

I accept before she has to mention clean clothes and regular meals.

"I take it I'm not the first street musician who's been installed to finance Virgilio's poetry."

"One after another for years they are coming. Some are still in Barcelona working. Pepe stays with us now, the conductor. He looks after the dogs."

We're strolling to my place to fling some *rubias* at the Galicians and gather my things. She's swinging her hips and hanging onto my pants pocket. I feel so good about being a provider that her stories are whizzing by me like some ruckus at a bar. I'm only checking my impressions and letting her enlarge upon the right ones. About Pepe, for instance...

I've been right from the beginning, the greasy little fake.

Before he starts "conducting" he puts down a thick, belted bundle of music paper. A closer look reveals black-winged figures riding the staves. I've never been close enough to hear them sing but Marina tells me the notes—actual crotchets and quavers—have been sprinkled at random. They're starlings on a power line. Traffic noise.

Pepe's baton is real and above standard length, or seems to be — Pepe can't be much over five feet. His greasy hair is combed straight back, he has battle scars around his eyes, his brown suede jacket is full of dark shiny places and his hands tremble when he's not conducting. Every city has its Pepes. When they sidle forth from dark places by the side of the road passersby reach into their pockets for a coin, hoping whatever they come up with will be conclusive.

As a scrounger Pepe is OK by me and I've helped him to buy wine, but I've never reached an understanding with Pepe the conductor. I've run him off twice in the same day only to deal with him again the next morning.

By the Wayside

Pepe's memory problems are no hindrance to his conducting. He's always conducting for the first time, I doubt he could keep a nursery rhyme in his head. No matter, certain master musicians at the Tapas Bar think Pepe is a genius who can conduct anything...Lover's quarrels...Street repairs...

Sometimes I doubt my common sense. In the short time I've been doing my street pitch I've seen a chorus of Catalan boys and girls in uniform take direction from Pepe while their chaperones, one of whom must have been their rightful conductor, looked on patiently... I've seen him conduct an Andean flautist and force the bottler, a girl in costume, to dance round him to collect. A tone-deaf Greek-islander played a broken bouzouki for half an hour grinning at Pepe and then split with him cheerfully, handing over what looked to be an eighth of the take.

Pepe has boasted to barmen that all the pitches make more money when he's conducting. If this is so it's because he creates a traffic jam and experienced pedestrians will sooner part with a little pocket money than line up with those who hold street performers to be a blight on the city, a waste of money, irritating attention junkies, or the "disguised beggars" of French law.

We buskers are too strong of body and will to be beggars, of course, but in one sense we're all hustlers, no better or worse than Pepe. Consider: without me to insist, no one in this blur of people with a destination would have a song from me.

Sometimes the police are consulted by soreheads or timid souls who resent having to leave the sidewalk because of a brief congestion caused by my admirers. I'm not sure we're being protected by a law, but we're all being protected, even Pepe, by the Guardia Urbana, who would rather get rid of well-dressed soreheads than ragged musicians.

I force the crowds to confront my voice, but even the operalovers want to give money and hurry on before they discover what landed me here with my thumb-dark anthology and my shaggy beard and my two shirts under a once-expensive jacket. The ones who don't know opera may have questions about my credentials, but they think I should be compensated for trying hard. My fellow buskers don't understand me any better. The ones who credit me with a good education think I legitimize their musicianship. The master musicians consider me a mere talent and no doubt some of them would like to see me perish of throat cancer for adapting so well to air pollution and cheap wine. My friends like to try their English and hear anecdotes drawn from my life as a vagabond in the "land of the free."

I'm a mystery to no one but myself.

30

The home for anarchists is another flat like Hewitson's that rambles through a mysterious old building. A mezzanine can be reached by skirting a light well. Here it's not so easy to get lost. Window-awareness keeps life on the oblong, and there's a nice north-south east-west feeling despite the sun's vague peripheral visits. (The light well has been built over and is dark with primitive plant-velvet.)

Where Pepe stays with the Great Danes there's no carpet—shit smeared everywhere. Sometimes Pepe can't find his way home and Marina will take over his feeding chores, but she hasn't got time to exercise the dogs.

I find it incredible that Pepe could exercise them all at once.

"They chase him?"

She won't let on.

"Virgilio is keeping him for sport?"

By the Wayside

I'm recalling stories recently told me by a new pillar of the Tapas Bar, a lesbian brickmason from Islington who was held captive by a Fleet Street journalist she calls The Flesher. A labyrinth with one savage dog was involved, though it was the journalist who took the bites out of backsides—in the account told me, the backside of a customer in a public bar. What went on in private was relegated to future installments and predicated upon greater intimacy with the brickmason, but I'm definitely curious. This woman can take care of herself.

"Virgilio collects people is true."

The reason I was suspicious in the first place.

"Everyone in the whole life is to be chewed into poetry."

She assures me that her dogs are devoid of these poetic aspirations.

"This is the only way they show they like," she says over her shoulder, leaning into the scrum. She's more Basque than ever at the moment, holding back the three of them with her strength of back and leg. I brace her by fitting myself around from behind, wondering if the brutes have protective instincts, wondering: how long before they feel deprived of food?, from living together so long in appalling conditions have they devised any collective bargaining mechanism?, is the idea of what constitutes appropriate food well-ingrained?, will the Great Dane's well known stupidity make it more or less likely for them to break the food chain?

Marina's dog-wrestling goes on long enough to convince me she's a friend of the dogs here. A tentative erection is complicating the pressure against her. In spite of her tight seams I can feel her loins wobble. She's pushing back hard now, it's a blood-filled presentation, I'm being surrounded. The dogs are yelping, confused by the way she seems to be backing off while remaining braced against them. I have no choice but to keep pushing or we'll come down with the dogs on top.

One of the dogs, no doubt their leader, having weighed the resistance, comes over to our side, mounting me. I think of the sandwich we're making and the smell of dogshit is over-

135

powering. The congestion in my crotch subsides. I slip away and the lead dog replaces me on Marina's backside. She spins out of the huddle and we leave off-balance, slamming the door.

The child is already asleep. Oh, for a shower together before dinner...

We could take a shower together, she says, that will offend no one.

And I thought it was going to be hard to get to her! I tighten my arm around her waist as we pass the old anarchists peering from their cluttered rooms. I want us to go naked in front of them, proclaiming the new order.

"I know what you are wanting, and I am too wanting it very much," she croons. I remember the first promise she made me and the mere month I'd had to wait for its fulfillment. Given the obstacles she'd overcome to get to me then...

The main thing is, she keeps her promises. I shouldn't have long to wait now, even if the shower is out of order.

The shower's not out of order (as I was sure it would be after her diplomatic language). Nor have the anarchists hit upon a means to make it impossible to have a private shower. There's no hot water, is all.

I was already used to cold water only. Except for Hewitson's I'd been without hot water since my days of luxury at the fascist's.

"Is it room temperature at least?" I've been considering all the busy kitchens in this vast building.

"No, the *tubos* are outside..."

My year in Sarriá taught me how cheap it is to repair plumbing or electrical fixtures here in Spain. These oldtimers must think a hot water heater is the height of luxury, something they want their grandchildren to enjoy when peace and anarchy have finally descended upon the land. I'll have hot water to their bathrooms at the rate of one installation every two weeks if I continue to enjoy fair weather and good voice.

The sprinkler head in this shower is the kind I recognize from public beaches and it's so low I have to bend my knees to get under the stream. I have a history of avoiding cold showers even at the risk of smelling less than fresh, especially when they are all that's available during a run of bad luck in a slum. In the mountains of the American west I've submitted to cold showers without anyone's urging, have even been known to plunge into icy mountain streams, etc., after bouts of climbing.

Marina is squatting more drastically, warming my penis for me, my shriveled balls snug against her chin. In under a minute I'm so numb from the icewater that my world, my universe is inside her mouth. She's well-schooled in cosmology...

My thoughts continue independent of my refrigeration. This isn't the first woman I've known who wanted to be pals with my penis, always reaching for it under restaurant tables, inflaming me through pockets, jamming a cold hand straight into my pants, or bringing it out to suck on in taxicabs or during car trips to the country. There's something the same about all these women, but I can't think what. "Not all redheads," is the best my memory can do, plagued by spirals. Were they nurses? Physical therapists? Germans?

After an eternity or two Marina regurgitates me and turns off the water. Instantly I'm warm where I had been numb, but it's a treacherous To-Build-A-Fire sort of warmth known only to those who have returned from the dead by means of a thaw.

The blood suffusing my brain is heavy with the past. Two of my penis's best pals had been cooks, another had been a waitress, and one woman let go of it for eight hours at a stretch to shampoo animals for a pet-pampering firm. A toy poodle, a wire-haired terrier and thou...

The air in this bathroom is the exact temperature of the wash-water and there's a wind-chill factor now that she's got out the towels. After chafing each other there's blood on every square centimeter of surface and enough left over to charge lips and nipples and even her old pal. I'm well-disposed toward the latter now, it having returned from interstellar space bulging with data, eager to be emptied and reprogrammed. Pal, indeed! I'm proud of my faithful subject for all the wonders he's brought home to me without wavering, content with my control.

Marina and I have stopped toweling off to hold each other and this is my first experience of the fit which will no doubt be as familiar soon as a favorite chair.

Away, gloom. The problem to tackle now is how to get inside her before there's pounding on the door...

No! She's dropped to her knees, she's warming me with her mouth all over again, tossing her hair like a wet dog.

Ah! Tired from too much fluttering, her tongue has given the job to her neck muscles.

If we had all night this would be perfect...

I see the need for a disorderly consummation here in the bathroom. The floor is a big improvement on the dog-pound. Whatever she wants to do is going to have to include much more of me. I'm tired of being a tidbit. I'm jumping up and down with frustration. This is the long-awaited night, we're both clean, sober and rested...

And we may as well be going to bed together in our winter clothes...

"Hey, down there!" With both hands full of wet hair I ease her off.

I'm able to bring her to her feet without pulling, though it's like having my way with a horse, and she gets skittish when I won't let go of her head.

I crush her against me, expecting tears. So many women have been hurt...Ever since it was possible for women to talk about the abuse, the pain, about being patronized and under-paid, the rage has been accumulating. The more it flares, the more it seeks fuel. It's the Watts effect. When Watts was ablaze the good burghers ready to make concessions couldn't understand why more was never enough and refused to address the reason rage renews itself, the reason it can never be appeased. Women don't need anything given to them, they're tired of the whole business. Women need to be in a position to give.

"My teeth are bad..."

So. "You're afraid to let me kiss you...?"

"Some are needing to be pulled out, but where you can

see, only this one, the others I keep." She outs with a horse-chuckle and taps a gray eyetooth. "I'm afraid to have not one tooth of my own like Virgilio. I am saving for this, you will excuse there is a smell for the time being."

The poor darling. "But I've kissed you before and didn't smell a thing..."

"You are taking beer. I am watching when you are drinking beer especially, this is a good time to kiss you."

Our nakedness is pitiable now. My once-sociable prick is ready to turn up dead in the water. The pink is leaving her skin, her nipples belong to baby. Irreparably sad is our need for socks.

There haven't been any tears. I have to figure my hugs aren't putting her off. I hug her again under false pretenses. When her arms come around my back I sneak into her ear...

Contact! She's groaning and doing the hokey-pokey. I'm having so much success I'm inclined to think she's walking in place to keep her knees from buckling. Her groans are enough to make me come before I'm aroused, low-pitched mudsucking. They're sure to bring one of the old folks with a full bladder.

But no. There might be ears pressed against all the walls, but privacy is fine here as long as you're noisy about it.

It sounds like an orgasm approaching, a sound precisely right for the painful loss of something she wants to get rid of. Amazing, she doesn't need rubbing to get off.

I'm determined to get in on the celebration before it starts, but she pushes me away.

"I can't! I'm not protected!"

"Not again! Damn you, Marina, I just wanted to be there at the big moment. Why make everything so complicated? So what if you're a gothic novel at the moment with an unfinished stairway that ends above a black abyss..."

"No, is not. *Es un mecanismo*! Is scientific! I will take no chance with another baby. I want my job. I keep it, yes. My words and numbers I adore."

"Have a tubal ligation, then..."

She knows the term. Her eyes get wide.

"All right, you want to feel like a woman..."

"Is the most stupid thing I ever hear. If I know I cannot have a baby, Nature cannot make me crazy."

"Good point. I've refused a vasectomy for the same reason. Procreation is the only good excuse for my excesses. What about a diaphragm? The pill?"

"The pill make me sick. The diaphragm is how we have Ana. I love Ana. You know how much."

She forces me to nod before she goes on. She towels herself absently. Then me. For warmth, our skin is dry.

"What about a...what you call in English? A preservative?"

"Yes. Well, it's against my religion, but I guess we'll have to try."

"You will please. You know how to make it work? No mistake?"

"I haven't dealt with one since I was eighteen, but I think I have the necessary expertise."

What a note.

"Thank you for giving me your ear, Marina. Even if there's an abscess in it that you're afraid to tell me about, it was wonderful..."

She wants to be pals again. I feel her bush up against my hip.

"It will be so good if you can fuck me sometime, like a dream. The pill, the device up in, you know, he is making me have growths of cancer, or not, what you like. I am so depressed all the time. It is almost a year since I have normal fucking with a man. Another *callejero*, not Virgilio."

There's no mischief in her eye. As long as she's not trying to make me jealous I don't care if she's had every busker in Barcelona. Still I want to know, "Who was the last one?"

She won't tell me. I sense I've made a mistake. I shouldn't have asked, I don't really care.

"I fuck Frankenstein, you know. He is one of the first man Virgilio is bringing home. I think Anita is from him."

By the Wayside

There's no question she's trying to scandalize, never mind her lack of expression or mine. Yes, the cheek of her, protecting herself from Frankenstein with a rubber rainhat.

I seem to be communicating my disbelief.

"He is the only man who ever have me here in the cold water."

"Did he look as bad then?"

"He is already missing the tooth."

She taps her left incisor, one of her healthy specimens.

"His hair is not so long then, more blond ones. Clean, he is goodlooking, and he is very intelligent before alcohol take away his mind."

I make a note to ask someone besides Hewitson exactly what alcohol has taken from Frankenstein's mind. He's never been anything but reasonable when I see him at work. Granted, he's crazy to sing so loud and beat up his guitars. He never gives possible benefactors the chance to approach unawares. By the same token, if he'd do something about his appearance people would get close enough to make a drop no matter what kind of noise he was making.

According to Hewitson, Franz is mad, and might have definite ideas about the kind of person he wants to take money from. I'm not attracted to this line of reasoning—too many people think I'm insane. And Franz's ideas about people are quite different from mine.

I love the ones who hobble by, the old ladies who smile, the weary work-worn or war-torn old men who may not smile at me but seem to be saying, "Keep your pecker up" by putting out their chests, squaring their shoulders, trying to stand taller and facing me down with a faraway look in their eyes.

I wonder if Frankenstein with his missing incisor and wild hair prematurely gray isn't giving me a preview of my condition when I am no longer Marina's lover. No, I can imagine a lot of scenarios where self-destructive behavior might prevent my success, but singing for my supper isn't one of them.

I've been watching her dress. In spite of her squeamishness

about procreative sex, which I see as a distrust of technology brought on by a failed diaphragm—she's not self-conscious dressing or undressing. She bends to put her pants on and points her long foot while her hair, starting to dry, falls wild about her. She's very slender, and would be bony if she weren't so strong. Her breasts are just full enough to sway with her movements.

I dress quickly and watch her finish with her hands over her head. I love the hair under her arms, and I'll kiss her there while she's denying me her mouth. The pink start of her nostrils. The folds of her eyes. Wherever she welcomes my tourist tongue.

But nothing should interrupt the beauty of her putting on her clothes.

31

Pepe doesn't show for dinner. I'm told he never comes to dinner with the family. He wouldn't be turned away, Virgilio assures me, but he prefers to eat with the dogs.

The last obstacle to happiness here has been removed. Breaking bread with Pepe would lead to fellowfeeling, and Pepe only makes contact with his fellows by pointing his stick at them or asking for money.

I'm being made to feel like a guest of honor.

It's my first supper here, I don't expect my welcome to last.

The seating arrangements are sensitive. My lap has been made accessible to Marina's left hand. Virgilio is to her right, should she want to pinch him for some reason. Nuria sits to Virgilio's right.

By the Wayside

The suffering elder circled by Virgilio during our first long talk yielded his body to cancer ten days ago, and his room to Virgilio. Nuria was installed the same day the body was carried out, doubling the general excitement. Death, disease, accidents, infidelities, wild behavior induced by wine or drugs or dementia—any change at all in the status quo is an occasion for hilarity here.

There are a few with a sneering, "I told you so" attitude. It's my feeling these are the ones who aren't expected to last long. Only the ones who help changes along are heeded, the ones who cackle and squeal.

Dinner is what I remember with the Boches and their relatives during my first days in Spain. Here at the other end of the political spectrum the food is the same. Salads with olive oil and salt. Fresh bread, strong wine, stewed legumes, fried potatoes and onions (or the famous tortilla), well-done meat.

I'll be eating with the first shift, always. The oldest anarchists are held in high esteem, they have the best stories, but it takes them too long to eat. Whether or not a story is being told it's normal for one of them to stop chewing suddenly and stare at the wall for twenty minutes.

With the first shift food's the thing, not stories, and we all talk at once—politics and gripes, horrors of the day, possibilities tomorrow, it's all jumbled together and made offhand by our busy knives and forks. So far I've made a rule stick (which might be quite an achievement here): no one is to stop the flow of Spanish to explain his drift or deeper meaning. Let all of them drift at will. Where I think they're going, where I think they are is of no importance as long as the plates of food keep coming. I'm just another mouth to feed.

"But you are a singer of opera, no?"

This from an old guy who's much too quick for the second shift.

I tell him that I will sing for him anytime. All through dinner if he would like. "I never need encouragement to sing, my friends. Here in Spain it's all I'm good for."

Oddly, Virgilio and Marina would just as soon I keep

making my operatic statements outdoors, but Nuria is more of a fan. Our paths have crossed before. She once asked to hear me on a Metro car.

Nuria and Virgilio, Marina and I sit up late in the parlor adjoining the *comedor*. Nuria sits with an arm around Virgilio and a leg over him. There's nothing to hide here. Two old anarchists look on wistfully from their huge chairs, their hands resting on their upright canes like a purpose in life.

Things get lively when Virgilio brings down a book of his poetry and reads lyrics that everyone seems content to hear again, though it's clear he's reading them for my benefit, wrapping his mouth around each word to get as much love as he gives.

Later he tells the story of his family with evident pride, while Nuria is thumbing his book of poetry and Marina is resting her eyes. The elders are still staring and blinking.

These anarchists of his are Sephardic Jews who settled in Spain before the Inquisition—possibly before the Muslim conquest. They survived the Inquisition as wily *marranos*, though as far as he can determine from his family's oral history, no one ever took either baptism or his Jewish tradition very seriously.

Virgilio is proud of his family's ability to survive without being useful to the powers of the times. Their tradition of independence may have extended to growing their own turnips from time to time—a loving and fearful nurturing, like our modern cultivation of contraband. He's proudest of the impoverishment of his line, which dates from the Dark Ages. For the Jews who chose to stay in Spain money commonly had the importance of land in conveying security and guaranteeing one's posterity...

"Yet my ancestors were never more than small tradesmen who left nothing when they died!" he exults. "Behold them now!" He's on his feet. The old men are blinking valiantly. I'm not sure they understand everything he's saying, he still speaks good English or fair French to make his important points. "Wine, woman and hatred of authority is all anyone needs in this life!"

The two old men glaring at Virgilio over their canes aren't even blinking any more, afraid that any response will keep him going. He caught them sewing coins into their coats? He's noted my interest...

"What a shame you can never know how well these men have satisfied their love of life." His voice is still loud, but he's making a gesture of dismissal. Maybe he's winding down.

Suddenly one of the old men with a cane spits on the floor, right in the middle of a big red tile, and the sound brings a granny, rag in hand, from the adjoining room.

32

The sleeping arrangements in my new home are less of a problem than hot water.

Ana sleeps with her mommy and the double bed is much too small for the three of us, but another double bed turns up in a storage room. There's a sag in it, but after I come home with a piece of wood and a mattress to match the one she has, after I lash the bedframes together and pin the mattresses we find ourselves with more room to thrash about than Americans in a king-sized.

Thanks to an Oriental woman with two daughters this isn't the first time I've had a frisky three-year-old in bed with me at night. I'd be happier with more to go on, but I have a hunch children aren't curious in their sleep.

Marina's like my Oriental love in another respect that's reassuring. She weaned Ana late and still allows milk from a bottle *con tetico* at bedtime while reading stories to her or inventing them.

For years I've been attributing marked success in school and leadership ability to my old love's methods. She once told me her people's way with children was "to spoil them, then to unspoil them."

I doubt late weaning plays more than a small part in adult decisionmaking ability but there was always something magical about that Eurasian girl's self-confidence and high spirits. Anyway, here's Anita growing up the same way, with the same exuberance, dancing through her days, more eager to find out for herself than have you explain.

I'm only on the sofa two nights before the bed's ready. Except for the cane-dependent anarchists, all have been in to admire our new sleeping arrangements, and there are faces I don't remember from mealtimes. The place reminds me of certain pensions in the *barrio gótico* where old folks go to be forgotten, sitting in dim light clutching one blanket, pre-occupied with the small family of a manager or resident owner, the only family, the only children, the only apartment-dwellers left to know.

Not one comment is passed about the possible deleteri-ous effects of two amorous adults sleeping with this beautiful child.

I've been told by women with a keen interest in the mechanism that I have hard-ons in the night, they come and go, and the same women are able to coax one from me in no time without waking me. Complicating the matter Marina's nearness and frequent potential availability has me reeling up and down the corridors of my uncomplicated days in a state of permanent semi-arousal.

I tell Marina my concern that the slightest accidental contact in the night might cause an eruption sufficient to wake Anita and turn her world upside-down.

She has faith in the lined bathingsuits of Virgilio's I'm wearing to bed now. They're cul-de-sacs, these sacs-de-cul. Since all my boxer shorts have fallen apart after the grannies' first laundering I'll be wearing these bathingsuits in lieu of underwear for the time being. Virgilio wasn't fatassed when he had need of them; they're hard to pull off even when I'm wide awake.

Marina quickly disposes of my suggestion that she sleep between me and the child.

"Anita will crawl between in her sleep. Between two *adultos* is always where she like to be."

So much for slipping something into Marina from behind. So much for any of the subtle maneuvers that have been hatching out of Metro cars, or causing me to lose my train of thought in front of my friends.

All along I've thought anything possible with Marina as long as it can be done is such utter silence that the child's sweet breath can be heard. Anything—as long as our movements are so subtle that the slightest shift in position of the sleeping child will register on our merged mattresses. Anything—as long as the dull gray robe that has been flung over the child by the faint streetlight at the window isn't slit by the white of an eye.

What a waste of the imagination. How could I have not foreseen that Anita would be our bundling board? Always a threat to wake up screaming...More than any Bluestocking would have bargained for...

I can discharge into her mother's mouth whenever I like, I'm told consolingly by the mouth in question. A day won't go by without a host of blessed moments alone. I can discharge into her hands, or if I want to be fastidious (you English!) into my dinner napkin. If I'll tell her when I need to piss...

These giblets of esteem are meant to end in sex with a condom as soon as I can get the details right. Marina assures me that any scenario is all right with her as long as I've got a condom...

I'm used to her complaisance. The truth is, it's impossible to get to her unless I'm willing to risk a public spectacle. There'd be more privacy around here if something were taboo to these people...

33

All of the toilet basins here are porcelain and seatless. Before I needed them for coitus I'd thought them a big improvement on the plastic-seated kind in cafes, where someone above two hundred pounds can worry about falling in. On seatless toilets of this kind I've learned to keep my weight on my feet—an aid to expulsion, incidentally—since the commode lip is much too wide for sitting unless you're a broadhipped Spanish granny.

On the day we first attempt a union there are four anarchists in our bedroom, it's a popular place for naps, but we've got the minutes and we've got the condom. She doesn't want our first fully-protected, grown-up-type marital penetration to take place on the bathroom floor, nor do I. But I'm doubtful about having her on my lap because of the wide commode lip I've described. With mere seconds to improvise I solve the problem by covering the toilet with my *maletín*, which is never far from me.

All the foreplay she wants is the second or two it takes to get me hard—she only has to point her tongue at it—and the additional seconds to install the condom, which we do together, muttering apologies.

The utter lack of amorous preparation may account for the fact that it takes her a few more seconds to work it in, while we watch and hmm and throw quick smiles at each other.

It's deliciously dirty to watch it go in with its absurd rubber stormgear, as it would be for her to install a dildo for my benefit, quickly checking my reaction each time she twirls it or changes the angle or nudges it further.

On the tropical journey to her cervix I congratulate myself for thinking of my music case. I'm higher than I would be on a conventional toilet seat and her movements to surmount me have less in common with squatting. When I nudge her cervix and lodge beside it she takes the weight off her legs with a groan and for a split second our souls are united like two bubbles out of a pipe.

By the Wayside

Then the heavens open, or there's thunder at least...beneath us! Much louder than any conceivable bowlnoise when the WC is being put to its customary use by erupting, flabby-cheeked anarchists...My music case has collapsed along with the thunderclap, but it takes a second for me to put the two together.

After her initial shock Marina chooses to ignore the noise and the subsequent rattling of my ratshit—my *rubias*, that is—which reminds me of the Latin band...

Our union has endured for seven or eight seconds before I've stabilized the situation by digging in my heels and taking her weight on my thighs, but the moment I do so my music case—the culprit is the incredibly durable material known as Samsonite—bounces back. In spite of the huge noise this is only a customary buckling and unbuckling, as normal for Samsonite as the taking on and off of pants.

She's raising herself by means of hands joined behind my neck and hurling herself at me. Each time she connects the *maletín* buckles, the ratshit goes flying inside and I have to renew my precautions against what is beginning to seem like the inevitable destruction of my *maletín*, water damage to certain music I can't replace in Spain, not to mention my pitchpipe, which won't even float on the toilet water, and the loss of everything I've struggled so hard to achieve with Marina when I'm so low in the bowl she can't follow.

I bought my *maletín* when it was just a large briefcase in Palo Alto. It's provided with a range of sewn-in file dividers and secret pockets, some with zippers, which must appeal to business types who have more to ferret away than us buskers. I make use of the zippered places to store the ratshit which accumulates inexorably while I'm working, but there's always more ratshit than I have room for, so that I end up spilling it in behind the ratty sheet music I have on file. I'm not concerned about the noise or the weight of it as a rule—all I'm trying to do is keep it out of sight so that the people of the town won't think flinging ratshit is an acceptable way to encourage me.

In my susceptible frame of mind it seems as if the ratshit

149

is in the service of a new musical instrument created expressly to taunt me. Because of my running battle with the Latin band the music makes my neck hair stand. Their maracas man is after me, the one with the gaptoothed grin who wears a backwards baseball cap. Because some of the ratshit is contained and some can fly freely about in my case, one of his maracas is bursting each time he knocks them together. Marina is filling his gourd with seed. He scatters and she gathers, it's only a game to them. The thunder is only cumulative for me...

After more than thirty seconds into our union, after a month's worth of rent in my old pension has been heard from, it's clear to me that Marina is content with the mechanics of our lovemaking and I've got to get ready for the long haul. Her oohs and ahs are still trying to get somewhere.

So far there's no sign of prick letdown, but to make sure I keep watching where, wrapper and all, I'm being devoured.

Before our long-awaited coming together has lasted a minute my fears are uppermost again. I resolve to raise her while she's on me, and though I won't be able to fuck her standing up without risking a tumble into the tub, if I can get us to the open place between the door and the washstand we can end it on the floor.

She doesn't understand what's happening and struggles like an animal about to be sacrificed. I'm rough with her, strong-seeming, since she's a threat to make me fall down backward by hooking me with her heels.

When we make the floor I see relief on her face in spite of the jolt the cold tiles must be giving her.

I'm trying to end it quickly now, which means I'm doing the slamming with everything I have, as if she has something inside we're trying to pop open. She's screaming and there are voices outside, but the door has a lock and neither of us wants to stop unless an axe comes through it or there's some other indication that the building is on fire. A note slipped under the door...It's hard to exaggerate the forbearance of these anarchists.

As when woozily leaving a cafe there are crescendos in the hubbub which may have nothing to do with me.

When we hear Anita's voice my prick melts out of Marina onto the cold floor.

"No grita, mami.." A thin wail. Marina's screams have quickly become groans.

Anita back so soon? These seconds I've been enumerating must have been a much bigger part of a minute.

She went with granddaddy to the corner store, a half-hour's trip. Granddaddy was turned around by something he forgot, probably money, possibly shoes, and was coming back down the corridor with the little girl when he heard Marina begging for her life...What a relief that everything is all right...

Not even close. Granddaddy never really left, was still trying to connect with the anarchist who had asked him to go to the store. If it wasn't tobacco it must have been something one of the women wanted. (Was he again being trusted to go to the store?) All the screaming made perfect sense to him, but of course, Anita was just a child...

34

It doesn't surprise me that our first attempt with a condom has turned out so badly. Condoms invite bad luck, I've always known it. Nor am I surprised to find that Marina is the sort of woman who goes crazy as soon as she has a prick in her—after having acknowledged to herself that she's ready to have a prick in her. It may be possible to slip it in her from time to time, I end by thinking, but if she's caught unawares she could hurt somebody.

The only thing that was right about our first time, with my

maletín for support, was the way she loved to watch it go in, the wonderful way she manipulated herself and me for maximum lewdness, her eyes twinkling with extinguished sin.

Given the circumstances it was a fine bit of sinning, if I do say so. There was an aborted consummation, yes, but I'd still achieved much more than I would have thought possible for an unbeliever. To be able to sin at all seemed such a blessing.

Ach, isn't the true horror, the true hell on earth reserved for those who've taken the sin out of life? No matter how comfortable they try to make it, life would seem to be unbearably dull and sad for the people who call themselves sinners, the people who never sin. Some of them are so far gone they can't even be seduced. They think about sex all the time, I'm told, and I expect they play with themselves in public toilets where they wouldn't expect their gods to follow, but they're virtually incapable of touching someone they hardly know without legalistic strategies such as suntan oil and congratulations. They're sadsacks, the lot.

The only problem with sin is that it's hard to manage twice in exactly the same way without making a fool of yourself. That being said, going to bed each night with Marina and her child is changing my outlook. Sin doesn't seem to matter as much and I reach the point where I can think of the wonderful hairy center of Marina without a stirring, without so much as a twitch from my old pal where he's nestled in Virgilio's bathing trunks.

Anita is brought to bed asleep. Marina starts her on the side away from me. Sure enough, the child sleepcrawls over her mother and gets between us again.

She goes to her mother to cuddle, she cuddles her pillow, she comes to me. She comes to me and I can see her beautiful sleeping child's face in the gray light of the window. She can never give more than her presence, but it's the presence of what they call god.

I'd actually lied to Marina when I told her that a sexual response to a child was impossible. I can remember such

horniness, such deprivation, that anything in my lap could start
a hard-on—anything alive—even a black-gummed, drooling
dog. The response was real, and sexual circuitry had something
to do with it, but my sexual imagination had been left out
completely.

Animals, men, young girls and boys have nothing to
worry about. The only people who are likely to have trouble
from me are women who've engaged my sexual imagination,
and it's a peculiarity of my imagination that it can only be
engaged when a woman is pleased by my interest. I'm
probably what's known as a straight, which in my milieu is a
word to spit after. I keep it quiet.

Beyond the beautiful still face of this sleeping child
Marina is snoring lightly and her rotten teeth are stinking and
her poor beleaguered body is fending off the nightly onslaught
of micro-organisms. And I'm loving her.

My love has little in common with what I feel for this
child. I have awe for this child, I even have awe for my feelings
about this child, but I know that what I'm feeling for Marina is
love, too. It's fully worthy to be dignified by that name even
if the women's magazines keep it at arm's length, hold it by the
tail like a dead prawn.

I love in her what I love in myself. Our willingness to be
absurd, to be clowns, idiots, and still find some good in each
other's bodies. I love the little we've got and the little that lies
in store. If I never have another chance to fuck her and I have
nothing to look forward to but more giblets, scraps from the
table of the sexual feast going on in our heads turning up in odd
places like cat food...It's enough. There will be another day at
the window soon. We'll just keep trying.

Even the knowledge I'm beginning to have that our
circumstances will never be anything close to right is no
deterrent. The whole point in being clowns is to escape the tit
for tat business that can make life a hell.

As it was in the beginning, is now and ever shall be:
nothing is mine. Goodbye Marina, sleeping with your back to
me.

35

I've never expected any good to come of staying at Virgilio's, so it's working out fine. Marina thinks I need plenty of practice if I want a reunion with Elena and the baby, who might be three before I can get it right. Perhaps by then I'll be able to admire the mother Elena is, respect the lover, give her time.

If that time comes my neglect will be sincere. I won't secretly be waiting for her to bestir herself. Marina's put her finger on the problem: expectations paralyze.

Marina and Virgilio are in perfect agreement about my role in Anita's life. The child will no longer spend her days at home with the grannies while her mother's at work and her father is busy wandering the city being in love with Nuria and dealing with his responsibility to be poetic. Anita will spend her days as my assistant while I'm doing my street pitch.

She won't collect for me, but she'll dance whenever she feels like it. Perhaps continuously. The recorded junk seeping out of the shops is enough to start her twirling. She'll entertain the Barcelonians who want to stop and talk politics. When she has to be taken to the potty the whores will oblige, they're never far when I'm at work and they've got healthy maternal instincts...The best to be found anywhere, for children they don't know, at least...

The grannies are giving me hard looks now that Anita is going to be snatched away on my account. I resent it that they're wondering aloud what Marina sees in me, especially since I've been buying the groceries. Of course Virgilio has always been their hero. They anointed him and sang him to sleep and played with his weewee when he was a child. I may call myself an anarchist but they know better. They saw through me from the first. They know I'm a nothing. I'm not even Jewish. I can't speak decent Spanish. I'd be in big trouble if it weren't for my voice. I'm counting on the musiclovers here to protect me. They aren't many, but I do have a couple of champions.

By the Wayside

Anita and I are off to a good start. She hates the Metro...It's so big and noisy, the people all look like the dead trying to come back to life. She wants to walk all the way to work...

We're way off in the eastern part of the city. This is a big distance, but I love walking and I can always put Anita on my shoulders if she gets tired.

Too bad Anita can't carry me on her shoulders is what I'm thinking by the time we reach the center of town. Since she never goes anywhere without turning circles Anita has walked an incredible distance for a child. Now I'm worried that she's going to get tired turning circles while I sing and there won't be any place for her to lie down.

The hell with the take. When she can't stand I'll carry her to a parkbench, take off my coat, wrap her up in it. She'll be as snug as an ear of corn. It stinks under the arms, but she's used to the smell, it's the normal thing where she lives.

When I take my first ten-minute break I'm already tired of watching her. Here she's had a breakfast of chocolate and those greasy *churros* and she ought to be turning into a fiend by now like all kids who get into grease and sweets.

But no. She hasn't got an ounce of fat on her, either. She's got to have energy stored where it can't be seen. She's a pint-sized Owen. God help me.

I'm pleased to note she stops dancing when I stop singing, she knows she's not the whole show. This is great stuff for a three-year-old. She'll soon be four, though.

Between songs she plays with the coins in my music case. She separates the beautiful big fifty-peseta coins from the substantial twenty-five peseta coins which are my bread and butter...From the five-peseta *duros* that are already getting to be more trouble than they're worth, though inflation is holding at 12-plus percent.

If there's any beer-drinking going on at quitting time I get into it with my *duros*. I can pay for meals with them at the Tapas Bar, Gloria and Esteban always seem glad to have them. *Duros* are cheerfully accepted at any of the bars where I change

155

my money. As much as Anita likes to count and organize
things she's going to be a big help when I've got to get all my
duros into stacks of ten. I love to count my money the same
way she does, thinking of all the things I'll be able to buy. It's
shitwork, and everyone should have to do a little shitwork from
time to time.

Trouble or no, it's clear that my life revolves around these
little coins.

Anita likes the ratshit best of all. She knows where it
belongs and likes to put it away, but she also likes to throw it
at people she doesn't like. She knows I'm only keeping up
appearances when I fuss at her while her victims are picking
ratshit out of their clothes.

There's usually a wall behind me to rest against between
songs, and Anita doesn't always want to count my money.
When I hit the high note, race through my cadenza and finish
off she sometimes stops dancing, runs over and leans against
the wall with me, her hands locked around my knee, her head
against my hip. I slide my hand around her shoulder then, or
feel her warm cheek, or take off the little beret she insists on
wearing to work with me and lose my fingers in her warm,
blond curls.

Halfway through my first set, which starts at noon,
Marina turns up to start her four-hour lunch break. She takes
Anita to the Picadero to eat the big meal of the day which the
Spanish, with cave-man economy, call *la comida*. Marina has
already had a snack at 10 in the morning. Today a tortilla with
a glass of beer, and then when she ran into a friend some fresh
anchovies with white wine. She'll be able to hold out for the
big meal till I pack it in at two o'clock.

When I show up with my sea of small change Anita has
eaten and her sweet sleeping face is in Marina's lap.

Marina tells me that Anita was very excited about everything that happened while I was singing. Did I do as well
as she said?

Anita will help me count up later. I finish her food while
mine's on order. No, I keep telling Marina, there was absolutely

nothing extraordinary about our first day together, it was the same old shit. "When it's the same old shit for Anita..."

"Then we can't be meeting in restaurants to eat. Is OK if you want a small plate of something, eat and run how you say, but she cannot sit through big meals like this with wine, she will start molesting everyone who eats. This is why I am taking her home to be with the family, why I won't see you at the *comida* every day. You know I want to..."

"What's wrong with a picnic, though? Twice a week or more I go down to the beach to eat, we pick up food on the way through the Barceloneta. Why not a picnic whenever the sun's out?"

I explain that "we" is Zoe the brickmason (who is known to Marina by reputation), a French magician and a guy from New Zealand who got here on a blackjack system.

Marina thinks the magician has "shifty eyes," doesn't want to meet the New Zealander, but she's eager to know Zoe. The look in her eyes closes the book on us. Zoe might as well have gone down on her already. It's already happening in her mind. Who cares where or when? In one of the abandoned buildings out at the end of the harbor where the beach begins. Ruins would be just right.

Every girl in the Tapas Bar wants Zoe to eat her out by now, there must be a line, and that includes some Spanish girls, not just the usual Danish sluts, so that there are more or less constant rumblings from the drunks at the bar. Because I'm perceived as a friend of Zoe's, and rightly, I have to listen to these idiots, sit there and pretend to be scandalized...

Or not. I've crossed the line. I'm telling them to go fuck themselves, that it's no concern of theirs what Zoe does as long as the girls ask it of her. Zoe's not after the young ones, her admirers are late twenties, we're talking about the girlfriends of her detractors.

"You're jealous because you're not getting any..."

They're jumping up and down.

"Or not getting it any more..."

I've got to make sure my escape.

"You ought to take lessons from her."

They'd be coming for me if it weren't for the improvement in my morale.

36

Marina's starved for sex that won't get her pregnant and she told me once when we were getting to know each other, "I like it better when a woman eat me, there is no beard."

I was mildly shocked, but hid it like the good bohemian I was trying to be. It's curtains for my sex life if it gets out I'm not pansexual. I don't want the survivors on the street to start thinking of me as a suspicious character.

Wanting to have sex with Zoe would be wanting to do the right bohemian thing, but Marina wants more. She wants an alliance, and she's not the first one.

Zoe's been a hero to the women in the barrio from the time she started dancing naked on tabletops and flaunting the scars around her shoulders and hips, elbows and knees, where her body was sewn back together after an auto accident.

The men are resentful of the nice tits Zoe has, and that's not all. It's the look of a body-builder that Californians would recognize. Thick, sinewy arms, lumps of muscle on her shoulders, bumps on her belly, ripples on her back. There's no waist at all and she's got a great butt for pants with strong seams. (I've never seen her in anything but jeans.) The Spanish girls love her scars. So do the men, though they'd like to see more of them.

Zoe's tough. It's not easy to keep her out of fights. The night we met she called me a cunt because of something I said, grabbed my hair and forced my face against the table; then held a full bottle over me, threatened to break it over my head and cut my throat with what was left. When she apologized the next day, telling me she was ashamed to have been so pissed, I knew we'd be fast friends.

Zoe's vulnerability is what gets me. It's manifest by more than her scars: the cocky way she stands up to the men after she's been going around squeezing the girls' tits. The way she stands up to Gloria and Esteban, who want to keep her out whenever one of the Spanish men has a knife. It would be so much simpler to bar her permanently, but as Gloria puts it, "She's got a good heart."

Her exploits are revealing. Going to court in England to fight the Value Added Tax on tampons. Others have had a humanitarian tinge, but she did time for stealing a double-decker bus for her personal use during a spree. She worked for a loan shark who owned a sex club. She wasn't required to do any of the rough stuff, but she had to look the other way, and she doesn't repent of what she did (or failed to do). She took up an honest trade, yes—became a "brickie"—but must have been a tremendous pain, working in her knickers with nothing on top till it was really cold. Still, when news of her accident reached the pubs where she was tolerated there must have been heavy hearts all around and visible relief, if not cheers, when it was known she came out of it so well.

Zoe is unique, and if there were some way to have her in small doses half of London would be in love with her. I think of the way she was sewn together, and the jaunty way she moves now, and couldn't be prouder if she were a brother of mine. Yet I resent her for making me want to intercede and stop the bad end I feel is coming. It just doesn't make sense to create so much resentment unless you don't want to live.

Zoe came here because of a Catalan girl she fell for in London, and the affair has gone on for years. The Catalan girl has someone else now, but she still has Zoe, too, and is on some kind of power trip, it would seem. She lets Zoe come back to her from time to time but always breaks it off again when she's satisfied that Zoe is helpless to stop loving her.

I've seen the girl on the street, and she's pure sex, the physical things that Zoe talks about are all there, but the eyes are full of malice, and not just because I'm a man and I'm Zoe's friend. This is a woman who wants to cause pain, I know it, and because I know it she's afraid of me.

Zoe's twice as tough as I am, but the bitch isn't the least bit afraid of *her*.

And no wonder. Around her Zoe tries to act courtly and ends up bumbling, falling all over herself like a teenager with an older woman. From the way she acts and the way the bitch treats her I've got to think that Zoe's never even roughed her up.

"Beat the shit out of her," I always tell her when she's having her coffee next to me at the Tapas Bar and I'm supposed to be sopping up her spilt milk.

She just smiles at me as if I'll never understand. How can someone as smart as she is be so blind to the truth?

She is smart, no denying it. She can quote more original verse than anyone I've ever met. Sure, low stuff, limericks. Still, she always knows who's heard just what and is a born raconteur in spite of the many listeners who are just putting up with her stories to get to her tongue.

In the brightness of Marina's eyes when I mention Zoe I've seen the end of the little family I've helped to form.

But maybe not. I've been on a tightrope so long I don't need the ground anymore. That is, I may never have to compromise with the real world of childrearing and meals around a table and sleeping arrangements sanctified by columnists in the entertainment section of the family newspaper. Maybe we can work Zoe in. There's plenty of room in the bed.

In a flash I realize what's wrong with the arrangement...Anita will have to sleep between her mother and me, and this isn't just accepted practice, a psychologically sound arrangement that can be altered by switching newspapers, this is Anita's idea of how things should be.

With Zoe out of sight on the far side she and Marina could

By the Wayside

carry on all night. Lesbian love is capable of such subtlety that Anita and I would both be oblivious.

Don't I want Marina to have pleasure any way she can? Yes, but I would miss being part of the scenario, having something to do. If Marina's not in my clutches I'm sure I'll be supplanted. I've been uneasy from the start about all the sucking and playing around. The only woman in my experience who preferred sucking to penetration was every bit as lesbian as Zoe.

It rankles to be able to see what's coming, to see Zoe coming, and not to be able to do anything to head her off. The situation as it is right now is made to order for a tenderhearted bulldyke. Zoe's already told me she loves me and likes to hold my hand when we're off to the beach or the British consulate, where she's taken me twice to listen to accents and altercations. And damn it, Zoe attracts me in some way, I can't deny it. There's a deep inner tingle at the prospect of knowing her better and having her near-naked in bed with me, even if her place in the bed is clear across the room.

I've been expecting something to go wrong at Virgilio's. I've always mistrusted communes since my San Francisco and Berkeley days. Nothing is so exciting as the first days or weeks in a new commune getting to know so many people all at once...Then the process of getting to know each other reverses itself and people start erecting steel barricades to protect little secrets about themselves that are completely without importance. Before long a program of mystification is in full swing with all the commune members trying to become mysterious strangers again. Flower children turn into lesbian sadists and musclemen are on their knees.

As usual I have no choice about going along, no chance, or very little, of influencing the outcome. There's something murky and scary going on inside when Zoe takes my hand and starts pulling me along, and I realize it's the woman in me she's seducing. My fear must be like a virgin's on her wedding night...I know I don't have the strength to call it off. I want her to hurt me a little and get it over with, I want her to wake up the

161

man I thought I was before I met her. But even as I own this
I know my thoughts about what should be and what I want are
weak hitches, last-ditch attempts to protect an image of myself
that no longer has meaning.

I'm ready for Zoe to possess me, though I can't imagine
how she's going to do it. I know she wants it, too. There's
something fierce about the way she takes hold of me, she never
clings. That's the reason I've been letting myself get in deeper:
I can tell she doesn't want me to hurt her. What exactly does
she want, though? We all know what's in store for the girls.
Why am I not as useless to Zoe as I am to myself?

The mysteries of the human heart—what a pain in the ass
sometimes. Tomorrow I'll crawl to the altar myself and let
them rip it out of my chest while Marina's got my cock in her
mouth and Anita's telling me, "I'm taking care of a little
worm," in her Spanish that I understand better than Marina's,
showing me a matchbox, "This is his house." Zoe will
approach with the blade, testing the edge with her finger,
taking off the white down on her cheeks, but when she bends
over me she's not the Zoe I remember, she's got her girlfriend's
eyes...

37

My Zoe worries seem premature when I almost lose my
life to a 60-year-old crippled fat lady who's an accomplice of
my worst enemy—a woman who sells lottery tickets. About
sixty herself, crippled as well, the Loto lady sits in the same
place all day near one of my favorite spots. She's there when
I arrive and she's still there when I'm off to more festive
regions to wet the rags in my throat.

Singing near the Loto lady is one of the few times I haven't got a wall behind me. (From now on I'll need an accomplice of my own to be the eyes in the back of my head.)

It's been a daring move to take this spot (I'm told). The regulars at the Tapas Bar, including some fellow buskers, admire my pluck. I'm careful not to get a swelled head when in the company of fellow street artists, some of whom are my age and have been working the streets from the time they learned to sound their instruments and ran away from home. I've been saying, "Pluck is nothing for an opera singer. It's taken for granted. No one will even teach you unless you've got pluck..."

"Pluck? I'd be afraid to open my mouth without it, but standing in front of that planter box, see, the acoustics are so much better. That's what gave me the idea."

What gave me the idea was the way the street fills up at midday between the Plaça Catalunya and the Galerías Preciados, the big department store whose peak business hours correspond to mine. I'm something like a pigeon outside pecking around for a grain of something that's been chased along the streets by speeding cars, while the Galerías, figuratively at least, is busy cracking purses like clamshells and sucking out everything inside.

When they close the Puerta del Angel to all but foot traffic at these busy times, the street's full of shoppers. Anyway, there's a bulge in it, so that the prospect from in front of the planter box is unmistakably that of an opera house to a singer onstage. My platform is a waist between the backstage area and the sea of faces to be sung to. Of course, in an operahouse all the faces would be facing me. No matter, I'm good and I'm loud, and it's a challenge to see how many heads I can turn.

The only possible objection to staking a claim is the effect on my brother buskers if I'm able to fill this space. But acoustical peculiarities having to do with open cross-streets and the angle of reflection of buildings above and beside me are in my favor. Most important, perhaps, there is no stone

163

surface straight ahead, no back of the house, so to speak. The hum of voices and scrape of feet overcome the sound I'm making before it interferes with the guitars or tinwhistles that are courting pedestrians leaving the Galerías or headed to the center's two most important cafes across the street.

The Loto lady's words were unintelligible forty years ago. None of the Catalans on the street can tell you what words these are. Everyone knows she's selling Loto tickets just the way everyone in Nice or Marseille knows that the *vitrier* wants to fix your broken windows. Some poor souls probably feel reassured about their old culture when they hear this pre-verbal racket.

She has a voice like a man's with a reedy whine at the center of it. I can never hear it without wanting to shove something in her mouth, say an umbrella. Shameful way to feel about a crippled old lady, I know. What's more, all of my brother buskers know how I feel, and take my side, and wish me well.

At first I'm not competing with the woman even though she makes as much noise as I can, and she makes it at thirty-second intervals while I sing, completely unaware of me—or so it seems.

Then I notice subtle adjustments in her timing. She is covering my decrescendos with her screams, all my soft high notes, my ornaments. She was sticking to the thirty-second intervals while she was learning my repertoire. She has a great ear, I'll give her that. After one hearing she can spoil every song I know.

Certain shopkeepers in the vicinity vouchsafe that the Loto lady has made the corner her own for as long as they can remember, since they started the Loto. Clearly she's the reason the planter box has never become a traditional spot. She destroyed all the musicians before me who tried to play here. But why? There's no point in having a battle to the death. The way we slow the passersby is good for her business. She can strike up a conversation with people who stop to listen.

Pure and simple malice is why she destroys us.

Trying to fight back by singing louder won't help. I'll lose my voice. Never in all the years she has left will the Loto lady lose hers (and I expect her to see a hundred). Ignoring her won't be easy, either, but it's my only choice.

So far I've been careful not to make what I do on the street a conscious spiritual exercise, yet there is truth in what I told Virgilio once. All the breath control creates some strange and wonderful states—states that I feel sure will offer some protection against the Loto mojo, or maybe just drive the bitch out of her mind.

When I work for a while I reach a point where it is hard to know whether I'm controlling my breath or my long breaths are controlling me, when it's anyone's guess whether I'm using my music to make a little money, or the music is using me to amuse the ghostly old composers of it. Considering the usual outcome for people conducting spiritual experiments it's a wonder brickbats aren't a daily occurrence.

Does the Loto lady have a contingent? I'm ready to concede that people who come this way regularly for lunch or coffee or more crap from the Galerías have become inured to the siren-blast, it probably doesn't bother them any more than the screams of the mutilated in a schoolyard every day at recess. I insist, however, that she is starting to annoy the (by now) sizable number of Barcelonians who are operalovers or are becoming operalovers thanks to my exertions.

Even so, she'll never lack for a majority to take her side. Sales of her tickets have probably never been so high. There's something pathetic about a crippled old lady trying to drown out the likes of Wagner and Caldara and Debussy with feigned insanity.

Anita is the reason the deathblow is aimed at me, she has to be. Good people are afraid for her. I'm viewed as an obstacle to happy childhood, my grind-it-out style of life as an impediment to childishness. Yet there is no danger of her dancing too far from the planter box and being trampled by the beasts of noon. I'm always capable of creating a respectful dead space when I let loose full voice into the throng, especially when I stand well out in the street, staying above the bobbing heads on my wooden curb...

Not once has Anita strayed from the eye of the hurricane in front of me. Parked bicycles and motos complicate the path behind. Tired drunks and wage-earners eating a brought lunch are clustered around the planter box, the benches are jammed. I'm used to having a crowd like this behind me when I work this spot. The only times I'm ever approached from behind are when these people want to make a drop.

I have no idea what hits me.

When I come to, a policeman has got the Loto lady's bodyguard by the arm and he's holding a heavy cane with a design cut into it. This may be the cryptic sign of Satan-worshippers...or perhaps the fat bitch is keeping score of the number of people she's killed with it, the number of vegetables she's created, and the number who just walked away with a goose-egg.

An angry crowd has gathered, but it's not clear at once who's angry with whom. Surprisingly, I don't seem to be the reason for their anger, though I'm sure my fate depends on the outcome of the argument that's raging and I can't see how I'm going to come out ahead with so many maniacs on both sides.

With a start I realize I've lost Anita...

No, there she is, she turns up after I painfully roll my head and my eyes. She has her arms out to me, but she's being restrained by a woman of means, late middleaged, wearing what looks to be an English suit. The woman's been heard from in Catalan and she's got the expression of a judge while the struggle is on. Whether I live or die isn't the point. She's looking out for society's best interests. What's to be done with this sweet little girl?

The policeman asks me in Spanish if I want to press charges. At least I think that's what he's asking; everything is still blurry. Apparently Anita hasn't said I'm her father. I'd have been flattered, but if I had been her father, concussion and all, I'd get to my feet and take a punch at the woman who tried to kill me. Wrestle the cane away from the cop and put a dent in her. I know the cop and he's all winter coat.

I've got to get some kind of defense going in a hurry. I'm not thinking straight. Of course it would be clear to all present that I'm not the little girl's father. We don't even speak the same language. Yet she's still trying to escape the clutches of social justice, trying to succor me.

"*Habla inglés nadie? Francés?*" I scream. Maybe it's because of all the noise the rest of them are making, but I seem to have lost my voice, it's a fragile croak.

Now I'm dealing with a dapper Catalan about my age who can probably speak 15 languages. The streets of Barcelona can cough up someone like this at three in the morning. Only the Germans rival the Catalans in assimilating languages, and the Catalans don't go hiking through foreign lands all summer, they learn right here with their faces in a book while they ride the Metro.

"He wants to know why she hit you," the linguist asks me. "What was the provocation?" Hardly a trace of accent. This would have been one of my friends if I had plenty of money in the bank and expensive clothes. We'd be sitting in one of the cafes up by the university where Elena had *horchata* with her professor friends, discussing locutions that originated in the Tidewater or the Pine Barrens of New Jersey.

"Provocation? The nerve of that little jerk. He knows what I do here. Wagner, Verdi. That was the provocation."

I hear him say something in Catalan with Wagner and Verdi in it.

"Don't be so literal," I try to scream out. "Tell him she's an accomplice of that loudvoiced bitch that's hawking the Loto! They're trying to put me out of business!"

He looks worried now. I know what's up, he was hoping for a gentlemanly rejoinder, perchance a few dry words to make everyone laugh. He doesn't like what my ravings will sound like in Catalan.

"You were singing, no? What has that got to do with the Loto?"

He's probably not a dolt. Spanish people just don't understand competition. "You can't see her for the crowd, but on the corner yonder sits a woman who sells Loto tickets—a fellow cripple, I think. I don't know, I've never seen her on her feet. Someone's riding her piggyback, maybe, or she's lowered out of a window. She's still sitting there. Even if the blow took care of me and everyone knew she was the one who ordered it, you wouldn't catch her crawling away. She'll be sitting there long after you and I are gone, screaming gibberish. As for the fat bitch with the cane...The one who carried out the hit? There are two possibilities, tell the cop. Either she's a halfwit who will do anything the Loto lady tells her, or she's being paid."

My disappointed intermediary is finally translating some of this. The crowd is quieting, you can hear the bad drivers on the Plaça Catalunya, there are so many feet in the foot traffic I feel like a wino on a subway platform. It's time to get up if I can, lay claim to Anita, and get on with my wasted life.

There's no telling what I'll be able to do for a living if there's brain damage. Even if there's beggary ahead I can count on Marina. That's one of the advantages of being in love with a woman who wants something besides a stiff prick in her, who may not want anything the rest of her days but the chance to be near, the chance to breathe the same air in roughly the same place. And Virgilio won't scorn my earnings as a beggar. I'll be guaranteed my food and a place to sleep at night. Pepe the conductor doesn't bring in a penny. Caring for the dogs is his only contribution, and if it's food he wants and not just wine, Virgilio will feed him right along with the dogs, he's told me so. I would have to be in abysmal shape not to warrant the same treatment as Pepe. I'll have more going for me, physically at least, even if I can't put out my hand for alms without some help from my friends. With a physique like mine in ruins...I could rake in more money than all of the beggars around here combined if I had my eyes looking in different directions and my tongue hanging out.

I'm trying to get up and there are strong arms assisting

me. The crowd is noisy again, another argument. Some think I should stay put, evidently. I hope they haven't called an ambulance, I might end up getting thrown out of the country.

Thanks to the assistance I'm able to stand. I get the feeling the crowd is murmuring, "Oh, the operasinger," "Oh, him." Perhaps I haven't been recognized by some of the gawkers without my beret. My beret...The man who restores it is the same who helped me up, a sturdy fellow with a beret like mine. A Basque...a real one...So what, I don't mind being an imposter, death is the same in all languages...Ugh. Oof, perhaps, when it's a bullet in the chest. A yip, a brief expulsion of unsupported breath. Then while the darkness spreads and the spirals of sex uncoil for the last time, a sigh.

I tell the dapper linguist to translate the following: "Let the fat bitch go. She'll never get to me again, I can hire someone to watch my rear. I bear this woman no ill will, and won't try to cut her throat under cover of darkness. But please tell her, and tell the cop to tell her, I know full well who's behind this, and vengeance is mine."

All this is duly translated, supposedly. At least some of it is. The cop restores the fat lady's cane. She starts back through the crowd to look after the Loto seller who, God willing, has been violently robbed of everything but her life by this time. The cop is really getting into it, shouting at the fat woman as she departs, as are certain crowdmembers—the artlovers, I imagine.

"What about the little girl," my Catalan translator is asking me now. "The officer wants to know your relationship."

"Es la hija de mi novia." I scream at the cop. I'm not sure a woman who's given me a three-year-old should still be a mere girlfriend in a place like Barcelona, but the cop is buying my explanation and so is the lady who's been here on behalf of the People of Catalunya for Social Justice. It doesn't hurt that Anita runs to me to be picked up as soon as she's released and wraps her little arms around my neck and starts kissing all over the side of my aching head.

I'm smiling in spite of myself and so is the cop, and so is

the translator, even though he has more reason than anyone to think I'm insane, and there's even applause from some of the onlookers who approve of the way the incident is ending. Catalans are peace-loving sorts, in spite of the way they love to argue. They like trouble to start, make no mistake—a lot of them will be leaving today glad to have seen the fat lady tag me with her stick, they wouldn't have missed it for anything. But they're glad I'm still alive and they're glad that the little girl with the blond curls has a mother even if I'm her boyfriend.

Anita's first inkling of what her mother means to me may not have come till I told Mr. Policeman that her mother is my *novia*. For Anita to call me a friend wouldn't have been good enough for the authorities. Not when the friend is a *callejero*, and a foreign one, at that.

Best of all for the crowd, I'm sure, is the fact that I'm willing to forgive the fat lady. Give her another notch, what the hell. If it weren't for people like her with victims like me life on the street would stale. Wagnermongers must be made to suffer, the people demand it.

Grateful, the onlookers come forward one by one, but so many that they seem to be coming in lines, to drop money in my *maletín*. I stand to receive them where I do to sing, a yard back from the open case, the child still in my arms, nodding my thanks as usual when someone bends to make a drop. There are so many notes I can't see the change at the bottom.

There aren't many whores in this part of town at midday but the two I recognize are looking at me with unaccustomed awe.

Ah, they must have thought the fat lady was *my* accomplice. Or maybe not. I'm well enough known by now. Someone to reckon with. How else to explain the child in my arms? I must be a good man in some way they don't know about.

The child may confirm a suspicion they've had about me all along. I'm not on the street because I'm a bad-guy. Maybe I'm not only educated, but respectable. Not singing here because I have to, but rather like some rich American fooling around. Fellow Americans at the Tapas Bar might help the rumor to spread. They know nothing of the hardships or the rewards of the busking life. As far as they're concerned, I sing on the streets because I'm too lazy to give English lessons.

It's impossible to read the eyes of a whore on the street regardless of Hewitson's or Marina's pronouncements. I'd never taken what she told me about Maribel and the others as anything but romantic twaddle. Sure, maybe there was a kind of collective melancholy that was palpable around a bunch of whores, but it wasn't much in evidence when a girl was chosen, even when it was me choosing and all I had to offer was a cup of coffee. Out of the hundreds of girls I knew by sight I doubt there was one who could have loved me even if she wanted to for a fleeting second between fixes. I was a clown to them, a fantasy, a joke.

Looking into the eyes of the two whores I recognize, who may have witnessed my beating, or may simply have happened by while I was being visited like a tomb and given money for my upkeep, I see that I'm being taken seriously for the first time.

I recognize the look from my days in France when I wore nice clothes and sang in operahouses, and walked down the streets of a town with other young men in nice clothes and looked into the eyes of women who wanted to sell their bodies to me, and saw respect in those eyes, and the hidden pleading, and the hatred still deeper, the bottomless hatred I'm seeing now.

38

How can we resist a picnic...It's March, the weather's cold, wet, windy...But at the end of the near-deserted beach are piles of rocks high enough to hold off the wind and there are places to shelter so near that when it rains we'll only wet ourselves with the first warning drops. Oh, and there's garbage a foot thick wrapped in driftweed to keep the child busy.

We've got the magician and the gambler with us on our first picnic. I don't want them to turn up at the beach and find me there with someone else.

The sun comes out as we set off and it quickly becomes almost hot.

Marina and Zoe are paired off already and I'm walking with Pierre and Trevor. They're glum about the child on my shoulders, afraid they might be asked to watch her for five seconds.

Along the harbor front of the Barceloneta Zoe and Marina are walking hand in hand and they're such different types a lot of prawns stop in midair to launch dark eyes like flies. Anita's riding on my shoulders still, pounding on my head, shouting for attention.

Anita slows our progress because of all the things she wants to do or see but she quiets down and plays alone when we reach our sheltered spot, trying to understand the collage created by long strands of seaweed and left in heaps among the rocks.

Pierre and Trevor go for a run on the wet sand in their bare feet and disappear from sight. The dry sand will keep their feet warm on the long trip back, which may be much later.

I stick to my routine, eating a few bites with the others, sunning a while, then working out, hoisting rocks every way I can think of, drawing on my experience as a weightlifter when I was away at school and should have been studying.

The slight advantage over my fellow man I enjoyed because of my strength has been reversed. That's the way it is with early advantages in life. Even in Barcelona I see frail types chauffeured about in big cars while types such as I was and still am in spirit are bent from the strain of too much muscle and too much will—arthritic joints, bad backs, all manner of broken bones and old wounds that still hurt.

Nevertheless, I take pride in the muscle mass which enabled me to hold my own as a soldier, and in hundreds of other useless occupations between bouts of blessed dissipation where I was given still more reason to be grateful for my iron constitution. Let the runts and weaklings ride. They rose to power because the people on top weren't afraid of them. I'm not in harness in spite of all their clever attempts to put one on me, and I look out on the world with my own eyes.

Zoe likes to lift rocks, too, and today she's outdoing herself—she's doffed her knickers for Marina's benefit. Anita pays her no mind: naked is close enough to partly naked, which she saw all last summer when she went to the beach.

Marina's all eyes. Like other Spanish women I know she gives her complete attention to anything being exhibited for her benefit, laughs if the exhibition has a commercial purpose, learns if someone wants her to, becomes sexually aroused if the purpose is to titillate...

The way Zoe's high breasts shiver and point as the muscles ripple beneath is the definition of "to titillate." I can't take my eyes off her and I've seen the show before. Small back muscles at a brisk boil, bands shuffling, levators bunched. When she bends for a new rock she watches Marina from between her legs watching between her legs.

Anita is still puttering in her terrarium, not a single embarrassing comment. She's picking over the driftheap as I should have known she would, dragging a horseshoe-shaped piece of something for mommy to see which turns out to be a toilet seat from the Age of Wood. I put it around my neck like a horse-collar, the better to play the fool. Anita can't take her eyes off me. I'm cracking her up with my "water" as she calls it, pronounced "bahter." Meanwhile Zoe keeps inviting Marina's attention with the slow, regular movements of her body, her jitterbugging musculature, and sudden displays of the well-organized little mollusc between her legs.

I keep checking Marina's reaction, and Marina never takes her eyes off to catch me checking. She's ignoring Anita, who is still sifting through the driftweed. As for me, I'm aroused by Zoe, but she's not the only thing in my head, there's also a crazed abductor with a knife.

I end my workout before Zoe. Jealousy has such a grip I'm not good for anything. I remember penis-envy and hope Freud is turning over in his grave, raising the earth over himself with his fetal contortions. Now, clitoris-envy—that made sense. I never admired anything so much in my life as Zoe's huge clitoris with it's parka. A brickmason's clitoris if I ever saw one. The air of honest toil about it.

When I visited her once in my old pension above the Tapas Bar she gave me a pep talk meant to get me to take better care of myself.

"Every night I wash out me knickers and put 'em up to dry before I have me wank and go to sleep. In the morning, soon as I've had me wank, I have a good wash before I put on me knickers..."

Zoe wasn't a reader and it should have been clear even then that when she didn't have a glass in her hand or a story in progress or a woman in her lap or on her bed she devoted all her attention to her sex apparatus: grooming, wanking, she probably even talked to it. With all this private attention, and the girls who'd been sucking her ever since she could find girls who wanted to suck, no wonder her clitoris was such a handsome, athletic specimen. If it were possible to trot it out like horseflesh at the start of a race those with inside knowledge would have known at a glance what a dependable steed she was riding.

The basis of my envy. I'd bet anything that not once in its long history of arousal had Zoe's clitoris failed to provide something thick and hard to lodge between herself and her partner in tribadism, a fit too delicate to be duplicated by the ill-favored organ of the male. I'd bet anything that Zoe's apparatus had never faded in the course of a morning wank because of the sounds of the alcoholic next door vomiting or choking on his own blood. I'd bet in all the years she'd been wearing Levi's she'd never caught it in the zipper.

Bulging all over with expectation Zoe finishes her workout while Marina stares and Anita prospects and I eat a *bocadillo* over a foot long, with olive oil smeared on it and the guts of a tomato squeezed on it and slices of *jamón serrano* end to end, thinking I've never eaten anything so delicious in my life with less appetite. And when Zoe plumps down on the blanket next to Marina I get up and tell them, "Anita and I should be going. I want to catch the crowd on the way back from dinner. If Anita gets hungry I'll get her something in one of the cafes when I take my break."

Marina's contentment has deserted the sand and gone racing to her head. It's dawning on her that she can have me in her life as a sex aide and surrogate husband and father and still fool around all she wants. One of her big goals in life is to avoid friction in the home. "You two should get to know each other better," I throw in for good measure, with a wink.

"What about the boys without shoes..." Marina doesn't know what she's saying. Nothing should be this easy and she wants to discover the hitch while I'm still here to deal with it.

"If they catch you doing something naughty..." careful, now, "you'll just go way up in their esteem. They only know you as a mother. They don't even know you're the wife of Wingnut, the well-known anarchist poet."

I only call him Wingnut in English. To escape persecution Virgilio's family had taken the name of a tree (some Jewish families took mere colors), a kind of ironwood that bore a hanging wingnut.

"I didn't know you were Virgilio's wife," says Zoe, touching her arm. Marina's arm looks frail in her red grasp.

"You see, there's lots to find out about each other, starting with your last names."

A few minutes later I'm pausing behind the seawall to try to hear them on the breeze but there's only the raucous laughter of the gulls. The relentless descent of beaks.

And the faint footsteps of a child.
"Stop... Wait..."
"Come, Uncle Gordon..."

39

Not only is Zoe installed at the anarchists' that very evening, she's sitting to the right of Marina at the dinnertable, supplanting Virgilio. I'd thought Virgilio's and Marina's places at table were traditional or I'd have pushed him out long before this. Being righthanded, I could have had my fill of Marina and matched her relatives bite for bite.

"I'm aware of another aspect of socialism thanks to some affluent friends." The anarchists have been having a heated discussion and I'm in a mood to blurt things. As usual Virgilio jumps on my response like an owl on a mouse. Everyone knows I'm in a dangerous frame of mind, everyone knows why.

"I mean Hewitson," I tell Virgilio. Zoe has somehow caused Marina to sit up sharply. Zoe and Hewitson hate each other.

Virgilio tells them a little about Hewitson. He knows a lot, but he's never been to the house, never heard any stories. And he doesn't know that Lidia's father is E.-R. When I say the name implements are put down quietly. The great man recently died.

"Such a noble, cheerful man. Such a good listener, and he was dead drunk when I met him over at Hewitson's. Some people can only savor the things that they've earned, the things they've become able to afford by sweat of brow, but I suspect you and I are different, Virgilio. The food given us by others, and paid for by them, will always taste better than what we can arrange by our own devices. By the same token I'm convinced that some men have the ability to impart freshness and sweetness to the things they possess."

When this thought catches up with the old anarchists some of them hurl their forks down in disgust. Lentil halves are flying. Wine is spilled, but the grannies are too mortified to spring into action.

"I'm convinced that as long as E.-R. owned those enormous buildings something of the past would survive, it would still be possible to go home with some new friends of an evening and get lost for three days. Now that he's dead and the buildings will be sold to pay his debts, those great old flats will be chopped into five or six apartments each. Everyone will know their way around but no one will feel he belongs. The thought of having to take one of those old elevators to the same floor with someone you don't know..."

None of them has ever thought me capable of harboring such sensibilities. Of course I'm just getting a rise out of them. Zoe knows what's going on. Everything's ticklebum for her and me—sex, religion, politics. The only suitable serious business for the dinnertable is chewing. Farts made more sense than their interminable spew about mutualism in '36.

"Now that the socialists are in, listen to what's happened to the Hewitsons," I continue. "They've left the labyrinth and moved to pop's old flat. It isn't as big, but it's grander and the maintenance won't cost them as much. Now they're on easy street, right? The money will come rolling in to them instead of daddy? No. The government is getting everything since the Hewitsons don't have any liquid assets and can't keep up with taxes. All the parasites that surrounded Lidia's father in life have carved up his estate. Lidia owns an entire town in the low Pyrenees, but all the rent of it just keeps them even against their taxes. The town hall gets all the buildings it uses for seven hundred pesetas a year, so the Hewitsons are subsidizing the local government. They've got Rembrandts in safe-deposit boxes, but they can't sell them because the government would charge a whopping tax and take the rest of the proceeds to pay off their arrears. Right now they're selling off antique furniture and heirlooms piece by piece. If it weren't for what that brings in they'd be as poor as the likes of you."

"He's having you on." says Zoe. "Life with you lot would be a big step up for some people I know..."

As it turns out mutualism takes care of Zoe's political thought. Like our hosts she thinks the human being is basically decent and good for something. In line with radicals of all stripes she thinks people should contribute to the community according to their ability and take from the fund of available goods and services according to their need. She distrusts politics that get complicated, like the rest of them here. There's an anarchist simplicity about what Zoe wants to give to mankind. She wants to lick her way to social importance. She'll erect brick walls if she has to, but she'd much rather service her social contract in small installments like a snail, leaving someone she cares about glittery with her nocturnal visits.

Fortunately Zoe has a practical side which may account for the fact that Virgilio is so delighted to welcome her to our bed. She's renting her flat in London and has begun to receive the rent here in Spain. As Virgilio must see it she's a better candidate for a long stay than I am. In London she might not have been able to live on her rent from the flat without doing masonry on the side, but she can easily live on it here and support all the rest of them besides. With Marina and Zoe and me all bringing in money the simple life so dear to Virgilio might be imperiled. But maybe not. A lot of things need fixing. In fact, it may be some time before they acquire anything that isn't badly needed. Life with the bare necessities has gone on for so long, and has been so good, they're incapable of whims.

Zoe doesn't know the history of anarchism in Spain. She doesn't even know what an anarchist is—what makes the people here different from anyone else. In the political gatherings after dinner, which soon fill up the large sitting room, having attracted active anarchists from down the street, Zoe's constantly speaking up for the communist point of view by mistake. As soon as her errors have been explained she'll say, "Well, that's all right, then."

I gave her *Homage to Catalunya* the day she came and tried to get her excited about Orwell. She was bored. I gave her *Down and Out in Paris and London* and she read the whole thing, but "there weren't any naughty parts. I can't believe it...I can tell the man was no poufter by his picture. Looks well-educated. That's a big advantage when you're down among the poor. Why aren't there any tarts? Except for the one in the scene with the monster. Unfeeling swine, that's all they are, that French lot. Parisians are the worst. I never 'ad a decent French 'ore in me life. I'll stick to the Spanish sluts. Something dodgy about this Orwell, though. You've been down on your luck as much as he ever was and you never stopped trying to get your leg up on a woman, now, did you Gordon? With a geezer like him who hasn't got a character you like you're better off not reading the kind of thing he writes..."

The rest of them are pushing Proudhon and Kropotkin and Bakunin on her and slipping her tracts, but she isn't buying. They aren't her types. She hasn't discovered any character flaws, she's got nothing against these authors, in fact she'd been against government of any kind from the time she found out what it was, but she's never been one to join a group...Even when there isn't a group to join, she doesn't like to be on the same label...

A lot of her feelings are shared by the people here, who might as well be called dropouts as anarchists. True, the older ones are living in the past, they remember a movement, real plans of action, real action. As it is today anarchism is a kind of mold on the political infrastructure that turns up in dark places. In a complicated old culture like Spain's there are dark places everywhere, and nobody cares how many black flags begin and end in the darkness as long as the dark places stay the same, there aren't any new ones, there aren't any bobbing flashlights or bubbling bomb labs.

As all the anarchists here are quick to point out, the identification of bombthrowng loonies with the anarchist movement was the doing of the sensationalist press, particularly in America. In spite of a handful of assassinations early in the century, anarchists have always been peace-loving, near-pacifists, hard to provoke, but brave when the time comes to fight for their beliefs. There hasn't been any violence here to speak of since the Civil War, and as everyone in Barcelona knows, that was a time when, thanks to the communist traitors as well as the Falange, the anarchists did more than their fair share of dying.

Zoe, who never had a political thought in her life, is the darling of all the anarchists in no time, even the rabid. She's an example of the kind of free and independent-minded person who can be trusted not to subvert a community of equals. She's got a clear, egalitarian idea of what she's good for and what she deserves. Compassion is practically an instinct with her, it was one of our first points of contact. I had a hell of a time stepping over people on my way to work, but it wasn't till Zoe fell in beside me that I realized something could be done to help the fallen. We couldn't get them on their feet, perhaps, but we could prop them up for a bit.

She's a type who can talk heroin addicts into keeping her company at mealtimes and then hound them into eating a square meal. Three heroin addicts at the Tapas Bar are strong in their support of her when they're not nodding. Their leader, the worst, the wreck of a noble man, is one of her best friends...Paco. At one time they could be seen once a day making the rounds of the bakeries and delicatessens putting sandwiches together. Paco knew exactly who had the best and where it cost less, though I have no idea how he found out.

He'd been addicted throughout his twenties. He didn't look that much older than his 28 years, but he already had cataracts...

If Zoe's a star in this hotbed of anarchy, I'm an unknown quantity. I'm respected for my singing voice, but I definitely lack the anarchist chic that Zoe possesses in abundance.

I'd started well. Nothing could be better than an affair with Virgilio's wife to get these particular anarchists on my side. It showed contempt for the institution of marriage, of course, but more importantly it showed trust in my friendship with Virgilio, and what it stood for. We reaffirmed Marina's right not to belong to anyone by refusing to fight over her. All of us had kept each other's humanity in our sights and defeated our petty feelings of jealousy, wounded vanity and pride of possession.

Then I had to muck everything up. Not content to get between Marina's legs with Virgilio's blessing I had to win over his three-year-old and supplant him as father, too. This showed no respect for Virgilio's fragile sense of himself as a family man.

Virgilio wanted to be necessary to as many people as possible—he had a special gift for bringing people together and making them useful to each other. He'd be reduced to being a kind of pimp if his wife and daughter looked to me for all their needs. And I was more than adequate to be their sole provider. My take on the streets could keep them in what would have to be called luxury by any standard they'd ever known.

There was a flurry of excitement when Zoe arrived. All the old folks wanted to see who would win the battle for Marina. I hadn't been around long, I hadn't worn out my welcome at all, but I knew I didn't have any anarchists on my side.

The fight's about over as far as I'm concerned. Anita doesn't care what kind of arrangement we have when the dust clears as long I'm still in the picture, including her and doing her bidding, so she's the real reason no one can conceive of my leaving. And Anita's making the best of Zoe's ascendancy.

From the time she was born she's had a crowd of women fussing over her, and fussing over her mother, too. Zoe might be the most welcome attendant she and her mother have ever had. There's beauty, strength, clarity and comedy in her fussing.

I'm not sure Nuria is adjusting all so well. She's an old-style Catalan—larger than average, but typically quick-moving and keeneyed on the street. I wouldn't be surprised if she'd like to pair off with Virgilio for the rest of her life and the hell with all his relatives. If Marina and the child will leave with me her way would be clear. She makes enough to support herself and Virgilio by selling sandwiches. A room in a pension would be a big improvement on the family home. All she wants is a straight shot at his body and the chance to end the politics and return Virgilio to the poetic realm where he belongs.

Since we've been together at the anarchists' there hasn't been any hankypanky—zero. Nuria is taking my side, though. I can sense her support. She's probably influencing Virgilio. Nuria might be insulted because of Zoe's exclusive interest in Marina. I heard her say something about "promiscuous lesbians" for Marina's benefit.

Marina knows Zoe's reputation, so it's all the more remarkable that Zoe is completely devoted to her. Oh, Zoe notices other women. No matter who's along when we're out walking she never lets a pretty girl go by without asking me how I'd like to "get my leg up on her." But she's not pulling strange girls onto her lap any more.

After dinner it's customary for Nuria to sit partly in Virgilio's lap and partly on the arm of his chair—she really is large. Marina is on Zoe's lap, the child is asleep on mine.

The same arrangement holds when Zoe insists we leave our smokefilled room and our useless talk of politics and take over a large table at one of the cafes in the neighborhood, as she increasingly does on mild nights. We may start with our own chairs, but after enough wine....

Anita's no impediment to a late night drinking wine

outside. Sleeping children abound in Spanish cafes, and not because of unwillingness to give up the glass, there's plenty of wine at home. On a mild night there's no pleasanter place to be than right in the neighborhood at some cafe sitting outside. No tourists, no drunks, no fellow buskers, no whores—or at least, no propositions. Zoe and Marina get their share of shrugs, but these workingpeople seem to think it's a privilege to be able to look in on lesbians so far from the center of town. The political talk goes on all around us, of course, but it's pale. The passionate sound of these opinions means nothing, they've been culled from the newspaper.

The times I've had insomnia after these mild evenings I've kept an eye on Zoe and Marina in the big bed, and they never touch intentionally, not even when there's only one of them awake. They're getting together in the daytime, somehow. But where do they get the discipline to turn themselves on and off this way?

40

A big picture of me appears in the *Vanguardia* along with smaller ones of some other buskers, and an article which is meant to gain public sympathy for us poor unemployed misfits and foreigners who are stuck here, and for those among us with a grain of musical talent—real musicians, frustrated musicians, but people who would rather raise their humble voices or pluck their humble instruments than go on the state...or back to mom...or blow their brains out and give the author a chance at the front page...

Hewitson has had nothing to do with this affront, it goes

without saying. I remember a couple of months ago when a man who identified himself as a journalist wanted some pictures of me. I said, "Sure," the tourists were taking pictures of me all the time, a dozen a day at least, and I enjoyed the thought of them being developed in places like Sweden and Australia and Nova Scotia. I should have had the sense to know what was coming. I'm larger than life around here and not just because I'm a foot taller than everyone else.

What's bothering me is the certain knowledge that my notoriety as a street performer will stand in the way if I ever decide to go legit and sing at the Liceo.

I have no worries about being accepted to sing parts there. My voice is getting stronger all the time. I'm outstripping my ability to be comfortable with so much voice. My personality is geared to provide backup for someone who's good enough to be given the first lead, someone who deserves a break. I can picture myself slacking off if I get my just deserts.

I'm used to having people above me with inferior skills, people with connections, rampant injustice holding me back...Nature rearing Her ugly head, twice as much bitterness and frustration as the human being can endure. *This* has been my claim to fame: in spite of setbacks, and too much time in harness, I've stayed the course. *Why* calls my sanity into question, and while so much of my story remains untold, perhaps it's best if I don't look for definitive reasons.

Oh, I'd done starring roles before. I did a United States premiere of a decent Leoncavallo opera, took the baritone lead. Premiere—at least that's what it was called in our publicity. It was done at the Met shortly after it was written and maybe by a host of other companies whose publicists had lacked the effrontery of ours.

Anyway, the top is a terrible place to be. All the cliches are true—no place to go but down, no one you can trust. It should be noted that in the opera field top billing is a life-or-death struggle in the kinds of shows where all the programs get thrown away and the performers themselves don't keep them

184

in their scrapbooks. Things can get really nasty when an unknown singer is doing a big role and a well-known singer a smaller one...Or when a well-known singer and an unknown are both Rhinemaidens...The truth is, there's plenty of room for nastiness no matter who's doing what. An ability to take nastiness for granted is the sine qua non for people who want a career in the cruelest of professions.

If it were up to me and there weren't a Nena to consider or an Anita I'd probably continue to sing on the streets as long as the Guardia Urbana would let me. That's not the same as saying, "I'd make streetsinging my career." The lady with the cane was still lurking by the side of the road, or someone like her. Something terrible would have to happen, that's all, to make me unhappy with my lot, unhappy enough to face the maestros again, and all the other perfectionists who knew more about music than I did...even if they were in love with my voice, one and all, and wanted my success more than I.

But for my child or my children...

I'd been a no-account long enough where children were concerned. Losing my travel money the way I had when Nena was born had been the last straw. Until I was memorialized as a streetsinger by getting my picture in the paper I'd been toying with the idea of shaving my beard, putting away my beret, buying or borrowing some new clothes and walking into the Liceo with nothing but my voice to recommend me and a plausible though deliberately vague account of all my years in the business.

People don't really look at me out on the street. But they would have studied that picture of me in the paper. My ears are showing. Enough right there. "Where have I seen a dramatic baritone with ears like that?"

In France I'd been warned by *administrateurs* in three French cities about singing in public. At the time I'd only been engaged for small parts. Never had I accepted anything but free drinks when I filled the public squares of their cities with Wagner and Verdi. Still, "We must think of our reputation, *monsieur!*"

I'm surprised when, after my picture has appeared in the paper, I have another visit from a little guy who's been trying to recruit me for the chorus at the Liceo. He's birdlike, he hops around, it's always been fun to watch him. He keeps blinking his eyes, he's probably the only hophead second tenor in history. I just laughed at him the last time. Someone with my voice sing in a chorus? He could see for himself how much money I could make this way, "singing solo the whole time!"

On this visit I make him wait while I sing an aria that would be a showstopper if I weren't the whole show.

He gives me a piece of paper, the name of a man, a time to see him. I'll be expected...today, tomorrow.

Why the urgency? He gets a commission for each throat?

He's gone. I won't see him again until I join.

I go that afternoon, I sing, I conquer. I have no résumé. None is asked. The men hearing me know what I can do. One of them heard me almost three months ago on the street and has been dispatching the birdman to collar me.

I can keep my beard and my beret. "I'm not trying to be difficult," I tell them in French, after asking to keep them. "I'll buy some new clothes, shoes. I'll buy some language books and master Castilian and Catalan now that I know I'm going to be here for a while."

"We will pay you 45,000 pesetas a month to start. You have done *Lucia* before, forget the staging. The *Fidelio*...That you have done, too? We trust you, but this is a German cast, you'd better know the opera..."

"Then you don't trust me. Yes, and *Tosca*...a continental breakfast. Look, your season only has three months to run and I've done every one of the operas you've got left. Call it fate..."

"We don't know you, *señor*. We don't understand the tragedy that has brought you to the street, but you are not an alcoholic like so many of these men..."

If only more prospective employers had sized me up from across the street.

"You are too old not to have done leading roles some-where. With your voice...Frankly, we would like to give you some parts next season. We will do this if you can prove yourself reliable in the time which is left."

"I'll never be late. I'm living on the outskirts of town, but I won't do any commuting. I'll trot right over after I've worked the *merienda*. There's a nice flurry in the early evening that I can't afford to miss. What you're paying me will pay for a cab home every night, a luxury I've always wanted ever since I moved away from the center of town. I've got a little girl to support...Is there any reason my little friend can't watch from the wings?"

The man in charge, a prince with a black beard, takes my request seriously.

"I'll see what I can do. Some of the choristers have this problem."

The one who made a face when I mentioned Anita is the chorusmaster. He may have resented his boss's flattering remarks about my voice. Chorusmasters like what's ordinary in a voice, what blends. With the power I have to drown out two or three sections I may have just stepped out of his worst nightmare.

These are honest types so I ask them for 5,000 pesetas in advance to prove it. "A tradition in my country when employment is being tendered."

The prince quickly give me the money out of his pocket. Good, he's never worked in America. I make a note to dun him for cabfare after I've been on time to rehearsals for two weeks.

41

Anita can tell a celebration is coming when she looks up from her wooden seat by the concierge. I tell her I have a job. Thanks to Virgilio this is a cause for confusion instead of rejoicing. Weren't women the only ones who were supposed to be excited or at least relieved to find a job? "The job is nothing, more singing," I tell her on the way out, for the benefit of the concierge as well. "But look, Anita, they gave me 5,000 pesetas just for thinking of them first! Just so I'll promise to come back soon and do my singing here! Come, let's find your mommy and Zoe and have dinner. We'll see, maybe a show."

Marina leaves work a bit early because of this emergency and we have no trouble finding Zoe, but it's hard to decide where to celebrate if it's a show I want with dinner. Zoe likes to watch the 70-year-old strippers who can fling their tits over their shoulders, but it's probably not right for Anita, who needs to be taught respect for the elderly. The Flamenco shows are too touristy and all the big stage shows cost too much. The celebration would be over the minute we got in.

We settle for a place I know of on a quiet, treelined street in the Ensanche. Friends of Elena's had told me about it, it's not far from the university. There's a classical pianist, Catalan food that we can afford. My 5,000 pesetas will buy a big meal for us all, three bottles of good wine, a present for the pianist.

I'm recognized from the picture in the paper. The pianist asks me to sing. I tell him I've lost my voice from so much singing on the street today...Wine after hours of singing swells the cords, that's the real reason I'm not in voice. No one insists. The ones who haven't heard me are relieved.

Zoe's indifferent to the music, but she likes the treatment we're getting. Anita has stayed awake for the music and eaten all her food which is like a rave notice to someone trying to feed her or entertain her at this hour of the night. After ten o'clock it's hard to get on her good side, hard to get her to admit she likes the things she says she likes. ("Well, you liked it two minutes ago...") She's only perverse when she's tired, though, and she only cries and acts put upon when she's hungry. Given that it's quick and easy to feed her or bed her down wherever you are in a city like Barcelona, Anita is almost too well-behaved, too good to be believed. The little ones I remember were always trying to get something out of you.

Anita would seem to feel no need to manipulate, and there's something unnatural about that to an old whore like me. Anyway, these are gloomy thoughts that don't seem to be connected to anything once I'm about my business, careening down the street. When for example...

Anita begs me to buy her something she wants and I tell her, later, we don't have time, and she sulks. Then ten blocks further on she gives me a dirty look when I have time to rest on a parkbench and watch my hands while the people she should have had for parents or playmates trail laughter as they dance by. Now I know she's all right and that my fears for her are nothing but a form of amazement for a mind schooled in mistrust, a mind that has distinguished itself by seeing bad outcomes to which our hale and hearty pleasure-seekers are blind.

42

I have them where I want them now.

It's the triumph of the small man with a small mind, an Edward the Second unfurling his claws.

Virgilio starts to lubricate whenever I'm around and tries to slip his flattering comments inside me like oysters. The anarchists are asking for voice lessons along with more dinner music, making much of my treatise on singing and welcoming my revolutionary theories into their oral history. Nuria is touching my arm. Zoe feels me up outside the can she favors and tells me she likes to lick men's balls.

Marina is looking at me with her one contact lens and I remember the looks I was getting when she was willing to brave Galicians in their pyjamas to get to me.

Anita's small hand has deformed my sleeves.

Fine that I'm gone all day singing in the streets, fine that I never give their long midday picnics more than an hour, but I've become a fixture in the evenings as Anita's lap, as sounding board and organ grinder for the anarchists, as the sole reason, since Zoe never has an opinion, for Virgilio's display of mastery in French and English, and as the sine qua non of the relationship between Zoe and Marina. Without me the two lovebirds would have been looking for a future together, there'd have been nothing furtive about their fooling around.

And Zoe would no longer be able to kid herself that we're brethren of some kind, men of Athens, when it's clear that I'm more of a lesbian than she is, or more of a woman.

People have tried to make me feel indispensable before. Probably I've been weak enough to believe them for a second or two when with cocktails in hand and crumbs on the floor the society ladies of the dress circle or the golden this or platinum that have told me that no voice they've ever heard could have done such a splendid job with the bit part I'd just sung, what a shame I hadn't been in town ten years ago when Otello was given and some nonentity had been the Montano...

These anarchists and fellow clowns think they need *me*, but they only need a little more money to get by on. They love people, however, especially oddballs, and they're much too goodhearted to think of themselves or think of each other as types who only need to know me because of my money.

Their faces blot the light in the high windows as they watch for my cab to pull up late at night after rehearsal.

"How was rehearsal?" one of them is sure to ask as soon as I make my entrance.

Half my life people have been asking me "How was rehearsal?" It's maddening.

By the Wayside

"Absolutely nothing of importance happened, it was just a rehearsal," is my reply, or something like it. "The girls were all dressed to be noticed, but it was just a rehearsal so we all watched the conductor instead..."

Something *has* been happening at rehearsal, however, but very slowly: the glimmer of a process that will take much longer than I have to live to complete itself. Something between me and the chorusmaster. He's so adequate he frightens me. I took him for a yes-man the day we met and we took an instant dislike to each other, but I think we're ready to be strangers again. My willingness to sing piano and blend in has turned him a tenth of a degree.

Political discussion in the big room comes to a halt while I regale all present with stories that made the rounds over a coffee or a beer, which the singers may drink during their breaks.

Anita never comes along on the nights when I'm rehearsing, but when I've got a performance the company has made good on their promise to let her watch from the wings. When she wants to see a show I pass her off to someone's husky mother while I'm onstage and she's handed back at the end of my scenes. She likes the loud music, the costumes, the spectacle. With so many people around her made up and in costume, she feels that she is taking part.

It's April, Anita's turned four, she's still young enough to see what's new and exciting in my routine, especially when we're doing a new opera. And she loves the long cab rides home through the dark city while she nestles in the crook of my shoulder and smells my cold cream.

It's only midnight when I get home, the second shift is still eating. It wouldn't do for the celebrity I am now to eat with such an unresponsive bunch. I eat on my lap in the big room and answer questions with my mouth full. After a few weeks of this it's clear that my operahouse is more boring than the street I sing on and discussions of general interest begin again and quickly become arguments or shouting matches as of old, with the difference that Virgilio keeps up a running translation

191

now, and I don't need it as much.

Fully aware of the effect on Marina and Zoe I'm not there for them in the family bed anymore, either. I sleep like a stone, not changing position the whole night, my legs drawn up, my hands pressed together under my cheek like a Hindu greeting gone awry. The child's beautiful sleeping face is always there when I wake, more often turned to me than to the lesbians, who lie next to the window. The stillness around her nostrils, her stub of nose, her eyes that keep seeing behind their silken curtains, the contours of her tiny face grace my sleep like the sight of a desert landscape at night from the windows of a hurtling train.

We never touch. Nothing disturbs the smooth, cool flow of sleep, the trickle of sand from the dunes.

43

I'm not surprised when I get the invitation. Marina and Zoe have been trying to bring me back ever since they began to lose me. They want a tryst, says Zoe. They want me to share the bed they go to in the daytime.

Invitations like this are nothing new from Zoe. She used to ask me to take a whore with her. With some subtlety considering the proposed arrangements, she's boasting that she knows her way around a man and woman in bed, this wouldn't be the first time. There will be plenty for me to do, I won't be "lying doggo."

Managers (as they were called) were recruited thus for

games at school—the boys with towels and buckets of water who stood on the sidelines, chosen for their ability to remain anonymous.

"Not interested. I've hated group sex ever since it spilled over onto my mattress at a crash pad in the Haight-Ashbury. When sex becomes impersonal you don't even know who gave you the disease. Just say '33 Hunt Street' and my blood runs cold. That was the clinic where we waited for our shots of penicillin and listened to conscience-stricken guitar music, folk songs with respectful pauses before the fingering. I'm not going through anything like that again..."

"But we love you, Gordon. That's different, innit? Marina's under your skin, admit it, she still is. You're too knackered at night to miss her is all. Think what it'll be like to be in her at eleven in the morning, when you're fresh!"

"That's when Anita and I are walking to work. Where?"

"A friend lets me use her kip, an English teacher."

"She won't want a man coming up, I'll bet."

"She's straight, that one."

"I don't believe you. Look, I wouldn't change my way of going to work for anything. It's my favorite time with Anita, now that I can make the trip without getting blisters on my feet."

"What about lunchtime?"

"What happens to Anita then?"

"Why can't her father watch her for a few hours?" She's getting red. "What's a father for?" She lets that hang in the air long enough to start us both laughing. "Admit it, Gordon, Virgilio carries it too far, being a good-for-nothing. He'll be glad to have Anita if we ask. It's that bitch Nuria that's been holding him back. I saw what she was straight off. Could only love a child if it were her own."

"I don't know, Zoe. I don't want Anita to get the idea we're trying to get rid of her."

"How can she think that when it's her father for the job? He's not some geezer we picked up off the street. Let me ask 'im. I'll make it good for you, Gordon. I can hardly wait."

She slips an arm around my waist. I know she's sincere, but when it comes to skin on skin she's nothing but a comrade. I can feel her backing off even while she's got her arm around me, struggling to keep up the pressure, trying to like the feel. I take her hand away, feeling sorry for her, certain I'd never be able to get hard for someone so tentative. I keep her hand in mine, though, and that revives her a little.

"You'll give it a try, won't you?"

"See what Virgilio says. And set it up far enough in advance that Anita starts to look forward to seeing her father then. I'll try anything once. As soon as someone gets hurt, I quit. I've been trying too long already to work something out with you two."

"Like 'ell, Gordon. You've been freezin' us out ever since you got that bleedin' job."

"I never take my eyes off the music. There's no one..."

"At home. At the beach. You act like you don't even want to touch her. Never mind, we'll fix it up. You'll see."

Zoe's more persuasive with Virgilio...

No, that's not it. Virgilio's behind the project like an outboard motor. He'd love to see more of Anita, especially now that the rest of us will be too busy. He and Nuria can give her their full attention.

I next see Zoe when she comes for Anita. I'm working the last crowd before it will be time to drift over to the operahouse and start eating *tapas* in the little cafe across from the stage entrance.

"You're going to get to spend the morning with your father tomorrow!"

Nothing has changed the child's smiling face when she looks up.

"I asked you to give her time to get excited."

"*No quieres acompañar tu padre mañana?*" Zoe asks, doing no better than I would.

"*A donde?*" asks Anita.

I want to see Zoe get out of this one. She knows Virgilio won't take her to the beach. I can't picture him on a beach in any season, though I still have his trunks...

Yes, I can: a young man reading under a blue umbrella, burying his butts in the sand. What's really not right for a poet of his stripe is the picnic.

"Tibidabo," says Zoe. I think she's improvising.

"Don't make me laugh," I tell her. Tibidabo is an amusement park high in the hills behind the city and built entirely on stairs. It's the least amusing place someone in bad shape could spend a morning in Barcelona.

Anita is clapping her hands.

"Maybe you'll have to settle for the funicular over the bay," I tell her.

Anita chooses not to hear me. The child must be as tired as I am of hearing her father say he doesn't have the money to take her anywhere.

("Go to the beach with mommy, Zoe and Gordon. They can buy you anything you'd like.")

Zoe's laying it on as best she can in her limited Spanish. Her dad's going to spend more time with her every day from now on, but that doesn't mean she won't be able to go on the streets with uncle Gordon anymore...

Before she takes her back to the anarchists' Zoe confirms my suspicions out of earshot of the child.

"You know I have to pay the bleeder to take her—he wouldn't have fare for the underground if I didn't. Small price to bring a father and daughter together..."

"You're bringing the three of us together," I remind her.

"Us, too, but why be onesided? Keep an open mind. How long will you be kippin' at Virgilio's? How long will a life like this go on?"

I recognize the lie while it's still in my throat.

"The streets won't keep you. I know how it is here, but if you don't believe me, ask Marina. They start enforcing a law and you're out on your bum. What happens when you start to get somewhere at the opera? You've told us how much you'll have to travel when you start doing leads. Where does that leave Anita? Why do you want her to think of you as a father?

You've got your own little ankle-biter to think of...What's going to happen to Anita when your flesh and blood is back? And I see it coming, all you do is work, we never see you pissed any more, your clothes are always clean. You'll be doing star turns soon and that Cuban lady will hear of you. I'll keep helping Virgilio to make sure Anita gets everything she needs. I love her, it's not just Marina, remember that. I'll never forget Marina no matter what happens, but Marina wouldn't let me help her if there was nothing between us but memories. She's not like her husband. She'd let me help Anita, though, and that might mean a lot someday. When you love someone you always love them, and any connection is good enough for me...Who knows, someday Anita might call me Auntie and I'll be like a member of the family.."

Returning home after rehearsal I take Virgilio aside to find out exactly what Zoe's done to his mind.

"Tibidabo is my idea!"

I may not respect Virgilio, but I like him too much to call him a liar.

"Look, I know Zoe's giving you money..."

"Of course, how else can I afford to take Anita there? But I am excited like a little boy to go there again. In my childhood this is a big extravagance. Fond memories await. I will enjoy giving my child the fun-house experiences of my youth, the wild rides..."

"She's never been?"

"Alas, with me, no. Marina has taken her, but this is no place for a hardworking woman, the climbing is very difficult." He shows his brown teeth in a smile. "Even for me! I am afraid after so long I will not have the strength to keep up with such a healthy child. All the walking with you has made her very strong..."

I've heard enough. Virgilio wants to be first father again. He's had it in him all along, but lacked the money to nourish his instincts. He's incapable of doing anything for money. Thanks to my American background, and my childhood grubbing for self-sufficiency in people's gardens, I'd always dismissed Virgilio as a shirker. A good poet, maybe, but lazy.

Other views are possible.

Virgilio likes to think of himself as a repository. Very few people care about his poetry now, his last collection appeared six years ago, but his books began to appear when he was twenty. At twenty he saw himself as a nexus of tradition and fresh language and stopped trying to have new experiences. In all the time he's mulled over the ideas of others he's made important discoveries, but nothing will change him, he's just trying to fit everything in. He's never worn any hat but his own, so he's never seen himself as a person who has economic significance.

There are only two possibilities in his feeble struggle to survive. Those who know him and need him for something, not only family but friends all over town who look forward to his arrival from time to time the way they would a journal of opinion, will give him a little food, a little coffee, a little wine. Or else those who don't know him or need him will find him useful, and take up the slack left by his friends and loved ones.

I can't read Spanish well enough to need him for his ideas, but I'm given the benefit of the doubt, of course—that's the core of anarchism and it always has been. Virgilio thinks no less highly of me because he has to provide me with food and roof, woman and wine, even though the woman is his wife. Far from it, it makes him feel rich to have so much that someone else would want, especially one such as I, the independent type, whose talents, under the current deluded scheme of things, bring such a high price.

I can tell he's pleased with Marina for wanting me to share her lover. He thinks I'm bored. He knew exactly when I stopped having the hots for his wife, and he knew exactly why.

"You have no doubt discovered my wife's obsession with little holes..."

"Little holes?"

"Little holes in the birth control device, little holes in her teeth..."

197

"I don't know, that might be too tiny a way of looking at it. She had Anita because of a hole in her diaphragm. And she's afraid of losing her teeth because of little holes she didn't start worrying about in time."

"We had some good years before she began to worry..."

Virgilio's smile is unutterably sad when it sits on his face with nothing in it.

44

I'm alone in the older streets of Gracia, the narrowest of the Ensanche, but Gracia is a spot on the lung. Slum-breath already lurks in its dead ends.

I should let them "get something started," thought Zoe, before I show up, so I'm wondering what they've got started.

"They." Marina couldn't start anything these days. She never has anything to say, drifts around like a kid with its mouth full of sweets.

The sound of her is what I remember best about our time together in lavatories or on the little bed I once had under the low beams. That's what I'd like to see started, then. A moan in her throat. Hectic respiration.

I'm canny enough about sexual encounters to know it never helps to dream or plan anything. The unforeseen in a sexual encounter is often what's best. Only bored lifemates can make expectations work by planning knock-down, drag-out fights first.

Yes, I'm scared of what I might find. I might chicken out if I were on my way to meet Zoe and some unknown female.

By the Wayside

I've admired her right along without trusting her.

It's a top story walkup, one of those brainstorms that has a different roof for every room.

They answer the door naked, Marina's hand on Zoe's shoulder. Zoe is flushed the way she is after one of her workouts on the beach. Marina is slightly walleyed with desire, something I might have been too close to notice before. Her nostrils are huge and she's breathing hard. As soon as I've got the door closed behind me she scoops Zoe's breast into her mouth, where its buddy would appear to have been moments before.

"Peel off, Gordon," says Zoe, unspecifically fingering the wild woman's hair behind the neck as one would a longhaired dog. The suckling sounds are having an effect, helping me to suppress my biggest worry. "You want to watch us a while, then, luv? I'll bet you've never seen her the way she gets with me."

I'm following her into a large room with a window onto a portion of the roof where clothes have been hung out to dry. The whites are blinding. It's not much darker inside. There's a mattress on the floor, lots of pillows, a couple of beat-up chairs. Zoe's motioning me to one.

"Take off your clothes, luv. We'll want you ready when the time comes."

She watches me pull off my pants, oblivious of Marina, who's got half a breast in her mouth and her hands keying on Zoe's front and back doors.

"Look, isn't he sweet," says Zoe as I pop out. Marina is shaking her head and rededicating her fingers. Zoe's forcing her to walk backwards so that she can get near enough to give me a tug. "Owww...Do you think I could get him to do something?"

I'm sure she's made them stand before and she's acting nurse-like on purpose. Still, there's no disgust on her face.

Marina's gurgling has the continuity of a scenic attraction.

I finish pulling off my shirt. I've already got the socks

off, they went with my pants. A man in socks can stop an orgy cold. And my feet are all that Marina's had a chance to see since she answered the door.

"Come on, sweet one, give him something to think about." Zoe's settled back on some large pillows and discarded her legs. Marina's on her like a terrier into a burrow. "That's it, luv. Coo, that feels good."

Zoe should be ashing a cigarette. Surely Marina has enough English to know perfunctory when she hears it. At last Zoe has her hands on her, she's patting her shoulder, staying with an ear. If this is passion I've seen as much in the shopping appraisals at the Galerías.

"Enough, sweet one, save yourself. This is just a preview," Zoe says to me. She's prying Marina's head loose. "Look at this, Gordon."

I flop down beside them. Bugeyed, with her nostrils as big as 25-peseta pieces and her tongue out I'm reminded of a small animal picked up by the skin of its neck.

I lean to touch Marina's temple lightly.

"Don't do that, luv. It has to be my way today. She can't do this at all if you're going to take over."

"Take over? You mean, touch her."

"She just wants you to see what she likes to do."

"I'm convinced. You're great together. What do you need me for?"

"Don't make me count the ways...Listen, I've always been an exhibitionist. Lot of good she can do me..." Marina's already burrowing again. Zoe puts a calming hand on her head. "This won't be some slap and tickle, either. You'll see."

Forcing Marina's head back again so she can see, Zoe sticks her tongue out slowly. As it emerges Marina retracts hers.

I've never seen anything like it...Probably because I haven't bought any of the magazines where it's on display. If Zoe is half the exhibitionist I think, her organ of speech is pointing from dirty bookstalls on five continents.

She's learned to control her muscles so as to erect a

conical object that's as thick as any man and perhaps because she's practiced sticking it out for hours alone each day, or on the job with her conquests, it's adequate to go deep.

I recline Roman-style to take in what follows, keeping to the edge of the mattress so as not to take an elbow in the face. (They tend to scramble when they lose their footing on their charge to the top.)

What Zoe's doing with her arms is déjà vu. It's the bench press she practices at the beach every day. Instead of a huge rock between her hands she's got Marina's hard rear end. Quite a feat, since Zoe and Marina weigh about the same.

Marina's groaning so loud I'm checking the window for clothes with something in them. Only the wind.

Zoe has been strong and silent throughout—even the endless melonchopping is a faint sound.

Marina's turned away from me, but her tongue lolls out each time she looks back, a pale pink novice.

Giving her a workout this way Zoe has been deliberately cheating me of the look on Marina's face. Zoe must know that the expression there will be more erotic to me than any of the stark grinding no matter how imaginatively conceived.

The girl who lives here might be a university student. She's invested in good hi-fi equipment and books and she's got her prints nicely framed but her furniture and the clothes peeping from her bedroom closet weren't much to begin with.

Zoe is getting to her feet. She's got Marina in a shoulder stand while she takes a breather, the "Queen of Positions"...Ah, now it's the rowing exercise...In combination with a shoulder shrug and rise on toes. When her staccato notes are too fast to sustain she slips into a less urgent rhythm and rebuilds.

Marina gets heavier and heavier until Zoe is nearly bent double, trying to start a dead weight lift she can no longer manage. Meanwhile Marina, whose lower back is now in contact with the mattress, is coming full circle, digging in her nails, hoisting herself, trying to mount an assault from behind. Now something like appreciation is going on, something less appropriate to a gymnasium.

It occurs to me I've been a voyeur very seldom in my life. In a wistful, drunken state I'd landed in porn theaters a couple of times, but I'd been forced to leave out of boredom and disgust with the foolishness of the performers. Instead of being delighted by the opportunity to be a fly on the wall, as I was at laundromats, thoughts of death had been crowding in as I left, and I found myself consciously suppressing the images I was taking home, longing for the lost darkness of my mind.

For months I've been worried about Marina's increasing silence and Moonie affect. Fine if she was in love with me in some way, fine that she's fallen for Zoe, but she's become too uncritical. It's as if she's had news of a fatal illness and is trying to keep from thinking about the approaching end.

Sure, in love it's important to let go, but abandon shouldn't be entirely passive. That's the kind of let-go that afflicts an animal about to be torn apart by a predator. It's a passivity that asks for destruction, it brings out violence in the male. If love triumphs over a man's instinct to violence he'll try to hurt a woman's feelings, try to breathe life into her by rousing her self-importance.

My love for Marina, and Zoe's, had upset her, confused her. Love of a woman was too new. She'd been a virgin bride, too modest to let everyone know how happy she was. She'd seemed sad because she didn't want the rest of us to feel poor in the presence of her new wealth of feeling.

Well...?

Now Marina's like someone bouncing in a cart. Zoe is trembling all over from fatigue and her refusal to subside onto her lover and destroy their gentle contact is generosity itself, and all the more spectacular when you realize she reached her destination an hour ago.

In spite of my fear that she's been lobotomized by her desires I can't help enjoying the sight of Marina while she's forgotten all the forced moves of motherhood and become a child again. Of course that's the rightness in it. There's a childish innocence in their escapades, an exploratory abandon, childish wonder, a childish refusal to stop, to be brought back to duty.

This is oral sex, after all—I should have seen the child-ishness all along...But I was so infected with knowledge about sex, the knowledge of militant procreators like my father...I'd learned to think this very sophisticated behavior indeed, a technique to be learned, scores of dos and don'ts to be dealt with. And the end result of all the knowledge and training and the practice was power over the woman I loved. I wanted her to be putty in my hands, I wanted her to do things that would have been unspeakable to her only minutes ago.

I insist that degradation was never a factor. I wanted her to help me shatter the complacency of all the bozos like my father who'd made up their minds about good and bad, and what was to be done and couldn't be, on the basis of some crap they'd heard or read, starting with their parents, back when people were running around in long underwear and sex really stank.

Suddenly I'm not a watcher any more, at least not completely. Hope is dawning in me the way it did when I realized that love of some sort with Lena was still possible, that the love I felt for the baby wasn't necessarily doomed.

"Ladies, could I get your attention?"

Nothing. They've forgotten all about me.

"Bancroft, remember? Your guest, Gordon?"

Thanksgiving at the Salvation Army, sounds like, and I'm stuffed.

"Listen to me, you crazy bitches! Or tell me to piss off if you won't!"

Things are getting out of sync, but they're far from grinding to a halt. Speech might be a long way off.

I stumble to the window, steeling myself for a face pressed against it or even a dozen, but there's no one. Maybe the girl who lives here owns all the clotheslines and the roofspace, takes in laundry. I pound on the glass and shout, "Police! Police!"

"What are you on about, Gordon? Bloody hell!" Zoe's flipped Marina off and is looking up at me from a sprawl with one hand on her throat and the other propping her up. Now she's looking for pillows to slide under her head.

"Here's your chance, luv, can you get him hard? She'd love to have the doggie behind while she's doing me."

I've had the same idea. I hike Marina's bottom into the air, but I've still got too many second thoughts to be hard enough.

"If you're worried about getting her pregnant, luv, you needn't be. She's had it fixed, haven't you, my darling...Don't stop...Hmmm. Yes, and I've had some stoppings put in her teeth, which weren't that dear here in Spain, as you'd know yourself if you weren't so stingy...and too squeamish to kiss her. A week it's been since she got fixed up."

"You should have told me.."

"You weren't there to tell. No, you've had your head in the clouds every night at the opera..."

"Not fair. Do you know what a problem her tooth decay has been? And her fertility? Sure I should have done something...I didn't think she wanted me to..."

I'm waiting for Marina to back me up but she's only aware of Zoe, as usual, and now Zoe's eyes are starting to roll up...

The price of admission is five seconds forgetting myself while I watch and listen.

45

Since Marina has four hours to be eaten for lunch we're still at it two hours later, or Zoe still is. I'm on my back thinking of pileups in contact sports, and how I have more in common with the floor beneath me than I do with these two screaming dames.

Marina's facing the ceiling as well, and has all her weight on me and her hair in my face so that our only important contact is coital.

Zoe's hogging her breasts. I keep trying to take one away. Zoe lets me tug the nipples from time to time, but only to show off her handiwork.

Finally Zoe goes into a bonafide endgame and the breasts are all mine. I don't know what she's doing to Marina down there but she's touched a deeper chord and the woman's bucking like crazy. I've got to keep hold of her breasts to keep her from bucking my prick off, though I'm not sure losing a breast is deterrent enough.

Zoe wasn't kidding when she told me she knew her way around a man's balls. At first she just sailed in on tippytongue to let me know I wasn't forgotten. Now she's hopping back and forth from Marina's clitoris to *mine*. That's right, she's found a spot I didn't know I had, just where it would be if I were a woman. Maybe it turns Zoe on to have at it through all the loose clothing, something like a giant foreskin for her to play with. All I know is, what she's doing to me will keep me inside Marina until I have my heart attack. Ejaculation isn't a possibility thanks to Zoe's teeth, a clear presence in the casserole, sharp tines nudging my sweetbreads.

Meanwhile Marina, with nothing but my prick to stimulate her, has gone into a begging frenzy, seems to be kidney-punching Zoe with her heels. When Zoe leaves me to go back to whatever she was doing Marina's frenzy isn't subsiding, it's turning into a fit. I'm half-persuaded it would be best to let go of her tits, let her dive through the window and run the rooftops for a while.

She's dying? The thought panics me and my cock starts to hurt like crazy, a sure sign it's melting. It always hurts like this after it's been numb for hours. Poor thing, it's totally bewildered by my expectations, as I would be to wake up one morning and find myself back in basic training, the toe of a boot under my bunk and "motherfucker"'s filling the morning air.

Is she bucking to get away? Is Zoe trying to bite

something off? Am I an unwitting accomplice to a sex crime?

I loosen my grip on her tits and she lets me know my mistake with a fierce backward butt that catches my upper lip.

I know the moment the blow lands I've lost a tooth, the only question is which.

Zoe has let go my scrotum. I'm limp enough to slip out from under without any fanfare. Free at last I scamper back to the chair where the madness began, where I was still, comparatively speaking, an innocent bystander.

Damn, it's the left incisor. I've been given the Gap of Franz. I've been Frankensteined.

The two maniacs are still all over each other and the hell with me. Well, the hell with them, damned perverts. Lesbian swine.

Why had I not had sense enough to stay away from a jailbird like Zoe? What did I expect to gain by getting mixed up with her? She was having sex the only way she knew, and it was a good thing she had so much to offer the other girls in prison, she'd probably been a bringer of sanity in that milieu, giving her cellmates something to live for. But prison was the only place for her shenanigans, anyone could see the danger of them. It was a miracle I hadn't already had my balls bitten off...The same miracle that had cost me one of my front teeth!

Why had I abandoned Marina to the clutches of the *tortillera?* A bright woman...a beauty...no longer traumatized by potency...whose breath no longer stank...

She could have been mine! What a fool I'd been to expect her infatuation to wear off. Or maybe not such a fool. I'd thought I'd get her back when Zoe went too far...As she was sure to do, she was the most excessive person I'd ever known. If someone at the cafe told her to lay off the dirty limericks he'd hear all eight hundred and seventy-nine.

"Gawblimey, Gordon, it's rude what you do. You can't just quit us like that and sit there. I thought you'd gone out for a Brahms and Liszt."

"I'm finished with you two," I tell her, noticing that my *sh* is coming out like a double *s*. I fake a big smile.

"It's a tooth, then. Don't take it so hard. What's the loss of a tooth compared to everything you've had today? I'd empty my mouth for a month of her fanny." She lunges forward and slaps Marina across the face. "Don't pull my hair like that, bitch, or it's worse you'll get!"

Zoe's hand swizzles dreamily while her tongue gives in to a narrative impulse.

"Marina tells me a Basque is a very different piece of work from a Catalan. True enough on the surface. Isn't she sweet? Montsy couldn't have taken the half of what I've just given this one. Why I wanted your help. She's been frisky today, right enough. Too neurotic. Well, I've done my bit. She'll get used to you and settle down. She's wonderful when she's all wonky as she is most days. Till it's time to go back to her job."

Zoe whacks her on the flank.

Before Marina's crescendo is ear-splitting she glissandos back to a groan. It's remarkable that such a simple musical pattern could have so much in it.

"It's hard for her to stop unless I turn up the heat. You could get me the switch, Gordon. Bottom drawer under the clothes."

In spite of myself I'm getting excited. I'll play along and watch Zoe chastise the screaming mimi. God, anything to see a muscle in Marina's face again, a frown, a stitch in her brow, a bit of sophistication about the lip. As it is she's moaning "No," now, her first intelligible word today, but Zoe's not imprisoning her hips, and she's not trying to escape. It's just a complicated game.

What's this? A small bundle of Pepe the conductor's batons bound together at the big end. The thin ends of them make me shudder and I realize I don't want to see Zoe use them. No, I do, if she'll tease. It's the damnedest thing, I can't be honest, I want to see Marina get stung, and I don't...The oven-men of Auschwitz might have begun this way...First there are two questions that create confusion...Then there are no questions...and there's no confusion.

My blood runs cold while I watch the preparations. Zoe's pulled Marina to her feet, but my old love can't stand without help, and she can't spare a hand to help Zoe, she's got them both between her legs for continuity. Zoe's got an arm under her ribs and drags her along as she forages for pillows. When she's made a mound of them in the center of the pallet she dumps Marina over it, face down, and reaches a hand out to me. All her movements seem spur-of-the-moment...Her deadly efficiency doesn't come home till I've put the grip-end across her palm.

I bite my hand when I see the first red welts. Zoe smiles back at me. "Don't worry, luv, she has to have it. Let her tell you herself sometime how much it means." She turns lazily but she's bringing another hissing stroke with her that sets up a grid. "If it didn't hurt where she sits she couldn't stop playing with herself," says Zoe over her shoulder, raising her hand again. "You know how it is in an office. Types and answers the phone, poor thing."

Now after the sound of power lines singing there's a groan no different from all the ones before.

I pull my clothes on fast. The room is suffocating. The sounds continue as I start down the short passage to the door. I'm filling my lungs with something besides air, or if it's air, I've lost the power to get rid of it, I'm being floated off my feet. I regain some weight clattering down the stairs. I let myself fall and feel the landing come up fast. I'm thirsty and hungry but I'm halfway across town before I stop at a cafe where no one knows me.

How did I let this happen? How did the Spanish woman who helped me find my way here in Barcelona get handed over to this goodhearted criminal with the soul of an older sister...? A panty-sniffing older sister, at that, who wanted to hear everything.

"Tell me all about it," she used to say when she was pulling a woman onto her lap in a cafe.

46

It was always the same with the important women of my life. They had to be the type called whore, tramp, slut. Such a woman was my destiny, or so the angels told me from the time I was thirteen, whirling in their light blue velvet tuxedos, snapping their long black fingers in unison.

It must have been decided before prep school. No dinnertable for Bancroft. No little faces near the edge of it. No little thumbs pushing food onto fist-held forks. No woman sitting across from me beaming or at least smiling to herself. Someone like Zoe in a dark roadhouse nudging my balls with her big toe.

Lili St. Cyr could have been the reason I was condemned. If I needed someone to blame...She had me thinking about her almost exclusively while the other boys were thinking about what they wanted to be when they grew up, content to ponder the bra straps of the girls sitting in front of them when thinking about girls couldn't be helped.

I found Lili by the side of the road on my way home from junior high school, the pages of her flesh stuck together by a forgotten rain. I took her to my camp in the woods where she came apart with small popping noises in the near dark while the air was feathery with honeysuckle sex and mosquitoes.

Lili took off her clothes for a living. Striptease. I knew about it from a magazine my parents had brought back from Europe. Over there they had stages full of people like Lili, but Lili was enough for America all by herself. She was as American as hamburger. She was my meat. She ate billions and billions of my thoughts.

I entered the reproductive phase of my life with my thoughts tugging at Lili's G-string, seed beginning to cloud the pearl at the end of my sore prick, my fist a painful tourniquet I couldn't remove while I was still flush with the victory of swollen tissue and seed.

I kept Lili in a watertight box next to a dead tree, under a thick clump of honeysuckle where life was at a crawl.

I may have been confused at thirteen but I knew that Lili was the reason for the unseasonable intensity of my feelings. God or Fate or whatever wanted me to fumble with the bra straps. I was supposed to be shy and clumsy at my age. I was supposed to make the girls giggle and burn and want to know me better and refuse to entrust their bodies to me for a split second.

Lili the stripper didn't attract me because she lay still. It was the world she brought to mind, the fact that there were women in it who were so sure of their beauty they could cast a spell.

The girls I was pawing were afraid of their beauty, even the so-called sluts and whores who wanted everyone to paw them. The last trusted their beauty least of all because their reputations were like fancy clothing. They were afraid that without them they wouldn't be noticed at all. There were similarities to Lili, and God and the parents and the rest might only have seen the similarities, but I knew there was a world of difference between women who could hold men at bay with the power of their beauty and women who needed to be needed so desperately that they didn't care if the consequence of being needed for a few hours or minutes would wreck their lives.

By the time I was at prep school my head was a library of pornographic situations and variations among the female of my species and I consulted it more often than the one full of history books where forebears watched from the walls and yellow light dribbled down long tables burnished by sweaty young palms and the pages rattled like moths at the window on a moist night. The library in my head was already potent enough to banish the collective achievements of mankind in the very spot where they had been collected. I was a library within a library, a small island of hell in a sea of ennui.

Try as I might I could never find the Lili within Sandy, the Lili within Stephanie, though I knew it was there.

The naked woman was already a reality to me and memories of Sandy, Stephanie and Sheila Burke occupied rooms of my library. All of them had had a naked woman to show me. Promising to let me do everything but "it," Sheila Burke had shown me things only her doctor could know about and made noises I associated with death and babies when "not it" became naughtier than "it."

It had been much too easy to be the person they wanted me to be. It would have been worse than ungentlemanly— perverse, cruel not to fulfill such meager expectations...Or for that matter, to expect more from them than they wanted to give. Make no mistake, they had put a high value on the flesh they yielded to my already expert hands. My cool appraisals frightened them, my overwrought responses tricked them into riskier exchanges. None of them knew that it was their confidence, the Lili in them, I was trying to rouse, and that things had gone awry between us because I resented the way they'd come to think of their bodies as a piece of meat to be thrown to me.

Then I drowned in the passion of a woman slightly older than I was...Jan...and I forgot Lili. I've forgotten her so completely by now that I can't even remember what she looked like. When I discovered women of passion I emptied the shelves of my library and the few surviving photographs are full of washstands and sepia maidenhair, the bleach of time having done a more thorough job than all the quick little purifying fires of guilt combined.

I had a lot of living to do before I understood that sex and love were one and the same the way the women insisted. When sex became less important in a relationship it wasn't love that remained, it was attachment. Sexual love, love, was a function of freedom. Whether out of fear or fatigue, the ones who became attached to each other were celebrating the end of freedom every day when the same old things hove into view and they heaved their sigh of relief.

I'd taken freedom as far as it could go. I didn't belong anywhere. My appeal was to the eyes and ears—hearts and minds—of people I didn't know. In spite of their cavorting, my friends were all fellow pilgrims to who knows where, quite serious about the unknown, or courageous in facing it.

Gratitude for freedom is quite different from the gratitude one feels coming awake for the chance to own the same things for another day.

The slut says, "Go back to her if you want, but love me now," and that's why she's my colleague. The past hasn't been agreed upon, the future hasn't been arranged. Whatever is, is now. I couldn't deny Zoe because of her boldness. We'd always be going the same way, we'd always be pals no matter how the situation was sorted out from moment to moment.

I'd failed Marina, though. My precious scheme of things was a failure. It was time to give the other side a chance. Attachment. Bonds. Marriage.

Family life. A steady job. Not just because the kids needed stability in their lives. Maybe there was such a thing as too much freedom.

How could I have thought so from my experience, though? I was immune to jealousy and capable of endlessly discovering the same woman, which passed for loyalty among the living dead.

The term "sexual addiction" hasn't been invented yet, we're a few years behind the times, so I lack a pat explanation for what's bothering me about Marina.

When Zoe came to the anarchists' and Marina stopped talking it disturbed me, yes, but only because I knew she was in love and wanted to forget me. It was a silence not unlike Elena's during pregnancy. She wasn't keeping a secret, that's another kind of silence—it's playful, and there's nothing in it. This was a silence caused by something growing within, something more profound than the certainty of addiction.

After a few Voll-Damms I'm wondering if it isn't power that has been growing in Marina, a power she'd never had over another person. Sure, she took the switching at the end and Zoe dished it out, but there hadn't been any goggle-eyed delight on Zoe's face when she landed her blows. Given her background a switching such as the one she gave Marina would have been child's play. If she'd hung her from the rafters, made her helpless in some way while she received her portion of pain...But no, she went out of her way to make her comfortable, to make this a dessert course.

Granted a tendency to take Zoe's side to spite Marina because of the way my Spanish friend was ignoring me when I was inside her, I still think there is more to be said for the depth of Zoe's love than the depth of Marina's. Sure, Marina kept caressing or clawing Zoe through hours of orgasms, even while she was having seizures at the end. What better reason to suspect that her caresses were mechanical, and bubbled out of her like froth from a rabid dog?

Compare Zoe, who exerted herself much more in trying to manage Marina and never stopped trying to satisfy her even though a moron could see the woman was insatiable.

Making allowance for Marina's inferior strength it still makes me suspicious that she gets so much more than she gives. So what if Marina is addicted to Sapphic love, or say "stimulation in general, including pain." What's to prevent her from seeking such stimulation elsewhere? Since her affair with Zoe she's slimmed at the waist, which was the only place she had an ounce of fat. She doesn't have Zoe's defined musculature, of course, but there's more meat on her bones, she has a tan from the beach and a pink glow on her dusky skin. All the sex is increasing her appeal, and now her teeth don't even stink. It makes me nervous. The last time an ordinarily attractive woman turned into a beauty right before my eyes she gave me a dose of the clap.

After a few more Voll-Damms I figure I've got to save Zoe from Marina, it's the decent thing, even if it means we both lose her. We'll have each other. If she'd give me a chance she might see what a lesbian I've got in me.

After today I'll never stop thinking of all the hardness and softness of her. Sure, I'm afraid of her and the light might shine from her more strongly for my fear. Still, I feel something has to be done to stop her endless doing, and I feel I'm the one to do it.

Dammit, my manliness might be at work here, getting me in trouble again. I haven't been a lesbian for long. I recognize the brutality I feel coming, the need to make her yield, the need to see the fear in her eyes when she wonders how far I'm going to take her and if she'll ever get back. I want to stop the chitchat, her clicking tongue, all the knitted mischief. I want to search the darkness with her beyond the little place where we're entwined.

I try to counter the effect of too much drink by staying too long on the street that night. I don't make my call and step on someone going on but all's forgiven. My colleagues might be relieved that I've finally had an accident. My story is known to all.

Here I am, a little sodden, trying to keep the conductor out of my mouth. Myself again. The shell of something.

47

My missing front tooth is changing my life.

I must have been clinging to the notion that people who mattered, the ones I'd want to know, were taking me for a man of parts. It's a comedown to look like I belong here on the street. It's making me uncomfortable everywhere else.

Fortunately the opera season was just ending when I lost my tooth and I only had to avoid smiling for a week. They knew, they'd seen it, I was much too spontaneous around fellow singers not to smile once in a while, but they knew I was trying not to and had the delicacy not to ask what was wrong.

A part of me wants to quit the streets and make a new start. There are times when naturalized lesbianism seems all wrong and I feel as if I'm suffocating again the way I did after my maiden voyage. However, Zoe has turned out to be a true friend. She of all people is the one who seems to understand the way I feel now.

Those of my fellow buskers who want me for a comrade are glad I'm gaptoothed. There's no question in most people's minds that I've found my *métier*. The loss of a tooth isn't such a big deal in a place where so many people are missing a leg. Even Marina can't understand why it upsets me so, but what should I expect? She'd given career advice to Frankenstein.

Zoe knows what's eating me. We've talked about it.

I've been used to having my experience of life in disguise. I never trusted anyone to care about me who knew where I came from. And I was happy playing the part of busker. I'd never felt the deprivations the way my friends did. That wasn't really me out there.

Maybe my "busker look" will give me the push I need to do something besides busking. Though it's hard to stop playing a role when you're good at it, it's easy to think you're better than your type.

Zoe can't be typed either. She's the only friend I can be sad with.

We have strange pastimes: looking at apartments together, pretending we're married and that someone is watching our child. We talk about staying together. We even came up with a wedding announcement once, but we were too well known in the barrio to fool anyone and almost ended up newlyweds just to prove that our friends didn't know us as well as they thought.

Zoe knows about my correspondence with Elena, which I've been able to sustain through the Tapas Bar. Virgilio and Marina and of course Anita have not been told anything new about my little family in the States. Anita's still my good pal, though she spends more time with her father and Nuria now and seldom comes to me on the street.

In the beginning I was able to check my feelings of loss and destitution by putting Elena out of mind and forcing myself to deal with my present situation. I tried not to think about going back to my country and erected a flimsy Cio-Cio San scenario to take care of the future. Yet our correspondence dragged me into another future, one even flimsier, as it turned out. It's a poor summary, full of distortions if not outright lies, but without it we'd never have got back together, and it's very much a part of my story.

Dear G.

I'm surprised by what you're doing (on the streets) because you lack the common touch.

No, I will never go back to Spain, even if you have a big success at the Liceo (though I'll be very happy for you), even if you come into a lot of money somehow and have a nice house to offer us. Nena thinks my mommy and daddy are hers, and that's best for now. I don't want her to know there's something abnormal about us until she's three or so. By then who knows where you'll be and what's possible for us? I guess what I'm saying is, I feel no urgency to change my life again anytime soon.

My "persistent vegetative state" as you put it is about to undergo a change. I'm to begin work soon as a bilingual paralegal. Not full-time at the office, however. A lot of the work involves translations that I can do home in bed.

I'm not sleeping with anyone yet, nor am I inclined to. I don't have sex urges anymore. Nature must feel she's got everything out of me she's going to get. If I sleep with my new boss it will only be to protect my job. I'm getting more money than I'm worth.

By the way, you'll have to be honest about what's really happening in Barcelona if you expect to correspond with me. You're doing a lot more than fieldwork for your treatise on voice, and I think I'm entitled to know just what. I gave up any thought of a life with you a long time ago, but I'm still susceptible to being amused by your adventures—please don't spare me the details. In fact, the juicier, the better.

Every day Lenita gets cuter. She's so naughty. No one can stay mad at her, though—not even my poor parents. Raising a child is hard at their age and I sometimes wish I weren't such a sybarite and you weren't an artist doomed to aspire until you expire. I hope it dawns on you one day that you can stop being a failed artist and start being a success at something secure and lucrative here in California and I'd consider vegetating with you again.

No comment about what's happening with your voice because it sounds like it's all in your mind. *Besitos...*

As always both pages are embellished with afterthoughts. That is, covered with cobwebs that lead to words in the margin that represent what she's really trying to say, alternative spellings and so forth, though a lot of these words have parenthetical question marks next to them. The afterthoughts serve to make her letters time-consuming and maddening. I want to kill her when I finish reading. I launch a series of aerograms to make a start.

E:

I can only respond with anger to what's in your letter and hurt at what's not. I write on because I insist you take me seriously as the father of our child...And I assure you that, should I return to the States, Nena will quickly discover who her real father is. Though a response to you is impossible I still want you to know what I'm doing with my life. I insist I have a purpose here and I firmly believe that my purpose will ultimately affect our child no matter how long we're estranged.

My voice continues to strengthen. I can do things with it I didn't know were possible for any singer. I'm breaking all the rules, of course. Singing full voice most every day for at least five or six hours and sometimes as many as eight. McCormack said that one must never sing full voice more than half an hour at a time...and never outside. That has been said by many of the greats, but it's folklore. I can last an hour going full blast and two hours at a time by saving myself. I've found eight dependable focal positions that change the muscular adjustment and I go from one to the other to stay fresh.

At the risk of extrapolating from singular and somewhat feverish personal experience I will say it would do any singer good to work outdoors. You hear yourself differently...It's harder to entertain yourself by capturing some of the sound...Another way to describe "interference with the emission." The sound is *out* and what remains with you is a creative satisfaction. Sometimes it floats you right off the ground.

I remember how you used to deplore the technical discussions I would try to have with you about voice (for the good of the book which it appears I will never finish but endlessly revise) but I think I've found some images now that will help someone starting out.

When you were a child did you ever blow into the top of a pop bottle to make it sound? (I'm sure you never touched the stuff when you came to the States, but you had Coke during Batista's time, *no es verdad?*) Remember how the stream of air has to be controlled? I get just the right feeling by imagining such a bottle out in front of me a ways. For a high note pianissimo I can imagine trying to "play" a bottle that's clear out in the middle of the street.

The pop bottle brings in a horizontal plane, perpendicular to the plane of the body's midline. Trying to "sound" the bottle we should think of thinning the stream of air horizontally and approaching the top of the bottle on the level. It's a refinement that some of the stream is lost to right and left around the lips of the bottle, only the heart of it produces a tone. And of course it can't be pushed or withheld or the sound won't explode. Intensity is a subtle struggle.

From all you know by now about how images control the involuntary muscles, you've probably deduced that the effect of what I've described is to stretch and thin the edges of the vocal folds producing a sound that is more distinct and intense than what you're accustomed to hearing from singers who try to make more sound by increasing the pressure of breath against increased muscular resistance in their throats. Mine is a sound of enormous carrying power which can be heard over the traffic in one of the important commercial sectors of

By the Wayside

Barcelona.

I'm glad you'd like to hear some dirt. It appears you're trying to revive your sex drive, if only to make it easier to deal with your boss's. I'm glad because a sex drive will give me something to work with if I make it back. I'm prepared to spend six months in a health spa before you'll let me put my hands on you, but I understand the problem—dirt doesn't travel well unless it's on a page of some kind.

In France I suffered the usual quietus. In the past there was episodic interest in Frenchwomen when I was the new singer in town. There were choruses full, cafes full of the pretty things and the fashion czars were letting them put their nipples on parade then, nipples that could have pushed up pavement. It took a while to get jaded...

During this last trip the only time anything remotely erotic happened I was turning pages for a buxom accompanist and singing through the entire role of the Dutchman.

Here in Spain I don't have much time to do anything about my base nature. I'm singing on the street all day and in the chorus at night. I task myself for not finding work here while you and I and the baby were still together. At the time it was easier to imagine a big success in France where I'd been so close to one before.

You wanted the juicy details. I've been involved with a woman with a four-year-old daughter. A prostitute, of course, but so far as I can tell, not addicted to anything but sex. The father of her child no longer pimps for her but has gone on to become one of the most respected figures in the Barcelona underworld. He can still boast of never having lifted a finger to make his living. The daughter of this union has become more precious to me than life itself, but of course that could be said of everything I care about. More indicative is the fact that I babysit her while I'm busking.

I 've run through my repertoire of pleasing indecencies with this woman—she's very beautiful, but not too bright—and found a lesbian staring me in the face, hand in hand with her lover, a three-toed Cockney from Islington. (I'm tempted to xerox her very British passport: "Identifying characteristics: three digits each lower extremity.") Trying to make love to both of them has just resulted in the loss of a front tooth (it was a head butt from the mother). The lovemaking is all standard lesbian fare, though I feel I'm being cheated on the oral end.

The Cockney is very clever and I wouldn't be surprised if she has long range plans for me that include a steel collar. She's already talking about suspending me in air. So far she's made good on all her promises of increased sisterhood and pleasure, so what can I say? (Show me the father-figure who could help me with this one.)

I fear it drains my limited supply of machismo to give so much of myself vocally day after day. I don't mind looking wrung out or neurasthenic on the streets, it helps the take. However, it won't do not to put my chest out and strut when I'm at the operahouse—that's expected of someone with so much voice. My colleagues have been trying to decide why I'm not a big-name baritone by this time in my life, and rumors that I suffer from stage-fright could become self-fulfilling if there's open season on my mettle.

Owen sends his best, but I'm afraid he thinks you're "not right" for me, and can't understand how I ever thought you would be. He thinks I'd be better off "marrying lesbian." Perhaps this is wisdom he gained learning to respect his grown daughter, and shouldn't be heeded by one so recently become a father.

I'm not sure I ever loved you or respected you, but I never doubted that I could, or that I wanted to, and I never doubted my desire. Nena deserves better from both of us.

I will come to you if you won't come to me. I don't want to start getting along with the loss of Nena the way I do with the hole in my mouth.

PS: It occurs to me in reading this over that there are only two lies, but I'd better fix them or you might check with someone at the Tapas Bar and start disbelieving everything I write. It hurts to have to be so honest to someone I hold in such low regard, but the mother of the girl I described was never a whore and is quite bright (or was until she became sexually insatiable). Her ex-pimp and the good-for-nothing gangster father of her child is really her husband, an anarchist poet who's in love with someone who sells sandwiches on the Ramblas.

Honeybear:

Thanks for the long letter. Sorry if something in my last letter made you angry, but I know you don't mean all the things you say when you're mad at me because you're really a gentle bear.

I do want to complain about the voice lesson. It's such a waste of your time. I suppose I know enough to find the things you have to say mildly interesting but you've simply got to stop pretending that I'm your student, it makes you pathetic. I wouldn't think of training the little voice I have, as you well know.

I can appreciate how happy you are to be able to live by singing, and how hard it is to give up on yourself when you're improving. Nevertheless, I think you're making a mistake to limit yourself to this kind of livelihood. I remember the things you said about age as it pertains to careers in opera, and it appears that someone over the age of 35 hasn't got a chance in a million of getting started. Why do you want to be a candidate for so much rejection and disappointment? Aren't you hitting your head against a wall? Wouldn't you be happier having realistic expectations?

I'm still adamant about not returning to Spain, and I'm afraid I'm still against living with you if you come here, even if you can get a decent job and stay with it. Nena's too happy with my folks and I wouldn't think of yanking her out of here and forcing her to live with someone she doesn't know.

I know how much you dislike being told what to do, but it's so obvious. Get a job in Silicon Valley. Live in Palo Alto within walking distance of my folks. They'll make you welcome if you'll behave yourself, and their place will be like a second home for you. You might look at the arrangement as providing you a lot of free babysitting and free food. That should make it less painful for you to give us half what you earn.

We've got Nena the most adorable Easter outfit. She's crawling all over and googoos a lot. The enclosed pictures will tell you better than I can how adorable she is now. My parents stop the stroller for everyone we meet.

Maybe it's out of responsibility for the child that my habits are changing. I'm not sleeping so much, I'm on time to work, I'm doing a good job. It's probably not essential that I be such a model employee since I'm quite sure my boss is in love with me. He's on cloud nine whenever we're alone together, especially if I let him fool around. My sex drive is still not what it used to be but it's good for my self-esteem to know that this guy is crazy about me and his place in the clouds is something I'm letting him keep. I'd never blackmail him, but he's incredibly naive. He talks about leaving his wife for me and I haven't done as much with him as I did the first night I met you.

Incidentally, I'm glad for the chance to tell you how things really are with me and I hope you'll keep being honest, too. (Please no more voice lessons.) We're not married, so we're within our rights to fool around. It's probably a duty that I do so to try to find someone who can help me provide for Nena's future. I never thought for a minute you were telling me about your whores and lesbians to try to hurt my feelings. (So there's no need to tack on apologies for the truth.) I never doubted you'd take up with whores when I was gone, and take pity on one with a child, or with child, or both—you do the checking.

Please don't think I'm trying to get even in some way by having sex with my boss. Money means a lot to me. It goes right into the bank for Nena's future. And when I say I don't feel anything, please don't think I'd be guilty if I did. I remember what sex used to be like for me. Well, so can you. If it's still like that for you, then I guess I am a little jealous, but

I doubt you're getting anything from the women you go to that would compare to what you got from me. You could never trust a whore to have real feelings.

I agree that Nena deserves better where you're concerned. I'm giving her much more as a mother than I thought I had to give, however, and I can truly face myself in the mirror and say, this child is better off with me than she would be anywhere else with anyone else I know. Still, I'd never write you off as a father, or even as an opera star, which, under the circumstances, is quite a vote of confidence.

Dear Elena:

A lot has been going on here. The reason it will be hard to correspond with you from now on, except in matters pertaining to Nena, is that I'm planning to get married...to Zoe (of the three digits).

Of course it's just for a joke or she'd never go through with it. She's interested in things like free drinks at the big party we're throwing, who will come, and so forth. (An awful lot of people are skeptical.)

You see, I haven't "changed" her. We'd never be anything more than pals, but I think that bodes well for people thinking about marriage, where convenience is everything.

I realize that marriage looks like a bid for respectability on Zoe's part that will cost us our standing as bohemians, but my arguments in favor have persuaded her, so maybe they're worth hearing.

1. Our sex will always be wonderful because we won't be having it with each other.

A. Keeping it hard to satisfy M. (mother not whore) problem no longer.

B. I like oral sex as much as any lesbian, but think how much more effective I'd be with Zoe to spell me.

C. Zoe's younger, so when I run out of gas I can still contribute to our marriage by attracting women into our parlor, women who might never have a lesbian experience otherwise. Knowing what Zoe can do to a woman I already feel sorry for the ones who are going to miss out. (Give her a try! You'll be glad you did! Step right in!)

D. When my presence is no more obtrusive than a housecat's, my pre-retirement years, which will probably be my last, might be very comfortable indeed: feet up, nursing a beer, Zoe skating away on her latest flame, who's making those noises that are better than any music.

2. Elimination of possessive behavior will mean greater freedom and happiness.

A. I still cling to the definition of love that came to me once in a Southern jail: delight in the freedom of another.

B. As above, there's no danger of Zoe ever becoming a sex object, a possessive object, or being objectified in any way because I'll never be able to think of her as anything but a co-subject.

C. Our circle of friends will be much larger than mine alone could ever be. Zoe's compassion and her criminal record make instant allies of the downtrodden everywhere. Thanks to her I know navvies who would have been put off by my uncalloused hands, and heroin addicts like Paco (her trusted delicatessen guide and sandwich man).

3. Philosophical compatibility. Vastly different experiences of life have led us to the same point of view.

A. We're anathema to our countrymen and vice-versa. We look out on the world from the bottom. Zoe was born on the bottom, tried life in all the other milieux and in other countries, usually because of searches for a soul-mate, stayed loyal to her origins. Growing up I heard a lot about *noblesse oblige* and being a good Christian, but not to be a hypocrite about the high standards one professed was to be a fool. Among the downtrodden I saw nobility of spirit, charity, compassion and all the other virtues, though the noble manner was missing and no one went to church.

4. Loyalty possible at last, promiscuity no longer inevitable.

A. B. C. D. E. F. G. Because of Zoe I've understood why sluts were always the right women for me—women who respected their sexuality and gave love when it was there to give rather than the sort who denied what they felt between their legs out of respect for some contract or notion of private property, some tit for tat, who preferred a living death to the uncertainties of freedom.

Zoe's the first person I've known who's total about love, who gives the lie to the idea that sex and love are different mechanisms. If it takes her ten hours to reach the heights with the woman she loves she's ready to take eleven hours tomorrow.

I still believe the heights are what's important, not the person you come with, but because of Zoe and lesbians in general I see that a new kind of "true love" is possible. Out of a deep feeling of friendship and "what is right" the lover takes responsibility for the ecstasy of the beloved.

The tongue is the tool of choice, no doubt about it, because it's not such a taker, such a squatter—it doesn't come crashing in and think it has rights because it's the one and only, the first planted pole. On average the tongue is more respectful, worship with it is easier, and it has staying power that even I wouldn't have thought possible (had I not known Zoe). Incidentally, Zoe can give quite a phallus imitation during the first five or six hours of lovemaking, while she's breaking down the inhibitions of heterosexuals.

Enough of my outline. I need to wind this up. Zoe's kindness, her heart, is what draws me to her more than anything. In spite of our common perspective we'll always quarrel a lot because our bearings have been quite different going through life and we've never shared any goals. (Except that whatever comes our way has always been good enough.)

If we do have one important goal in common at the moment it's to keep alive the life we found here on the streets, to make a commitment to it. True, most of my fellow buskers are crazy. Not to think that of them would require me to gloss over behavior that can be downright alarming at times. What draws me to them is their kindness. All these renegades are so goodhearted, and so are the Spanish people who compose the society we're parasitizing.

I've thought and thought to decide what's so different about this place and a lot of things come to mind, but there's no way to put your finger on a feeling like this, it's too subtle. But it's a feeling that makes all the difference in the world. If you've got it you leave your house in the morning eager for the events of the day to swirl around you. If you haven't got it, you're dragging your ass.

I know myself well enough to see that I'm trying to consecrate my friendship with Zoe as a way of showing loyalty, showing which side I'm on, and very romantically, perhaps, I'm trying to keep alive the hope that this feeling will never leave me.

I want to keep feeling that I've stepped out of the plastic bubble of my Americanism, and that I will never return to the land where the status quo is king and all its deliriously happy subjects are slaves. I suppose you can forgive the masters for boosting and trying to perpetuate the illusion that all is as it should be while they're on top, but what gets to you after a while about life in the States is the way the most aggressive defenders of the status quo are well-fed slaves. Worst of all are the American poor who vote the rich man's pocket—the fools who elect our Ronalds.

By the Wayside

Here there is no status quo, simple as that. If it exists it's in the minds of people who have the sense to keep their mouths shut. Nor is everything going to hell, as certain American tourists might want us to believe after peering at us for a week or two out of the glass bottom of their identity. Here the cultural bedrock is solid, perfect for dances and capers of all kinds. It's a place where people would rather entertain each other than compete.

I wonder if you knew the Spain I'm talking about when you were here? I didn't. No inkling.

The best solution for you and the baby will no doubt sound as crazy to you as my engagement to Zoe. Come back and live with us anarchists. (The nuptial bed is in a commune, but there's lots of room.) We'll have a *ménage à vingt-trois*. If your parents object to our unmarried state, I can divorce Zoe. (We have an ally here who can arrange divorces and marriages for us at top speed, and it's a good thing. If we try to marry in Gibraltar Zoe's sure she'll be "nicked.")

I know you're going to encounter objections from your parents if they find out what's going on, but let the sybarite in you do you some good for once and ignore them. I'm not sure if you've had any experience with lesbians but with innocence and experience already side by side in the bed that awaits you, your adjustment can be as gradual as you like. If you don't fit in somehow, you could have a room rent-free and use every penny of income from the ranch to buy sweetmeats—or to hire a half-dozen nurses for Nena (though I see no harm in the fact that our grannies are sometimes heavyhanded).

Please give a thought to returning. I know you could be happier here with us than you could possibly be with your parents, especially after having given them such a hard time during your first dependency. I know what a big thing security is with you, and I suspect some of your reluctance to return to Spain is because you feel security is something I will never provide. Zoe is twice as tough as I am, and reasonably kind, so I hope you'll give serious thought to enjoying a higher quality of communal life.

Dear Gordie:

The P.O. tells me they can't promise overnight on this but I'm spending top dollar anyway because I want you to know that I think you're in serious trouble and I care about you enough as a brother to want you to get out of it.

Elaine sent me copies of two letters you wrote her (and she sent copies to MOM). She wants us to use any influence we have to keep you from throwing your life away. Elaine's letter to me sounded like she was going off the deep end, so I gave her a call. I only met her once as you know and can hardly remember what she looks like so it was embarrassing to have to talk the way we did on the phone. I did tell her that you've been throwing your life away since you left college and the amazing thing to me is that there's anything left. Which maybe there is if you'll stop your crazy antics and start living like a morally decent human being.

I'm a Christian again and Sally right with me and I'm bound to tell you that the kind of thing you're doing over there just wouldn't play in our small town. I'm afraid I can't invite you to come and stay with us while you get your life together, and it's not just Sally and the kid. I know you better and I'm sure you made up a lot of the stuff in those letters just to shock Elaine or hurt her feelings for taking the baby away from you. Central California just isn't like L.A., though, and even if you don't drink the way you used to, all you'd have to do is step out of line once around here and it would be all over town.

I've got an idea how I can use you in my business and give you a place to live which will also be an office to work out of—probably the only way you'll ever be respectable enough to work in an office! I've been renting a mobile home to a chick on the outskirts of L.A.—don't worry, it's not what you think. She's moving out and I want to sell her home, which will be a lot easier if someone's living there to show it. These homes are a bitch to sell, by the way, so you'd most likely have a roof over your head for some time to come. If you could sell it, though, don't worry, I'd put you in another of my homes.

Working out of this mobile home you can sell loans for me. I've sewed up some of the biggest lenders in the state and they'll go 80% of the value of mobile homes, so I'd like to work you in as a specialist in mobile home loans. A lot of people are so strapped for dough they don't mind refinancing their homes. You should make a lot of money, but don't be surprised when credit is tight again, that's the way it is in the loan business.

I might have a job for you as a mobile home salesman during the lean times. I am opening a huge new lot on a major highway, and your Spanish would come in handy. Affordable housing is the name of the game, or call it the low end, so I could use someone who knows how to talk to the rough element that doesn't speak English or embarrass easy. I'd start you right away, but my new lot won't be open for a couple of months, and I need to sell that home in L.A., so it's too soon to let you live around here. Let's see if we can't put your family back together before that happens.

I've been on the phone to mom to try to calm her down. She's very upset, Gordie. It was a big mistake to give her so much to think about in her old age. I've been telling her it was a joke. I'm telling her that Elaine's an incredible slut and you just threaten her this way because it's the only language she understands. Don't worry, I'll think of something better if I have to.

As for Elaine, let me work on her some more. She says it's crowded living with her parents, but she still needs to keep the ranch rented and has no plans to move out. If I could get you a triple-wide to go with the job she might feel different about staying with you. Of course it all depends on how you do on your new job. I say "your new job" because I know you can do it if you set your mind to it. You could make an easy fifty grand a year. So no more talk about marrying lesbians with a criminal record.

Sally sends her best. Lisa remembers you. Love ya bro'.

Dear Gordon:

Tom just called and after a long talk I feel well enough to write. I was so sick from the news of your behavior I haven't been able to eat or sleep. You know what I'm talking about, don't make me give a name to your disgusting activities. You write about them without a trace of shame and I feel like the mother of one of those mass murderers I read about—a mother who's telling everyone, "That's not the boy I know."

Tom says you wrote these horrible things as a joke, but it's clear that he's trying to protect you. I was on the phone with the woman I thought was your wife...

Another sin. Lying. How could you do it, Gordon? Calm as you please you wrote me from Spain last year to say that you and Elaine were going to Gibraltar to get married. That poor sweet girl. When I think how I was taken in by you, too. What kind of son did your father and I raise? I'm afraid to know. You were such a caring child. I'll never forget all the baby birds you tried to keep alive. And you were twelve and thirteen when we were taking the foster children and you were such a help to me. I remember how you used to babysit for our friends all during your teenaged years. Your father was even worried that you were what they call gay these days, in spite of your size, but surely you'd never done anything to make him suspect you were the kind of person who would dream of the abominations in your letters. It would be one thing if you were confessing this kind of wrongdoing to a professional, but you sound proud of it, there isn't a grain of remorseful feeling. I can't believe how badly we failed you.

It's my duty as a mother not to give up hope. I will pray for you every day. God grant release from the evil impulses that are ruining your life and causing your loved ones to suffer. God grant you the courage to face up to your terrible mistakes and change your life before you cause any more pain to that sweet girl or deprive that darling child.

48

"Señor..."

When a cop comes up these days it's usually to talk politics or ask how my drops have been. I'll be on my knees opening my case, filing loose music, arranging large coins for bait and I'll know the cop by his shoes. He'll let me set up unless he's come to tell me, sorry, I can't, another busker close by was taking a break when I showed, or it's the old man with the child's keyboard again, the one who hides in doorways and starts playing nursery rhymes when he hears me clear my throat.

"Señor...no se puede..." is all wrong.

I've never seen him before. Let him ask one of the others...Learn where the spots are.

I ask him why, tell him I'm here every day, or there. He can see I'm angry.

He is telling me something about a license.

I've always known there was a license gathering dust somewhere, a fine example of the printer's art, the craftsmanship of a bygone age. I've always known I will never obtain this license, and that no one else will, and that no one ever has. It's been someone else's department ever since it was issued.

I recognize the address he gives me. It's the same office that takes all the wallets full of ID that I turn in, wallets I find on stairs and landings dropped in transit by heroin addicts.

I tell him, "I know, I know," hoping he can see I'm wise to him, since I don't know the Spanish for "runaround."

Content that I'm all packed I watch him join a lady cop waiting across the street, also a newcomer. I follow them down the broad concourse till they turn left for the cathedral. There haven't been any other buskers to move on, which I find strange. By now I should be as quick as any of my colleagues to know when the Catalans are up to their tricks, closing off the street in honor of some wretched saint so they can dance their beloved Sardanas and put all the street people out of work.

Forget us musicians...A crowd of beggars sitting in

puddles of their own making did more for Barcelona than these platooons of reverent Catalan nationalists with their medieval mojo.

Ah, some saw the Sardanistas differently. I'm aware of resident foreigners who dance with them. English teachers, of course. The cafes are full of them, even the Tapas Bar has its share. Recently arrived women on the lookout for more recently arrived women to take to their favorite shops.

I double back toward the Plaça Catalunya to find a policeman I know to tell me what's going on. Near the Galerías I encounter two more on patrol, neither of whom I've seen before. I ask them, where are the buskers here, the street musicians?

"Down at the bottom of the Ramblas, sir..."

"Nonsense, that's a circus. I mean the real musicians, the guy who sings opera here everyday..." If I don't know them, maybe they don't know me.

"Nobody is to sing here without a permit...All the way down the Ramblas..."

The nearby Metro stations are dark holes I'm afraid to fall down. I worked there in the beginning, before I knew what I was doing. The various stone tunnels caused me to compete with myself. There were places in the warren where I was a cacophony. The drops were always terrible, restoring my belief in humanity, but there weren't enough dirty looks. People shouldn't be reminded of going under on ether when they're trying to catch a train home after a hard day.

Of course the Ramblas are out, particularly down by the turnabout where motorists are trying to make time and the only pedestrians are hardship cases—machine-gun-carrying, Catalan-hating officers of the *Policía Nacional,* pregnant whores, tourists asking each other for directions, Christopher Columbus, poor people who can't afford to ride and still have a long way to go.

I head to the Tapas Bar expecting to find a crowd of malcontents. They've come and gone. This is more desperation than I'd expect to find after three days of rain. Rumor has it my

By the Wayside

friends are taking the Metro to the far reaches of town. There
might be busking in Sarriá tonight, or Pedralbes. Groups are
hitting the open-air markets.

Bad news has been left at the bar. Phil was arrested.

"He wouldn't move on?"

Gloria's heard all kinds of reasons. Arresting Phil would
be as hard as moving him on. Spots to play have become
traditional because of him. Gloria thinks he might have swung
on the cops with his crutches, he's been doing that a lot lately
with friends, but no one ever takes him seriously. Hash could
have been found on him...(any time you looked...)

By now I've seen Phil on the street with six instruments.
The person running through *Porgy and Bess* on the top floor of
the Bar de Pi turned out to be Phil. He can turn up anywhere
doing anything...disguised with hats and dark glasses. The
disguises are an inside joke. He lost a leg at mid-thigh. All the
pedestrians of Barcelona know who he is and have been
following his downward slide for years.

On the way to the jail to see if I can do anything for Phil
I try to prepare mysef. He'll probably tell me to piss off. He's
so tired of being pitiful that he only wants money. Best if it's
shoved under the door, but he'll take anything he can con you
out of, no shame in that.

I once carried him to a room in my pension, shocked by
how light he was. His guitar case would have been the same
trouble. He disappeared into his room for three days. He
wouldn't answer when I banged on the door, but I knew he was
in there, and the Galicians said he was. They heard all the
comings and goings, but particularly the goings. They could
hear thoughts of home steal into the night.

I wonder why I care about Phil. He's the best musician
on the streets and maybe the richest thanks to the conscience
drops, but I don't pass the time with him when he's working.
If his money's out of sight when I meet him he'll say he wants
drinks with me, but can't pay. He hustles all the people who
ought to be his friends.

This is my first trip to the jail. Here are the same old

brownshirts with machine guns that greet you whenever you're on official business, but I have to go down some steps on the side of the building. I remember using the front entrance of this building on Layetana but I can't remember when or the reason...

Police eyes are all over me before I realize that I don't know Phil's last name. No, "one-legged musician" should ID him even though I don't know what instrument he had with him today...

Guards are blocking the room ahead. I have to clear a table in the vestibule. There's something suspicious about a table off to the left.

My question about a one-legged musician produces a nod right away but he wants to see my passport.

That was my business here! Fear is rattling my prepared speech. He's talking about "taking" me, too, while I search my pockets for the paper I was given when my passport was stolen, a carbon copy with a blue seal, they'll recognize it.

They're very interested.

I tell them I'm waiting for my new passport at this very moment...It may be ready today...

"How did you lose your passport?"

"Robbed."

"And you reported this to the authorities?"

"Right upstairs in this building! They gave me a copy of the report. Aha!" The paper curled and was crushed into my makeshift wallet, one of Hewitson's old checkbooks. Surely there can't be any problem now...The ape is studying hard, though, trying to find one.

"You still haven't told me how you were robbed."

I give the word for ambush, lacking the one for mugged.

"Where?" He doesn't look up...He's been staring at the report of loss the whole time, taking the curl out of it with rhythmic sweeps of his hand.

I tell him, down by the port near the Estación de Francia...I'd been on my way to the moneychangers, thought they might still be open. I had some Dutch money...

"So late at night..." It occurs to me that he's checking my story against what I told his comrades upstairs that night. "That's a very dangerous place to be...anytime. Why are you wanting to exchange Dutch money if you are English...?"

"A very generous...loan. Look, I was the victim..." I've used *herido,* wounded, and appear to have made my big mistake.

"How were you injured?" At last he's looking at me. The moustache makes him look young, and he's got clean teeth, but his eyes have seen a century of trouble and want more. I smile back at him mechanically before I remember the hole in my mouth. Bingo! I point to it.

"You should have reported this."

I see that he's been cheated and take heart. He's staring at his large hand, now at rest on the document which he knows better than I do. I have the sense of having been here before. The memory games, the questions begetting questions...

I'd been under suspicion once before in Spain. During my palmy days in Sarriá I'd been picked up in a cafe for trying to get an Argentinian to say something in English about the Falklands War. For my own protection the police had arrived and put me in the back of their little car. My American passport made no impression. They drove me all over town and dumped me near the bullring on the Plaza España...They knew just what they were doing and refused to telephone Elena. With no corroboration, then, I had to explain to Elena how I could leave on a shopping errand and end up lost at the other end of town. Needless to say, Elena was a lot more clever than any police investigation unit. She knew that long disappearances with nearly empty pockets were best explained by another woman...Someone who cared about me enough to give herself for nothing. ("How long has this been going on?" "Since the war in the Falkland Islands...")

"What is your business with this man?" he asks me at length, and I try not to show my relief. At last I've broken through to the kinds of questions he asks of everyone who comes here.

"He's a musician. I have property of his...I need to pay his pension for him or they'll put his things out in the street."

"Ten minutes," he says, looking at the guards.

"Can you give back my document? Now that I realize how much I need it..."

"When you leave."

They let Phil come down the stairs on his crutches. For the first time since I've known him he seems glad to see me. He hides the look quickly and for the rest of my ten minutes will be trying to make me think I'm wasting his time.

I'm shocked to hear that the police brought him in because he couldn't produce a passport...He has only one errand for me, to the owner of the tiny pension where he now resides. Should I lack the readies I can sell another guitar, but I'm to let Colin, one of his English friends, decide which one.

In the dwindling minutes he answers my questions about the crackdown, but not without sneering first and saying I wouldn't have to ask if I'd been on the street nine years instead of nine months. It's always been a policy of the city authorities to reassign their beat cops every now and then so things don't get too cozy...

Phil means too cozy for cops as well as the corps of hustlers who depend on the street policeman's good frame of mind. Sure, Barcelona would be in a terrible fix if the cops kept getting their *cafés con carajillo* at the same bar every morning.

"How long before things get back to normal?"

He smiles and I can see the bastard's going to love riding out the emergency here in jail. He says that the spots on the Puerta del Angel will open in a week...Maybe two...It's all the tourists flooding into the city in spring. They want to see some new faces...I'll see for myself, if I stick it out. A lot of my friends will go somewhere else. Up to France, even to Switzerland.

I trudge back to the heart of the barrio noticing the stampeding summer dresses, but my thoughts don't bother to get inside. The ladies in their summer dresses are skipping over the places I've known, the places I've been with my music case open. No one will bother me in the Metro, Phil has told me. No one will bother me anywhere tourists don't go.

Phil's smile was even clearer than his advice. "It's not as easy as you thought, is it?" He'd heard of my missing tooth, no doubt, but we'd been avoiding each other, this was his first chance to see.

49

The crowd at the Tapas Bar is thinning out. We've lost the droning Greek and a half-dozen marginal guitarists. Two sax players have stopped their wheezy honking. Except for Franz and Geet with his Pan flute and Eduardo pounding his conga and Pepe the flamenquista we seem to have lost the colorful, day-in day-out crowd. The streets have been filling up with showmen, however.

I'm getting my first look at the big-time buskers, itinerant musicians who never stop long enough in one place for the cops to do anything about complaints. On a Tuesday afternoon they fall out of the sky and a hundred people make a circle around them, two hundred. Even the young ballbusters on the Guardia aren't going to try to move on someone with a crowd that size. Cops have political instincts along with all the others.

One recent arrival stood the city on its head for two days, a Frenchman with an "orchestra."

I was trying to get twenty minutes of drops while there weren't any cops around and he tapped me on the shoulder. He wanted to play at a spot way down the line, and I thought he was being sarcastic about my loud voice. I gave him a serious answer in my best French since I didn't know him. Still he held back..."My orchestra is very loud."

"I can compete with an orchestra. This won't be the first time."

As it turns out I can't compete with him. He's the whole orchestra, of course. As soon as I hear the racket I've got to run down to see what.

It's a great show. His top hat has a lid...There are joints all over him that make noise. He's got cymbals between his knees, things to tootle affixed to his bass drum. The drum beats itself when he prances around, his hands have more important things to do. He marches in a circle almost as wide as the street and only stops to make the kids squeal with a raspberry. There's an exaggerated seriousness about everything he does that smacks of pedantry and has the crowd squealing.

I cheer with the rest, but I'm envious. He's doing a better job than I ever had with the character I'd been trying to create long before I went on the streets: the shabby gentleman, the genteel disgrace. I'd started work on him when I was a teenager, altering the best impression I was able to make with a patch on my tuxedo, a dandelion in my lapel, and engineer boots.

The French one-man-band is a prince, but I can tell he's not comfortable here. Anyone capable of making that much noise all by himself would have a keen nose for trouble. When he hitches a ride out of town with Mary Poppins it turns out everyone's a fan.

50

One of the reasons buskers patronize the Tapas Bar is so they can have what they need on the slate till the rain stops or the heat or cold suits their clothes. Tonight Esteban looks preoccupied as his place fills up with street people, few of whom have any coins they want changed, all of whom are talking about the crackdown and how the cops have been treating musicians in Tarragona or Madríd.

It's customary to pay a staggering surcharge on bills here for the privilege of longterm credit, but if everyone is run out of town at once Esteban might be ruined. According to Gloria she and Esteban have twice before fallen victim to such an exodus. Most of the musicians settled their bills when they got back to town. Still, some were never heard from again and their names are kept alive by those of us who are still paying for their flight.

Being honest in money dealings and prompt to settle our bills is a way of showing respect for each other, then. In nine months on the street I've seen a lot of musicians come and go and they're honest on the whole, probably more honest than anyone would credit them for being—anyone except the small businessmen who extend them credit. The English teachers are honest, pay off weekly. The screevers do so well they don't need credit. The jewelry sellers are shifty except for the hippies who are proud of their scant needs. The beggars just take, take, take, but as soon as someone is revealed to be a beggar his credit is limited, and people like Esteban know beggars at sight and never get stuck in the first place.

Everyone's aware of Esteban's demeanor tonight and Esteban's aware that they are aware and is trying not to be surprised by anything that would loosen him up.

It's hard-luck tales all around. Apparently the police are running off the musicians in places where no tourist has ever been except by mistake. Jokingly it's suggested that a crime wave might change the new policy. But it's too soon to do anything, we all agree, except keep trying. Surely the guardia doesn't want to arrest all of us...Nor do they want us all down at the city hall clamoring for a license. We're not ready to put them on the spot.

My connection to Zoe is well known so I'm being told to get with her tonight when I go home and have her make good her reputation as a firebrand. It's also well known that, prior to falling for Marina, Zoe sucked off a high-placed Catalan in the city government, perhaps the highest-placed female politician in Catalunya. If Zoe's as good as the Danish twins have been saying, the politician can be enlisted. A word in the mayor's ear would have everything right overnight.

Perhaps, but it's tricky to deal with a lesbian in love. Right here where her exploits are legendary Zoe might be the first to say, gone are the days, no more bit of crumpet. She'd do anything for Marina, however, and Marina would do anything for the *callejeros*. By this time we all think of Zoe as having a passkey in her mouth in spite of the gradual accumulation of unopened arrivals since she left the pension upstairs. Petty jealousies are forgotten...All of us are proud of her entree to the mayor.

That night when Zoe tells me the politician in question is just a secretary I regret all the drunken jabbering during our "meeting." In politics, however, a secretary can be someone quite important. It turns out this one hates her boss, and if he's the one who gave the order, we can get all the information we'll need to do him in.

I realize I'm being drawn into an assassination plot. To an investigator I might appear to be the brains. I'm the one who contacted Zoe. There's no dearth of people at the Tapas Bar who'd sell me for a glass of beer or change to play the fruit machine. If Zoe does manage to identify the author of the crackdown and do away with him, even *I* will be harboring a suspicion that I'm the one who put her up to it.

I'm one of the few who knows how far Zoe will go, knows her criminal record, knows how much she resents the idea that there's anything she hasn't got the guts to do. What's at stake is her feeling that she's superior to most everyone because of her unique mix of endowments, male and female.

The only defense that comes to mind isn't convincing: my involvement in the plan was limited to reinvolving Zoe with her girlfriend in the administration. Motive: jealousy, despair. I never dreamed she was serious about helping the musicians get back on the streets. STRONGWOMAN AVENGES GIRLFRIEND'S BOYFRIEND OUT OF WORK SINCE GAG ORDER. Suspect Inside Job.

Telling my friends the next day about Zoe's willingness to help I try not to sound as if I take her seriously.

No one is taking her seriously, but every one of us is afraid she'll make us wish he had.

We wouldn't lift a finger to stop her, however, even if we knew she were stalking the mayor this very moment. My friends take the attitude that they're going to pay with their lives no matter what the future brings. Especially prone to such thoughts are the sensitive souls who realize they're their own worst enemy. There's nothing to be done about us, that's common knowledge. We can play the notes, it's all we're good for, it's all we can get excited about, and if the future is filling up with our forgotten troubles, fine, we don't expect them to be urgent until we're unable to play the notes anymore.

Unable, I say, but not prevented. Prevented from making music, as we are now, everything we've let slide for months or years is catching up with us, faces of children in cracked photos are gnawing at us, our patrons and supporters, the cafe owners who used to wish us well are all starting to look more like creditors. The people on their way to work, the English teachers zooming to their appointments, the tourists dizzy with destinations are no more interested in the instruments we pluck idly or tune than they would be in what a flock of winos is having for lunch. All those who ignore us now are bringing home a truth we never wanted to face in our busking days. Ostensibly we're given money because of the music that issues from our mouths or hands. That's the little fiction that sustains us. We're not being given a *duro* because we're good artists who want to keep creating music, playing better, singing

better, composing new songs. Where we sit in silence we don't
warrant a glance, or if we happen to attract one for some reason
or no reason, no one ever knows us.

For once I'm part of a special-interest group and allegiance
isn't a problem. For once I'm on the side of the idiots and I
don't care who's got the most right or who's got the best taste
or what the longterm effects will be of a contemplated action.
In all the months I've been left alone by the side of the road my
music has made a place for itself. I'm as much a part of the
Barcelona street scene as the guy who only knows *Oh, Susanna*
and has green plastic lizards on his hat. The visitors have taken
me home along with the ornate façades and the pitted stones
where the anarchists were shot.

I have no idea who gave the order, or what he might look
like, but I doubt he's heartless. Nothing has been done to stop
the beggars from putting out their hands. They're right where
you'd expect to find them wearing their dark glasses, kneeling
on the same old cushion, holding up the same old sign or
wearing it around their necks.

If we want to start begging, fine, we have as much right
to beg for something to eat as anyone else, nothing will be done
to stop us. He's not attacking us then, he's attacking our music,
he's attacking the friend in our arms, or in my case, the friend
in my throat, the faithful companion of long days in a place
where no one really knows me.

Walking down the street he must have heard my friend
Geet playing the Pan flute, his head whizzing back and forth.
He must have stood a while and wondered with the others still
listening how the man can keep going like that, gasping for air,
and he must have come to the same realization as the others
when twenty minutes had passed: something extraordinary
was happening that couldn't be explained.

He hates his own job, always has. He thinks of all the
asslicking that has landed him in office and continues to keep
him there. He knows that only fools hold him in high regard.
He knows he has never for five minutes been as free as Geet is
all day long.

Geet: real name, Norbert. Father a Hamburg butcher. For reasons he cannot explain, having nothing to do with something he read, he became a wandering musician, and a follower of Bhagwan, a *sannyasin,* a vegetarian, a man of peace. Geet even brings peace to the cafe under a beer sign deep in the barrio which serves the cheapest food in Barcelona, where a large black dog which belongs to a German with peroxided hair chases under the tables after the greasy tissues with which poor Spaniards have wiped their hungry faces. Geet sent his beautiful blond girlfriend back to Hamburg because he felt she was too young to understand what he was doing here in Spain by the side of the road again this year. Geet: followed by children wherever he goes, who tells me everything about himself and is my friend because I'm not for or against anyone, because I don't mind being silent with him, sipping tea. To look in his eyes, as I have at odd times, is worth everything I have ever done with my life. There's more space in his gaze than there is over my head, but there's no invitation there, I'm not being taken. Nor am I being rejected. I'm being given back to myself as I really am: free.

Someone besides a child should value the freedom that is Geet's to give. Couldn't we come up with a manifesto? We don't even have a leader. We don't have an organizer. We're full of ideas about how to live an interesting life, but we completely lack the ability to tell others how to do it.

51

Since nothing has come of Zoe's efforts to find someone to assassinate, and we buskers are incapable of mob action, we're resigned to finding a new way to survive. I am, I should say. Others are going elsewhere. For some of them busking is not only a way of life, it's the only way they've ever made a living. There are men among us who wouldn't know how to live off their mothers.

An English speaker with my background should start teaching English, that's what everyone is telling me, even Marina and Virgilio. Zoe wants to put me in touch with lesbian teachers of English she knows. Owen has a host of contacts by now and wants to repay me for taking him in when he came. The teachers that frequent the Tapas Bar are getting close-mouthed when I'm around, anticipating competition. I'd like to enter the field for a lark just to find out who my real friends are.

A ballet dancer from California is helping me to balance these inducements. She's had what Americans like to call a "good education," and gave up a lavish lifestyle to get away from her boyfriend, who was "into drugs," and to get her child away. She became a star in the milieu a few days after she came when she tried to go Zoe one better by dancing naked on the tables for the *men* present.

A few days later she threw away her welcome with an impassioned speech containing the opinion, "all artists are psychopaths," which perked up ears. Further discussion revealed her belief that the buskers here were "addictive personalities," and styled our method of making a living "full-blown dependency."

These observations would have been cause for laughter if the psychopaths in question weren't being prevented from pursuing their addiction by tight credit, and weren't completely cut off from the guarantors of dependency thanks to the recent full-blown enforcement of frivolous licensing laws. She could have been torn limb from limb, and probably should have been, but she was beautiful, she really could dance, no one wanted her to stop doing that even if we had to put up with more lectures. In addition, her little boy had a beautiful sad side and a pitiful, raspy voice.

The advice she's tailored for me is: I should be earning my living honestly by teaching English, "since that's the only game in town."

I've been trying to think of another game. All that has come to mind is an old hustle Pierre the Magician learned from an Algerian pimp. To trip a big payoff on the fruit machines, a thread is taped to a coin and the coin is given a tug when it has dropped a certain part of the way down the gullet of the targeted machine. All the skill is in identifying this split second of opportunity.

My job has been to block the machine from view while Pierre goes fishing. So far he's collected a couple of jackpots from places where we'll never be seen again, but I don't like the way my face is becoming an unpleasant memory all over the part of town where I most like to show it.

Pierre will give me a third of the take but I haven't got the stomach for earning a living this way. All the tension while I get in position and Pierre starts feeding the machine coins he's letting it keep...All the fake exclamations of defeat until the trick succeeds and there's nothing false in our cheers...Or in his...

Pierre's very proud of his sensitive hands. It's the pride of a prostitute in the apparatus that is keeping her alive at the moment but is going to end by giving her AIDS.

An English musician named Colin (Phil's friend) set off on a trip around the world yesterday to be financed by tin-whistle playing. He's been planning it for years, he says. He was back in the afternoon, not a word about what went wrong. Probably got halfway to Tarragona before he forgot what he was supposd to be doing, or thought he must have been going to Sitges and missed his stop.

He was an aeronautical engineer before he steeped himself in acid. While there was still something left he'd learned Sanskrit and Tibetan to advance his studies of religion. One follower and he could start diverting the mainstream. A small crowd of them and he could change the world.

Colin is telling me he likes Barcelona, he's "going to stay and teach English."

The teachers present are restive, some have the good

sense to leave before they'll have to answer questions. Without exception the English teachers here are sane, therefore more interesting in a group. If people like Colin start teaching they'll suffer a further loss of cachet.

In general the teachers are like Owen—immaculately groomed, gracious and well-organized as they zoom around from dot to dot. The teachers belong to a lower caste than the buskers and that's why they're expected to answer questions about rainfall and holidays—expected to be almanacs. Or if they've spent a few years in college and their knowledge is encyclopaedic, referees.

Yeah, but they're obsessed, they're money-hungry as hell. It's embarrassing to walk with them anywhere near the port because they're sure to start asking how many pesetas would be in it for them to help unload a certain cargo, or "Do you need anyone to crew? Does anyone speak English?" The last is a trick question because they're trying to get into a conversation with someone who thinks he can speak English so they can let him know he ought to learn to speak it better.

Unfortunately Barcelonians in droves are still learning to speak English or trying to brush up what they had in school. English teachers are swarming all over town. It's alarming to see a teacher twice during one of my linear days—almost sinister, as it would be to come upon a curiously marked pigeon in a seething flock at the heart of town and then all by itself on a doorstep in the suburbs.

In spite of their low standing among streetpeople, the teachers are well-received by Gloria and Esteban at the Tapas Bar, as they would be in any cafe where they chose to hang out. How can a cafe owner not enjoy providing a haven for people who are aggressively clean and neatly dressed, whose very livelihood depends on a complicated network held together by *café con leche* and messages left at the bar?

With texts provided by Owen I give some lessons to a cafe owner down the street. Free lessons—the man came to the Tapas Bar once with a large sum of money that had spilled out of my pocket when I was paying for a drink. I attributed his honesty to the fact that he came from León, which went down very well. His place is a cut above the places I frequent but I try to stop for one of something from time to time to pay my respects to the honest man.

I give this man his first lesson at a dark table in the rear. For two minutes we discuss the books we are going to use, the method of study I've chosen. We spend the rest of the hour discussing, by every linguistic means available, his wife's incurable illness. I understand his beautiful Castilian Spanish perfectly. His wife is suffering from lupus erythematosus, which I know something about, unfortunately.

My second pupil is one of Owen's rejects—a woman of means who's looking for a husband of English extraction. She's miffed that I'm an American. I think she's been trying to tell me she was fooled by my arch way of speaking.

We don't complete the lesson. She wants to learn British English, doesn't want to "learn wrong."

I agree that the British are more capable speakers than my countrymen, but I still expect to be paid for the full hour of time I'd set aside.

When she came she asked me not to forget to sing for her. "I've heard so much about you."

I give her a snatch of Wotan's Farewell.

Owen thinks the problem is all in my mind. I should have shown some interest in her as a person.

52

My brother's offer of a job arrives in this unhappy time and I only think for a minute before I write to accept.

Dear Tom:
Your letter couldn't have come at a better time. I've been having survival problems.

Thanks for interceding with mom and Elena for me and making room for me in your company. I never thought I'd see the day when I'd be pleased by the offer of a job like the one you describe.

When I make California I'll need a few days off to rest and digest the things I've done and seen. Then I'll be ready to work for you doing anything at all.

I feel bad about leaving. It's sad the way this scene is folding. It's not pleasant to talk about it, but there's a big difference between me and most of the others on the street. They have to be there and I don't. What they do with their instruments or their hands is the last chance for a lot of them, there's nothing ahead but beggary. Here full freedom becomes abject dependency at the stroke of a pen, but we're used to this kind of thing. Our best performances have gone unnoticed, our worst have filled the music case.

I know I'm tough enough to take what would be ahead if I stayed, but I guess I need to work for more than survival. Freedom at the discretion of some bureaucrat isn't free enough for me.

Thanks again for all you've done as my intermediary. I sincerely want to do you some good as an employee, but I'll tell you up front that Elena will view life in a mobile home (even a "triple-wide") as one step up from a dumpster. I'll have to kidnap her and try to fool her when the blindfold comes off. From the bed she'll think she's in a real home.

For what it's worth in overcoming buyer objections, I think the "mobile home lifestyle" you're always talking about wouldn't be half as frightening if people didn't have to start looking at your homes from the outside—the crummy lots with the ass end of so many cars in their faces, all the Astro-turf and cedar chips, and the doors they open without feeling any weight in their hands.

I know you sell these things and I don't want to offend you, but if you could figure out a way to blindfold your buyers and get them inside for their first look at a mobile home, you'd outsell everyone in the state.

Anyway, I applaud your business instincts for starting me on loans and working me into sales at the low end. The way I see it, the crappiest homes you've got will be the easiest to sell, especially to people with large families who are just looking for a place to hole up, and those people, especially the Spanish speakers, are the ones I want to do business with.

Thanks again for all your help.

Dear Gordie:

OK, you're on the payroll as soon as you get back. I'm going to advance you the cost of a one-way flight. I get the feeling from your letter that you might have an attitude problem, but I'm going to train you. You've got natural ability, a phone voice, brains, you know what I mean. You might straighten out when you see some green.

The real good news is that I've got your wife and kid back. Elaine is a bit of a hardnose about the living conditions she'll accept but you might budge her if you keep hammering. I know the type. She told me she was going to write you a letter to explain what you'll have to do to keep your end of the bargain. She doesn't want you leaving Spain till you've read it through and agree to everything.

Mom's willing to put you up until I get the home ready, but don't expect a friendly reception. Can't wait to see you and hear what you been up to but for now I gotta go.

53

Dear Gordon:

You know by now that I've been in contact with your brother because he's delivered several messages from you. We reached a sensible list of conditions that you will have to be willing to accept before I'll let you take responsibility for our child.

1. Drinking. You will not touch a drop of alcohol again in your life or the baby and I are gone. I realize that you were only out of line two or three times when I knew you, but one time, when you were robbed, was crucial, and I'd been counting on you. Your brother's the one responsible for this condition. He knew you when your drinking was out of control and says there are people all over the state that are still upset by you.

2. Housing. I know that part of your brother's business is selling mobile homes and this might be an opportunity for him to rent one he can't sell. No deal. Our quarters will have to be an improvement on my parents' because I don't want Lenita to get the idea we've come down in the world. She's a very smart girl.

3. Money. You will give all your paychecks to me. All the accounts will be in my name only. This may seem strict, but the only way I can be sure you aren't running around is for you to ask me for money whenever you want to do anything. Obviously, with a baby to take care of I'd be handicapped in trying to check up on you.

4. Singing. No practising in the home. No playing your opera records. Rent a studio, get a tape deck and listen to opera in your car. The baby probably wouldn't care, but I never want to hear another opera as long as I live. The tiniest excerpt on the radio brings back the whole miserable time that I was holed up with you in Sarriá, pregnant and at the mercy of your music.

5. Food. No more weird diets. If you're going to do the cooking, no more margarine in place of butter, no more brown rice sweeteners. No more seaweed hidden away in the soups and casseroles. No more bits of raw garlic in the spaghetti sauce at the last minute. No more raw garlic period. No more comments about the health-giving or life-prolonging qualities of the food you eat even if you've got nothing to say against mine. I make you sound like a fanatic, and maybe you don't see yourself as one. You'd never done all the cooking for someone before, and you *were* a fanatic in a quiet, insistent way. Now you know better.

6. Exercise. No more pushing me to walk with you or climb with you when I'd rather ride. No more attempts to massage me when you're supposed to be giving me *frôlage*. Let me die in peace, and preferably, in bed.

7. Hygiene. You must promise to take a shower at least once a day and brush your teeth whenever you've had anything to eat. If you've eaten raw garlic you won't be permitted in my presence (or the baby's) until the smell has worn off. Never wear an item of clothing more than one day. Sit down to pee unless we're outside. Always carry a handkerchief.

I might seem picky trotting out such a long list, but I'm sure that's only because 90% of men already behave the way I want you to. As for neatness, I remember what a slob you were when we started living together in the States. Granted, you turned into a neat freak when the house was yours to keep clean. Now you'll be working hard and no doubt will expect me to keep the place clean for you, and I'm willing to keep everything picked up while I'm with Nena, but you'd better not go back to your old ways.

If you do everything I say I'll try living with you again. A word of advice: go slow. Don't try to change all at once. If you start thinking "I can't remember all this," stay the hell away for a few hours or even days. Let's try to be a good example for the baby. Maybe I'll even start desiring you again someday.

Let me know in writing if you agree. If you think I'm not serious and you can slide by, ignoring the above requirements, we'll need a contract. If you're up to the challenge and ready to work hard to change the way you live, *bon voyage...*

54

I'm not telling anyone of my departure, just quietly settling my accounts. I'd love to be the reason for a party, but I don't want to have to explain why I'm leaving. I'm only half-convinced I know.

We're getting moved on by the police less frequently now. The edict banning us from the Puerta del Angel has been losing its teeth, the Guardia Urbana is too flabby to enforce it. The music you hear on the street now is subdued the way it is in distant memory or dreams. There's no vying, no showing off, no repartee. Instead, a lot of closed eyes and clean clothes.

Hard times are forgotten when the rat circus comes squeaking into town. They set up right in the middle of the Puerta del Angel and stop traffic all the way to the Plaça Catalunya without a word from the police. The pope didn't command this much respect, or the Three Kings.

All the usual street performers are out in force, even the hungry ones are glad to be missing work. We've taken over the inner circle of a huge audience like the guests of ancient Greece. Franz is front row center sitting crosslegged, someone the rats may recognize from prior stays in Barcelona, wild nights away from the cage.

By the Wayside

Not only have the buskers called a halt, most pedestrians are saying the hell with their destinations. The mob completely blocks the street and the police are watching the circus, too.

These circus folks with their capes and sequined costumes look too respectable to be seen with us and no amount of winking will fix the disparity.

The disparity is just right. There isn't one of us who doesn't identify 100% with the performing animals, small and furry though they are. We all know what it means to jump through a hoop.

The circus seems to originate in Germany to judge by the accents but Geet tells me there are French people, too. There are some geek-ish touches, rat-swallowing and regurgitation. No sleight of hand here, the little devil is soaked with gastric juice and clearly irritated. (For obvious reasons, this is the smallest rat. Maybe they all started this way...)

The minor acts are enjoyable. No matter what the rats do they get screams from the kids. They jump through hoops, they jump through flaming hoops, they walk a tightrope. There's music the while, with the leading human performers taking part, the most notable being a muscular fellow with long peroxided hair, a yellow bathingsuit and a purple cape and tights, who plays the saxophone.

The *pièce de résistance* is the suicide rat, and for my dough this is a better animal act than anything you can find under the big top. It's for damned sure far above any of the animal acts to be found in Barcelona, with the possible exception of the albino gorilla at the zoo who likes to smear shit on the glass of its cage.

Until now the best thing with animals on the streets has been a gypsy who plays a trumpet while a little goat turns a circle atop a stool. The suicide rat has more talent than a tribe of gypsies, more showmanship—you name it. As soon as I see what it can do I'm a fan for life. I want to take it home with me like my pals, but not to put in a cage. I'd put it in silk pyjamas and let it play in the crib with my little girl. I'd put a silver spoon in its mouth a hundred times a day.

For the suicide rat's act a ladder eight inches wide has been erected far above the heads of the crowd—a hundred feet or more, I have no idea how they're keeping the ladder still enough for the rat to climb. I keep waiting for it to buckle and arch into the top of a building. Atop it is a tiny platform from which, of course, the suicide rat is going to dive.

Since nobody expects the poor thing to live there are groans when the sax-man/superman urges him higher with his long thin whip. Theatrically, the rat pauses from time to time and looks down as if he can't make up his mind. Perhaps life with the man in the yellow bathingsuit isn't as bad as all that...

At the top the rat is a speck to the straining faces below, and can barely be seen inching out on the little platform, hesitating before he leaps to certain death. The flash descent is just the same old shit for this rat, but it's a giant step for his kind.

The screams intensify when the man in the yellow bathingsuit catches him. The pistol-toting policemen are clapping their hands right along with the children. It still seems to me an amazing thing to have done...Catch a thing so small moving so fast. Relief is making the rounds. We could have been spattered with blood.

By far the best part of the act is the suicide rat's jubilation at finding himself among the living—running in circles, leaping up and down to acknowledge the applause. Geet and I stay through another complete show to see the suicide rat again. When it occurs to us how many shows the rat circus puts on in a day we wonder how many rats they've gone through in training...If the suicide rat gets to retire...

No one sees me go. Buskers often depart without saying goodbye. It pains me to think of running into Hewitson. Surely he's in the crowd somewhere, the rat circus must be one of the big events of his year. Perhaps he's too busy with all the people he's brought...

No one but Hewitson could talk me into staying. In five minutes he'd have me feeling sorry for all the fat cats back in the States. He'd have me pledge myself to Spain till all my teeth are gone. Better to gum my way here than run around with a smile on my face wishing one and all a nice day.

He'd be right, of course, and he'd be sure to latch on to me until there was no chance at all I'd turn my back on him.

I keep telling myself I'll be back. After all, the Liceo has a job waiting—I'll do parts next season. In three or four months I can bring Elena around. I'll be sure to write Hewitson a long letter in advance so that he'll be available to help her settle in.

I'm seen leaving by some anarchists, but they must think it's a weekend trip, they're all smiles.

I'm no longer myself as the cab is bouncing out of town. There's nothing I want to say to the driver. For now there's nothing to live for. It's exhilarating, but so what.

CALIFORNIA

55

I didn't phone Elena for four days after my arrival in California. I spent the whole time at my mother's cottage soaking up sun on the patio in back among her American roses and gardenias, listening to American hummingbirds and the hum of traffic on a freeway I couldn't see, perhaps quite distant, obscured by the sick foliage of royal palms and walnut-infested walnut trees.

"Well, I'm back, what's left of me," I told Lena when I finally called.

"I thought you were shacked up somewhere."

"Resting here at my mother's. My brother's advancing me enough to cap my tooth. I can't start work for him till I'm a new me."

"Sounds like you'll have time to paint my ranch."

"If you won't drive me too hard, maybe. I think my love of Spain may have been masking a wasting disease of some kind."

"We've been telling Lenita about you and she's curious to see what you are exactly. After all his hard work as a father daddy has started calling himself *abuelo*. I think that's quite a concession..."

"Yeah, there seems to be room for me linguistically, at least, or until I run out of paint."

The thought of being rejected again as a father was the spur I needed to start eating everything in sight and doing calisthenics. My new tooth was on rush order. The day it was seated I drove to Elena's to start painting.

It was ten at night when I pulled in. Nena was having a bottle. Enrique was in bed. He was a "morning person."

"In other words, you told him I was coming and ruined his evening."

"I told him, but he's always in bed by ten o'clock and up at 5:30. You'll see. My mom's coming down."

That would have to be Isabel making the floor nervous above our heads. I remembered her tread.

Nena was more of a person, her features more definite. She was groggy with all her milk, but her feistiness was coming through. She'd give me an argument soon. The helpless babe I remembered could hold her own bottle and throw it at you when it was empty.

Mama steamed up to the crib and put her arms around me. This was what I'd expected from Elena, not the cheek she offered.

By the Wayside

I told Mama how good it was to be back, and managed to sound convincing.

Like many immigrants, I suppose, I was still in awe of the sizable houses that so many American families had contrived to have all to themselves, yards where there weren't any secrets, a wealth of flowers and gadgets on view like a set table, automobiles twice as big as they needed to be. I'd returned from long stints abroad before and knew that all too soon I'd be seeing waste in the bigness of things, and in spaciousness the very reason competition was so deadly here, a loss of community.

Before long even the flowers in these gardens would be as hard and malignant as jewels that give confidence to a transaction. Ownership would be a frenzied refusal to allow anything alive—whether plant, animal or idea—a purpose of of its own. I'd be ignored by all the well-heeled people scurrying around the shopping malls, for instance, and feel important only to salesmen. I'd vanish into my job and by denying myself all the things everyone thought I had to have, save money for my escape.

Mama was impressed by my Spanish in describing the America I was so glad to see again, but on her way to heat up the manzanilla tea she spoke to her daughter about me and I couldn't understand a word.

I was more robust than her mother remembered, Elena explained. "She thinks you're a survivor, and that's a good quality in a father."

Elena bent to slide the rubber nipple from the sleeping child's mouth and I saw that the breasts she no longer nursed with had remained full. They remained inaccessible, too— still full of maternal purpose. The way she swooped to the child and slowed the caring act to get it just right I saw she was happier with her identity as a mother than she had ever been as a student or a lover.

Now Elena took care of the baby. Her bed was beside the crib. Isabel trusted her enough to sleep upstairs. With Enrique in the house the women couldn't have been putting on a show for me. "See what a good mother Elena has become." I'd been wrong about her, that was all. There were things in her I had missed completely. She knew I had been scared by the thought of leaving Nena in her keeping, we'd been over that ground before I left for France. Why hadn't she spoken up for herself?

More to the point, why did I think people had to protest their innocence and their competence the way I did, as if every person I met had seen my dossier?

While we were having tea and passing around photos of Nena and Mama's face was squeezed so tight with pride she reminded me of the dog that's all folds, I was having some unsettling thoughts.

What if Elena had tried to fool me with her decadent behavior when we met, correctly perceiving that I was jaded and that procreation would have to be incidental? What if she'd taken to her bed on purpose to elicit paternal instincts that were the best part of me, or the only useful instincts I had left? (In Elena's view, my need to express myself in song just got me in trouble, and my need to give pleasure to a woman gave them the means to make me miserable.)

"No, you can't sleep in here with me," she told me after bedtime tea. "We're not married."

"Surely...Don't they know we're planning to get a place together?"

"They don't. My father thought we were married in Gibraltar before Nena was born. My mother didn't have the guts to tell him it was a lie. It took a long time for Mama and me to find the courage to tell him."

"How long? When did he find out?"

"Last night. He says he suspected it all along, but I can tell he's worried. He says it will be harder to get money out of you if we have to file a paternity suit."

"Do you want me to sign something? You want to get married in Reno?"

"Shush! Last night was the first time I told him that you expect me to move in with you if this job with your brother turns out to be something besides a sales pitch."

"He didn't sell me. He needs me."

"Daddy doesn't like the idea, so you'll have to bring him around. One way to start is to very humbly sleep on the living room floor until this painting job is over."

"You think he'll have more respect for me if he has to step over me on the way to the kitchen every morning at the crack of dawn?"

I knew Enrique's early morning espresso ritual from our first overnight visit, just prior to leaving for Europe.

"Lower your voice! He'll hear you. You might wake the baby. Try not to stir up a hornet's nest while you're here."

"At least you know what it is. We've got to have our own place."

"In the morning. You know about the daybed. Take whatever covers you want."

Yes, I knew the closet where these things were kept, and as before I'd be using only a mattress because Enrique had taken the bed apart to store it and a corps of engineers couldn't have put it together again.

"Just answer me one question. How can a guy who knows 30 languages let his daughter run off to Europe with someone he hates and get pregnant by that same someone and think, gee, I guess that someone wasn't an honorable fellow, he must have slept with my daughter nineteen months ago, he must have raped her. I'm not going to let that happen again. These are the thought processes of one of those old country guys who burns candles before icons. If he's really as backward as all that we'd better elope."

"Go to bed. We start work tomorrow and he's bound to wake you early."

56

I heard Enrique on the stairs. He was a wisp of a man, but Mama had all the lumber in the house commenting by this time. I had to feign sleep so he wouldn't think I was laying for him; wake when he made a ding in the kitchen and tell him how glad I was he woke me.

I could sense his disgust as he circled the mattress in the living room. There was a light breeze, his bathrobe snapped like a flag.

The ding for round one.

"How have you slept?" was his opening jab.

He was readying the old sock to make espresso, or call it a pastry bag—duck made dark with the years. He put sugar in the fresh-ground coffee. The result was so good my mouth was already remembering it.

"I had a good sleep, thanks. Wonder if I should risk waking Nena to try to put that mattress away..."

"Six-thirty will be a better time. The baby will be hungry then, and her screams will wake Elena. It is thus every morning."

"Elena wakes up at six-thirty—on a Saturday? Without going back to sleep?"

"Yes, her habits have changed." He'd got the water hot and smiled at me through the steam. "She stayed with the same job for six months and learned the discipline of coming to work on time. Also, the baby's hunger has taught her to listen to the needs of another. Someday she will make someone a good wife."

I was leaving the open kitchen for the dining room when I took this rabbit punch. I came right back to let him know my head was clear. "After her childbearing years, I suppose. A lot of women remember their husbands then, see the need for a companion as they start to decline."

"Quite so. I only hope she will choose well. You see where companionship has got her thus far."

"We were more than companions, Enrique."

"Let me set these down and we will talk, but not too loudly. You have a loud voice, I have noticed, perhaps because you've been singing opera recently."

He came to the table taking small steps, the tiny cups making his hands huge. As light as he was there was no up-and-down motion at all as he drew near, which made him seem deep in the water, as if I were only seeing the top of him.

"My daughter tells me she never loved you, nor you her," he said after a lengthy first sip.

"That's a superficial account...We were certainly attracted to each other. She was better to travel with than any woman I know. Made to order for an itinerant musician."

"There's the baby...I would say she's made to order to work as a temporary legal secretary, by which means she will have the chance to meet an employer she respects."

"It's nothing new for an opera singer to travel with his family."

"I'm not aware that opera choristers travel at all. Isn't that what you're doing now, chorus work? As I understand it, your dreams of being a soloist were dashed when you tried and failed to gain a position in provincial France. It must be very hard to give up the ambition to sing when you still have a little voice, but I am not naive about the world of professional musicians. Choruses are full of people who once wanted to be stars who could travel from place to place as you imagine yourself doing."

"Wait a minute. I took the chorus job I've got now because I was promised parts next year. After I've done a solo role my employers will have a hell of a time keeping me off the road. Offers will be coming in from all over the world."

I was painting this rosy picture to rattle his composure, of course. Till now he'd been giving me his wisdom with a crinkly, old man's kindness, the snake.

"These are mere dreams," he said, starting to hurry his words. "You are asking a woman with a small child to stake her life on the favorable outcome you expect whenever you deign to open your mouth in song. It is most surprising that you have got all your teeth."

"I didn't lose that tooth to a critic."

"I was not aware that you are missing a tooth."

"Sorry. I'm not, anymore. I didn't know how much you were told."

"You are speaking nonsense. However, your words do not matter to me. Your actions have already spoken much louder than any noise you have ever made on a stage. You are a drunkard and a ruffian! I do not begrudge you a certain talent, and a good appearance. Here in America I predict success for you if you will find work as a salesman. Is this what your brother is offering? Who is this brother, anyway? No one ever mentioned him to me. What is his business that he can offer a job to someone like you?"

"He's a millionaire. I don't know everything he does."

"Is he legitimate? Under what name does he do business?"

"Something with 'dream' in it. He has a loan business. He sells mobile homes. He has a transportation business and a construction business, I think to move mobile homes around and keep them from blowing away after he sets them down."

"He wants you to sell mobile homes, then?"

"Not right away. Loans. 'Sell loans,' that's how he puts it. Try to get people to refinance their mobile homes. I admit there's a crazy sound to it, but he swears there are people out there who want to do this. Anyway, it's certainly prescient of you to think I would make a good salesman. After my brother you're the first person who thought I could sell anything. I'm sure you're right, too. I'll have to be a good salesman to get out of the hole I'm in, so I will be."

"You are in debt to someone? This is the hole?"

"No, I mean my situation with Elena..."

"You are not referring to this habitation?"

"No, I'm only trying to say that I can get out of a hole as fast as I can get in. It's not a euphemism for anything nasty, at least not to me..."

"There's nothing funny about such wordplay in respect

to my daughter. I wish to inform you that I have a forty-five caliber revolver and I will not hesitate to use it if you do violence of any kind during your stay..."

"I'll try not to drop the toilet seat..."

"My daughter invited you to paint her house. In return for your work I've agreed to provide food and a place to stay in my daughter's name. When your work is finished you will leave and contact my daughter through the mail. If it is up to me you would have been in court already and by now she would be visiting you in jail."

"Yaaa.."

That was the baby. "Saved by the yell. I'd better get that mattress put away and see if I can help Elena with her toilette. Unless she's drawing her own bath now..."

"If you disclose the subject of this discussion to my daughter or my wife I can no longer extend my hospitality."

"You mean, I can't be your dartboard anymore? Hey, Rico, baby: I reckon I'll have to extend my fist in your direction before you throw me out, and I don't pick on people half my size, so stop pushing me. And I'm going to bring Elena up to date right away. I want to make sure she knows about the forty-five, at least. She once told me she's scared of guns."

"If you frighten her I will call the police..."

I laughed in his face and went for my first look at Elena awake at 6:30 in the morning. She hadn't exactly jumped out of bed when she heard the baby, but she'd been moving closer, and had a hand on the crib rail when I came through the door.

"She needs changing..." Not only were her eyes completely open, there was love in them.

"I know all about these things. All the foster children when I was a kid, remember? I've already spotted the changing table. Now that Isabel's out of our hair and there's room to move around I'm going to show you what kind of a father I can be..."

"Papi," said the baby, who'd stopped crying to hear what I was saying to her mother in a foreign tongue.

"She wants my father," said Elena, but the baby was

263

letting me take her. "How'd you two get along?" Nena squeezed my nose and grinned.

"We hit it off much better than I expected. I got to the bottom of my demitasse before he threatened to call the police. There's only one threat on my life to cloud the horizon. Are you aware that he's keeping a forty-five?"

"Oh, he's had that for years. I don't think he knows how to use it. He just keeps it on hand to show solidarity with Reagan and the right-to-bear-arms types. But honey, please don't do anything to get yourself shot till you've finished painting the ranch..."

57

Isabel was minding the baby and Elena was doing a little work, the first I'd ever seen her do. When I could see her from where I was trembling on my scaffold her arm was always moving. Slowly, true, but where did she get the strength to keep it lifted so long while there was a brush in her hand?

Scaffold, what a joke. One slender board trying to rid itself of me.

I slopped on the paint at top speed, seeing nothing sinister in the fact that I was trying to overcome my fear of heights by hurrying the work. The more I got done, the sooner I could take on sewers and trenches—I was ready for anything. "Terrestrial employment, is it? I'm your man!"

I could see Enrique didn't like the look of us coming home together in our old clothes with the same color of paint splattered on them.

We brought him around by playing with the baby. Nena

was walking a little, determined to get it right. We would play a game with a soft rubber ball where Nena would point at the adult to whom the ball should next be thrown. She let me have my fair share of catches, but she gave her granddaddy more than his fair share, perhaps sensing that this kind of game was a big yawn for him.

It would be going too far to say that Enrique enjoyed a sense of family when all of us were together, but Isabel clearly did, and she was wearing him down. He was embarrassed by her giggly good humor at first, then he tried a tight smile. By the third day of fun and games he was begging off. This wasn't his idea of fun, and Isabel had to remind him how important it was for little Nena to have a father.

"In other words," I told him, "if I hadn't come into your daughter's life when I did your precious playmate would not be punctuating your dark, linguistic days with her sweet cries."

"Why don't you go to a movie," he countered. "You have spent your money on this kind of thing before. Dine out if you like, though I assure you, what my wife cooks is better than anything you will find in town, no matter how high the price. You haven't seen each other in a year and all you do is work."

"We have lots of chances to talk, though," I continued. "I'd rather not go back to the spendthrift ways of yesteryear. I think it would be smarter to pattern my behavior after you. I rather like the feeling that I can gain some control over my life by being tight."

"That's easy to say when you haven't got a dime," Elena told me earnestly, preventing her father from saying the same old thing too nicely.

"As you well know, Lena, my means are sufficient for what the new day may bring, and every wise man from Lao-tzu to Yogi Berra has told us to take one day at a time, or one pitch, that is, offering. I don't need to hype my brother's employment offer. Consider the record. I've worked for low wages before and still managed to save half my earnings, make a stake, start over in a different state or country. If my dreams are bound up in a child's future instead of my own..."

Enrique cut me off then with a hacking cough. Last night he'd left the table to flush the upstairs toilet after a suitable interval. His tolerance was there for all to see. I knew exactly how miserable he felt. I felt the same way when one of my less bright busker colleagues would ask me to teach him to sing the way I did so that he could improve his drops.

Castro had perverted Enrique's sense of security when he threw him out and it had taken the poor man a lifetime of scrimping to regain enough faith in a temporal authority to believe that what was his was his.

He was constantly telling me how I had all the opportunities that he lacked when he was my age. I was tall and goodlooking, I spoke English without an accent, I had a brother who was already a millionaire, contacts from my schooldays to use. I had more going for me than most Americans my age. Psychopathology therefore was the only plausible explanation for my having sunk so low as to become a housepainter for nothing, with a future in selling people the chance to make unwise financial decisions.

At dinner before what was likely to be my last day as a housepainter Enrique made an all-out assault on my sense of having done a good job, of having restored his daughter's confidence in my ability to provide and care for my small daughter. I had no *political sense*.

It hurt to hear those words. Mama had outdone herself with a spaghetti sauce she had spiced herself with hot peppers and comino. I knew we'd be shouting soon. It was impossible to eat spaghetti in a flying rage, which was undoubtedly the reason Italians so often forgot why they were shouting.

"Politics have nothing to do with the choices I've made, Enrique." This in a quiet voice. Elena wasn't eating, either, she knew an eruption was imminent. Mama looked pleased with her sauce and who knows what other things that had turned out well today. For example, today, over Elena's objection, I'd told her that I wanted to marry her daughter as soon as the practical problem of finding a grand enough house and a way to pay for it could be solved. Mama Isabel had no patience with

Enrique's hatred of me, whether unreasoning or all too reasonable.

"Politics has everything to do with your failure to prosper in this country. You're a malcontent. You're dissatisfied with your government. You turn a blind eye to illicit substances..."

"Not that again..."

Enrique felt that the residents of the townhouse one down were paying too much attention to particular plants in their backyards. He would never say anything, he would never call the authorities. He wouldn't call the authorities if he saw them burying someone. He disapproved, all the same. Tolerating the use of marijuana was worse than smoking it. When he was called as a substitute teacher he had to contend with teenagers who had smoked marijuana right before coming to class.

I'd given my opinion on the subject last night. I'd always taken it for granted that teenagers would smoke dope for a year or two when it would do the most damage to their minds, ruin their chances of getting into a good college, and so forth, partly to take the edge off the future, restore a little blurriness, dispel the feeling that they were about to be punched out of a machine, but also, and perhaps most importantly, to satisfy themselves that they were not going along with the wishes of someone like Nancy Reagan.

I'd loved wine, women and song too much all my life ever to get addicted to hard drugs, but even an oldtimer like me, someone who'd tasted the best things in life and wallowed in them as well, would have been tempted to go on heroin before nodding at the wisdom of a word from Nancy.

Tonight Enrique wanted to up the ante. He was convinced I was an "immoralist," with apologies to Gide. "Someone who doesn't say no to drugs is saying yes!"

"I'm sorry you've been stewing about this, Enrique, but you've missed the point. Many kids are obliged to say yes to drugs as a way of saying no to Nancy Reagan. Seriously, would you want someone like Nancy to be a role model for Nena, for example?"

"Papi," said Nena with a smile in my direction. I fancied she was old enough to enjoy someone who could make her granddaddy show this much life.

"Do you realize you're talking about the wife of the President of the United States?"

"I realize you're a big fan. Yes, Ronald and Nancy rule the country at the moment, but that's no reason the rest of us should be afraid to tackle complex issues..."

Enrique was so carried away thinking what he wanted to do to me he couldn't think of anything to say. While he hesitated Elena piped up.

"Gordon's right, Papa. The Reagans are idiots. It's time someone had the courage to tell you so."

"Courage?" sputtered the old man, brandishing the knife he used to cut up his spaghetti (the rest of us ate like Italians—no spoon, either).

"It's the wrong word," I told him. "I'm glad you take exception to it, Dad. That's what America is all about, criticizing authority with impunity. I'll stick my neck out...I don't think courage is ever involved in expressing a political opinion in this country. Forget what you read about political courage. If this were the kind of country where I could get in trouble for putting DOWN WITH REAGAN on a billboard, then we could talk about courage."

"I'm not so sure," said Elena. "Maybe we'd be talking about foolhardiness. If someone could convince a jury that by DOWN WITH REAGAN you meant KILL REAGAN they could put you in prison."

"Stop it, Elena! I won't have this kind of talk in my house! What if someone were listening? We're all naturalized citizens of the greatest country on earth!" His wild eyes discovered me winding my spaghetti. "You've done this to my daughter! You've turned her into a fuzzy-headed liberal!"

"No, she's right on the money. Anyone would be a fool to take a chance on a jury today for any act remotely anti-Reagan. The percentages are against you all the way. These are the same people who put the Reagans in office. Considering the regional vote there are good odds you'll come across a jury every now and then that will be composed completely of Reagan supporters."

"Halfwits, in other words," said Elena.

"I prefer the term 'naif.'"

"You're calling me a halfwit in my own house!"

"That was your daughter's word."

"She's just a puppet for your liberalism. So this is the meaning of the low voices I hear downstairs each night while I'm trying to sleep."

"Daddy, you're making a big deal about nothing." Elena told her mother in Spanish to reason with him, and Isabel told him to calm down. She'd been pleased to see Elena and me on the same side of an issue, whatever it was, and was letting Enrique feel her irritation with him.

"I don't see what you've got against liberals, Enrique," I went on. "If the liberals had carried the day back when Castro took power we'd have been trading with Cuber...helping her to find her way...You might never have had to leave."

Enrique jumped to his feet, threw down his knife, put back his head and screamed. Then he ran from the table.

He might have been after his pistol, but he had both women on his heels.

The baby was saying "Papi" again and coming to put her arms around me.

She might not have understood any of the words but she was as quick as Isabel to understand the situation.

She knew I needed protection.

58

Elena had some Seconal on hand she'd bought from an old friend from a philosophy class "in case of emergency," so Enrique was able to get some sleep that night.

Mama said no to the offer of a "red" and could be heard snoring minutes after her husband was off. I doubted the baby's screams would have awakened her.

The baby was soggy with sleep. If she did wake she'd make noise a long time before she was conscious.

Elena wasn't ready for bed.

Neither was I.

Elena was naked except for her robe. She slept naked.

I was down to my skivvies, which would have to be on in the morning, but could go on and off all night, quick as a cap.

"Look, I've promised I'd go away with you. What more do you want?"

"I want to know why you cover up like a boxer every time I get within striking distance. The few times I've kissed you you don't open your mouth, or if you do, it's just for a moment, till you think better of it."

"You'll just have to be patient. I'm not ready to have relations yet."

"If you'll be straight with me I'll be as patient as you like. You weren't screwing your boss, then? It was all a story to piss me off?"

So far she'd refused to say anything on the subject.

"All right, I lied to try to make you jealous. Just the way you did with your whores and lesbians. You should have seen that guy. He had the hots for me, though. Don't worry. I'm not going to make you lie. I'm sure you went with a whore or two. It's different for men. After having a child...I don't know, something got switched off. It's an animal thing. If it doesn't switch on again I'll see a shrink. But you be honest, too. How did you lose your tooth?"

"You won't believe this, but a woman hit me over the head with a totem pole."

"While you were singing on the street?"

I nodded.

"Oh, how funny. She swung for your mouth while you were singing?"

"No, she knocked me unconscious and I broke my tooth when my head hit the street."

"That's a scream. Did anyone do anything?"

"The police let her go. I was too woozy to see any danger in letting her go free."

"Good. We need more types like that. She tried again?"

"No, one hole in my mouth gave complete satisfaction. Look, Lena, when we leave...I've seen the mobile home, it's roomier than this place, everything's clean, you'll love it, but I'm not going to pressure you, OK? I'll never say a thing about sex as long as you'll promise to play with yourself."

"Don't worry. I want to feel the way I did before...Then I don't want to. I'm sorry, but the truth is, I like all the mothering stuff."

"I've seen that you do. I don't want you to be the sybarite you were."

"And I don't want you to be the ascetic."

"We'll find common ground as parents. Spread the blanket, and when Nena has chased her butterfly into the deep grass..." She pulled away again. I was only trying to plant one on her cheek. "Give me your hand, then. Can we talk holding hands?"

"We really ought to get some sleep."

"Tomorrow might be too late to fine-tune our plans."

"We have all day at the ranch to talk. Or until you finish."

"You're right. I just wanted to say...Look, I'm sorry about your dad. I had no right to goad him that way."

"I don't blame you. I wish I could do it. I hate having to put up with his patriotism day and night."

"No, it was wrong of me. I owe him a lot for taking care of you, and all of you have done a great job with Nena. I feel awful about being away so long and awful for the things I thought. Maybe I learned something. If we could look in on the people we know while they're far from home we wouldn't recognize them. The way you acted in Sarriá was your behavior for dealing with me. You'd organized all your resources to deal with me and didn't waste them anywhere else. It was the isolation that did us in, that little island of opera and linguistics. If there had been a crowd of people who knew us on hand we wouldn't have seemed to helpless, we'd have had more respect for each other. As it was, we were a couple of monomaniacs, you looking for a womb, me looking for a whale. What's that?"

Her soft palate jump-starting a snore.

59

The morning had been full of dread and wavering, a Sunday, a terrible day to finish anything. My glitches were all where none but sparrows and mud daubers would see them. Done, then. Still I was reluctant to leave the old place.

I probably knew that I would never see it again even though she might keep on leasing it for years if it wouldn't sell.

Boxes of my correspondence, unfinished novels and rare books were still rotting in the crawlspace under the bottom level of the house once inhabited by raccoons. I couldn't bear a close look.

I waited for Lena down by her mailbox. She'd said she'd be back at one but I waited till two. In spite of all the promising changes in her personality simple errands were still hard for her.

While she was driving fast down the hill I realized that I didn't care what had happened to the things I was storing, and therefore didn't have to see. The house on the hill would no longer have any meaning for me unless she needed me again to do menial work.

There was to be no more work.

Her father gave me the news...I still had on my work clothes and was looking forward to a shower. He was still in pyjamas. On Sundays he didn't change out of his pyjamas unless he had to, a surprisingly loose arrangement for someone who clipped articles from Time magazine and wrote the date received on all incoming correspondence.

"She doesn't want you," he told me, seeming to smile sincerely.

"We've been over that. I'm hoping she will soon, and I think she is, too."

"She doesn't want to live with you. She told me so."

"She's wavering, then. I have to talk to her. She's worried about money. She's worried because I won't be a millionaire overnight."

"She has told me she doesn't care how much money you will earn, where you will live. She wants to stay with her mother and me. It will be better for Lenita. She doesn't love you. Her precise words were, 'I don't love him. I would never love him, even if he wasn't such a loser.' She may have meant, 'if he weren't.'"

"Where is the bitch? Why are you telling me all this? I want to hear it in her own words."

"She will not return until you leave. If you continue to use such disrespectful language I must ask you to leave this moment, and deny you the benefit of a ride to the bus terminal in my car."

"I get it. I was set up. Elena rigged this whole scenario so she could get her ranch painted for nothing."

"And for months you were not living off her in Spain, contributing nothing and inviting vagabonds into her house?"

"I was writing at the time. You don't get money right away for work like that."

"You were writing a book of voice pedagogy. You, who cannot be hired to sing chorus parts for provincial opera companies..."

"I wasn't trying for chorus parts."

"Of course not. You wanted to be a soloist. How else could you presume to tell others how to sing?"

"Because I've been encouraged by great singers of the past who think I'm on the right track. Granted, it's a difficult field, a lot of people don't make it. All I want is a chance to try. If I can get somewhere with my voice I'll have a chance to offer Elena and the baby a good life. The alternative is a low-paying job with no future. I couldn't even be a housepainter without covering her with shame. I know what you think of people who work with their hands."

I had him dead to rights, he couldn't reply. There was the small matter of his wife's being a slave for more than twenty years while he waited for the phone to ring, his reference books spread out before him on the diningroom table.

Elena could have set me up to paint her house, or she could have reconsidered living with me when she saw how much I liked to work with my hands, how I didn't complain about being asked to sleep on the floor, and so forth. I'd disappointed her, that much was certain. I should have seen the blow coming. I'd worked myself out of a job before.

"All right, then. Let everything depend on how I do working for my brother. I had no right to expect her to soften right away and want to move in with me. I'd taken her wish list too seriously, it was a clever trick. If she refuses me the next time she'll be saying no to everything she's always wanted."

At the bus terminal Enrique gave me a sealed envelope.

"She didn't want you to read this while you were still capable of damaging my house. Say what you will about my daughter, she is considerate."

Dear Sweet Sweaty Bear:

This letter is to thank you for the beautiful job you did on the ranch, and to tell you how sorry I am that I'll be unable to leave with you the way we planned.

In the first place, the planning wasn't thorough enough.

By the Wayside

Even with your brother's financial help it would traumatize poor Nena to be uprooted from her peaceful life here.

I know you're grateful to my father for all his help in caring for our child, and you understand that his politics don't prevent him from being the loving father to her that he was to me. In fact, she thinks his emotional outbursts are cute.

I was very impressed with the way you took care of Nena, too. I think you've come a long way toward being someone who could be her father. It's sad that you lack the means at the moment to prove how much you're willing to sacrifice for our happiness. You say you want to take care of us, but I've never known you when you were in a position to help someone else, and I think you'll have to agree with me when I say that you haven't done too great a job taking care of yourself.

Compounding the sadness I feel about our situation is the fact that I'm now sure I don't love you. The only reason I ever thought I did, undoubtedly, was the sex we used to have. Without sex to blur my mind I see a recklessness in you that scares me. It's the same reckless *joie de vivre* that attracted me to you once. I don't think you can do anything to change it and I don't think you should try. Just because I don't feel it anymore doesn't mean that the attraction isn't there. Ideally, you should attract a woman who doesn't want a child by you, who doesn't mind moving around a lot—someone who wants your kind of life. There must be someone out there.

This isn't goodbye. I may have been experiencing a prolonged case of postpartum depression and it may be possible for me to respond to you again someday. If you're still available I might want to try. And I will make it possible for you to see your daughter if you're up our way, but I'm sure you can understand why my father's door will be closed to you for all time. We'll have to work something out on the sly.

Until then I'll always think of you fondly and wish you every success on your new job.

PS: I'll never discourage Nena from saying "Papi" when she points to your picture.

60

I stopped by Tom's on the way south to learn more about my new job.

"I'm going to let you take over the mobile home and work the territory I told you about, selling loans, but you should think of this as probation, Gordie. If you do real good, I'll keep you. But even then, don't get carried away. I can't bump you any higher, there's just no room. Earn all you can. Save it! Then think what you're going to do when it's time to move on. If you can sell the mobile home you're in, I'll help you get started in some other line of work..."

Much to Tom's surprise I was a smash hit as a loan broker. Or at least I was better at half of the job than anyone who'd ever worked for him. Quite by accident we discovered that I was a master at getting people to do what Tom wanted when I talked to them over the phone—perhaps because it was precisely what I didn't want them to do.

"Mrs. Brown?"

"Speaking."

"You sound like an intelligent woman, Mrs. Brown, and that's why I'm sure you'd never think of taking a new loan on your home."

"I live in a mobile home."

"That's why my brother asked me to call you. His bank will lend on 80% of the value of that home of yours."

"You mean refinancing. We've talked about it."

"Why, if you don't mind my asking? Wouldn't your payments go up?"

"Sure, but we'd get some cash out of this place. It might be our only chance, because it'll be worth shit in a few more years."

"But if you need cash, that must be because you have a hard time making ends meet."

"You've got that right."

"Then it would be stupid to raise your debt. You'll just end up giving the cash back and losing your home."

"Yeah, that's what Ralph and I decided."

"There's a five year call on our loan, by the way."

"I knew there was a catch."

"See, you are intelligent, and Ralph might be, too. I'm sorry I wasted your time with this call. I'm under an obligation to my brother or I'd never have bothered you in the first place..."

"Wait!"

There were hundreds of variations, but this was often how it went when I could get someone to talk turkey...Twenty percent of the time, maybe—a huge "hit" rate according to Tom. My misses were uniformly of people who slammed down the phone as soon as they heard the word "loan," or didn't talk to strangers—the intelligent ones.

I tried to be happy about my success but it was depressing to realize that twenty percent of the people I called were eager to ruin themselves to help Tom and me. Foolish was the only word for them. I stopped flattering them in my pitch.

"I'm sure you're not dumb enough to want to refinance your home..."

"Not so fast!..."

"That's right! I called you dumb before I heard a thing you had to say! See what this job is doing to me?"

"About refinancing..."

The half of the job I couldn't handle was facing these people. Since I was now living a hundred and sixty miles from Tom he had to hire a closer who was willing to say, "I spoke to you on the phone." Almost never did our customers change their minds about what they had told me they wanted to do with their lives.

"It's bad enough interviewing these lemmings..." I was telling my brother.

"Easy, now, bro'. You're doing fine. Anyway, they're not lemmings, you're telling 'em which way to go."

"No, I'm not. They're telling me. I'm like a momentary obstacle to them. They swarm past me and meet up again at the edge of the abyss."

"Well, isn't that what it's all about in finance these days? It's the perfect image. I'll use it to pump up my district managers. There are hundreds of thousands of people out there willing to commit themselves to new debt. All we have to do is get in the way long enough to make sure they're committed to us when they take the plunge."

"As long as I don't have to watch..."

"Bernie loves doing it. Good man, Bernie. He knows they're all pre-sold. He's just putting out the paper, picking up signatures. I might let him keep the job if success never goes to his head."

"As long as he deals with the office and stays away from my place here. I meant to talk to you about that, Tom. I work best in privacy..."

61

This was no dream, but my first experience of the "mobile home lifestyle" which my brother was forever touting but had never experienced firsthand.

As I saw it there was nothing wrong with mobile home living as long as you stayed in one place all day like certain oldtimers or young paralyzed folk. There was no way of telling if the floors would buckle under your weight unless you walked on them. The walls looked perfectly solid until you put your hand through reaching for the thermostat.

Daydreams don't often tend that way, but if you could imagine yourself small enough to inhabit a dollshouse or any of the flimsy habitations given to kids these days you could get some idea of what it was like in my ersatz home. It wasn't quite as brazenly plastic as children's toys and it hadn't been scaled down near as much but the feeling of make-believe was strong in there.

If I hadn't stayed glued to my desk making my calls my mind would have drifted off and in a week or two I might well have been playing with dolls. As it was, all I thought about was making money in the loan business. I only put down the phone to eat or clean up or do calisthenics. Calisthenics had always bored me but in my present circumstances they gave me my most exciting moments. Moments of unbearable pain, moments of triumph as I surpassed yesterday's numbers.

So much self-contained healthiness and hard work made me think of life in a penitentiary, and how well-suited I would be to it, which might yet prove to be a good thing. I couldn't exclude the possibility that I would go back out into the world one day and pursue a life of crime. My stay in the mobile home was like living without an atmosphere, with a weightlessness of attitude. Turning somersaults in this limbo I had no idea how I'd be headed when I got out.

From time to time I did venture forth to resupply myself with potatoes, yoghurt, bread and fruit. I went to the pharmacy to take my blood pressure. At the pharmacy I came upon the magazines which would be one of the deciding factors in ending my existence as a bivalve.

They weren't sex magazines. I lived in a depressed area, or at least a depressing area on the eastern outskirts of L.A. There was an impressive range of mountains overlooking the mobile home park, but the people who lived here never had time to look up at the mountains. They only had time for human-interest magazines while they visited their hair salons or waiting rooms or other pit stops. They were all business as they went about their business, and pleasure only came to them under cover of darkness, like an incubus. Devils swooped up and down the street, in at the window, looked out of the husband's eye, commandeered the wife's claws. All over the neighborhood one could hear the sound of blows and flimsy beds, cries of pain and ecstasy vied.

In my dark penitentiary I masturbated, the dim sky of my

mind filled with the glittering personalities of *People* magazine. As I had in adolescence, as Zoe had, I could see the point of keeping my libido at bay. It wouldn't do for me to start noticing women at the supermarket and following them home. Nevertheless, I felt repugnance for myself when I was housekeeping again after these minifrenzies.

Benumbed as I was by compulsive work, eating and exercise I was still capable of realizing that *People* magazine was erotic to me because I needed to enter other people's lives, enter their homes, be a direct object for them or a dependent clause. Perhaps because I hadn't been to any of their movies I wondered what the female stars or starlets would look like without their clothes.

My sex drive thus resuscitated I began to think about Elena and wonder if I'd be able to waken a sexual instinct in her and nourish it. Ostensibly I was working hard so that I would have more to offer Elena and our daughter—someday, maybe, a home of their own. How did I get closer to such a goal by denying myself a sex life, even the company of others? Why did I need to be numb?

Deep down I was afraid it was really over with Lena, that her father was right, that she never had cared for me and never would. Nena would be lost and I'd quickly go back to my old ways, aimlessly drifting from embrace to embrace, making sure that my partners only wanted the experience of making love to me, which was all that I wanted of them. How unbearably empty that life would be now that I had a little one who needed me, a reason to settle down and work hard, now that life as a family man was so nearly possible for me.

62

"Don't quit me now! This is the best you've ever done at anything!"

"It makes me sick is all. This place would be perfect for Nena to run around in."

Tom had driven down to my mobile home the minute he realized that his star employee's loyalty was wavering.

"Think how happy Nena would be to live in a place she could tear apart with her own two tiny hands..."

"I hope you don't talk about it like that to potential buyers."

"What potential buyers? One in three months. I'd have called right away if anyone was interested."

"I know, I know. Look, at least hang on until I can sell this place. I'll give you a huge commission. Without somebody living here I'll never get rid of it. People are suspicious of a new lifestyle and it helps to see someone else manage it, especially a single guy who doesn't look like the domestic type."

"Seems that's just what I ought to look like. All I do is tidy up in case someone sees the sign and wants a look inside."

"I meant to tell you: I appreciate how neat you're keeping everything. I never would have thought you had it in you. I'm impressed, Gordie. Forget what I said about no room at the top. I'll make room. I might even cut you in on the corporation. You've done a great job down here, and not just selling and putting out the name. You're an inspiration to everyone in my organization—in the lower echelons, at least. None of 'em can believe it's possible to make so many calls in a day and hit on such a high percentage."

"How much do you stand to make when you sell this place?"

"Ten thou'. Five is yours. If you're really gonna quit me, if you haven't got the stomach to do a decent job with everything I'm paying you and a two-bedroom house thrown in...You know what it's like saying? Nothing America has got to offer is good enough for you. You'd rather be back in Barcelona living in a Spanish whorehouse with syphilis growing on the walls and AIDS in the drinking water..."

"It's not that simple. I did like the simple life back there, don't get me wrong. But the point of working for you, living here, wasn't just to help your business. You may remember that you didn't think I was going to be much help when I started. The point was to offer Lena an alternative to living with her parents, a secure future, a place to raise a kid in."

"So this park's not good enough for her? A rec room, a pool table? There's going to be water in the pool again when they find out what went wrong. Isn't there a slide out there into the pool?"

"The park's not an issue, Tom. She wouldn't live in a three-star, four-star or even five-star park. She won't live in a mobile home. She won't live in a 'stick-built,' as you call it. She won't live with me."

"So forget her! Live for yourself! You could make a fortune down here just doing what you're doing. There isn't a secretary in my organization who wouldn't marry you on the spot, or file divorce papers to make it possible. They haven't even met you, but you've got the sweet smell of success about you and they've smelled it. You want babies? Any one of them will give you a baby, even if they've already got a dozen at home. Wake up, man! Forget this commie bitch and her little beaner..."

63

Being up against the wall hadn't always put me at a strategic disadvantage. Tom probably thought he had me between a rock and a hard place when he got me to agree not to quit him until my home had been sold. Long experience of hard places had taught me that Providence never backs an enterprise until one is resigned to the worst of all possible outcomes—nay, cheerful about it.

Even as I was telling him, "Yes, Tom, I'll stick it out until this place sells," I sensed that there was a buyer just around the corner about to make an offer, and such was indeed the case.

As far as Tom was concerned I'd accomplished a miracle in selling "that shithouse" and it was time to take me off loans and put me to work on one of his lots for "the big money."

"Before I get excited about making more money," I told him, "I need to figure out how to get rid of all this money I've got."

Tom left the ground..

"What have you got? Twelve thousand? Peanuts. That'll be gone in a week up in San Francisco if you hook up with those old friends of yours. Not one of 'em has a second pair of shoes. Anyway, the Cuban'll have half of it before you put one foot in Hennessey's. You're hopeless, Gordie."

He called our mother anyway. By this time he was good at getting her to put his case. Every time I visited my mother she had a list of things for me to do so that Tom and I would get along better.

"You and Tom are fighting again, Gordon, and this time I have to agree with Tom that you're at fault. You've simply got to give his business a chance. You've had a little success. Tom says you have a real talent on the phone. Well, of course you do. You've got your father's phone voice. Every time he'd call I'd forget all the things I wanted to say..."

"I've given his business a chance, Ma. All I'm doing is helping a lot of people lower the quality of their lives. It's immoral."

"How can you say such a thing? Your brother is one of the most respected mobile home dealers in the world. You can read that much in the Los Angeles Times."

"It's the line of work he's in. In another line of work they'd be calling him Blackbeard."

My mother's face assumed the bitter resignation which had given it most of its lines. "I wish it meant more to you boys to be Bancrofts."

"It means a lot to me to be who I am, Mom, that's the whole point. I was never able to be what you and Dad wanted and I'm clearly not able to be what Tom wants and escape with my self-respect. All the same, aren't I somebody?"

"Yes. A drifter. A debauchee."

"Oh, come off it. I'm a good singer. My songs used to make you cry."

She started to cry. "The thought of them still does. The thought of the voice you used to have."

"What do you mean, 'used to?'"

"That's over, Gordon. Can you face it? You've got a wonderful talent, but it won't keep you alive, or your wife, or that beautiful child."

"It's got to, that's all I know. I came very close to losing my mind while I was working for Tom, and it wasn't the immorality of what I was doing. I just thought that might be something you could understand. I was going out of my mind because I wasn't singing."

She'd been expecting something worse. Little boys, maybe. After the letters from Spain she was guarded around me, especially when I was talking.

"Who was to stop you? You were alone..."

"I couldn't do it. I couldn't open up. In Spain I let loose in front of all the different types that Barcelona has produced and the tourists besides. But I couldn't bring myself to start making legitimate sounds in my mobile home and start the tongues wagging in all the other mobile homes jammed in beside me."

"You need an outlet for your voice. A community theater..."

"I've had enough outlets. None of them are big enough, the explosion just keeps building inside."

"Don't say that!" She'd risen half out of her chair in a somewhat unnatural way, like a cobra. "Don't look like that!"

"Don't look scared of you? Take it easy, Ma. I'm working it out. As long as I keep singing I'll be all right. I've got a plan. I'm going to pay Elena what I owe her, but I'm going to give my voice one more chance. If she'll live with me all my money will be at her disposal. If I succeed with what I want to accomplish as a singer I'll give her still another chance. If I don't get anywhere with my voice, I'll see if Tom still wants me."

"That money won't last long if you plan to study."

"Study? Mom, I'm not a cub scout anymore. I'm not even a boy scout. I can go back to Barcelona and I've got a paycheck right away for chorus work while they decide what roles they want me to sing. I might get substitutions. I can sneak up to France for auditions between shows if nobody recruits me. I can get an agent."

My mother had been brightening as I ticked off my options. She loved options where I was concerned, especially if I could afford them or employers were offering them in writing. She was such a ripe breeding ground for pleasant images that there wasn't room on the surface for a single memory of my operasinging days to come floating up like a corpse.

64

"Promised you parts?" Elena didn't look up from her plate.

"They wanted to see if I could be an on-time chorister and keep my hands to myself. I made them promise me roles all over again before I left. They didn't tell me what roles, but I might have the chance to step into a big one if somebody gets sick. I didn't tell you before because I was serious about working for my brother. I wanted you to see that I could stick at something disagreeable for Nena's sake."

"But now your opera career is at stake."

"It's my best shot. It's what Nena would want if she grows up to be as fairminded as she is at bounceball."

"She'd want you to quit a job where you were making more money than you ever came close to making before?"

"I can go back to work for my brother anytime."

"For how long? You'd never have quit if you thought it was something you could do for a living. But I've always known you could make a good living if you wanted to. What you haven't shown me is that you want to be a provider."

"You wanted me to be a provider without anyone to provide for. I could have stuck it out if the mouths I had to feed were where I could feed them."

She took another small bite of her lobster thermidor.

"You just wanted company in your misery."

"I know you'll see me differently if I'm a success at something I want to do...for all of us."

"Look, the last time you were off trying to do something for your family you were nearly killed by an old woman with a stick."

I was still considering the accuracy of the way she'd been reading me, and having trouble denying the truth of anything she said. I'd had no intention of doing the kind of work my brother was giving me for any longer than it took to prove that I could do it.

"Maybe you're right about me, but I'm back in the States where all people do is work. If I've got to be in harness anyway, by God I want something to pull. There's still time, Elena. Decide now and I'll go back to my brother. I'll take care of you."

"I don't doubt your ability to take me for a ride of some kind, but where are we going?"

"When I want to take responsibility you think I'm being sentimental."

"Of course I do. You were happy as a clam over there in

Spain, and you'd be there still if the cops hadn't been making
it hard for you. Look, Gordon, I don't hate you for being the
way you are. I just don't want to have to depend on you. Say
what you want about me for having a silver spoon in my mouth,
and depending too much on my parents. The truth of it is, I'm
the one with the money. They need me."

"The hell, they've got their savings."

"Not enough for them to feel secure, I'm afraid."

"Security again. Why is security such a big deal for you
people?"

"Because we were thrown out of Cuba and lost everything."

"Well, of course. But that was decades ago. In all that
time you've never trusted anyone to care about you?"

"Never. Certainly not you. Not someone who's trying to
succeed against all the odds and make up for the years he's
thrown away..."

Chewing. Drinking. Hygiene.

"It's all too neat," I said, finally. "Granted, if what I had
to do to provide for my family was cajole people into making
irresponsible financial decisions I might end up resenting you
for my legitimacy."

"I'm sure you would."

"Lena, I must have something to give."

"You do. Money. I thought that was the point of all this."
She took in the dining room with quick looks to left and right,
then nudged her plate with its plundered bright orange cara-
pace. "The nerve of you trying to pay me back." She sat back
in her chair, chuckling.

"Why are you amused? Figure the cost of my support
while I was working on my treatise. That way all my caretaking
will have been a gift. Then figure what I should be paying for
Nena's support for the year to come, till my next career
decision."

"It's ridiculous. You expect me to take money from an
ascetic? I had to go to Barcelona to study. I couldn't have
found a cheaper place. I could never have managed to eat as

287

cheaply as we did together thanks to all your economies. Nena doesn't cost much these days...You can make a contribution to her college fund, start an account in her name. No, forget it. You'll need every penny if you're serious about your opera career."

"I've just told you, the parts are there for me..."

"What parts? I've heard you say that leading roles are the only ones that pay. You'll need to keep auditioning between the breaks in your shows, and travel is the one expense you can't cut back on. The only time you ever wanted to spend money on comfort was when we took that audition tour through France while I was pregnant."

"We weren't considering *your* comfort? That was the first time I'd ever stayed in a three-star hotel in over five years there."

"Yes, but I remember you telling me that you had to feel cosseted to give a good audition. Wear clothes fresh from the cleaners, take taxis..."

"Well, it helps not to call attention to cheap clothes in a place like France. When everything is clean and creased the French won't look so hard. Damn them for being such lookers. It's hell to get them to listen."

"I'm right, though, aren't I? You'll need money to keep trying for the top, and going back to the streets to earn it probably won't be the best way."

I acknowledged the truth of her observations, feeling more like a beggar than I ever had on the streets.

"If I have some success, though..." I knew I wouldn't have to complete the thought.

"I don't know what I'll feel like by then." A smile eased onto her cheeks and she was even more beautiful. "As it is now I feel as if I should make up for lost time. I've been taking better care of myself. Exercising a little. I'm starting to get interested in sex again." She cast down her eyes in mock-modesty. That is, her smile was still there. "Sex is never at its best unless you can play the field."

I tried to control the bleeding in my jugular by force of

will. "If Nena doesn't have a father, isn't this a hollow victory for you?"

"That depends who's interested," she said coolly. "Having you want me as much as you do is no victory at all. Not just because I've always known that you do and take you for granted. I'd never feel quite as important to you as that sound you're after, that perfect tone that's in your head. You'd never have let your health go and taken all the other risks of life on the streets for *me*."

"I was having a great time. You've got it wrong..."

"You thought you were. I saw what came back from Spain, and that was after a long rest and good eating. You were killing yourself. I knew from the moment I saw you that you weren't the man for me. As long as you were sacrificing a great deal you'd think you were making me happy."

The victory was all hers, and the hollowness of it was vast, as big as the world, and there was so much laughter echoing out of it I couldn't hear myself think.

Lena thought I was the big winner tonight. As I hobbled away to seek fame and fortune she congratulated me for being able to give myself another chance.

Something she said near the end stayed with me.

"You've no chance at all of succeeding if you don't focus your energy, so if it helps you to think you've got a wife and daughter, go right ahead..."

BARCELONA

65

A well-dressed American man with two large duffel bags and a music case checks into a well-known hotel near Barcelona's Diagonal and spends his first afternoon making calls through the desk to numbers written on scraps of paper or printed on business cards. Late that afternoon he takes a taxi to an apartment building in the Corts district midway between the downtown area and the northernmost urban community of Barcelona known as Sarriá. The driver waits. Returning the man asks to visit another address in the Corts district, another apartment building. Later he visits two more apartment buildings in the district known as Pedralbes, in the direction of Sarriá.

On the following day, wearing dark glasses, the man takes another taxi to the stage entrance of the Liceo, now more frequently referred to in Catalan as the Liceu, Barcelona's world-famous opera theater, which is tucked away on the Ramblas next to one of the worst sinks of depravity in all Europe, if not the world, the *barrio chino*, where people get together on the street to buy drugs, or ask where to buy them, or to buy sex, never having to ask where, because the people they ask are selling it, because toothless old ladies are selling it down on their knees in alleyways.

The man is not recognized at the stage entrance, though he knows the concierge and has laughed and joked with him for three months last season.

After the man introduces himself the old concierge says, "Señor Bancroft! What a surprise! How different you look without your beard, without your beret, with short hair." The old man is laughing and biting his lip at the same time. The hello which started with a handshake ends with a hug.

When Señor Bancroft leaves twenty minutes later the old

man pats him on the shoulder and watches from the entrance as he walks down the sidestreet and picks his way across the southbound lane of traffic. On the pedestrian mall he turns north and is lost in the scrape of tourism amid the screams of caged birds.

Seeming very happy about something Señor Bancroft stops beside a large cafe terrace and spends a long time looking in every direction before he sits. He orders a *café con leche* from the waiter and waits for it with his hands over his face, shifting in his chair, seeming to look for someone he doesn't want to find.

While Señor Bancroft was strolling up the Ramblas a moment ago something about him caused a beautiful young girl to pause near the entrance of a hotel where she has just sold herself. She has followed at a distance searching her mind. His gait is familiar, he's so tall, there's something about the way he carries his head and swings his arms...

When he sits at a cafe terrace she watches him from behind and finally identifies him.

When the waiter is off nodding with the man's order she comes forward. (The waiters on the Ramblas all know her, and have been known to correct a customer's impression. "She may not look like one, *señor*, but she is a whore...")

Nearing the table she realizes she's having fun and wants to be overbold to tease him.

"Hi, Maribel," he says as she crosses in front of him, taking off his dark glasses.

She quickly circles the table, then presses his face into her cleavage.

A lady at an adjoining table, probably English, is wide-eyed. So is her husband when he turns to see.

Slipping her hand under Señor Bancroft's chin Maribel forces his head back and shows her tongue before she completes the kiss.

"What a welcome," says Señor Bancroft when he can breathe, speaking clear, accented Spanish. He pulls out the chair next to him, but she drags it away and sits facing him too far from the table to rest her arms. He catches the waiter's eye and points from his coffee to the woman called Maribel.

"Where did you go? You vanished."

"Back to my country. I was a prostitute for my brother."

"So your days on the street are over."

"I'm here to succeed, not just to survive." He tells her he'll be doing solo parts this year.

Her coffee arrives. The waiter puts it down with precision and a pinched face. He looks at Maribel as if in doubt that he's done his job well. After a glance at her companion's unsmiling face he's on his way.

"So you won't have time for your old friends..." She has turned in her chair slightly and begun to slide her leg up the vinyl armrest.

He smiles. "I'll never forget that time of my life." He says this looking directly at the inner thigh just revealed. Maribel slides her leg slightly higher while smiling into her drink. Then she sips and looks at him fixedly over the rim of her cup. A tongue of reflected afternoon sun is lapping cream from her upper thigh.

"I'm more than a memory, no?" Her soft, plaintive voice can scarcely be heard over the sizzle of streetnoise. He's watching her lips and the nudges of her tongue which loose words like bubbles.

He motions for her to come closer to the table, then leaves his hand in mid-air between them.

She ignores his hand and raises her leg higher still, revealing a violet, lacy bulge with a tiny pink adornment. Now the bulge is rhythmically contracting, the pink silk bow is acknowledging him.

"Maribel, stop. This is ridiculous..."

A glint comes into her eye. She reaches under her skirt with her right hand then leaves her chair to touch his upper lip with two extended fingers in a kind of kiss. On the zephyr created by her brisk movement there's a perfume that closes his eyes. His past life drops like a wrecked building, all the secret rooms of his experience giving up their fragrant secrets.

By the Wayside

He opens his eyes and peers around him wearing an idiot grin. His grin is answered by a newsvendor in a dark kiosk. Customers are buying, cafe-sitters are drinking coffee and talking, passersby are steadily approaching distant destinations, their attention firing blind about them. There's no acknowledgement when he's hit.

He puts out his hand again.

She stands to let her dress hang, slides her chair close to his, covers his hand with hers and guides it to her leg as she sits.

He takes his hand away when the waiter appears. After paying he gets up to leave. She looks in his eyes until he passes behind her. She looks at her hands and her skin heats as the moment expands. Then his tongue is entering her ear. She bounds up, laughing, and hits him in the ribs.

Loosearmed, holding hands, they walk up the Ramblas. The hurrying people coming toward them and overtaking them are heaping them with subtle intimacies, softness when their arms touch, messages at the wrist. Then she puts her arm loosely around his waist, he puts his around her shoulder. They take each other's weight and match steps. At the top of the Ramblas, on the Ronda Universidad, they get into a yellow and black taxi.

He gives the driver the address of an apartment in Pedralbes. On the way to the Diagonal he changes his mind and gives the address of his hotel. The driver nods, there's no immediate change in his plan.

Now the man in the back seat reaches to the floor to squeeze a shapely foot and to pick up the lavender lace panties that lie next to it in a tiny heap.

293

66

Later, when all their clothes are off, while the intensity of their first carnal reunion is wearing off, his fond gaze drifts up from the thick hair of her pubis and finds a new fullness in her belly. There's a new firmness to the touch. The change is minute, but he'd looked long and lovingly at her once late at night as he lay impotent beside her in her small apartment off the street of whores and he has resorted to the sight of her many times since, just as she was.

"Do you know who the father is?"

Her head moves very slightly back and forth on his pillow and her lips press together and thin.

"Could you have it?"

Again she shakes her head. "I'll go to England for an abortion in two weeks. It's all arranged."

"Do you have enough money?"

"More than you, probably. I have no vices." There's no trace of a smile on the face she turns to him. "What could I do with all the money I make? I save. I will buy a pension with the money someday, but not here. Up in Calella, perhaps, where I will take in German, Dutch and English vacationers in the summer months. I will live there all year. I love the Costa Dorada in the off-season, when there's nothing on the beach but some trash blowing and shapes remain in the sand for days."

"Why not buy a place on the Costa Brava? It's more beautiful. You could have your own beach, your own *caleta*."

"There's no sadness there, no craziness. People are clinging to the hillsides and Nature is boss. I like the resorts where workers go for vacation, where the signs are silly, the menus ungrammatical or badly translated, the buildings ordinary but fresh with paint. All the Spanish people who stay through the winter will be my family. We will be sad together while we wait for the craziness to begin again, like parents waiting for children who are away at school."

"But Maribel...If you have enough to make a start...You

could have a man. You could have a kid."

"You would be my man?"

"Sie sei mein Weib!" He sings the line in half-voice. Since Maribel knows German, but not the Dutchman, he corrects the third-person singular and then tells her something about that line, "the silliest of all the operas."

"I will only tell you that I wish I could have a mad marriage to you," she says in her beautiful, soft Spanish. "You have a crazy mind like mine, and you have a heart. But no man can stay with me. My craziness is different from yours. It's the kind that doctors know about, but for which as yet there is no remedy. Depression. They give me the drug lithium, and I think it is helping sometimes, but I know I cannot fool the disease very much longer with the same trick."

"I thought you were using what we call 'downers' in English."

She laughs, but her face is neutral again when she says, "It may be close to what you think. I try not to analyze my illness. It helps me to think it is the doctors' problem."

"They know how you live?"

"Oh, yes. What good would it do to lie? My first doctor is still a client of mine. He pays well and only wants me to suck."

"Who are these idiots to think they're helping you if they won't try to get you out of the life? Incredible. Just the thing for depression, a succession of Spanish maniacs breathing beer and anchovies into your face and trying to mangle your insides. I don't buy it. You're not just some beautiful slut, you're the most intelligent woman I've met here."

"Think about this, Gordon, and stop saying silly things. With the danger from my maniacs, as you call them, I feel alive. They want to see me more often, but the closer they come, the more I reject them, the more I deny. Driving them crazy keeps me sane. You are not like them, my friend. But you are not the best kind of lover for me. I can tell how much you are trying to please. There's no brute in you. No anchovies, if you like."

"As long as I wouldn't have to knock you around I'd do any kinky thing you like. People don't get less complicated because you know them better. If you don't type somebody and stop thinking about them you can spend a lifetime reaching the core."

"I can't share my life with a man, Gordon. It makes no difference who it is, my disease will start to change him. I will know the instant he starts giving me special consideration. The more he cares for me the more I will hate him. I do know men, Gordon, perhaps better than you, and I know that my problems make them think they should own me."

"Bollocks. I'd treat you like a queen and I'd be the one owned."

"I would never let my sickness rob you of your freedom."

"What is this sickness? You were always in a good mood when we saw each other."

"I'm an actress. I pretend to be cheerful and get into the part. I forget the shit in me, but I can see it rub off."

"This sounds like a classic case of *angst*, if you ask me. Nothing sick about it. It happens to all of us with half a brain. That's a pretty shitty world out there."

"Think what you will, but when I look into people's eyes, when I'm seeing them clearly, I can read their minds. I know what they're thinking."

"You're hearing voices?"

"Never. But their thoughts are going through my mind. How can I impress her? What will I get from her? What can I do to her that will make me feel good? Their thoughts answer these questions. When I was younger I hated myself for not loving life more, for wanting people to be better than they were. If I had to live with them as they are the sickness would rule me, I would close the door on everyone and waste away. Or wait for the courage to kill myself. As a whore I live with them. That's my identity. That's what I am. I'm a whore and I won't give you the chance to find anything more in me."

"I don't think you're giving yourself that chance. Look,

I had an experience with depression when the army got rid of me—all because of the drugs they made me take. Really, the whole misery. Couldn't eat. Saw death in everything. The people around me, even my parents and my poor brother, were monstrous. I lost the power to love."

"What happened to get you out of it?"

"I got a letter from a school chum, a very funny guy, telling me of his experiences in the Marines...That's a military group..."

"I know who they are. I fuck them."

"Right. Anyway, I had to respond to him with something funny. We were rival wits, wanted to be writers. Finally I made myself laugh with some of the things I found to say and the clouds lifted. I remembered how helpless I'd felt prior to writing that letter—for long months, in fact—and it seemed ridiculous of me. How could I have been so narcissistic? How could I not see the humor in all the maniacs at that army hospital who were trying to convince me I was insane? How could I have made it so easy for them?"

"I understand what you mean."

"So whenever I feel the blacks coming on I start finding things to laugh about, starting with myself."

"For me laughter is like falling into a hole. I get dizzy. I panic. I drink alcohol. I look for a man who will treat me very badly. I don't start to feel alive again until I am sore between my legs and I feel a heaviness in my stomach. I want the feeling that I'm carrying something there that doesn't belong."

"It makes me dizzy to hear you. Maybe you are one sick puppy. Well, I guess an abortion is best, then. It wouldn't do to raise a kid when maniacs are threatening the mother's life on a daily basis—or hourly."

Disgust is curling her lips when she says, "I'm afraid I would kill my child before I'd let it know me as I really am. I feel less like a murderer getting rid of an embryo...This is the third time, you know. It is murder, I know that. But if there is a god I want him to recoil at the sight of me, I want him to be sick to his stomach with the knowledge of what I've done.

297

More than any man I hate the Almighty God Who makes me
live my life like an insect fluttering at the mouth of an abyss.
I want to give love so badly. To a man, to a child. I want to be
good for something, I want to do some good with my life. I've
ached for years and soaked my pillow so many nights when the
last of them has gone. Why do I need the danger so? Why can
I only thrive on a diet of abuse and degradation? Why am I a
whore to the depths of my soul, always looking for the beast in
a man, and until I find it, feeling less than alive?"

"Have you considered suicide?"

She laughs. "I don't have the courage. Death will have
to be a surprise. I know I can't count on you." She laughs
again. "I feel no threat from you. You least of all. You're the
man I would love if I weren't sick in my mind."

"I wish you'd try. Loving me, I mean, not suicide."

"Maybe someday they will have a drug. My doctors tell
me they are testing new drugs all the time and some are
promising."

"I hope they can do something for you, Maribel. Someone as sweet as you are, afraid to have a baby because you don't
trust yourself...It's too awful. Still, the way you were moaning
and groaning a while ago...It's hard to believe you weren't
enjoying yourself."

"Are you crazy? It's all I like. I can never be fucked
enough. I'm a sex machine. How can you be so naive? It
disturbs me. You thought I was like one of those girls with no
mind, who only wants money and tries to get the man off her
as fast as she can?"

"You do try to last it out, then."

"You know I do. I don't want the man to leave until he
doesn't want me anymore. I want to fuck his brains out."

"I really do think you might be suffering from a mild
neurosis of some kind."

Her laughter is deep-throated, coarse.

"I'm curious...what about a woman?"

"I avoid them. The softness of them...I'd rather eat
worms. The way they whimper and squirm. No, you must

298

believe me, I have to have danger. I have to feel the man is getting so excited he doesn't know what he is doing, he's out of control. Oh, it doesn't happen that often, maybe twice a month, but I get men who want me to eat their wives in front of them, or eat one of my girlfriends. I love it then, I feel so degraded. Once a man spanked my bottom after I gave pleasure to his wife, and he made me have orgasms while he spanked me. That was one of the best times..."

"I'm probably nuts enough to marry you, but getting the kinks out might take the rest of my life. Still, a child might do it. I told you about the Cuban woman who had my kid? I'm still battling to have my self-esteem back after that one. Anyway, she used to be pretty kinky before her mother's instincts took over. I would have noticed the same thing with hundreds of women, I'm sure, if they'd have been willing to talk to me after they became mothers."

"She still loves you? The woman who had your child?"

"She never did. I'm not as attractive to her as I think I should be."

She snorts. "You can have any woman you want. This Cuban is an idiot."

"That sure is good to hear, even if it's only part of the service you provide."

"It's the truth, but I still want you to pay me."

Señor Bancroft is silent a while.

"I was thinking of a woman for you because it seems you're in a rut. The one I had in mind is plenty dangerous, too. She might not completely turn your life around, but I can guarantee you 180 degrees."

"Zoe, the English bitch. In love with the *vasca* who used to be your girlfriend. She has been coming to me for a year now, once a week."

"I thought you didn't go with women..."

"I don't think of her as a woman. She is as strong as a man. She is crazier than most men, too—much crazier than you."

"She spanks you?"

"Do you think? No. Never. Isn't it strange that she never wanted to? The next time I will ask for it. There must be a side to her I never saw."

"Well, how much? I'll settle and give you the fare now, but I'll go down and put you in the taxi, of course."

"Ten thousand pesetas."

"Hey! It used to be two thousand or nothing when I saw you before."

"You were poor. I wanted to help you. Now you pay like the rich bastards."

"I've changed so much because of a haircut? These clothes?"

"No, but you are no longer a whore. When you were on the street like me, giving yourself every day, you were one of the family, I had to share with you. My pussy is a poor gift next to that voice you have."

"No man in his right mind would ever think so. Well, I hope I don't lose too many old comrades this way."

"You won't lose Zoe. She still talks about you. "

"She'll always be a friend, but I've got to stay away from her until I've got a few roles under my belt at the Liceu. And the kid. You know Marina's little girl?"

Maribel, who is dressing, nods.

"That girl saved my life once. I was her disciple."

"I remember her. I used to see her dancing beside you when you sang on the Puerta del Angel. I was afraid to be recognized, but I came many times to see the two of you."

"Anita would have loved you!"

"In the presence of such beauty and innocence I feel like my heart is being eaten by dogs. I enjoyed her from a distance. When she stopped coming I hated you."

"It was a bad mistake. But it doesn't work to fall in love with someone else's kid. We've got to love our own, even if circumstances make it hard. I haven't given up. I still want to be worthy of my little girl."

"You're worthy, but not tough enough. Stop giving these women so much power over you. Marina. Zoe! The Cuban bitch. They hate you for giving them so much freedom."

"I can't love someone who isn't free. It goes back to some words right out of your mouth, about owning. All you can do is give them freedom, and show your love, and be patient. It may not be as thrilling, but it's a lot more satisfying to love than it is to be obsessed, and believe me, the kids know when their parents are obsessed, and a sad kid is about as bad as it gets. Here's the money. I'll take you down. I love you, you know, but at these prices I hope I can control myself. Here I am talking about obsession and worried about how soon I'll want to be inside you again..."

"You can have the rest of the day and all night. I won't charge you more."

"No, I lost it when I heard about your abortion plans. I feel uncomfortable getting in line with the men who are making you a victim. I need to think of a way for you to escape."

She shrugs and kisses him on the cheek. Her face remains a blank as she leads the way downstairs.

67

María Angeles could no longer dismiss the rumor she'd heard from the sopranos who shared her dressing room.

The words were true. Gordon Bancroft, the American from nowhere asked to do Escamillo in the Liceu production of *Carmen,* had been seeing a *puta,* someone who sold herself on the lower Ramblas and worse streets in the vicinity. It was a Catalan girl with a reputation for keeping to herself and taking too many chances.

María Angeles showed no emotion about the news she received from her brother José, but flew into a rage after the rumor about Gordon was enlarged by one of several colleagues who were aware of her interest. To her face she was told that the American baritone she was "leading on" supplemented his income by working as a high-class pimp. The word was out about him at the Tapas Bar, the cafe in the barrio he frequented before he vanished and reappeared wearing fashionable clothes.

Her enemy felt he'd need a lot of money to horn in on established underworld arrangements.

"You know what they are?" María Angeles shot back. "You know what it takes?"

"He would need to protect himself," the other woman had gone on, hesitantly, but dabbing on her eye makeup with precision. "Hire people loyal to him."

"Maybe hi s interest isn't what you think," María Angeles countered. "Maybe he's trying to help his friend in some way..."

"She is making him pay, I am sure of it," said her best friend, Vitoria, who couldn't resist a chance to make everyone laugh.

"We all know the kind of interest it is," said another, a grandmother who often covered snide remarks with a sigh, as if remembering a harm done her.

María Angeles's chair scraping the stone floor stopped the chatter, but the women kept working on their faces, hoping that they could make her feel ridiculous before her hands came into their mirrors. With clenched upturned fists held in front of her she started down the room, then changed her mind and came back to kick her chair.

Silence never lasted long in a place where borrowing was a way of life and colleagues were needed to check things that couldn't be seen in a mirror. The dressers arrived then and the women who had finished making up went to the costume racks to further their transformations.

Wigged, they'd be safe. Even in a rage María Angeles wouldn't interfere with a performer ready to go onstage. She cared as much for the general effect as any stage director, and she was fierce about the production details she could influence.

It was common knowledge that she watched over her career with the same stern eye. The women who were jealous of her voice attributed her fast rise in the company to her talent for detail, her compulsion to get everything just right, her timing—meaning her ability to catch an important man's eye and make the right remark, though she could keep a beat as well as anyone.

María Angeles had the best voice in the company, and sang in the chorus (against advice) for something to do when she wasn't taking a part. Barring an accident or a health problem she would surely inherit all the glory of Caballé. Tall and beautiful now at twenty-two, with dark blue eyes, dark brown hair and an aquiline nose, she would still be beautiful when she reached stardom, everyone knew. Iron discipline on the way up was common in these days of increased competition for singers, and increased opportunity—more contracts, twice as many grand opera stages as in Caballé's youth, ten times as many opera programs in universities thanks to America, that opera mill across the water.

Once on top everyone in the company held that María Angeles would quickly ruin her figure. She was too big-boned. The way Basques liked to eat...Secure against her enemies she'd allow herself a small indulgence...rarely...and then more often. Her strong frame would exult with the added weight. Her stronger stage presence would be applauded.

In her bones she feared her enemies were right. Yet as long as her talent was adored she wouldn't care what people said about her body. She would still have lovers, or men who wanted to be her lover, rather. She was unlike most of her colleagues in the fact that the only lover acceptable to her would be someone who'd fallen in love with her talent, fallen under the spell of her voice.

So far only one man had made love to her, a young sheep farmer from her mountain village in Guipúzcoa. She thought of him as a shepherd at the time, though she was aware of his aspirations. She didn't think of him at all now and had convinced herself that what they had done one early evening in a high, secret place had been a dream. The land had been the commune's, the smell of the land had been theirs. They'd been celebrating something both had felt, something Nature had

wanted them to feel...that very evening. She'd taken the land
home under her fingernails. Her knees and elbows had been
dark with it.

Her brothers had been uneasy like animals in a barn when
a stranger enters. But her blood came and convinced
everyone who seemed to know about the secret place that
Nature had just been teasing. Once in a while She played
with Her people that way, and there was no harm in it.

Vitoria had helped María Angeles to keep her head when
the American baritone came last year. Someone who sang on
the street...with that old man's beret and unkempt beard...and
his long hair flying..."María Angeles, how will you be perceived by the men who are sponsoring your career? Don't you
think some of these men hold out the hope of having you for
themselves someday? They expect you to be attractive and
charming to them, and they will respect you for rebuffing their
advances. They would respect your decision if you married
someone who could help your career. To be involved with this
Bankrupt...It would be a slap in the face, an insult to everything
they have done for you. Never forget who you are, María
Angeles. Never forget where you are in your career. You can
be unreasonable about anything you want for yourself. Genius
has its privileges...Anything except a man. When you are a star
you can have a stage lover in every great operahouse in the
world without making yourself ridiculous...Or a dozen friends
like me. You can have them waiting in line outside your door."

Realizing the thought pleased her, she blushed. "I'm not
a fool, Viki. Do you think I want to get pregnant by him? I
could never let him touch me...I wouldn't let him take my hand
until he had a leading role with the company. Am I some kind
of slut like the others that I want this man pawing me? You
say I should remember who I am...Do you know who I am? I
will work to succeed, harder than anyone. Yes, I will be
charming when I have to be, when I can see the good of it. Just
because I'm a virgin doesn't mean I'm not a bigger cynic
than any of you."

The color came back to her face when she lied.

68

"Do you know what she is?" Vitoria was asking the man she called "Bankrupt" in her perfect English. "A complete romantic! A shepherdess! She knows nothing about men. Beware! The first man who touches her will be her husband. If she permitted a liberty and the man didn't want to marry her, she'd call on her brothers. After they were finished with him, he wouldn't be good enough for her. I ask you..."

They were having this chat in a scruffy cafe near the Liceu soon after the company announced that Gordon Bancroft would be taking the part of Escamillo in this year's *Carmen,* that the Frenchman G. deBois was finished, had canceled all five performances.

"I've had an inkling what she is," said Bankrupt. "I knew a soprano like her back in the States. She, too, had a high E and huge tits. I called her 'Madame.' I was so intimidated by her I'd drop coins and spill on my shoes at the canteen. I'd feel dirty even though I'd bathed that day. The clumsiness went away, it was a kind of homage. Still, I would play the part of oaf longer than necessary."

"Hmm. Oaf would be just right. Too bad you've outgrown the role."

Bankrupt ordered more coffee after they agreed they had plenty of time to get back.

Vitoria was a heavy, quick-eyed woman with a curled lip. She really cared about her talented, innocent friend and wanted her success at any cost. In Bankrupt's experience ruin was all that ever happened to singers who were taken out of an opera chorus to do leading roles and still permitted themselves the luxury of a friend.

"What a woman, my Madame..." Vitoria seemed receptive with her smiling face perched on a plump arm. "She was always on the way to glory. I couldn't look at her without thinking of the triumphs she had in store. When she looked at me her eyes seemed to say, 'Why am I wasting my time with you? You can't help me.'"

"There's no resemblance, then." Vitoria eased back from the table to a concertante of creaks from the wooden banquette. "María Angeles wouldn't look you in the eye long enough to say all that."

"Madame was ten years older then than María Angeles is now. Oh, you're right, though, I'm stretching it. Madame had already been through a hundred men. Still, there are similarities. The way she made way for herself with her elbows, the way she made an angry face when you had her in the corner of your eye. The way there was never too much to do to assure success. Thousands of things every day, and she knew exactly what they were."

"Well, as far as it goes..."

"I'll tell you what it is," said Bankrupt, suddenly weary. "She just didn't believe in doing anything that didn't make sense, and immorality seldom makes sense unless you're dying of something."

Vitoria clapped her hands, narrowly missing her demitasse. "You would be wonderful for María Angeles, a man of your experience, if only..."

"If only I wouldn't try to be her lover."

"Yes. If you could care for her talent as I do."

"But I do. And her heart."

"Yes, but her heart is more a child's than a woman's. I resent her sometimes for having been so sheltered. Perhaps I should say I envy her. She will find a man to fit her dream, wait and see. He might be very sophisticated, but with her he will be exactly what she expects."

"The lucky devil. That is, he will be if I don't get to her first..."

"Don't even think of it..." Her mouth had fallen open, her cheeks were sagging, but there was a fine point in her eyes.

"How could a man look at her without thinking of it? But easy as it would be to arouse her, even by accident, I'm not going to start squeezing and have to meet the rest of the family. She's just a kid. I knew a fourteen-year-old who was more sophisticated about sex. Her name, too, was María Angeles..."

69

"Stay away from him," Vitoria told María Angeles that same night. "He's a monster of depravity. He has gone with fourteen-year-olds..."

"How can you know this?"

"He told me. We had coffee and he admitted it. He can't leave women alone. He's ruined his life because of his *amours* with women of all nations. This is why he is not one of the top baritones of the day. We both know he has the voice, but what opera company will put up with a molester of children? Where except in Barcelona could he cater to such vices? He's here because he has to be. If you become involved with him you'll be unwelcome even in Italy."

María Angeles smiled at the hysterical note in her friend's advice.

"So you're afraid he's just right for me." When she triumphed María Angeles's smile never showed her teeth.

"You'll be ruined! He's much too smart for you. He's a surrealist, I think. Probably the worst things you've heard about him are true. There's not one whore but a string of them."

"I'm going out with him after the rehearsal tonight."

"He invited you! He defies me, then."

"Yes, he asked me during the last break. I'm sorry, Vitoria. I'm tired of the rumors. I must know who he is. I'm drawn to him. I don't start rehearsing my Amina for a month. Something needs to be decided before my feelings for him would be a distraction."

"Be careful. I sense this man is very dangerous. He is so cheerful...No one knows English better than I. There is something very wild in his way of speaking. He may be brain-damaged. All of life is a joke to him. He could be dying of something..."

70

Señor Bancroft takes María Angeles to one of his favorite restaurants in the Quarter, the Egipto. They have a polite conversation, glancing at each other, till the wine arrives. With a glass to her lips she is able to meet his gaze.

After a minute of staring at each other and letting the wine burn out in their mouths they can say anything.

"Of course I noticed you last year. I was stealing a peek at you whenever I could. Like all the men. I never saw you notice me, though."

"I am noticing. I am wondering, with what I hear you on the street singing I am wondering..."

"*Habla cristiano.*"

"My English is so bad?"

"Worse than my Spanish, anyway. I want your thoughts to pour."

"I was attracted to you from the first time I heard your voice. You were singing *Per la gloria,* just resting. I love those old arias, old and sad."

"I love them, too. They're my childhood sweethearts."

"I came to hear you three or four times. I saw you with that little angel. You understand, my schedule is so busy, I have so many classes, so much coaching, I have no time for a fantasy life. Art is all I have, and the body that I must keep clean, the hair. Piled around me is all this knowledge I must acquire. People are advising me, teaching me, pointing out my mistakes, applauding. No one touches me except my teacher, Joana, to feel me breathe."

"No one takes your hand?"

Smiling, she slides a large upturned hand across the small table. Their fingers curl and nudge between each other. Later the light breath of an index wafts across her palm.

"Stop..." He sees the word but can't hear it above the restaurant noise. Her hand remains on the table, however, the tips of her fingers lightly against his wrist, her long thumb locked against his while her cup fills.

By the Wayside

He has been watching her face during the minute caress. She opens her eyes when he stops stroking and he is still watching, smiling.

"We'll be good for each other. Ever slept with a man?"

"Only in a dream." Her cheeks flare and she curses her people, her upbringing. If only she could have been brought up among intellectuals like Vitoria what a happy slut she could have been. She'd have slept her way to the top by now and made the world glad that she had.

"We'll go very slow. I've felt you against me in the crowd scenes." He's looking down as he says this, stating a fact. He could have teased her. He could own her. Love flares in her bosom. She shifts in her chair.

"Everyone knows I've been flirting with you."

"I tried not to show my feelings."

"I knew I could have you if I offered my body. That isn't the victory I want." She tries to keep a fixed expression and to ignore the heat on her face. "I want your loyalty. I want you to protect me. I want to care for you, too." She grips his hand. "When the time comes I'm sure you will know what to do, and what to tell me."

Their salad arrives, the usual Catalan business, hearts of romaine, tomato, onion and olive, fresh as if it had been picked that afternoon. The salad speaks for a long minute.

"I know about the whore," she says, after swallowing her first bite. "Maribel. I know you see her. I don't know what for."

"Sometimes just to be with her so she won't prostitute herself."

"Good."

"With anyone but me."

"All right." Her fork stops exploring. She sets it down on her plate. "Do you love her?"

"Yes. She has a good heart, but she's crazy. She needs for someone to care for her, care as much as we could care for each other. She needs to be somebody's life or death."

"She'll be somebody's death, I fear, of AIDS."

"So you're afraid of me, knowing I have been with her."

"I'm not afraid to let you have me. A love like mine won't listen to reason, especially to the comments of house-wives, all the clucking hens at the operahouse. They say they are trying to save my life and secretly they would like to see me lose it with lots of blood. Fear will never stop me from doing anything. Love controls my thoughts. I love you too much to make it easy for you. I know I could give you pleasure, but I don't want to feel responsible for it.. I doubt I could think of anything else if I knew I could be giving you pleasure. My love tells me to wait."

"Love isn't usually so wise. In fact, if you knew anything about sex I'd say you were a fool..." She gasps. "And if you weren't such a romantic fool, you'd be a liar, especially as to the mechanism which controls your thoughts." She slams a fist down. "I believe you, though. I'm the same romantic fool. I want everything to be perfect between us. We could help each other to grow."

"Yes. Nothing else is possible for you and me except death. Perhaps fate has already been too kind to me, but I feel I will have you soon. We'll be together before I die, and that will be enough for me. As for the Catalan whore, do anything you like. If it gives you pleasure to fuck her, then the pleasure is mine, too. There can't be room for anything as petty as jealousy in a love as great as I want ours to be."

The waiter clears the salad dishes and sets down two casseroles full of gaping mussels, shells glistening black, steaming, swimming in a red nectar.

This course, too, has its say.

"You're very generous, María Angeles, as I knew you would have to be. You'll be the love of my life. We can't escape what we mean to each other. Still, it's confusing. If it's possible...Perhaps it would be best for us if I were celibate right along with you. Chaste... Though I hate that word. Gives me a chill."

"I knew you would want this. You are a noble man."

"I'm not sure. If you'll help with all my masturbation..."

310

She makes a face. Her dark blue eyes get darker.

"How can you even think of such a thing? Go with your whore, then. Please, I don't mind. I know how men are. I've got brothers." She drinks off a glass of white Penedes wine at a swallow, moves her head away from the table as if looking for a place to spit, then snatches up her napkin.

"I'm sorry to have offended you..." Señor Bancroft goes on, writhing, "but I was under the impression that we'd be sparing ourselves the responsibility of giving each other pleasure, not relief."

The small dark place at each corner of her mouth might be the beginning of a smile.

"How exactly is the Catalan whore crazy," she says at last when her plate has been pushed away and her heavy bosom is resting on the edge of the table.

"She's a manic-depressive. She risks getting herself killed by the men who take her. She sees an abyss up ahead that she's trying to escape, but the truth is, the abyss is within. She's afraid of being captured by her past. Her small attempts to have a life, to have feelings like yours and mine, don't have any more weight than daydreams."

"Did something happen to cause this?"

"Her father screwed her from the time she was nine and beat her because he suspected she was enjoying it."

"The pig. His balls should be cut off. Tell one of my brothers who he is and he's a dead man. This is nothing to do with our cause. There must be some honor in being human or we cannot live together under the sun."

"If it weren't for the penalties for such an action, I might be tempted."

"Penalties? Are you no man? You care about the penalty when a savage like this is still alive, looking at little girls somewhere, creating more Maribels?"

"Maybe you can bring me around to your way of thinking. Toughen me up. As it is, I'm afraid I'm not much for this business of cutting people's balls off. I'm a product of the 'make love, not war' generation. I know the world is crawling

311

with monsters, but compassion is our best chance of improving the situation."

"*Caramba!* Your compassion is no help to this woman, you say so yourself. You refuse to avenge her because of your high principles. What are you going to do, then?"

"Fix her up with this big-eared Englishman I know."

"What good is this big-ears?"

"He's a compassionate man. He's never been a hater. His wife ran off with another man, his daughter became a lesbian. He hopped on his bicycle and rode to Barcelona. He's still in love with a Scottish girl who dumped him and it's hell to get him to listen to reason, but if she's not charging him I think he'd be willing to give Maribel a try. She'll fuck his eyeballs out—which might be easier than you think. My guess is, Owen will appreciate her thoroughness and energy. If his fortunes as an English teacher don't improve, perhaps she'll let him be her pimp, and that would be a step up for him. The main thing is, he'd be able to look out for her. Owen is capable with his fists. He's been in great shape since I've known him, which can't be said of anyone else I've known here in Barcelona. It must be the cheap wine. I think he's someone you'd like to meet."

She talks to herself in *éuscaro* for a moment. "I've been warned about your flights. My girlfriend called you a surrealist. You think I'm straitlaced...Well, I am. If you knew how I was brought up...No, I'm sure you can't even imagine such a life. I knew I would be a singer when I was very young. My family knew. For this reason, when we traveled to San Sebastián or Bilbao or Santander or someplace I was watching the city life with different eyes, knowing I would live in a city someday. When I was older I saw Madríd and Barcelona and Bordeaux, also Toulouse. I went to the *Grand Théâtre* in Bordeaux when I was sixteen. This I can never forget. There I saw the life on the streets, the free life of the artist which has been with us since the middle ages. I knew that I could belong to this world as well. I never wanted to, but I knew there was a place for me. Knowing this has always been a comfort. For another Basque woman home is the only refuge in adversity, the only way to retreat. Because of what is in my throat there's no need to retreat, ever, no matter how badly I conduct my affairs. A man can put me out on the street with nothing, an *intendant* can make sure I get no work in Europe, it is OK with me, I will survive. I can sing on the street the way you did. Someone will hear my call. Someone will want to be my friend."

"Yes, and the street can destroy you just as surely as it did another Basque woman I know..."

"Marina's not a Basque. I don't care about her blood."

"You know her?"

"Everyone knows her. The little girl's mother? I've seen you with her, and with that well-built Englishwoman. It's been said of you that you slept with both."

"All lies. I might have wanted to...There was nothing...I never even slept with Marina in the normal sense of the word. We tried..."

"I have a friend who knows her better than I. Marina was in the paper once with her husband, the poet, the anarchist. I was told this. I was up on the mountain with my sheep when this was happening. Now, I am told, she too is crazy. I do not like this information now. All the women who enter your life become crazy."

"I don't know the word for what Marina is in Spanish, but it isn't 'crazy.' She's in love with the Englishwoman, you know. When she loved me there was nothing wrong with her mind. That might be a matter of opinion..."

"There is nothing wrong with love of a woman. I know about this. But this is why I say she is no *vasca*. I've never heard of such a thing in my province. In San Sebastián, perhaps. The French are there...the influence. Still, we love what we love. I know men who love their land more than anything, or their flock, or a particular animal, or a particular small child. We love who we love. There is no shame in love, no matter how it is given or who gets it. Except for love all things given are just to make business. Love is the only gift that carries the risk of pain and humiliation, the only gift that can make us ridiculous. It is the noble gift, then, and the singing voice is its handmaiden. Let them hiss and shout...If we sing with all we have to give, we are giving love."

"That's beautiful, María Angeles. OK—it's agreed. No more looking for love. You'll have mine, I'll have yours, and the hell with the next course, let's go for a walk. I want to hold your hand while we float down the empty streets."

"Are you crazy? You have some weeds and an appetizer like this and call it a meal? We will have at least two more courses, or three, and all must be heavier. These Catalans eat like birds, like French people. They are so small, so quick...They make me feel ungainly. They make me afraid to break their bones crossing the street."

After much more eating they walk hand in hand out of the region of narrow streets and all the way to her apartment. At the downstairs entrance they talk some more. Before he leaves, he kisses her hand.

71

The world loves a lover, perhaps, but a couple in love expecting to be smiled upon by fellow members of a professional opera company might be pushing their luck. They might consider themselves very lucky not to be the butt of practical jokes, not to be made to look foolish onstage, not to be tried by sexual provocations to which any response would be embarrassing.

Operasingers are expansive people. They can be generous with money, affection, praise. Yet an underlying anxiety dogs them. Anxiety about their voices, about their standing with their employers, the critics, the public, the choristers looking up and the conductors looking down. They are people who talk to themselves for reassurance, and they are distracted by lovers with their private smiles and private time sense. Brave is the couple who can show love for each other in the midst of so many people with a stake in appearing coarse and hearty.

Gordon and María Angeles are a standing joke, perhaps because of the childishness of their affair. They're never seen kissing, except when Gordon kisses her hand prior to brief moments apart. They never take their eyes off each other except to follow a conductor or a piece of music or a flight of stairs down.

They don't seem to care what anyone thinks of them, diminishing the general hilarity somewhat. They respond to ridicule with a dreamy smile, even when there's laughter right in their faces. They listen to advice with nothing to say. Their response is the same to a favor.

On the streets of Barcelona their reception is different. Waiters give them special attention. So do the older people in parks and cafes when they have found the odd half hour to visit. Gordon is keeping in touch with Owen and Hewitson, but is still avoiding most of his old friends. If he weren't avoiding them, surely they'd be happy for him, they'd see nothing amiss. Whether from hashish or wine or woman half the *callejeros* were stumbling and staring at any given time, there was nothing strange in it. Only in close contact with the lovers could there be something unusual in the softness of their huge voices, the gentleness of their strong bodies.

Prior to meeting Lidia Hewitson, María Angeles vowed she wouldn't be impressed. Learning that Lidia was planning a world tour to be financed by the sale of her Oriental rugs she became well-disposed. At the end of their second visit she is enough not herself to throw her arms around Bill, and cry for shame on the long walk home.

They walk a lot now, only taking cabs to the ends of town or to Gordon's apartment, where they sometimes go to prepare a meal with a kind of brother-and-sister domesticity.

Impetuous as any sheepherding swain her age Señor
Bancroft introduces his beloved to his mistress, the woman
María Angeles still calls "that Catalan whore." Foolishly he
believes María Angeles is as fond of Maribel as she says. With
the sophistication of a mooncalf he lets María Angeles persuade
him to sleep with Maribel twice, three times, to make bearable
the long wait for the right time to marry, which will be plain to
both of them, she says, when it arrives.

72

Bancroft tells Owen that he sometimes feels that his life
is in a ballet belt. "Maybe it's only a dream-state, but I ache all
over."

"What's a ballet belt?"

"Ballet belt is to jockstrap as girdle is to panty."

"I see. But you're knocking it off with Maribel, aren't
you? She told me you keep her at it all night, she's so sore she
can't work. I wonder if that's fair, actually. You're not the only
one with an ache."

"What sort of interest is this I hear?"

"Intense, I fear. How would it make you feel if you were
the only one having her for nothing? That's what puzzles me
about her sessions with you...Well, I'm sure I could last that
long if it meant not losing her to a rival."

"Don't worry about me that way. Without her services
I'd blow it with María Angeles, I'd never be able to control
myself. Maribel feels obligated to me. I introduced her to
you."

"Should I be considering myself a ponce, though? I'm
not sure I fit the image. I'm not entirely sure what I'm
expected to do. And I wonder if my Spanish is good enough,

quite frankly. I can make myself understood much better..."

"Owen, relax and enjoy her. You're using a condom, aren't you?"

"Of course. She's so adept I hardly notice when she puts it on."

"Notice! Notice before you put it in!"

"It would be altogether too petty of me to consider our sex less than satisfactory because of a bit of rubber between us. Anyway, Brenda was on her back all over town, who knows what I got from her, so many of the new scourges are late bloomers. Maribel might well be the one who needs protection from me. It's a gruesome business, sex, these days. Got to have it, though, haven't we? Sometimes I'm thankful I'm not one of the young ones. I can be grateful for all my good times, and with Maribel to soften the years ahead..."

During their fourth all-nighter Maribel confides to Gordon her true feelings about the Englishman.

"I don't love him, but he makes me feel safe."

"You'd consider him for a pimp, then."

"I will never be sharing my earnings with an idle man. You think I have no more sense than one of the drug addicts out on the street?"

"It's a problem, then. Unless I can convince Owen that there's such a thing as a pimp who works for a living. Ideally, he'll want to take you out of the life."

"Fuck his ideals, then."

"Maribel, I didn't spring Owen on you without plenty of forethought. Ever since you told me about your father..."

"I've been telling psychiatrists about my father for five years. My father is a kind of fiction to me now, a story I tell well. As for how I really feel about him, he doesn't exist."

"I'm convinced he does exist as part of the mechanism called will. I think he's right down there at the bottom of the things you do to yourself."

"So where does Owen fit in?"

"Right down there at the bottom with him. I think he

could help you to create a new past. An imaginary life if you like. You could be a creature of your own imagination instead of a plaything of so many others."

She thinks hard, then sucks him for a while. When she comes up for air she tells him, "It feels right. I wouldn't think so if this were only a conspiracy to help me to help myself. Truly, there is something very strong about this man...His English culture, his physique. I think I can be more precise. He is someone in despair, we have this in common. Pain has made a big hole in us and our feelings don't seem connected to us any more. They arise, they pass. They flutter a moment then they're gone on a puff of wind. Yet he has the determination to keep on, as I always have, without an important goal. He has no past worth going back to, no idea what lies ahead. He's content with his life, but he's not calling attention to what he likes about it like some pest of a poet. This is a very quiet man, but there is something happy inside. Yes, you can tell him he's my honorary pimp, if that would be good for his male pride. Honorary titles don't mean much, we all know that. He'll have to keep working. Harder, perhaps. You won't be paying for him forever, and I don't want to reveal your secret. I'd hate to have to ask him for anything when he thinks he's had so many complimentary passes. I'd like to see if he'll make me a gift, sometime. If he thinks enough of me to be obligated. The male ego is really something, you know..."

73

María Angeles knows the game that Gordon is playing, though he doesn't go out of his way to keep her informed. She wants him to succeed. She likes Owen. She pities Maribel, and might like her, too, if she hadn't become a kind of sexual necessity for the man she wants for a husband someday.

If he makes a successful Escamillo at the premiere she will give herself to him. She'll not promise him anything yet, but rehearsals are going well and he'll make a dashing Escamillo unless he falls on his head.

She considers a fall possible because of all the tricky climbing he must do in the smugglers scene, up and down a rickety stage mountain in the dark. If he falls and hurts his head she'll marry him on the spot and take care of him for the rest of his life. All that worries her is an unseemly declaration of her feelings.

Even if Gordon's star shines brightly for a while, as brightly as hers, it will fade while her popularity is at its peak— his age guarantees this. When he retires from the stage she wants him to become an important intellectual figure because of his discoveries in the art of singing.

She has read nearly half of the 4,000 pages he has written pertaining to voice. She has shown some of them to Joana, her teacher, who is enthusiastic. She wants to meet Gordon and has invited him to help her teach.

As the star pupil María Angeles has been able to persuade Joana to wait, wait until Señor Bancroft is known to the operalovers of Barcelona, until the people who remember him as a streetsinger, a kind of clown with a voice, have begun to take him seriously. Gordon understands that the time is not yet right for what he calls a "transmission."

She is physically sick from all the love coming up in her, and all the anger. She is sending Gordon to Maribel because it's easier to deal with jealousy than it would be to control her desire. She wants Gordon when she can afford to make a fool of herself. Until then she can only show her love by protecting him, and devoting herself to his work.

She is in awe of his voice, and of what he has written about voice. When his knowledge has been "transmitted" his ideas will be taught in all the countries where operatic training is given. María Angeles questions him closely about the meaning of things he has written in English about singing. She is translating his ideas, filling a notebook with them, changing them only for the sake of understanding—when she is sure she understands, and the English does not translate. She feels like a Renaissance scholar, sometimes, poring over an ancient text.

She too is trembling on the brink of an abyss, as Gordon says Maribel has been doing. She has the strong legs of a child of the mountains, however, and the strong will of a performer to stop trembling. She feels the same lightness that causes Maribel to seek alcohol, to transform the anxieties of her mind to a heavy queasiness she can carry.

Unlike Maribel, María Angeles is not afraid of the looming darkness, she's not afraid of being swallowed. She understands her uneasiness as a fear of the unknown, and she sees her perseverance, and the pen in her hand, and the trust she has as a kind of mechanism for bringing light. Each day she knows a little more, has done a little more, has written a little more. She wants the weight of her achievement outside of herself where she can handle it, open it, show it. She wants to give away everything she knows each time she sings.

It is thus with the weight of sung words, which Gordon has explained is a weight which must be felt far in front of the singer, where it seeks a tiny vacuum.

"It sounds like nonsense but the thought of EU becomes a place for you to sing to, what I've called a vacuum. Or think of it as a little crack in the world of related things, a miniature black hole of French EU out in front into which you are pouring the tension of your being and its cool shadow of sound..."

Late one night, practising—her practice room is corklined—much that he has told her becomes clear. Her mind summons images he has given her, her voice plays with them. Soon she feels a new emptiness. Her strong legs stop asking to be noticed. It's like being on horseback without a horse. Soon she is singing through tears of gratitude, tears that don't choke her. She hears Gordon's voice telling her in his heavy accent (that moves his ideas like a bullock pulling a cart): *"...Your cords are way out here, EU holding them back, OO stretching them into eternity. Don't think of words as things to be pushed around. Let them dissolve onto the cords. Only a ghost*

320

remains, an outline. Hold it still until the next word is superimposed..."

"Forget everything I've told you. Drink the voice, the way the Italians say, but drink with your belly. Think of the sound as filling a glass way out here, and give yourself some lips down here, say at the level of your navel. Take that glass in your lips and drink the sound at the same time you're projecting it into the house, sweeping it off your cords with a loose upper lip...Wait, sweeping the foam off your glass of beer, then. Have you ever seen that done? Remember, your tone is in the glass. Doesn't weigh much, but it's there. The house gets the foam off the top of it. Its liquid weight goes into the slit in your belly. Clamp down on the rim of that glass and tip it toward you. There. Feel the liquid that escapes spilling off to both sides, right here. The ischial prominence, if you call it that. As for the liquid that passes into your belly, it spills. Right to the floor with it. You're not keeping a damn thing. You can't even slow it down. There's your abyss, my darling. And that tiny vacuum out there? That's the other one. It's between those abysses, once you recognize them, that everything is possible, in words, in song. It's a scary place to be, but try to relax. I've been there, too. We'll be going out for coffee soon..."

She sings a long time before she feels an effort and comes to herself.

74

The night of Gordon's debut María Angeles makes up and dresses ahead of the other girls, leaving the top of her corset loose beneath her purple blouse. When she's put the finishing touches on her cigarette girl she leaves for his dressingroom. Since he doesn't make his entrance until the tavern scene in Act Two she doesn't expect to find him dressed yet.

He's naked to the waist. He has on his slippers, stockings and the short pants with their absurd encrustations. He's put on his makeup base and rouge and blackened his brows. The highlights will give him something to do later besides pace the floor.

She kisses each cheek and then holds his face in her hands to disown her greeting.

"Is Luis in the passage?" he asks.

"He's sure to be there."

"I don't want to be inundated with wellwishers. You know how I feel about talking before singing. Maribel might come. Are you prepared?"

She shrugs. With her back to the door, and her body angled so she can't be seen in his mirrors, she elongates the elastic decolletage and frees her breasts. She's breathing hard, excited by the sight herself.

He lowers his mouth reverently and she holds his head in her hands once again, digging her nails into his cheeks, into his scalp at the temples.

He pulls up suddenly. "Someone's sure to come in."

"Luis. Your whore. I don't care."

Orange makeup base clouds her pale breasts. "I want them all to know. Tonight will also be my debut. When it's over here I want you to do everything to me, everything you've done to a whore. From tonight I want to be the only woman in your life."

Reluctantly, then less reluctantly, Señor Bancroft does what she expects. María Angeles groans as if in pain. Where it has been forced out between the corset stays sweat is darkening her hideous costume. The makeup on her upper lip is becoming greasy. Pale rivulets explore her neck and then hasten to her heaving chest.

Maribel finds them thus and scampers between them to see.

María Angeles quickly fills her corset and adjusts her

blouse. The material would seem to be able to expand indefinitely, but the blouse looks skimpy trying to contain so much.

"Let me help," says Maribel, touching the soprano's makeup where it is too wet. She moves to Gordon's makeup box to find a base darker than the one he's using.

As if to underline Maribel's importance the first warning comes over the squawkbox in his room.

"WARNING, LADIES AND GENTLEMEN OF THE CHORUS...FIFTEEN MINUTES..."

Maribel dabs deftly at the face of the much bigger woman. Finished, she turns the face from left to right several times before she's satisfied. Then, with a hand on her client's shoulder and one on her back, she turns her to the mirror.

"Gracias..." María Angeles's chest is starting to heave again. Shutting her eyes to Gordon she takes the whore in her arms, gathers the comely body to her bosom.

"Don't cry," says Maribel, "or we'll have to do it over. There, see, it's good that I came. It's good to have someone."

"Dios mio..." It's Luis, the assistant stage manager, a lisping, gaptoothed creature valued for his intelligence and discretion. He's a friend to nearly everyone in the company, and on performance nights he's a friend to the artists he doesn't like.

"Off with you, Luis, we're under control," says Escamillo.

María Angeles takes Maribel back into her arms and rocks her back and forth.

Gordon decides the rest of his makeup can wait. He'll have the whole first act to worry about details and the mirror will be like still water then. Presumably Maribel will be watching the show and María Angeles will be struggling with the militia onstage. With their backs to the audience the supernumeraries of the militia will be attempting to cordon off the rioting cigarette girls and from the way it has gone in rehearsal Gordon is probably not alone worrying that the rioters will push some of these men backward into the pit. María Angeles is hard to control when she throws herself into a fight scene, bowling over the other girls in her attempt to get at these poor excuses for men in uniform.

The door opens again and nobody comes in. Then a short sound shows Gordon's delight as Anita comes skipping around the embracing women. María Angeles lets go of Maribel and faces Marina.

"So that's it, son of a bitch," says Marina to Gordon without humor. The smile on her lips is so thin it makes her look older.

Anita is in his arms asking where he's been, why he hasn't come to see her.

"America, my home," he tells her, sitting and turning her on his lap. "I've been too busy here..."

"Too busy screwing these bitches," says Marina in English to him. María Angeles has enough English to understand, but he may be able to persuade her she was confused and heard wrong.

"No dice tonterías, Mami," says Anita, sensing his interest as any true child of Frankenstein.

"That's right," says Marina, going into Spanish. "You didn't know he had two of us wrapped around his little finger. And I don't mean my daughter. No, with her at least, his intentions were honorable."

There are pink welts under Marina's eyes, as if she's been crying a lot recently, or staying up too late, or has contracted tuberculosis. She's dressed in a tubercular manner, Gordon thinks, but that's the style these days. Faded floral hysteria, lots of black, one white bird. She's washed her hair today. He loves the ripples when it's very clean. What they felt for each other was never properly consummated and he wonders if he doesn't still love her.

María Angeles has come between her countrywoman and her man. "I know about Gordon and your English girlfriend. You're not shocking me. You should think what you are doing, coming here like this minutes before his debut performance."

"Silly cunt," Marina says then, making Zoe so real to him that she might as well be standing there. Then in Spanish again, "He made his debut with me, I hope you will never forget it. I helped him to survive on the street, to make his way. He would be a toothless beggar by now without me to care for him. Do you think I respect his loyalty to you or to this madhouse? All these people rushing around, trying to act important, trying to fool each other into thinking they care about art...Bah!"

"I'm sorry you don't understand how much we care," says María Angeles with a new strength of tone.

"You country bumpkins make me sick with your Sunday dresses and your Sunday promenades with all the louts you can find and your male relatives walking behind. You won't be around long."

Maribel has come between the two *vascas*, crossing her arms. Anita is quiet in Gordon's lap now, enjoying the show. He's silently congratulating Maribel for keeping her hands off María Angeles. "You won't be around long..." Marina waits for the squawkbox to stop.

"LADIES AND GENTLEMEN OF THE CHORUS...TEN MINUTES...ZUNIGA, MORALES...WARNING..."

"I don't care how well you learn your lesson from this Catalan slut!"

"Mami!"

The back of María Angeles's hand has sent her older countrywoman reeling back.

Anita is struggling out of Gordon's lap.

He tells her it's all right, her *mami* wasn't hurt.

Maribel has both arms around the soprano and is trying to keep her body between the two women.

"We'll see how tough you are when I've got my friend Zoe to help me!"

Still leaning into the young soprano, Maribel turns to face Marina.

"Good thing you didn't bring her today," she says cheerfully. "She wouldn't be good for much after spending the afternoon with her head between my legs."

"What are you talking about, slut. Shit-eater! Anus-fly!"

Gordon releases the child, who runs to her mother's arms. It's too late to stop Marina's tears, he thinks, but the child might help her to tone down the language.

Like it or not, the anus-fly is in María Angeles's keeping, there's no way out for her. The soprano's back is to the long counter with its three mirrors. She looks helplessly at her onetime future husband, already afraid of the thoughts she'll have when she's alone.

Luis puts his head in and feigns lack of interest in everyone but María Angeles.

"María Angeles, they are screaming for you. If you're not out there by the last call they won't let you go on!"

"When have I missed an entrance, eh, Luis? Is this fair to me? Go tell them I will be down for the last call, but if I'm not, I don't care if it's one second to curtain, I'll be there. Nothing will keep me from doing my best job, not even a crazy bitch like this!"

Maribel turns to find out if she's the crazy bitch in question, and satisfied she's not, takes her weight off the big woman and faces the one who really does look crazy, nourishing the hate in her eyes with the comfort she gives the child.

"I don't believe you. Zoe will tell me the truth. You're saying this so I won't upset your friends before they go onstage. If you're telling me the truth you've got more to worry about. Believe me, you'll need much more help than you'll get from this stupid ox of a girlfriend or this poor excuse for a man. I know where to find you, don't forget. I know all your shitheaps."

"BASTA!" shouts Gordon in the strongest part of his range, jumping up like someone ready to fight. "At least some of you should know what shouting does to my voice! This is not the time to get to know each other and sort out your love lives! You're all good people and I would have been glad to see you if you came to wish me well, the way I've been glad to see Anita, but this isn't the time to try to get me to take sides. In fact, I'll take you all on, if I have to, to have some peace of mind."

He looks from face to face for an argument. Anita's grin causes him to slump down from his artificial height. "Look, couldn't we get together somewhere after the show?"

"I doubt there's a bedroom big enough," says Maribel, ever cheerful.

"Our bed is big enough!" says Anita, asking each stricken face in turn to confirm the brilliance of her suggestion, then turning to her mother to find out what went wrong.

"The bed is big enough," says her mother in English, "but is Bancroft? Zoe and I both notice. From the time we start screwing him he is shrinking. Keeping up like this he is going to be more lesbian than he think."

María Angeles starts for Marina carrying Maribel along. She's about to take a handful of Marina's hair when the sight of the cowering child weakens her resolve.

"You cover the Basque people with shame," the soprano is content to say. "You who pretend to understand artists. I could kill you for ridiculing his manhood before he has to sing an aria like the Toreador Song. I don't care if his manhood shrinks to this," she growls, letting a stub of thumb show above her fist, "he's all the man I will ever need!"

The toreador in question takes two steps backward, feels the edge of his stool, drops onto it and crosses his legs.

Maribel is asking both Basques to be quiet, pushing them further apart. "Such a discussion shouldn't be left to amateurs. I have more experience than a thousand women like you and I can assure you that our bullfighter isn't shrinking." This reassuring information is directed to María Angeles, Maribel's manner her mirthless bedside best. "Gordon is one of those men who has got a thermometer between his legs. If you get him hot enough there's no telling how much blood goes up." For Marina's benefit she adds, "You wouldn't recognize what he puts in me. Even if he weren't afraid your friend Zoe would bite it off, you would never see it bigger than it gets in the morning after a night of heavy drinking."

"I've dealt with those," says a voice from the door. "All they're good for is making you sore." Maribel has been sharing her wisdom with a beautiful Latin woman, a Carmen if there ever was one, who is holding a female child against her legs.

"On the whole I remember him as adequate, if not awe-inspiring," Elena continues, nudging into the room behind her child. "Even with his equipment in working order, however, he could turn me off with his spiritual facial expressions. Towards the end there was an embarrassing lack of lewdness."

"You were seven months pregnant," Bancroft adds, looking surly when he takes his hand away from his eyes.

"*Papi!* Daddy! Hi!"

Anita's look of welcome is undiminished by her mother's shrieks of laughter. "You're his baby. What's your name?"

"*La Cubana!* What timing!" Marina's highpitched laugh goes higher like a rip, again and again, while she points a wavering finger at María Angeles's stricken face.

"Mami, can we have Gordon and his friends on our bed tonight? And his baby? I promise not to tickle."

Marina ignores the tugs on her dress.

Maribel has crossed to Gordon. She pats him on the head, whispers encouragement of some kind and tries to leave.

Elena makes way by coming further inside. She's more beautiful than he's ever seen her, leaner. A California plaything.

She gives Gordon the baby, who's full of new things to say in Spanish and English, though none of it makes sense.

"This is too perfect," Marina is saying to María Angeles. "You didn't even know about her! The bastard didn't even tell you! I'm sorry you had to find out so soon. You won't have a year or two to waste on him."

Marina mimes spitting in the young soprano's face and leaves quickly, not even glancing at the new arrival she'd heard so much about and with whom she had once wanted to share her house and her table and even her bed, according to the anarchism of the day.

Anita is saying goodbye over her mother's shoulder, sad to be leaving, sorry that Gordon has done whatever it is he's done. The hope of seeing him again is somehow apparent by the way she opens and closes her hand in front of her face.

"So this is your lesbian," says Elena in English, looking

up and down the exotic purple specimen with its look of fear and fixed wide eyes. "Somehow I'd never pictured her so young or so tall...Should I miss the start of the show, then, Gordon? I suppose I'll have to if I want to see you alone."

"PLACES, LADIES AND GENTLEMEN OF THE CHORUS! LAST WARNING! FIVE MINUTES! MARIA ANGELES, POR FAVOR..."

María Angeles seems ready to leave, at last.

"Is this your child?" she asks Gordon in a pitiful, thin voice. "Your woman?"

"My child, yes."

"You never told me."

"I meant to, someday. I couldn't spoil what we had."

The baby on his lap says, *"Mami,"* and puts out her hands to be taken off.

María Angeles's pallor is causing her makeup to look mottled and smudged. Her eyes aren't as wide, but they aren't seeing. They follow her head unblinking as she turns away. She moves to the door too slowly for someone about to perform.

Gordon bounds to the door as she goes out.

"Remember the job you've got to do," he calls after her as she stumbles down the corridor. "You won't get close to the truth by thinking about it. Perhaps it won't be so terrible to face. I've lived with it, and it didn't keep me from finding you."

Nothing he says is going to turn her, but she's taking the stairs well. She's going to make her entrance.

"I seem to have come at the wrong time," says Elena, smacking her lips. Her clear delight has calmed the child, who is again putting out her arms to him. First indicating the armchair in the corner for Elena, he takes the child and sits again in front of the mess of his makeup kit. Its components fascinate his squirmy charge.

"My mother tipped you off, I suppose. It's the same old story. My mother would be the Antichrist if it weren't for her good intentions. As it is I'm never able to pin a thing on her.

Did she come, too? I'd love to see her."

"No, only mine. She'll take the baby back to our hotel. Are you sure you're going to be OK to perform? I'd hate to think that Mom, Lenita and I came all this way for nothing. Your mother paid all our expenses, incidentally."

"I've no doubt. Yes, it would be a terrible waste of your time if my performance should fall short of the highest standard. Dammit, that woman you just called my lesbian is the best talent in the company. Before long she'll be one of the best sopranos in the world."

"And now her coattails have slipped right through your fingers. 'Coattails' sounds better than 'apron strings' in this case, don't you think? I can't get it out of my head that she should be your lesbian in spite of her youth. What a bust, eh? Is she the Carmen?"

"No, she's a soprano—dramatic coloratura. A Norma someday. Another Ponselle."

"Then the one with the cute kid is your old *inamorata*, discarded in favor of the young soprano with a future."

"It isn't at all like that. It's the first time I've seen Marina since I got back. I tried to shut out my old life and concentrate on my work here. I knew if I went back to the streets I'd let myself slide. Freedom only works for me when I've got no one to please but myself."

"How is it any different when you've got a few women to please, too? Isn't the one with the cute figure and the natural curl another one? I seem to recall that pleasing women was part of your credo."

"Maybe it was never true before, but I feel my talent to sing is a responsibility."

"I have a feeling the Spanish soprano is behind this. I think you've finally found someone to sit at your feet."

"The show will be starting any minute. They might be holding the curtain. You'd better hand off the kid and find your seat. I don't enter till Act Two, but I'd like to get the rest of my makeup on...Thanks for coming, Lena. I don't care what kind of a mess I'm in because of it."

"I did it for your mother. She thinks Lenita ought to know you for some reason. Lenita doesn't remember you well but she was saying, 'daddy, daddy,' all during the flight. It's a new word for her in English."

"Daddy," says the baby into his ear.

75

Alone at last he stares at himself in the mirror and tries to empty his mind.

The music starts on the squawkbox and all of it sounds ominous, not just the Fate Theme. He wants to see how María Angeles is doing, wants to be assured of her self-control in the fight scene. He would be sure of success himself if she can do her part.

When he hears the women singing about *la fumée* he can pick out her voice. He will spare himself the embarrassment of an appearance half-clad in the coulisses, which would lend credence to the dire things that Luis has surely been saying.

A third-string Escamillo will be getting ready somewhere. Gordon knows about him but can't even remember his name. Roberto? Despite the expense the company has been rehearsing him separately. Luis has told him it will be a disaster if "Roberto" has to go on in his place. He's a lazy tenor, short and fat. The only way the audience could possibly enjoy him would be with a live bull onstage.

The women who have just visited him flicker into his thoughts and the music becomes a background instead of a precise extinguishment of time.

At one point it occurs to him that he loves them all, even Elena.

There is such a thing as a right woman for him, however, and María Angeles is that woman. She redeems the labor of countless hours that has resulted in his knowledge of the singing voice. She forgives the unsteady man he is and encourages the secure artist. She understands the difficulty of what he is trying to do. Probably she will even understand the problem that having a child has posed for him.

He will never abandon his child or his paternal rights, but he can't let anyone outside his field decide the best use of his time. The child must not destroy the artist he is in favor of another wage-earning man with outlets in community theaters. This was what his mother had wanted, and he'd defied her. He would have defied his father. Clearly his parents are still part of his life when he contemplates the child and thinks what to do for her. He wishes he had more to offer now, more on the horizon, the everywhere-accepted prospect of increased earnings and returns on investment and pension plans. All the things parents want for their children. Only unqualified success will palliate his mother's concern.

He can't ask for more time to show what he can do. He can't further strain the belief in him he has been asking of people who know nothing about voice and think of auditions as something like beauty pageants, rampant with favoritism. If he fails tonight and suffers the child to go away without a father he will be damned.

Only with María Angeles could he hope to have the understanding he has always needed to go his own way and continue to refute the authorities in the books about voice and the books about what's right for children, and the books about the psychology of defeat and addiction and alcoholism and co-dependency and psychosexual disorientation and all the other books by Californians for Californians that once helped the people who couldn't understand his work to understand him, or think they did.

María Angeles is too young...

Yes, and innocent. Her heaving chest. Her stricken face. Turning away like a child who's accidentally seen death, with no grown person near to sanction tears.

She knew there was no answer she would want to hear but she couldn't wipe the *why* off her face.

By the Wayside

She's an innocent 22 years old. All she knows of love is what she's given to her favorites in a flock of sheep. She didn't understand what was between her legs well enough to give it. Why she wanted to be taken. She wanted new meaning.

What's the good if it means a start to the haggling, the right price on her, a payment plan of mortgage proportions?

Better if her value remains unknown to her. Better she marries him at 22 years of age and never knows another man. He could complicate her pleasure to the point that she would never be curious about anything that could happen in a casual affair. If he could prevent her sexuality from making trouble she really would have a shot at being the greatest singer of the age. She might resent him someday for monopolizing her while there was still some good to be got from exploration. Let it be so.

No, she'd have to get hurt or there'd be no salt in her tone. She'd have to be free. Perhaps she wouldn't have to coarsen, though, become cynical like so many of her peers, if she had the chance to study life as well as art from a position of safety.

He can't stop thinking that María Angeles is still his, it's insane.

Of course he's lost her. After what she's seen...He would have to be present every minute to refute her conclusions. Even then it wouldn't be easy.

It's got to be over.

The beautiful little child he created will have what's left of him.

As it should be. How could he think for a minute that someone else should be there when the child says "daddy," as he'd wanted Owen to be once, as he'd even wanted Lena's father to be? Someday, if he's very careful and a little lucky his daughter will be lending her hands to the applause for him and waiting for him at the stage entrance.

He's closer to that dream, closer than he had been when Zoe and Marina were bedmates and Anita a perfect surrogate child of his and streetsinging not only a profitable stopgap but a chance to prove his theories.

All that was wrong with that life was that it was unacceptable to Lena, and hence to the child. He'd refused to abide by Lena's judgment of what was right, but he'd made strides in giving Lena authority and accepting it without bitterness. Lena is just as sure of what's right for Nena as he is.

True, he knows exactly what's right for *him*, and Lena hardly knew herself, or had no self to fulfill, only whims to indulge, but what relevance did that have to the question of what was right for Nena?

The tavern scene. The Toreador Song.

The dresser comes in to pluck at his costume and declare him fit to go on.

He follows the dresser out, placing one foot in front of the other.

He follows the ghost of the Escamillo he's been rehearsing to the familiar empty place.

Some of the stagehands are bobbing up and down like monkeys with the anxiety they feel for him. His composure where he waits is making them proud of him and a small crowd is forming before the TV monitor to see if so much composure before an entrance is a good thing.

The properties man has handed him a false pewter cup with nothing in it.

He enters on the balcony inside the tavern, merrymakers on either side. He waits for the introductory music to end, raises the cup to the people staring up or turned to him, and begins,

Votre toast, je peux vous le rendre...

A huge black sound slaps the back of the house. On the main floor, placid a moment ago, there are thrashing whitecaps. Choristers will later ask each other if they saw the operagoers in the orchestra seats duck their heads when he began.

After the first chorus Escamillo has a long draught of nothing, tosses his winecup, sees it caught. Then he swaggers down the stairs, merrymakers making way. As if on a whim he vaults the rail and crosses centerstage to the table where he will sing the second half of the aria.

He leaps onto the table...

And slides off the other side...

Into a clump of choristers...

Who promptly begin to chew their hands.

The orchestra, sensitive as a charging bull, keeps on.

His words fit the disaster wonderfully.

Tout d'un coup, on fait silence...

There is a black and dreadful silence welling up around him. The chorus has cleared a way for him to see the conductor. From the fifth balcony it may be possible to see which one he is. He can do no better than stand near the table while he sings. Trying to get up might cause another fall, one he might not survive—that is, "continue to sing after."

After the act there is much speculation as to what went wrong. He is tensely congratulated for having got through the aria, but feels this is the kind of praise reserved for generals who win battles by losing all their men.

Most theorizers feel that the culprit has had accomplices among the stagehands. The stagehands stoutly deny this and Señor Bancroft, at least, believes them.

He knows Vitoria is the the one. He'd seen the surprise when María Angeles's face found him as he slid off. For a millisecond they were together again and he took heart. Before he'd made his feet he knew how Vitoria had done it, bringing a vial of liquid soap onstage in one of her folds.

76

When the hubbub dies down outside his dressingroom Elena is left like the bit of something that causes condensation.

She is smiling but hasn't come to cheer him up. He knows the smile. He saw it after his close calls painting her house. It was the languid smile she used to cover her mild concern that Death was loitering near and she might be taken by mistake or changed somehow after being brushed by his cape.

They are between acts and choristers are cruising past for a glimpse of the Flying Escamillo.

"If I close the door," he tells her, "I'll be inviting the grassy knoll contingent to finish me off."

"You know what this means," she begins.

"It's my last chance to talk to you. I'm sorry I've only got twenty minutes."

"You won't need them all. I expected a better answer."

"What did sliding off that table mean?"

She nods.

"You may think it means that I'll be singing on the streets again."

"How could you?"

"It was a set-up. I have an enemy who's very fond of María Angeles."

"That goes without saying, but how could you get involved with all these women?"

He is silent.

"I thought you were finally going to put your career first."

"I frankly don't give a damn what you think. The only importance I want in your eyes is as a father. For the sake of a family for that little girl I know I could have been some kind of husband, but now it's too late. Still, in spite of all the evidence to the contrary, I'm tired of the way sex has been screwing up my life."

"It sounds good, Gordon, but I know you too well..."

"PLACES FOR THE THIRD ACT...FIVE MINUTES..."

"Don't you see that it's your pat understanding of everything that's causing all the trouble?" His voice is loud when the squawkbox stops.

"No matter what job you chose the singer would have been clamoring to come out and you'd have been distracted around the baby and me."

"Can't people change?"

"PLACES PLEASE..."

"You already have, for the worse."

"I'm reconciled to the fact that I have to be an economic success for you and the baby to have a decent life. I don't mean, be rich."

"You think you could make enough as a singer to support us? On the strength of what I just saw?"

"PLACES, LADIES AND GENTLEMEN OF THE CHORUS...WARNING CARMEN, JOSE, IL DANCAIRO, EL REMENDADO, FRASQUITA, MERCEDES..."

"Don't write me off just because of that slip. Maybe somebody important heard me sing and had sense enough to suspect a saboteur. Critics would understand. Staging mistakes are common with last-minute substitutions."

"There's no reason to give up on your voice, I agree. It was incredible."

"You think so? Then tonight wasn't a total disaster. Don't leave yet—you can see the rest of the show from the wings. I'll fix it up."

"I couldn't bear to see any more."

"Why, Elena?"

"I could never hear you without thinking of what might have been. If you'd wanted to make opera your life you'd have been a star a long time ago. If I had to stick by you now for some reason all I'd ever hear is, 'What happened to Gordon? Why aren't we hearing about him?' Let me tell you how it is for me and maybe you'll be smart enough to apply the lesson to other women in your life despite all the evidence to the contrary. Women don't want to be worshipped. They don't want their sexuality to be an end in itself."

"The hell they don't!"

"Sorry, I'll speak for myself, then, the way I promised. From the beginning I felt you wanted me to be your world. You were in love with the phenomenon of woman the way you were in love with Spain—a tourist who didn't want to go home.

Sexuality is to sidetrack a man, not to sustain him. You'll never know how much I despised you for believing my shabby little tricks were all that I wanted to be important about me."

"You can't tell me it was all a pretense."

"No, of course not. Once you got me started I went along. Women don't do much important thinking when they're aroused. But I hated what was happening to me. Because any woman will do for a man who adores women, I had to be all women to keep your interest. I had to figure out what you were looking for and give it to you. So much for kinkiness."

"The hours I spent..."

"It was my way of keeping you at bay and letting you worship at the same time. I knew you were hopeless when I saw how long even that could interest you."

"Elena, do you realize there's a baby's life at stake while you outsmart yourself this way?"

The stage manager puts his red face in and shouts, "I hope you're planning to sing in Act Three, Señor Bancroft. How are your legs?"

"Fine."

"You're not planning a spectacular fall of some kind?"

"No, a goat couldn't be more surefooted."

"I'll be back to escort you onstage. We're not taking any chances until you're ready to go on."

"That's kind of you."

He winces and leaves.

"I'd better be going, too."

"Wait, there's lots of time. I don't go on till we're fifteen minutes into the act. Please stay and watch...I plan to redeem myself."

"No, I made up my mind to leave after the fiasco. My heart might not be strong enough to watch you climb."

"Right, you've seen *Carmen*. The apes of Gibraltar would have trouble with the mountain they've given us this time."

"Don't say the name of that place. Good luck. Don't write. I'll get in touch with your mother about visiting Nena."

"You're not going to be in town for the night?"

"It'll save your mother some money if we turn right
around. I don't mean to sound discouraging. It gave me a thrill
when you came on and got the first half of your aria right."

"What are you talking about? I didn't miss a note all the
way through!"

"Maybe not, but you weren't as effective when we lost
sight of you. Take care of yourself."

He is too dazed to reply. She's gone.

The stage manager is back.

"Oh, come now, Bancroft, we can't have this. You're
ruining your makeup. We don't want Roberto! Please get
yourself together. They've got him in costume, you know."

The stage manager is homosexual, but has never let
Señor Bancroft see his nelly side. He clucks and mutters to
himself while he dabs at Escamillo's face. He has the makeup
right again in no time. The old man would stay to comfort the
baritone, but a kindness might bring tears of gratitude. He
knows the type.

77

Señor Bancroft is alone and sitting stonefaced before his
mirror when she comes in.

"Why aren't you onstage?"

"Vitoria did it! I could kill her! Oh, why did I tell her?"

"You had to tell someone."

"I saw your wife leave."

"She's not my wife."

"You're not going back with her? She hasn't come here
to stay?"

"I may never see her again."

"You could have told me, then. I would have understood."

"I wasn't sure how I felt until now. I still don't know

what's right."

"Your career comes first."

"It appears that it will have to, but I've got to wonder if it should. And making a career of some kind without self-respect won't be easy."

"Nothing is easy in the opera life."

"You're going to be in trouble for missing the scene."

"Bah, I'll make *them* apologize for harassing me all night. I wanted you to know how great your voice sounded. Everyone's talking. You can let your pants fall down the next time, nothing will prevent your success. Also, I'm thinking about our friend Maribel. Something about her touched me. We can have sex all three tonight the way you like. It's time I left behind my ways of a schoolgirl, which are becoming a pretense. I don't ever want to limit you again. There's nothing I'm afraid to try...Oh, how tired I am of taking advice from Vitoria when I know and have always known she is in love with me just as the Englishwoman is in love with your old friend. Nothing physical can happen now, but she would like that, someday. I need to break from her, and now that her enmity is in the open, I can do it by siding with you. She's been here a long time and has many friends, but she has no influence comparable to mine. It's as she says herself, there's an aristocracy of talent, and I'm the queen."

"See if you can't get into the scene. Forget this nonsense with Maribel, and don't turn on your friend. She only wanted what's best for you and I understand her feeling that you need protection from me."

He goes to her, takes her roughly into his arms and kisses her.

"I don't need protection from that," she says, pulling away.

With the next kiss he occupies her mouth until he feels her getting heavy. She staggers back and looks at him for a moment with her mouth still open.

"I want to have your child." She tips the words to him like someone trying to pour drops from a full glass.

"That's not for us to decide."

"God wants it, too."

"Let me tell you something about God..."

"Hold me...Whisper in my ear..."

Doing as he is told he whispers, "Like many creative types, God is a Lazy Slob."

She pulls away, digs her fingers into his arm and shakes him once, hard.

"Is this a time for your jokes?"

"He makes a mess and moves on, is all I'm saying. Surely you don't believe in a divine *Mr. Fixit*."

"I don't understand."

"Forget Him. He doesn't care any more what I do. As long as I'm lost and confused He has complete confidence in me."

"Please tell me you love me and you want me to have your child."

"I love you and want to make a baby with you even if Vitoria puts a knife through my heart before it comes into the world."

"It's Vitoria who is afraid now...After what she has already done...When I get my hands on her..."

"I doubt you're prepared to kill her, and that's what it would take. She's fixated, María Angeles. She thinks I have to be stopped. She's convinced no one could love you as much as she does. There's no sacrifice she wouldn't make for you, so maybe it's true that nobody could love you more."

"Then let her sacrifice her life!"

"Don't let anyone around here hear you talk this way," he says hurriedly, under his breath. "The staff, I mean. They'll be coming for me with torches."

"They will fire *her!* What do you mean?"

"What good is that if she can still do something foolish, or you can, trying to stop her? It would be easier to get rid of a foreigner."

"I would follow you...anywhere!"

"Go do your scene..."

"Kiss me again."

She's more demonstrative this time and he has to hold her away.

"I know I have to go," she says, panting and wildeyed. "Tonight, though. I won't let you escape. We'll make a baby."

She runs from the room and down the hall—like a kid, he thinks.

78

In spite of the pall that has come over the rest of the cast he's ready for the knife-fight in front of the smugglers' cave.

The cliff is as he remembers it except for the whites of offstage eyes. He gets his cue and starts down. The narrow trail is hard to find in the bad light, and takes some real climbing, but he's been clambering up and down for the past week to the point that he knows exactly where his feet will be at certain musical cues and couldn't have been any safer if he were twelve years old again and this were one of the trees in his backyard.

He's trembling. Someone who would sabotage the artistic effect of the tavern scene merely to give him a chance to break his neck is capable of anything. But even someone as overwrought as Vitoria wouldn't have hid in the shadows while the rest of the chorus left the stage. He doesn't expect her to do anything incriminating, he expects something to give way.

"Bravo," he tells himself when he reaches the stage.

Don José's eyes are twice their usual size. Their duet up to the knife fight is full of tension anyway, so he imagines it is going well. He's supposed to slip and let José get his knife over him. They've rehearsed it countless times, but Señor Bancroft is sure José expects to end up in the string section.

The scene goes pretty much as rehearsed except that he has to keep trying not to laugh at the leading tenor, a sad

Bulgarian to begin with, whose eyes are right for someone who's just been stabbed and is waiting to die.

When the gypsies, and María Angeles, rush on with Carmen and her pals he knows where to look for Vitoria but can't make her out. Nothing looks the way it did in rehearsal. The costumes seem too brilliant, the makeup too thick, the stage too dark. Anyway, he's supposed to be facing Death and it's the wrong time to try to pick someone out of a crowd.

When he says his general goodbye and invites this rabble to come and see him fight bulls, and has his parting shot at Don José, still popeyed, he's done his important singing. He's starting to breathe easy.

When he makes it back up the side of the cliff the ordeal is almost over.

He continues his exit and rests on a high scaffold just out of view of the audience.

A minute later he starts to sing a brief reprise of the Toreador Song, softly, as if already halfway back to civilization.

> *Toréador, en garde.*
> *Et songe en combattant*
> *Qu'un oeil noir te regarde*
> *Et que l'amour t'a-...*YAAAINHHH!